PENELOPE RICH
AND HER CIRCLE

BY

MAUD STEPNEY RAWSON

Author of " Bess of Hardwick," etc.

WITH 29 ILLUSTRATIONS INCLUDING A PHOTOGRAVURE
FRONTISPIECE

London : HUTCHINSON & CO.

Paternoster Row   1911

TO

MRS. JAMES SINCLAIR,

WHOSE GOOD HELP AND SYMPATHY AT THE
OUTSET HAVE SO SWEETLY FURTHERED
THE MAKING OF THIS RECORD.

CONTENTS

ILLUSTRATIONS

x   LIST OF ILLUSTRATIONS

PENELOPE RICH

AND HER CIRCLE

CHAPTER I

THE HOUSE OF DEVEREUX

THIS is the plain story, so far as public and private
documents and contemporary statements reveal it,
of a woman who was in her beauty both flower and star,
and at whose feet some of the most celebrated love
poems in the English tongue were laid. These gifts of
verse, passionate, tender, enchanting, are like undying
wreaths and posies to her person and her heart—garlands
and bouquets of immortal blossom, of gems in which
the stars sparkle for all time.

Her name is Penelope. It is true that she spun many
a web, that she was faithful—though not to her lawful
Ulysses. But she had not the full reward of the faithful. Neither was her lord a fit Ulysses. That rôle fell
to another man, of whom more presently.

She was Penelope Devereux, daughter of that great
Earl of Essex whom Elizabeth of England appointed to
the governorship of Ireland, and sister to the brilliant
Robert Devereux, whom the same Queen first spoiled
and then beheaded. The father, Walter Devereux,
succeeded his grandfather, Viscount Hereford, Lord

B

Ferrers of Chartley, Bourchier, and Lovaine. The family, as is obvious, was of Norman origin. In that province it ranked very high. Two young knights of the name—originally written d'Evreux—came to England with Norman William, to whom they were related, and acquired vast estates, respectively in Wiltshire, and Wales. From this point their family history is as rich in political and military prominence as that of the contemporary house of the Talbots, Earls of Shrewsbury. Their marriage ventures were also noteworthy. Of kin as aforesaid to the now royal branch of Norman nobles, a descendant in 1300 wedded the Princess Elizabeth, daughter of Edward I, and another, an heiress, in the following century married the sixth son of Edward III. This was Thomas of Woodstock, Duke of Gloucester; his wife was Eleanor de Bohun, and it was to her ancestor Henry de Bohun, the nephew of William, King of Scotland, that Maud, heiress of the Mandevilles, brought the earldom of Essex by right of her own family. Therefore it was upon royalty that a commoner —if one may use such a term in regard to the de Bohuns, themselves so strongly imbued with the blood of Scottish and English kings—conferred so notable a peerage. Eleanor de Bohun's sister, Mary, married that Henry Plantagenet, Earl of Derby, who became Henry IV, and her son was Henry V. This very brief and condensed survey will accentuate the fact of the high origin of the Devereux house. The Earldom of Essex lapsed for a time in the reign of Henry VIII, with the death of Henry Bourchier, one of the most impressive of the nobles who assisted in the pageant of the Field of the Cloth of Gold. He died without male heir, and the estate passed to his sister. Her grandson, Walter Devereux, re-earned for the family the earldom. He succeeded his father as Viscount Hereford in the first year of Elizabeth's reign. Everything was in his favour. His family had for some time been zealous Protestants. Many of their contemporaries had been driven under Mary to seek refuge in Germany and other safe havens on the Continent. Now they came flocking back. Among them were the Knollys family, of whom the head was Sir Francis, who appears to have held religious views of the most rigid nature. With his daughter Lettice young Lord Hereford, who had just reached his majority, fell in love. They married in 1561, and Penelope was their eldest child. Now Lady Knollys, the bride's mother, was sister to Anne Boleyn, which of course placed her in the position of first cousin to Queen Elizabeth, while Lettice herself was first cousin once removed. This was an additional point in favour of both families. Sir Francis Knollys at once took his place as a courtier in immediate attendance on the sovereign. Lord Hereford, however, had to wait for some time before he was chosen for special service. It was ten years before the Queen conferred on him the Garter, and restored to him and his house the Earldom of Essex.

He had in all five children. The youngest a boy, Francis, died in babyhood. The others were Dorothy (1565), Robert (1567), who succeeded him, and Walter (1569), who married, had no children, and fell in a skirmish outside Rouen in 1591. He was spoken of as a promising scholar, and entered Christ Church, Oxford, at the early age of fourteen. The three remaining children of Walter and Lettice lived to make history and a good deal of scandal. They saw very little of their father at the time they were growing and developing. All of them were scarcely out of the

nursery when Essex was offered his Irish commission—
the quelling of the rebellion in Ulster. If he had been
like his friend and relation by marriage, Lord Leicester,
he would have foreseen the sheer bog, military and
financial, into which this Royal commission, under
guise of a favour, hurled him. He volunteered in
1573, and the details of the official document on his
appointment are as interesting as they are amazing.
They are worth notice here as particularly affecting the
finances and influencing the career of Penelope and her
brother.

The Earl actually undertook to maintain half the
fighting force of twelve hundred men, which he took
with him, and was to bear half the cost of erecting and
repairing fortifications. In return he was granted half
of the county of Clandeboye, which included nearly all
Antrim and an adjacent mountainous tract in the north-
east ; he was to pay no duties, and to be immune from
all charges on the transport of arms, money, and necessaries. It must be remembered that whatever Elizabeth
gave with one hand she took away with the other. In
return for Clandeboye she asked for 800 marks of
land which he claimed through an ancestor, the Earl
of March.

Very rapidly, long before the Michaelmastide when
he was to start for Ulster, Walter Devereux saw
that the cost of the expedition required a sum of
no less than ten thousand pounds. This he actually
borrowed from the Crown, which behaved like a practised usurer. He agreed to the terms—ten per cent
interest, in default of which he was to forfeit certain of
his estates. So that from the very outset of their lives
his children were weighed down by this foolish and
unnecessary mortgage. The Earl was further ham-

From an engraving after an original painting

WALTER DEVEREUX, EARL OF ESSEX

pered in his office by subservience to the Lord Deputy of Ireland, Sir William Fitzwilliam. Essex was to have absolute control of Ulster under the Queen's Seal as Captain-General of the province. The Deputy contrived that he, and not the sovereign, should officially confer the office. The Earl became aware betimes of the hostility and envy which his earldom brought upon him. "I look," he wrote to Burghley just before leaving England, "for to find enemies enough to this enterprise, and I feel some of them already." Though he did not yet realise the share of Fitzwilliam in the affair, he suspected it, and tried to start on a peaceful footing, for he continues: "When your Lordship writes to my Lord Deputy of Ireland I pray you that you will desire his favour and furtherance to me in this enterprise. He shall find me as ready to do any service there to Her Majesty underneath him, and to get any honour unto him, as he shall find any man; he is a gentleman whom I have ever loved and liked well of. And I have good hope I shall find him my friend; and yet some suspicion have I had of late of it by reason of some speech that hath passed from his near friends."

A later letter announcing his leave-taking of the Queen is written in a very fine and temperate spirit. He sailed long before Michaelmas, and among his companions was Lord Rich, whose son is intimately associated with this story. The expedition started under the most uncomfortable and unpropitious auspices with a shocking passage. The little fleet was scattered and driven on the Irish shore in different places—the vessel of Essex near the entrance of Belfast, that of Lord Rich at Castle Kilcliffe, while others drifted a-coast as far south as Cork.

The difficulties of the campaign quickly disheartened

nearly all the noble volunteers under Essex, the first of whom to go back to England and his comfortable Essex mansion was Lord Rich. Meanwhile Essex laboured in the saddle and out of it, and nevertheless found time to interest himself with regard to the future of his children. For his heir Robert he schemed at one time to win as a bride one of Burghley's daughters. This union was not carried through, as the lady married the disreputable and vindictive Edward de Vere, Earl of Oxford, to whom further allusion will be made. Later on, Essex wrote to Burghley asking that Robert might be committed to his charge and brought up with the young Cecils, since he was now of an age at which it was well for him to leave his mother's influence and receive other teaching. This plan was effected.

The next point of importance as regards Essex's family was his petition that his friend, Sir Henry Sidney, should be appointed Lord Deputy in place of the now unpopular Fitzwilliam. His own claims for the same post were pleaded by one of his friends in a document which shines with his praises : " How uncorrupt he is, how painful in watch, in travail, in wet and dry, in hunger and cold, and how frank of his own purse in Her Majesty's service, I will not speak." All his supporters agreed as to his own fitness for the Deputyship and the tragedy of his present position. " It were the greatest pity in the world that so noble and worthy a man as this Earl should consume himself in this enterprise, which, by Her Majesty's countenance and no great charges, would be so easily brought to pass. Well, if Her Majesty did know his noble and honourable intent . . . so well as we do know him, surely she would not suffer him to quail for half her kingdom of Ireland."

Undoubtedly he was the right man for the supreme

From the portrait in the National Portrait Gallery. Photo by Emery Walker

WILLIAM CECIL, LORD BURGHLEY

post in Ireland. But jealousy prevailed, and the next best thing from his point of view was the co-operation of Sir Henry Sidney. In 1575 the office of Earl Marshal in Ireland, now held by the Earl, was conferred on him for life. He had asked that it should be hereditary, but this Queen never gave with full hands!

Just before this all his anxious toil had been annulled by sudden orders from Court to abandon the Ulster campaign. It was done in a subtle fashion by depriving him of all but a remnant of the men serving under him. Upon this he tendered his resignation of the control of the province, and asked leave to live quietly and exercise his influence in a corner of Ulster, " which I hire for my money, where, though I may seem to pass my time somewhat obscurely, a life, my case considered, fittest for me, yet it shall not be without some stay in these parts, and comfort to such as hoped to be rid from the tyranny of rebels." The Queen dallied over the matter, wrote him sugary and flattering letters which filled him with false comfort and hope, and finally cut his special mission in two. For a while he remained in Ireland building fortifications, and at last, in 1575, was allowed to return to England on leave.

Let us see what happened to his family in his absence. All this time the hand busiest against his interests was, apparently, that of Lord Leicester, who was perfectly aware of the charms of a beautiful woman, and had every chance of meeting Lady Essex while he was forgetting Amy Robsart, going through a form of marriage with the widowed Lady Sheffield, and allowing ladies of fashion and sisters by blood to quarrel over their passion for him. Lettice Devereux was in her full beauty and surrounded by her lovely children. Their headquarters in England was Chartley, on the borders

of Staffordshire, the property which came through the
Ferrers branch of the family. When in London they
appear to have been domiciled at Essex House, in the
Strand.

To London the tired, impoverished Earl Marshal
came for a short space to attend the Court, see his
family, and try to mend the holes in his financial affairs.
Thence he went to Chartley, also for the latter purpose.
Very soon after he was on his way back to Holyhead and
his ragged, Irish task. But he had not forgotten in the
midst of more pressing affairs the future of his eldest
daughter. He had set on foot negotiations to betroth
her to Philip Sidney, the son of his good friend.

The families of Sidney and Devereux had one great
bond of sympathy—their poverty. This and their loyalty
to the Sovereign drew very close the two fathers who
worked together in Ireland. Rarely have two men
of such eminence and principle co-operated in such a
complex political situation. Together they strove to
solve the Irish problem, pleaded for assistance from
headquarters, endured too long the gracious meanness
of their Sovereign ; and both died true-hearted, and, in
the main, unembittered, in her service. But in their
deaths they were parted by some years. Had the great
Earl lived but two or three years longer his Penelope
would have spun her web differently, and possibly
certain love poems would never have been penned.
The poetic impulse which enshrined her for all time
would have found some other outlet, and enriched the
world in a new direction. Yet it is with the death of
her father in Ireland, immediately after his return in
1576, that Penelope's story really begins. As in the
case of Bess of Hardwick, nothing is told of her babyhood or childhood. The Elizabethan child was not

From an engraving in Plott

CHARTLEY

brought to the fore, and only in letters here and there do we get scraps of child life, showing that it was much the same as now, except that our sports are freer, our hygiene more rational, and our punishments more humane. We may assume that Penelope learnt to ride and dance and curtsey, and read and sing and sew, loved spice and sweets and flowers, and was initiated in the housekeeper's art. She does not appear real until she was thirteen—a very important age for an Elizabethan girl of good family. She was considered eligible, and her guardians usually lost no time in match-making. At this age Penelope Devereux attracted Philip Sidney, eight years her senior, and the friend of her brother, the Earl-elect. This was in 1576, and Sir Henry Sidney, acquainted with her father's wishes, now formally proposed for her hand on Philip's behalf. This was not the first overture as regards Philip. When he was fourteen a move was made by his father to secure him a bride in Anne Cecil, Burghley's eldest daughter. She was only a year younger than Philip, and from Sidney's point of view it was an ideal match. But her father had, financially, bigger game in view. He courteously refused the match, as in the case of Robert Devereux. Nevertheless, Lord Leicester was approached, and the matter was not finally closed . . . possibly on the assumption that the boy would inherit his uncle's wealth. The scheme went as far as discussion of marriage settlements before it fell through. Philip was busy at the university, and Anne as we know was betrothed eventually to Edward de Vere, Earl of Oxford, with whom, in after days, Philip came to blows at Court.

It was at Chartley that Philip Sidney met Penelope. He was then twenty-one. He was cultured, travelled,

widely known already at foreign Courts. Chartley,
which by some writers is accorded the additional title
of "castle," was a very beautiful and elaborate building
before it was attacked by fire in 1781, as is shown by
the engraving here reproduced from Plott's *History*.   It
had not the towers of a castle—the original castle, in
ruins, stood on the estate—but portions of the roof
were "embattled," and it was surrounded by a moat.
Built round a court, it was an edifice of many gables,
and contained a great deal of fine and fantastic wood-
work, plain and carved.   The armorial devices of the
Ferrers and other branches of the family were worked
into the window and into portions of the exterior and
interior of the structure.

It was a good house for entertaining guests, and while
Essex was in Ireland during the first part of his mission
Elizabeth visited his wife there.   In connection with
this great honour one discerns the hand of Lord
Leicester.   There is every reason to believe that from
the beginning he did his utmost to remove Essex as far
as possible from Court and the Queen's person.   Similarly, if he had chosen to prevent her from visiting
Lady Essex at Chartley he could have effected this.   But
he courted the society of Lettice Devereux, and at this
time, 1575, he had a special opportunity of doing this
lady honour.   He organised the famous pageant of
Kenilworth for the Queen's delectation, and among the
guests was Lady Essex.   At Kenilworth also were the
Sidneys, Lady Mary, her son and husband—for Sir
Henry did not leave for Ireland till later.   It is not
probable that Penelope went to Kenilworth.   She was
probably too young for such an affair.   It was on the
return journey, after a stay at Lichfield, that the Queen
halted at Chartley, bringing in her train Leicester and

From a painting at Warwick Castle.

ROBERT DUDLEY, EARL OF LEICESTER

the Sidneys. Here was food for romance indeed ! Here
began a new love-story for the mother, under the very
nose of Elizabeth, and the first of several love-stories
in the life of Penelope.   There were truly inflammable
ingredients under that beautiful roof of many gables.
As a curious contrast to them move the figures of
Philip's mother and father.   The former was Leicester's
sister, and as widely different from him as balsam from
hellebore.   She had but one love—her husband ; but
one desire—to live honestly and with gay courage. And
she needed it in her poverty, through all the wreck of
her beauty.   Would Leicester ever have risked his
health disinterestedly in his Queen's service ?   Would
he have attended her fearlessly through smallpox,
braved the disease, contracted it, and emerged, still brave
and loyal, with a disfigured face, saddened yet unembittered, and with no hope of recompense for his devotion and sacrifice ?   This—as history repeatedly shows—
was the story of Lady Mary Sidney, and for this reason
and because of their poverty Sir Henry and his " Old
Moll," as she dubbed herself, were glad enough to escape
service at Court whenever possible.

Nothing in the nature of a betrothal came out of
this hospitality at Chartley.   One cannot believe that the
hostess was very happy over it. She was never a favourite
of the Queen, and the knowledge that Essex had gone
upon his errand at such worldly disadvantage must
have been hard to forget while Her Majesty walked in
the gardens of Chartley, over the estates which, should
Essex fall finally upon evil days, might slip into the lap
of the Crown.

The acquaintance with the Sidneys, however, was to
be renewed in London.   The Queen summoned Lady
Mary to Court, and the poor soul had to obey, while Sir

Henry went off to his new post in Ireland. So with her daughter Mary and Philip she took up her residence in London in the family residence on the river, Durham House,[1] opposite Paul's Wharf. Only a few paces away on the Strand was the mansion of the Essex family, so that the young people of both families could often meet. If Leicester could have kept his mischievous hands out of their joint affairs just now, the affair between Philip and Penelope, despite her tender age, would have been fanned into betrothal. Lord Essex already wrote of Philip from Ireland as "my son by adoption." Had the Earl had more leisure on his flying visit to England, and had Penelope been sixteen instead of fourteen, the parents of boy and girl would assuredly have settled the matter. Leicester's efforts to hurry Essex back to Ireland were certainly among the causes which prevented this happy union. It is further possible that as Philip was his nephew he thought the boy, if unwed, would be more useful to Elizabeth at the moment, and also Leicester might judge Penelope's dowry—if indeed such a thing existed—as useless to an impoverished youth like Philip.

For the whole of a winter, a spring, and half a summer then, Philip and Penelope were in constant touch. After this Philip, as a natural sequence of affairs, joined his father in Ireland. Thus the three persons most important to her life and fate in this hour were far from Penelope Devereux when the thunderbolt of bad news fell upon her people. Death crashed across life, across Court entertainments, pageants, the visits of lords and ladies, the Court plays, the gardens, the daily tasks, the prayers, millinery, embroidery. After a very short

[1] Originally the London residence of the Bishops of Durham. The site is now occupied by the Adelphi Theatre.

From the painting in the collection of Lord De L'Isle

MARY, COUNTESS OF PEMBROKE

and sharp illness (dysentery) Lord Essex died. He faced it quietly, he made his preparations with sweetness and fortitude, while those about him were paralysed with grief, shamed by his patience, unable to bear the sight of his physical suffering. His last letter to the Queen, loyal, humble, pleading, is irradiated by a light which may be truly called saintly. His children were constantly in his mind. Above all, he longed for the coming of Philip. It was one more bitter drop in the Earl's cup that the boy reached him just two days too late to hear from his own lips his wishes in regard to Penelope. But they were faithfully repeated to Philip, with the phrases in which the Earl hungered for his arrival: "Oh, that good gentleman! Have me commended to him. And tell him I sent him nothing, but I wish him well—so well that, if God do move their hearts, I wish that he might match with my daughter. I call him son—he so wise, virtuous, and godly. If he go on in the course he hath begun, he will be as famous and worthy a gentleman as England ever bred."

In his last prayers for his family the Earl made especial petition for his two girls. Chancellor Gerrard wrote of it to Walsingham : " For his daughters also he prayed, lamenting the time, which is so frail and ungodly, considering the frailness of women. 'God defend them,' said he, 'bless them, and make them to fear his name, and Lord give them grace to lead a virtuous life.'"

Full well he realised that he had left three women to the mercy of Court temptations, three complex, keen natures, with the heritage of great beauty, in the rich possession of youth, and the prospect of many years of life, for even his wife was quite a young woman, still in her early thirties.

All this makes it clear that everything was in favour of this pretty Sidney-Devereux love-match, except money. The Queen took the young Essex under her protection, everyone combined to sympathise and assist, including Burghley, while Edward Waterhouse, secretary to Essex, a friend of both families, wrote thus to Philip's father :—

" All these Lords that wish well to the children, and I suppose all the best sorts of the English Lords besides do expect [1] what will become of the treaty between Mr. Philip and my Lady Penelope. Truly, my Lord, I must say to your Lordship as I have said to my Lord of Leicester and Mr. Philip, the breaking off from their match, if the default be on your parts, will turn to more dishonour than can be repaired with any other marriage in England."

[1] That is, "look anxiously for."

CHAPTER II

THE HOUSE OF SIDNEY

THE family of Penelope's first suitor was, like hers, of French origin. In the train of Henry II there came from Anjou a certain William Sidney. He received the honour of knighthood for distinction in battle, was endowed with the manor of Sutton, and was created Chamberlain to his royal master. It is scarcely necessary to follow the long line of Sidneys in detail up to the Tudor period. The only ancestor here necessary is that later William Sidney, a lineal descendant of the original gentleman from Anjou. This second William carried out the family reputation for soldiering, for he was in command of an important wing of the army which won the field of Flodden for his country. This and other services brought him posts and estates. He was given the manor of Penshurst, as lord of which he was appointed to the control of the education of Edward VI, in the capacity of tutor, chamberlain, and steward. His death took place a year after the accession of Mary of England. He left a son, Henry, a plain esquire, with the elements of distinction in arms and in diplomacy. Holinshed describes him as a man of good looks and fine nature, of "comliness of person, gallantness and liveliness of spirit, virtue, quality, beauty, and good composition of body," in a word, "the only odd man and paragon of the Court." That is to say,

he was an individual who stood out from the mass of
courtiers by brilliant and high qualities, a man who
struck you as entirely in a different mould from the
run of his fellows. Four years before his father's death
he was knighted at the same time as his contemporary
and senior, William Cecil, the future Lord Burghley
Of Henry Sidney—"this right famous, renowned
worthy, virtuous and heroical knight, by father and
mother very nobly descended"—Holinshed further
tells us what he was "from his infancy bred and brough
up in the prince's court and in nearness to his person
used familiarly, even as a companion." At the early
age of eight Henry Sidney was actually in personal
attendance on Henry VIII, who confided the upbringing
of his precious royal baby son to the Sidney family
Sir Henry has recorded the fact very simply: "I was
by that most famous King put to his sweet son, Prince
Edward, my most dear master, prince and sovereign
my near kinswoman being his only nurse; my father
being his chamberlain, my mother his governess; my
aunt in such place as, among meaner personages, is
called a dry nurse"—for she was in constant attendance
upon the child, "so long as he remained in women's
government."

Henry Sidney, therefore, had greater chances in life
than almost any of his contemporaries. His career
opened brilliantly. He inherited Penshurst at the
age of twenty-five, and here his wife, née Lady Mary
Dudley, sister of Lord Leicester, bore him their
eldest son, Philip. At the boy's birth an acorn was
planted, of which the oak afterwards shaded—alas!
not Philip, but his brother, Robert, and to which
Ben Jonson alludes in his poem on this beautiful
house :

From the portrait in the possession of Lord De L'Isle

SIR HENRY SIDNEY

> " Thou hast thy walks for health as well as sport,
> Thy mount to which the Dryads do resort,
> Where Pan and Bacchus their high feasts have made
> Beneath the broad beech and the chestnut shade ;
> That taller tree—which as a nut was set
> At his great birth, when all the Muses met."

And the delightful attitude of the host and hostess to their neighbour is equally well suggested :

> " And, though thy walls be of the country stone,
> They're reared with no man's ruin—no man's groan.
> There's none that dwell about them wish them down,
> But all come in, the farmer and the clown,
> And no one empty-handed, to salute
> Thy lord and lady, though they have no suit."

This, as explained, Ben Jonson wrote of Sir Henry Sidney's second son, Robert, who in after days by James was given the earldom of Leicester, in default of any other heir to his famous maternal uncle. But it was as true of Sir Henry and Lady Mary Sidney as of their successors. For it was the older couple who called the tune of sweet friendliness to which their domestic and country life travelled. Had Edward VI only lived, their home would never have suffered the strain of poverty, their hearts would never have been torn between their effort to be loyal to Elizabeth and yet stop short of the point where such headlong self-sacrifice halts before the precipice called self-destruction. The young King was Henry Sidney's contemporary, his dearest friend. Alas! for great hopes. Edward VI died in 1533. That he died in the arms of his young and faithful servant did not mean that Sidney's career in the next reign was assured. He had to make his way first with Mary, then with Elizabeth, and it was very soon patent to him, as to all those who put fidelity before the fattening of their

c

purses, that the second queen was one of those sovereigns
who, unless pestered for solid rewards after dangers and
difficult enterprises, expected her servants to be content
with her glowing praises.   All through their lives we
see Sir Henry and his lady struggling for recognition
and recompense.   The latter was in every sense a splendid
comrade of the road, and it is interesting to note that
while their eldest son revered the stock from which his
father sprang, his mother's race was the one which he
prized most highly.   This comes out forcibly in a
paper which in after years he penned in defence of
his uncle, Lord Leicester, and of the family of Dudley,
in reply to that scandalous, anonymous publication
entitled *Leicester's Commonwealth*.   This work, a most
frank and unbowdlerised publication, which was first
issued on the Continent and vainly suppressed, set
forth in detail the rumoured crimes and licentiousness
of Leicester.   He was fortunate to have so fair a pen-
champion of his memory as this nephew.

   To these Dudleys, as all books of pedigree show,
belonged originally the Dukedom of Northumberland.
Twelve generations previously came into notice their
ancestor, a certain Robert de L'Isle, who revolted with
other barons against King John, and was deprived of
his estates.   These he regained on the accession of
Henry III, but his posterity, until the reign of
Edward III, were in constant opposition to the
crowned authority.   This Edward brought the family
better days and a share in the victory of Creçy.
Thenceforward, through lack of male heirs, the title was
linked with the various marriages of the de L'Isle
ladies, until late in the fifteenth century a de L'Isle was
given in marriage to a Dudley.   This gentleman was
beheaded in 1509, and his family forfeited estates and

From the painting in the collection of Lord De L'Isle

SIR PHILIP SIDNEY AND HIS BROTHER, AFTERWARDS
EARL OF LEICESTER

dignities. It remained to his son John to rehabilitate his house. He did this to such good purpose that he quickly acquired the Barony of de L'Isle, the Earldom of Warwick, and the Dukedom of Northumberland. But this ambition killed him. His son, Lord Guildford Dudley, had married Lady Jane Grey. Northumberland, for crowning her, died on the block, and his son and daughter-in-law were sacrificed for his treason. His three sons, John, Ambrose, and Robert, were imprisoned for supposed share in the scheme. On their release they fared but poorly. John retired to Penshurst and died within a few days. Ambrose, destined one day to reclaim his elder brother's title of Earl of Warwick, and Robert were penniless. The extraordinary speed at which the last-named climbed to wealth and favour as Earl of Leicester extracts from his most bitter critics admiration of his personality. Of the two daughters of this family Mary Dudley found, as stated, a good husband in Henry Sidney, while Catherine married the Earl of Huntingdon. Thus we see how that estate of Penshurst, which was originally the lost home of the Dudleys, returned to them through Mary Sidney. Philip, when he looked back on the nearer family history of his mother's line, could not have been particularly proud of it. His maternal grandfather had been executed for treason, his uncle Guildford likewise. Three other uncles had begun their Court life in prison, while Leicester was the centre of a perfect bouquet of scandals. And yet the boy could take up the cudgels and write thus :

" I am a Dudley in blood, that duke's daughter's son ; and do acknowledge—though, in all truth, I may justly affirm that I am, by my father's side of ancient and always well-esteemed and well-matched gentry—yet I

do acknowledge, I say, that my chiefest honour is to be
a Dudley."

Certainly he saw all that race through the kindling,
tender eyes of "that duke's daughter," in whose love
his life was cradled and whose wisdom he worshipped.
She was certainly a very attractive and delightful
woman, with an uncommon mingling of robust courage,
pathos, and humour. Anything more absolutely unlike
her brother Robert cannot be conceived than this
patient, strong-hearted woman, who loved not Courts,
to whom all immorality was foreign, who had no love
save her husband, and never sponged on the rich or the
more successful of her circle. She sacrificed everything
for her husband and her five children, and in addition
to the purple disgrace of her father's and brother's
tragedy, she had her bitter private sorrows. Two of
her children died in babyhood, and Ambrosia, her third
daughter, named after her uncle of Warwick, in her
teens. And yet Mary Sidney carried a steady face and
an untired heart through it all. She could even, as her
picture at Penshurst shows, play the lute and wear
brave garments. Fortunate, indeed, is it for the present
generation that such a portrait of her exists to show her
as she was before she yielded her beauty to the smallpox after nursing Queen Elizabeth devotedly through
the same disease. In modern days a queen would have
acknowledged such a service, not only by a special
decoration, but a stout pension. Elizabeth did neither.
And so Mary Sidney, face to face with the gallants and
lovely ladies among whom she had by right the highest
place, could not bear the consciousness of her scarred
face, and went at all times most unwillingly to London.
Perhaps the hardest moment of all was when she had to
face her lover-husband on his return from his second

From a painting in the possession of Lord De L'Isle

LADY MARY SIDNEY

period of official activity in Ireland, and reveal to him the loss of her beauty in her prime. There is material here for as moving a little drama as can be imagined. Her husband himself has recorded his shock and sorrow in a letter which is amongst the State papers :—

" When I went to Newhaven I left her a full fair lady, in mine eye at least the fairest, and when I returned I found her as foul a lady as the smallpox could make her ; which she did take by continual attendance of Her Majesty's most precious person, sick of the same disease, the scars of which, to her resolute discomfort ever since, hath done and doth remain in her face, so as she liketh solitariness, *sicut nicticorax in domicilio suo.*"

Her health was, after this, always indifferent, but she struggled ever by letters and by practical endeavour to improve the position of her husband. For twelve years he served in Ireland as Lord Deputy, for twenty-six he was Lord President of Wales, and, like Essex, spent his gold and health for Elizabeth. At intervals on his return his wife would bestir herself, hidden in the country, chained to her bed by sickness, having no news to write "but of my unrecovered and unhealthful carcase," as she called it, yet, as Fulke Greville put it so finely, sustained always by her " large ingenuous spirit," a woman " *racked with native strengths.*" That immense vitality in her she handed on to at least two of her children, Philip, named, let us remind ourselves, after the then Spanish King Consort, and Mary, named after his queen. She bequeathed to them also, in Fulke Greville's happy phrase, her " ingenious sensibleness." The way in which she set to work to procure the aid of trusty Court friends elicited from Philip the exclamation, " Before God, there is none proceeds either so thoroughly or so wisely as my Lady, my Mother."

Both mother and eldest son toiled to keep the name and the reputation of the father clear from blame and suspicion. A miserable task enough! For Ireland, in many senses, was in those days what South Africa has been, and is, to many an Englishman of the nineteenth and twentieth centuries—a grave—of hopes as of physical vitality, a land of snares, pitfalls, and treasons. In addition, this was one of the old time-worn instances in which foreign service, be it never so bravely rendered or so well done, is the begetter of envy, hatred, and malice on the part of more leisured contemporaries in the home country. Age after age history repeats itself dully and with contemptible puerility in this direction. Henry Sidney had not only foes at home to fight second-handed through his nearest and dearest, but, like Lord Essex, the jealous hostility of the would-be loyal Irish to tackle. The Earl of Ormond was chief among these enemies abroad. The position and political relationship of Ormond and Sidney was unique. The Earl's own brother, Sir Edmund Butler, headed the Irish rebels. Sidney's business it was to hunt him down and capture him. State papers are very picturesque in their statement of the situation and capture and escape of this prisoner from Dublin Castle :—

"There had seemed likelihood of one brother being presently lodged in the Tower as a traitor, while the other was being petted at Whitehall as a courtier. But Butler had managed to escape from the Castle by means of a cord, which was broken by his weight, so that he had tumbled down and got many bruises by the fall, besides slipping into a shallow river, where, through a long, dark winter's night, he had to wait, up to his chin in the water, for an opportunity of finally running away."

Not the Butlers only, but Sidney's own brother-in-

law, Sir William Fitzwilliam, with whom Lord Essex
had so much difficulty, worked against him, and the
latter with the assistance of Ormond's flattery of the
Queen—a sweetmeat of which her palate never tired to
her dying day—supplanted Sidney in his Irish post.
This was another of those occasions when Elizabeth
presents to my mind the picture of a too keen trader
who is bent on giving short weight to his customers.
Balance in hand, she weighed not virtue against worth-
lessness, or large merits against small offences, but
always her will, her fear, her suspicion against the services of her men and women. Herself an arch oppor-
tunist, she could expect nothing but opportunism from
her courtiers. Many of them could disguise it. Few
of them but cherished it. Of these few, the Sidneys,
even had they employed it, would have been found out
soon enough by their inability to cloak their feelings.
At this crisis the royal dispenser of praise, blame, and
office, balanced Sir Henry's work in Ireland against
a barony. Honestly she may not have thought she was
giving her servant short weight. But she was. Of
what use was a peerage to a man who could not support
it ?[1] "Other men," as Fox-Bourne reminds us, "found
Ireland a mine of wealth," but this good knight, the
erstwhile paragon of the Court, "returned from each
holding of the Lord Deputy's office three thousand
pounds poorer than when he went."

The family expressed its views on the subject of the
proposed honour very plainly and with dignity. Mary
Sidney describes her lord as "greatly dismayed with his
hard choice." He could not support a title, yet in refusing it would offend the Queen. He risked the latter
course, and resumed his post as Lord President of Wales.

---

[1] *Memoir of Sir Philip Sidney* by Fox-Bourne.

This, however, gave the couple more social leisure. They visited Lord Leicester at Kenilworth on the occasion of the famous pageant for the Queen, Lady Essex, at Chartley, during Elizabeth's visit there, and from time to time they were in attendance on Her Majesty, and obliged to take up residence at whatever palace she affected. In the present case, the winter of 1578, when Sir Henry had returned from Ireland for the third time, the *mise en scène* was Hampton Court, shockingly overcrowded and uncomfortable. Poor Lady Mary was in feeble health. Her constitution never recovered the blood-poisoning it had from " the pock." She had not improved matters by her devoted journey to Ireland to tend and assist her husband, who already, at forty-three, was an ageing man. She was obliged often to keep her bed. She knew the capacity of Hampton Court, and the utter disregard by chamberlains and other authorities of the comfort and well-being of the officials whose residence was commanded, and in successive letters she urged the family secretary, Edmund Molineux, to use interest for his employers' domestic comfort :

" I thought good to put you in remembrance to move my Lord Chamberlain in my Lord's name, to have some other room than my chamber to have his resort unto, as he was wont to have ; or else my Lord will be greatly troubled when he shall have matters of despatch : my lodging, you see, being very little, and myself continually sick and not able to be much out of my bed. For the night-time one roof, with God's grace, shall serve for us ; for the day-time, the Queen will look to have my chamber always in readiness for Her Majesty's coming thither ; and though my Lord himself can be no impediment thereto by his own presence, yet his Lordship, trusting to no place else to be provided for him, will be . . . troubled for want of a convenient place for the despatch of such people as shall have occasion to come to him. Therefore, I pray you in my Lord's own name, move my Lord of Sussex for a room for that purpose, and I will have it hanged and lined for him with stuff from thence."

The ideas of an Elizabethan Lord Chamberlain on these subjects are indeed amazing. In one chamber an important official and his wife were to sleep, carry on their work, receive not only private, but official visitors, of every sort and condition, and still be open to sudden visits from the Queen. And there would often be days when Lady Mary could not lift her head from her pillow. Was she then to hide within the curtains of the four-poster, or behind the tapestries, with all of which she was expected to furnish the official lodging at her own cost and out of her own meagre household store ? Apparently such was the placid assumption of the niggardly Lord Sussex. Every difficulty seems to have been put in the way of Lady Mary ; for again she wrote to Molineux :—

"You have used the matter very well ; but we must do more yet for the good dear Lord, than let him be thus dealt withal. Hampton Court I never yet knew so full as there were not spare rooms in it when it hath been thrice better filled than at this present it is. But some would be sorry perhaps, my Lord should have such sure footing in the Court. Well, all may be as well when the good God will. The whilst, I pray, let us do what we may for our Lord's ease and quiet. . . . Also, if you go to Mr. Bowyer, the gentleman Usher, and tell him his Mother requireth him, which is myself, to help my Lord with some one room, but only for the despatch of the multitude of Irish and Welsh people that follow him, and that you will give your word, in

your Lord's behalf and mine, (that) it shall not be
counted as a lodging, or known of, I believe he will
make what shift he can. . . . But when the worst is
known, old Lord Harry and his old Moll will do
as well as they can in parting, (sharing) like good
friends, the small portion allotted our long service in
Court ; which as little as it is, seems sometimes too
much.   And this being all I can say to the matter,
farewell, Mr. Ned."

In this letter, which closes, " Your assured loving
mistress and friend," the whole personality of this
delightful woman flashes forth.   We discern the sturdy
fighting spirit, her deep devotion to her " good, dear
Lord," her pathos, humility, and irony when she touches
upon Court ways ; her practical housewifery, her understanding of her husband's official requirements, and the
charming relationship—that of a mother to a son—in
which her qualities and position placed her in regard to
young minor officials in attendance on the Queen's
person.   It is extraordinary that throughout her close
intimacy with that sovereign her tongue was never betrayed into disloyalty, malice, or bitterness.   At the
most, a light irony is all she allows herself.   How she
kept not only her own body and soul together in her
various moves from Court to camp, from camp to
Welsh castle, and castle to Kentish manor, but also provided for the needs of her children, is a marvel.   A
household move in those days, plus a journey, was an
affair of indescribable cumbrousness.   All through the
domestic correspondence of the great ladies and gentlemen of the ages preceding the mural use of panelling
or the employment of permanent brocades, allusions to
the tapestries and hangings, which it was needful to cart
about England, fill the mind of a modern householder

From the painting in the collection of Lord De L'Isle

ROBERT SIDNEY, EARL OF LEICESTER

with dismay. And all this in addition to the launching of sons and daughters in the world !

Philip was the most expensive item in this reckoning. His great qualities, his many graces imperiously demanded a fair field and all the advantages which could be procured for him. Not only tutorship, but a "grand tour of European travel," were part of the parents' programme for him. And there were Robert Sidney, the next brother, and Thomas, afterwards called Colonel Sidney (about whom history tells so little), to be educated, tutored, and as far as possible also allowed European experience. Imagine, too, the details of wardrobe all this entailed—especially for Philip. There must be doublets, hose, scented waistcoats, cloaks, and velvet and satin plumed hats for the courtier, with a constant reinforcement of gloves and shoes. The young man's valet also needed what some modern ladies' papers would call "sartorial provision" over and above the garments which his screw could furnish him, especially when his master "lay" at Court, travelled abroad in the company of ambassadors, or, as a representative of the Queen, dined at home or on the Continent as the guest of princes. The shoes, the shoes ! If one could but gather all those which Philip alone wore in the course of his thirty-one years into a single parlour, what a romance they would furnish under the borrowed title of a *Salle des pas perdus*.[1] Yet were his comings and goings never "lost" in the sense of fruitlessness. His feet never carried him anywhere without high purpose, and seldom failed to bear him triumphantly through

---

[1] If history and State documents had only preserved for us the corresponding amount of dainty Court slippers worn by Penelope Rich, it would make a rare pendant to the list just quoted in the gallery of the world's fripperies.

his greatest errands.   Here is a shoemaker's bill which
the first volume of the *Sidney Papers* has preserved
for us :—

S<small>IR</small> P<small>HILLIP</small> S<small>YDNEY</small>

First, for two pairs of pantoffles and two pairs of shoes for yourself	6s. 8d.
Item, one pair of strong shoes for yourself	16d.
Item, for one pair of boots for Mr. Weddell.	6s. 8d.
Item, for one pair of shoes for him	12d.
Item, for four pairs of shoes for your servant the footman	4s. 8d.
Item, for four pair of shoes for Thomas, your man	4s.
Item, for one pair of white shoes and one pair of of pantoffles for yourself	4s. 8d.
Item, for one pair of Spanish leather shoes, double soled.	20d.
Item, for three pairs of shoes for three of the men.	3s.
Item, for one pair of pumps for Griffin the man	8d.
Item, for one pair of Spanish leather shoes for yourself.	20d.
Item, for one pair for your footman.	14d.
Item, for soling a pair of shoes for Thomas.	8d.
Item, for one pair of buckled boots at. the pair.	8s.
and one pair of winter boots for yourself	15s.
Item, eight pair of Spanish leather slippers for yourself	17s. 6d.
Item, for four pair of shoes for Thomas	4s.
Item, for six pair of shoes for Thomas, footman	7s.
Item, for soling a pair of shoes for Thomas your man	8d.

CHAPTER III

THE SPLENDID PHILIP

OUT of the conditions already stated the eldest son of the Sidneys had to build up his reputation, maintain his family's name, and learn the whole story of the sweet bitterness of Court service under Elizabeth.

As in the case of Penelope, his upbringing had been that of a sturdy Protestant. Unlike her, he had, of course, special advantages in the way of education. One does not imagine that Lettice Devereux ever encouraged a desire for deep study in her children akin to that which actuated that household at Penshurst, where Mary and Philip shared in youth and in maturity the joys of learning, the graces of legend and of literary rhymes. With this deeply serious habit of mind the boy possessed a deeply romantic nature, and the combination of these two marked him out very early for distinction. Naturally also he took himself very seriously, analysed his emotions and thoughts a good deal, was as keenly responsive to the events of the day as he was to all things vital and beautiful. An ardent idealist, he was rich also in energy, mental and physical. He was poor—poorer than ever, for on a certain journey to Ireland his father and mother were shipwrecked, and were deprived of nearly everything but their lives. "I lost," wrote

Sir Henry, "the most of my household stuff and utensils, my wife's whole apparel, and all her jewels, many horses, and stable-stuff." Hence Philip had his way to make financially as well as socially. At Shrewsbury—whither he was sent to school while his father, as Lord President of Wales, made his head-quarters at Ludlow Castle—he did well as to books and manners. Of his moral and spiritual sense, which developed so early, surely those two good parents of his assuredly laid the foundation with love and care. And from that spiritual sense again uprose his courage and sweetness, his fine "temper." One of his father's letters to him at school is amongst tutors and parents probably an oft-quoted and well-thumbed document, but I would have it framed in every English study. Here are fragments :

"Above all tell no untruth ; no, not in trifles. The custom of it is naughty. . . . There cannot be a greater reproach to a gentleman than to be accused a liar. . . . Study and endeavour yourself to be virtuously occupied : so shall you make such a habit of well-doing in you, that you shall not know how to do evil, though you would. Remember, my son, the noble blood you are descended of, by your mother's side. . . . Think upon every word that you will speak before you utter it, and remember how nature hath ramparted up, as it were, the tongue with teeth, lips, yea, and hair without the lips, and all betokening reins or bridles for the loose use of that member. . . . Give yourself to be merry ; for you degenerate from your father if you find not yourself most able in wit and body and to do anything when you be most merry : but let your mirth be ever void of all scurrility and biting words to any man, for a wound given by a word is oftentimes harder to be cured than that which is given with the sword. Be modest in each assembly. . . . Well, my little Philip . . . this is enough for me, and too much, I fear, for you. But if I shall find that this light meal of digestion nourish anything in the weak stomach of your capacity, I will, as I find the same grow stronger, feed it with tougher food."

This "little Philip" with his hot, high spirit, had graver dangers to run than those of a public school. Through heats and angers, loves and hates, trust and mistrust, he passed at furious pace, as a child runs the gauntlet of all its early diseases. All this his mother foresaw when she added a long postscript, slipping it "in the skirts of my Lord President's letter," in which she explains that she writes only a message of her own lest it should prevent her son from "reverently honouring" and fully appreciating the counsel of his father. From that she will not withdraw the boy's eyes, "no, not so long time as to read any letter from me." He is to keep his father's letter always before the "eyes of his mind," and to read it over at least once in five days.

Philip went in due course, at the absurdly early age of fourteen, usual in those days, to Oxford, as a student at Christ Church. This brought him into closer touch with the great men of the future, the official celebrities of the day. Sir William Cecil, not yet a peer, specially took note of him, and the boy spent his New Year vacation at Hampton Court with the family of "Mr. Secretary." Here as we know he met, not Penelope, but a very different girl, Anne, the eldest daughter of the Cecils, of whom his father was already fond. All his friends, young and old, spoke well of him. Cecil wrote to his father : "Your Philip is here, in whom I take more comfort than I do openly utter, for avoiding of wrong interpretation. He is worthy to be

loved, and so do I love him as he were my own." And
bis school comrade, Fulke Greville (Lord Brooke), put
it more strongly in later years, "Of his youth I will report
no other wonder but this, that though I lived with him
and knew him from a child, yet I never knew him other
than a man ; with such staidness of mind, lovely and
familiar gravity, as carried grace and reverence above
greater years ; his talk ever of knowledge, and his very
play tending to enrich his mind, so as even his teachers
found something in him to observe and learn above
that which they had usually read or taught."

His father called the boy "the light of his family."
He was in every sense, under all circumstances, life-
giving, a stimulant to all about him. This, with his
keen observation and scholarship, singled him out
from the very beginning for that diplomatic career
which was chosen for him. This began soon after he
left college in 1571, at the age of eighteen. He was
driven from Oxford by a fierce outbreak of the plague.
For about a year after this his movements are not quite
established by history. It is on the cards that in the
height of his fever for study he went to Cambridge for
a year. It is equally likely that he joined his family at
Ludlow Castle, and made good use of the time to finish
his earlier studies there. At the close of this epoch he
visited his old school in company with his father, and
Shrewsbury town gave them a good welcome "in wine
and cakes and other things." After this it was considered that the moment had come for the boy to see
the practical working out of those theories of government and politics of which, so far, he had only second-
hand experience through books. The Queen's projected
marriage with the Duke of Anjou, the younger brother
of Charles IX, gave him his opportunity, brought him

From the painting at Warwick Castle

SIR PHILIP SIDNEY

in after years one of his richest experiences, and resulted also in the penning of a letter which is one of the most remarkable ever written, and one of the most valuable of State papers. The Queen, while she played with the Duke and received the passionate and unbridled ex-pression of his devotion, called him, as readers of her courtships will remember, her "Frogg." He was a mere boy, and Elizabeth was thirty-eight. His face was pitted with smallpox; he was undersized and *chétif*. One wonders whether he really wrote those very masculine love-letters, or whether he employed an imaginative subordinate, a Court prose poet.

The English ambassador, who at the moment was Walsingham himself, had written to urge the marriage, the French Court smiled upon it, and the Queen sent over a special ambassador to discuss the affair. Philip, through Leicester's influence, was deputed to accompany this official, the Earl of Lincoln. The Earl was not long over his business. When he returned to England with a favourable report, which, even after centuries, astounds one, Philip did not accompany him. He stayed on to study Paris, make closer acquaintance with Walsingham, and enjoy and observe the volcanic atmo-sphere of the dazzling French Court. This was the beginning of a long tour. Therefore, it is conceivable that even while he was in England the Sydney-Cecil match went forward but slowly.

Thus, by the time Philip met Penelope in London and at Chartley, he was heart-free and ripe for love-fancies. He was a *preux chevalier*, intensely skilled as swordsman and horseman; while abroad he had made a special study of riding. A verse in Shakespeare's *Lover's Complaint* seems to be the very picture of him as he rode in attendance on the Queen, and curiously pre-

D

figures him as he must have looked at the battle of
Zutphen, when his horse was killed under him :

> " Well could he ride, and often men would say
> ' That horse his mettle from his rider takes :
> Proud of subjection, noble by the sway,
> What rounds, what bounds, what course, what stop he
>   makes ! ' "

Just now, moreover, he was at an age when ardour
flies to verse. One biographer suggests that a poem,
part of which is quoted here, represents his attitude to
love at this crisis :

> " Since, shunning pain, I ease can never find,
> Since bashful dread seeks where he knows me harmed,
> Since will is one and stopped ears are charmed,
> Since force does faint, and sight doth make me blind,
> Since, loosing long, the faster still I bind,
> Since naked sense can conquer reason armed,
> Since heart in chilling fear with ice is warmed,
> In fine, since strife of thought but mars the mind,
> I yield, O Love ! unto thy loathèd yoke."

The suggestion that he falls in love in spite of a stout
will and " stopped ears " is delicious, and quite in keeping with the grand attitude of vanity which a sentimental
boy loves to assume.

As a matter of fact, his head was full of many other
things. His man's destiny pulled him one way, his
youth's passion another. He was no loose-liver. Some
day he planned to lay his sword, his learning, and his
heart at the feet of a woman, he meant to abide by her,
to found his own family, and in after years find the roof
of lovely Penshurst sheltering his old age as it had
sheltered his babyhood. But just now everything in
his surroundings fired his ambition, claimed all his
diplomatic art, his courtier's hopes and proficiencies.
For three years he had travelled—visited Poland and

Belgium, been to Paris, and Vienna and Frankfurt, Venice and Padua, Prague, Dresden, Heidelberg and Strasburg, ere he came home via Antwerp. In regard to tremendous events in foreign capitals he had truly been well blooded. For he saw Paris through the red pageant of the Massacre of St. Bartholomew. And now, after the splendid Kenilworth masque, unparalleled in the history of such productions, and the winter and spring at Court, he was about to be despatched as a special ambassador to Germany. Early during his wanderings he had made a fast friendship and a rare one with Hubert Languet, ex-Romanist, and ex-professor of civil law. Paris brought them together, for Languet, a newly made Protestant, was, at the time of the Huguenot crisis, lying *perdu* in the city, waiting for a favourable moment to deliver to the French king an address from German princes. Languet was in the prime of middle age—the early fifties. To him Philip appeared as a resplendent spiritual son, a youth so precious that he would fain have a share in the making and shaping of his manhood during a period when new experiences were thrusting at once dangers, delights, and possibilities upon the gifted young diplomat. Theirs was a rich correspondence. His adoration for Philip was almost feminine. Above all was he desirous to see his darling married. In 1577, aware that Philip had no other fixed views in prospect, and certainly unaware of the budding passion for Penelope Devereux, the eager professor actually tried his hand at match-making, and there is evidence that he selected a suitable German lady for his friend. If Philip had fallen in love now, one has a vision of him settling on the Continent for ever, possibly as ambassador at Vienna or Prague, a father of future landgraves. England would have lost its first of gallants, one of its greatest romancists, most intrepid *littérateurs*, its finest military heroes. Fortunately, he was still very vague, as to matrimony, and thus escaped this plot of Languet.

After this, the young man went back to England for a very brief space. He was now (1578) twenty-three, and Penelope fifteen. Lady Essex was just emerging from her widowhood and going to Court again. Now was the moment to choose a wife and choose well. Alack! Philip, now a knight, had his eyes focussed upon foreign service once more. He wanted to fight in the Netherlands. Languet opposed this stoutly. Of what use, he argued, was it for a man so brilliant to risk his life and waste his force in work which could be accomplished by dullards whose lives were not so costly to the State? And it is in this connection that he urges marriage so seriously on Philip :

"In so large a kingdom as yours there can never be lacking chances of exercising your genius, so that many may see the good fruit of honest labour. You may be sure that praise and glory are the reward of goodness, and never fail of being duly paid. If you marry a wife and beget children like yourself, you will be a better servant of your country than if you cut the throats of a thousand Spaniards or Frenchmen."

This was not the first attempt on the old politician's part. Already in 1575, while Philip was, as Fox-Bourne phrases it, "walking in and out of Court in his white shoes" and in close touch with young Penelope, Languet had opened his attack. To wit, on August 15th, 1575 : "May God grant that our excellent friend Wotton's[1] new purpose of matrimony may prove successful and happy. He is going before to set you an example ; but I believe

---

[1] This young gentleman became secretary to the young Earl of Essex.

From the painting in the collection of Lord De L'Isle

HUBERT LANGUET

you are well inclined of yourself and do not need exhortation." In reply, Sidney seems to have treated the matter carelessly. So Languet replies on December 3rd (1575) :

" What you write in jest about a wife I take seriously. Be not too confident in your own firmness : more cautious men than yourself are sometimes caught. For my part I should be glad if you were caught, so that you might give to your country sons like yourself. Whatever is to happen in the matter, I pray God it may turn out well and happily for you. You see with what high courage our friend Wotton, has passed through this peril; his boldness seems to convict you of cowardice. Destiny has a good deal to do with the matter, and so you must not suppose that by your own foresight you can so conduct it as to be entirely happy, and that all shall turn out as you desire."

In a letter of January 8th, 1578, Languet returns to the attack, " beginning in jest and ending in very tender earnest." Sidney replies :—

" I wonder what has come into your mind that, when I have not as yet done anything worthy of me, you would have me bound in the chains of matrimony, and yet without pointing out any individual lady, but rather seeming to extol the state itself, which, however, you have not yet sanctioned by your own example. Respecting her, of whom I readily acknowledge how unworthy I am, I have written you my reasons[1] long since ; briefly indeed, but yet as well as I was able. At this present time, indeed, I believe you have entertained some other notion which I earnestly entreat you to acquaint me with, whatever it may be : for everything that comes from you has great weight with me ; and to speak candidly, I am in some measure doubting whether someone, more suspicious than wise, has not whispered

---

[1] The letter containing his " reasons " no longer exists.

to you something unfavourable concerning me, which, though you did not give entire credit to it, you nevertheless, prudently and as a friend, thought right to suggest for my consideration. Should this have been the case I entreat you to state the matter to me in plain terms, that I may be able to acquit myself before you, of whose good opinion I am most desirious : and should it prove to have been a joke, or a piece of friendly advice, I pray you nevertheless to let me know ; since everything from you will always be no less acceptable to me than the things which I hold most dear."

It is amazing that Philip did not now, in support of his willingness to take advice and seek opportunities of marriage, press his suit in the direction of Penelope, if she be the lady of whom he acknowledges himself as unworthy. True she was very much his junior, and during his vast experience of Courts and countries he may well have felt that his emotions were not actually concentrated on any one woman. Then there were family claims which, after his long absences, he could not resist. There was the betrothal of his young sister, Mary, to the Earl of Pembroke, and the financial distresses of his parents. As to this match, it was excellent—one of the few in which the Queen did not meddle, one of the few of whom all concerned approved, and, unlike the marriages of the bride's Devereux contemporaries, was not a clandestine matter, to be kept secret as long as possible from the ears of Elizabeth. It was not altogether a triumphant ceremony, for the bride's father could not be present. Even for such an important family event he could not get leave from his Irish duties. The couple settled, of course, at Wilton, and there Philip visited them. Thence he was forced to hasten back to Court to take up the

cudgels on behalf of his father, whom the Queen
accused of spending too much on his administration,
while his enemies further assured her that he and
Leicester schemed against her. Leicester, she was told,
planned to marry her and secure a crown ; Sidney, with
his help, was to seize Ireland for himself and reign there.
The main grievance was the cost of Irish affairs. Sir
Henry, it was stated, levied taxes on the rich for the
maintenance of fortifications, and so forth. Certain of
the Irish nobles, who by craft had succeeded hitherto in
avoiding taxation under the guise of being privileged
persons, whose services to the Crown exempted them
from such duties, accused the present Deputy of abusing
his powers and mismanaging the revenues at his command. It needed all Philip's force and brains to fight
single-handed against these Irish peers, the Treasury,
and the Queen, to prove his father's single-heartedness,
and in the end to show that his sturdy and bitter
complaint of personal poverty was pitilessly true. Out
of this battle of pounds, shillings, and pence the young
courtier came triumphantly, freed his family from all
slur, and greatly strengthened his own position at Court.

Is it not perfectly natural that after such a fight for
the honour of his house, with his eye on his own needy
purse, in face of the contrast between this, his own
ambitions, and the constant financial drain inseparable
from Court life, Philip should have been tempted by
gold-fever ? Those were marvellous days for voyages,
days of dream-travel, rich with hopes of the harvest of
new lands. Wealthy noblemen made it their business
to fit out prospecting expeditions, just as capitalists to-
day finance aërial experiments. Among these was the
Earl of Warwick, another uncle of Sidney's, whose wealth
helped the great, the sensationally popular Martin

Frobisher to his American voyages. Philip certainly heard the tale of these journeys from the adventurer himself, judging by the vivid way in which he poured it out to Languet :

"A piece of earth glittering on the ground . . . the purest gold, unalloyed with any other metal. . . . The island is so productive in metals as far to surpass Peru. . . . There are six other islands near to this, which seem very little inferior. . . . He has now returned bringing his ships . . . fully laden, and he is said to have brought two hundred tons of ore. . . . So pray, for the sake of our love of one another, send me your opinion on this subject, and at the same time describe the most convenient method of working these ores. Remember . . . so to write as that you may answer the great reputation in which you are held here ; for unless you forbid it, I will show your letter to the Queen."

Languet did write, of course, and very forcibly. Even as the victor in the old duels of savage medieval days rubbed earth and gravel into the wounds of his opponent, so did Languet, from the vantage ground of his age, experience, and religious philosophy, imprint the gritty dangers of that marvellous American ore into the mind of his young friend—and, indirectly, into that of the Queen :

"Who could have thought that the extreme north would supply us with such an incitement to evil ? You have stumbled on that gift of nature which is of all the most fatal and baneful to mankind. . . . I fear that England, quickened by the love of gold, will just empty itself into those islands. . . . Do I therefore think that you should reject these good things which God has thrown in your way ? Anything but that. . . . I am thinking of you. . . . If Frobisher's . . . hope of finding a North-West Passage has power to tempt your mind so greatly, what will not these golden mountains do, or rather these islands of gold, as I daresay they shape themselves day and night in your mind? Beware, I do beseech you, and never let the cursed hunger after gold, whereof the poet speaks, creep over that spirit of yours, into which nothing has ever hitherto been admitted save the love of goodness and the desire of earning the goodwill of all men. . . . What is the object of all this? you will say. That if these golden islands are fixing themselves too firmly in your thoughts, you may turn them out before they overcome you, and may keep yourself safe till you can serve your friends and your country in a better way."

Such a letter was a strong deterrent. It might still have not diverted Philip from his gold-dream. It certainly delayed him—fortunately just long enough to enable chemists to discover that this North American ore was practically worthless.

Frobisher sailed again, but Philip's ardour was chilled. He turned his attention to Court ceremonies. The old absurd business of *étrennes* to the Sovereign once more sapped his purse. New Year offerings of the Sidney family this year (1579) were well to the fore—far grander than those of Lady Essex, whose widowhood, perhaps, suffices to account for the poor show she was able to make with a little array of ruffs. Lady Mary Sidney presented gloves, perfumed, and twenty-four gold buttons with diamond centres. Possibly she also selected the gift which bore Philip's name, for it consisted of two very feminine items—a cambric chemise, with sleeves and collar embroidered with black and edged with gold and silver lace, and a pair of ruffs heavily spangled and adorned with silver and gold !

Penelope Devereux presented nothing, so far as I know. She seems to have been kept well in the background by her mother, whose own matrimonial plans were probably setting her head and heart afire. One regards the latter, Lettice, at this juncture in the light of a typical " smart " Society woman, who did not wish to be troubled much with the prospects of her daughters while her own youth and beauty were throwing spells upon the promiscuously amorous but never really conquered Leicester. If in this I wrong her memory, may her shade forgive me, and the tale of her many sorrows in the near future rebuild her dignity and restore her good intentions. She may well have desired a second husband. Life is always a hard struggle for the poor widows of eminent men, and she was not a shrewd, overpowering, dominant creature like some of her contemporaries—Bess of Hardwick, for instance—nor had she that steely strength and rigid purpose which later carried such a woman as Lady Anna Clifford through her long married life and her conjugal quarrels over property. That Lettice sought a high marriage as the only way out of financial embarrassment and the best means of warding off that which every great lady fears more—nonentity through poverty—is perfectly reasonable. That she should have let her beautiful eyes dwell so long on Leicester is amazing, in spite of his dazzling position, his accomplished powers of paying his court to the woman he most fancied at the particular moment. She must have known all the gossip about him. Even if she did not realise his scandalous treatment of Lady Sheffield, who, he declared, was not legally his second wife, she must have been rendered very miserable by the report—though quite unfounded—that the sudden death of Essex in Ireland was due to a poison administered through Leicester's agency. She may, on the other hand, have regarded this as an excuse for marriage,

by which the strongest proof of this lie could be given
to the world. While she contemplated such an act she
had to work very hard to win the Queen's favour.
Elizabeth's lukewarm regard of her at this period has
never been explained. Feminine jealousy, while as yet
no open cause was to hand for it, can have been the
only reason. If Lettice Devereux had wished to push
on Penelope's affair she had full power to do so through
her hold on Leicester. But she was unwise, and let the
opportunity slip. Meanwhile the Earl of Huntingdon,
who was actually Philip's uncle by marriage, had been
appointed guardian of her children, and Penelope and
Dorothy made their head-quarters with him and his wife
in the country.

But to return to Philip, whom we left but shortly
in the act of presenting New Year offerings to his
Queen.

His life, for the moment, was one of continual un-
rest. Never was he sure of Her Majesty's trust;
always was he placed as buffer between his father's
struggle to convince her of his honesty and her own
inexhaustible suspicion.

Once again Philip did respectful combat on behalf
of his house; once more, by his single-heartedness and
his winning graces, he kept his foothold near the person
of Elizabeth, and all the while his heart and head
were in rebellion. He was ever conscious of fetters,
of the narrowness and barrenness of his life and conditions.

Suddenly, like a lovely distraction, there came to
him a clear call to put his pen to paper, not for political,
controversial, or family causes, but for the gaiety of his
neighbours. With all his tragic seriousness he had in
him that really divine power to delight. He should

have been spared the greater strains, the weary fights, the strife of words which enmeshed him, and surely have come down to history as a sparkling soul formed solely *pour égayer les cœurs* in the ancient phrase. The elements of comedy and of satire were strong in him, but it is wonderful that in the midst of so much courtly turmoil and at such a grave political crisis they were not crushed out, or his spirit soured. Yet, in the whirl of all his serious activities, he found time for his first literary achievement. This was a masque, inspired, no doubt, by that magnificent " show " at Kenilworth, at which he had formed one of the audience. Once more it is connected with his uncle, Leicester, who undoubtedly encouraged the conception and fathered the production of it, for it was devised to honour and please Elizabeth upon another of her visits to that Earl.

The place of performance this time was Wanstead, one of the royal manors in Epping Forest, which Leicester had recently acquired by purchase from Lord Rich. It was a great occasion for uncle and nephew. The Earl had fitted out and richly furnished the old house, and in the high tide of spring Her Majesty, with full cortège, came as his guest. What better or sweeter title for occasion and season could the literary aspirant choose than *The Lady of the May?* As to plot, it is mild, not to say thin. Yet comedy and grace were in it, and it is chiefly noteworthy for the inclusion of a satire, not only upon the pedantic writers of the age, but upon the speech of those who parade as cultured folk. Philip was not, of course, first in the field in this respect. Already, in the second year of Elizabeth, his old friend and Walsingham's coadjutor in the secretaryship of State, Thomas Wilson, had penned his famous *Art of Rhetoric*, practically the pioneer of works of such criticism in this country. "Some," he wrote, "seek so far outlandish English, that they forget altogether their mother's language. And I dare swear this, if some of their mothers were alive they were not able to tell what they say ; and yet these fine English clerks will say they speak in their mother tongue, if a man should charge them with counterfeiting the King's English. Some far-journeyed gentlemen, at their return home, like as they love to go in foreign apparel, so they will powder their talk with oversea language." How inevitably in this context you sum up the favourite, tiresome colloquialisms of the Anglo-Indians of your acquaintance, or the newest Yankee idioms imported by Anglo-Americans ! And is it not so with the continental traveller of a certain type in our day, even as when Wilson wrote thus : "He that cometh lately out of France will talk French-English, and never blush at the matter. Another chops in with English Italianated. . . ." This assumption of superior knowledge invaded, in those times, the realms of the higher poets in a way that would amaze the present "hustling" age, which recks nothing of good verse : "The fine courtier will talk nothing but Chaucer ! " wrote Wilson. Again the infection has spread delightfully to the literary and professional classes : "The mystical wise men and poetical clerks will speak nothing but quaint proverbs and blind allegories, delighting much in their own darkness"—a delicious hit at the wilfully obscure stylists of all ages —"especially when none can tell what they do say. The unlearned or foolish fantastical, that smells but of learning, such fellows as have seen learned men in their days, will so Latin their tongues that the simple cannot but wonder at their talk, and think surely they speak by some revelation . . . and he that can catch an ink-horn term by the tail him they count a fine Englishman and a rhetorician."

If I have digressed a little further than I intended in introducing this bit of literary satire, I must be forgiven by grace of the really delicious phrases it contains, such as that "inkhorn term," caught and used by the unlearned in its most awkward fashion. This lively Dean of Durham, whose irony flogged the bookish vanity of his day, also brought down his inky scourge upon the fashion for alliteration. Fox-Bourne has culled for posterity a rare example of this :

"Pitiful Poverty prayeth for a penny, but puffed presumption payeth not a point, pampering his paunch with pestilent pleasures, procuring his passport to post it to hell-pit, there to be punished with pain perpetual."

And so Philip Sidney, when he imagined and pro-jected on the canvas of his spring pastoral the figure of the pedagogue Rhombus, had cause and precedent enough for this ingredient in the picture. The masque concerns itself briefly with the old question of the worth and merits of the men of the chase, the pursuers, against that of the men of the pastures, who do not hunt nature down, but cherish and guard it. The subject was naïvely introduced, while the Queen wandered in the grounds of Wanstead, in the person of a sturdy countrywoman, who complained to her that her daughter was pestered by two suitors. Instantly, the poor beauty herself—Lady of the May—was dragged out of a thicket by six shepherds, "hauling and pulling to which side they should draw"; in effect a regular game of "oranges and lemons" over the fair one. Upon this, an old

shepherd came to assure the audience that the brains of
two of his best countrymen had been turned by a young
woman of a "minsical countenance," but that the affair
would be far better explained—"disnounced"—by
Rhombus. Into the play of words, therefore, bounces
the pedagogue with a magnificent mouthful of welcome
and flattery to the Queen :

"Now the thunder-thumping Jove transfer his dotes
into your excellent formosity, which have, with your
resplendent beams, thus segregated the enmity of these
rural animals. I am . . . a pedagogue, one not a little
versed in the disciplinating of the juvenile fry, wherein,
to my laud I say it, I use such geometrical proportion,
as neither wanteth mansuetude nor correction. . . .
Yet hath not the pulchritude of my virtues protected
me from the contaminating hands of these plebeians ;
for coming . . . to have parted their sanguinolent
fray, they yielded me no more reverence then if I had
been some *pecorius asinus*."

After a little more egotistic digression he returns to
state the case. What matter have we here ? Why, "the
purity of the verity is," that a certain beautiful virgin,
who is "the sovereign lady of this, Dame Maia's
month, hath been hunted . . . pursued, by two, a
brace, a couple, a cast of young men, to whom the
crafty Cupid had . . . delivered his dire, dolorous
dart."

Do you marvel that at such a juncture the young
lady herself was made to interrupt the torrent of Rhombus, and suggested that the Queen should arbitrate in
the matter and award the girl to whichever swain best
satisfied Her Majesty in song ? Here came the pastoral lyrics. But the Queen's award was delayed by
another duel of words—this time between an old shep-

herd and a forester—as to the worth and status of their respective callings. This gave Rhombus another grand opportunity, and the gentle May Lady another chance of interruption. The wooers, Espilus, the chief shepherd, and Therion, champion of the huntsmen and foresters, came forward to learn the royal award, given to the former, and all strife was brought to an end by music and dance and the May Lady's epilogue.

A delicious scene and a delicious occasion! Who would not give much gold to know what went on at those rehearsals in the Wanstead gardens, with Philip, in his rich Elizabethan suit, as stage manager? Truly he loved the cult of the shepherd. The hatred of empty ceremonials and stiff liveries had never been so strong in him as now. Everything in him was straining towards those ideals of sweet life in green pastures, to which we follow him presently—down to Wilton, in and out of the literary circle which he and Mary Pembroke inevitably drew about them and through the mazes of his great *Arcadia*.

For the present let this gentle beginning, the May Masque, please the Queen and Leicester, and rejoice the pride of the Penshurst family. Details of it all certainly reached and delighted Languet, who had already been annoyed by the literary affectation and empty largiloquence of cultured England, and whose cosmopolitan nature and experience made him hypersensitive to such things. In truth, these foreign visitors of ours, who bring humour and sharp criticism to bear on our style and ways, are the best friends of an island people, all too prone to grooves and to over-seriousness in the lesser things, all too morbid where outside criticism is concerned.

After this incident at Wanstead the star of the

Splendid One seemed truly in the ascendant. Praise of his personality and capacity flowed from all sides. Two months later (July, 1578), the great Stadtholder, William of Orange—the Silent—wrote strongly to Elizabeth in commendation of Philip, urging that he should be employed by her in diplomatic concerns abroad, and that he, the Prince, "would stake his own credit upon the issue of his friend's employment about any business, either with the allies or with the enemies of England."[1]

But Elizabeth did not send him forth. She kept him at home to help her to entertain Prince John Casimir, son of the Elector Palatine, and dally at Court. In his leisure moments he could at least forget his chafing in literary circles. He flung himself now into the formation of a literary coterie—the Areopagus Club—in the hope of forming a new school of poetry. Edward Spenser had just completed his *Shepherd's Calendar*, and dedicated it to our young gallant.

Gabriel Harvey, now a lecturer, and erstwhile fellow-student and friend of Spenser at Cambridge, had extolled Philip in a Latin poem. Further, Spenser had closer knitted the trinity of friendship by introducing Harvey into the *Calendar* under the character of Hobbinol. It was a fine nucleus for an art circle.

Here we lose Philip awhile in a maze of books and friends. We catch sight of him again in the full glare of publicity, when he wrote his famous letter to Elizabeth, condemning respectfully the proposed marriage with her "Frogg," Anjou. It is not necessary to insert here this amazing letter, which at once delighted and scandalised the nation, the Court, and its European audience. It was the climax of the boy's pent-up

[1] Morley's *English Literature*, p. 372.

E

feelings of indignation, the flower of the deliberate observation which he had nursed while actively employed in the marriage negotiations. It was the outcome of strongly increasing purpose, of feelings which it became gradually impossible for him to hide. Such emotion would scarcely have leapt forth in so audacious a form as this letter, had it not been for the way in which, day by day, he saw the Queen's curious behaviour and apparent hot leaning to Anjou fed by the interested support of a large section of the men who attended her. It is in regard to this very matter of the Anjou marriage that a vivid Court episode in the life of the youth took place. It looks on the surface like a mere quarrel between two gallants, but in reality it displayed Philip as opponent, single-handed, of the French faction and the English courtiers who backed it. Of the latter the Earl of Oxford, a turbulent and vicious person already mentioned, was the chief, and on the wave of Elizabeth's seeming infatuation for the Anjou notion he had temporarily won the first place in her favour. This achievement was the more easy since Leicester's third marriage had clouded his glory, and Philip was manifestly opposed to the Anjou scheme. The Earl of Oxford, as an accomplished "trimmer," with no ideals and no object but self-aggrandisement, was the very man whom Elizabeth's mood required. Every characteristic in him jarred upon Sidney, who saw the whole situation and could thoroughly mistrust the Earl. Of this peer a delicious pen-portrait "in a rattling bundle of hexameters," by the poet Harvey, must not be omitted. It paints such a very strong contrast between Philip and the popinjay earl, who, on a certain autumn morning, strutted into the royal tennis-court and interrupted Philip in the game.

"Strait to the back, like a shirt, and close to the breech like a
    diveling,
A little apish hat, couched fast to the pate like an oyster,
French cambric ruffs, deep with a witness, starched to the
    purpose;
Delicate in speech; quaint in array; conceited in all points;
In courtly guiles a passing singular odd man."

Philip seems fated to have been cut out of matrimonial projects in youth by men of singularly violent
and unfavourable nature. It was only four years since
Edward de Vere had wrested Anne Cecil from his
younger rival. Truly he was a man "rich enough to
satisfy paternal prudence." His disposition seems to
have been blandly overlooked by Burghley, that arch-
detective of England. For he must have known as
much about the fellow's past as a confidential War Office
secretary does of that of every man and officer in the
line or the cavalry. A prose summary of a few of his
activities should be added here to Nash's poetical ridi-
cule of Edward de Vere. "He was well nigh the
gayest and well nigh the most brutal of Queen Elizabeth's courtiers. Treason in politics often estranged
him from his sovereign, and treason in morals often
estranged himself from his wife; but his fair outside
got him as often as there was need for it, in either case,
a woman's pardon. When he was young he killed his
cook. When he was old and had squandered his
immense patrimony, he persuaded Thomas Churchyard
to be surety for his lodgings, and then ran away,
leaving the poor poet to hide himself until he could
scrape together money enough for payment of a bill."[1]
This shabby trick played upon a worthy man of letters,
whose long life from 1520 to 1604 was one long
struggle for existence, who was forced to ask help from

---

[1] Fox-Bourne, *Memoir of Sir Philip Sidney.*

aristocratic patrons, and must have sat often shivering
and hungry in that social "bear-garden," the suitor's
ante-room of a great person, sticks especially in my
throat. On the whole I prefer Oxford's treatment of
his cook—killed, but not tortured and made a scapegoat.
And this Thomas Churchyard, let us remind ourselves,
was both a soldier and a leading dramatist, as well as a
poet—author of two famous plays, in the *Mirror for
Magistrates*—"Jane Shore" and "Wolsey."

If Oxford could treat a social subordinate (for so he
surely would alike judge the greatest of poets and the
most perfect of cooks!) in such a way, he certainly did
not spare his contemporaries. We see him now, "conceited in all parts," adorned with his oyster-like hat,
strutting into that royal tennis-court on a fine September day. He claims insolently a share in the game.
Philip takes no notice. The Earl reiterates his demand
with fresh arrogance. Sidney's remonstrance, courteous
and dignified, enrages his enemy, who orders all the
players to leave the court. Sidney's flat and dignified
refusal, based on the Earl's discourtesy, prefaced what
should have been a challenge here. But the Earl was
not man enough to do more than bawl "Puppy!" The
angry shout brought a crowd of courtiers, foreign and
English, into the tennis-court—foremost among them
Anjou's French Ambassador, Simier, dubbed by the Queen
her "Monkey." Philip demanded the reiteration of
the word. Oxford repeated it: "A puppy." From
Philip, "That's a lie!" For a minute the two heated men
faced one another, while Philip waited, hopeful of the
challenge to a duel. Oxford blustered . . . never gave
it. The other left the court and waited at home.
After the lapse of a day he sent a friend to ask when it
would be forthcoming, adding that his French friends

would teach Oxford, if he did not know it, what was the only honourable course to take. Even this tremendous stab had no effect. Meanwhile, Queen and Lords of the Council intervened, and a reconciliation was ordered, and ordered with recommendations and reprimands especially detrimental to Philip's sense of honour and his just pride. He was commanded to submit himself to his social superiors. He had the fine audacity to retort that a peerage carried with it no "privilege to do wrong." He reminded the Queen that even she bound her own conduct by the laws of her subjects, and quoted the action of her royal father in giving the gentry the right to appeal against arrogance and insult from the classes above them. There the matter ended, so far as Philip was concerned. He could do no more while the Queen's skirts sheltered Edward de Vere. Naturally that very shelter afforded her protégé of the moment an excellent screen, while he actually concocted a plan to assassinate young Sidney. He prepared the way for this by the despatch to his rival of a messenger carrying an amicable proposal that their dispute should be healed. Sidney assented. He was now living in London. Oxford planned to enter his chamber by night, stab him in his sleep, and escape by a boat ready waiting on Paul's Wharf. Some miracle saved the pride of the Sidneys from so shameful an end. The scheme was not even attempted. But it is stated as real two years later in State correspondence.

We return now to his additional protest—the letter about Anjou and the iniquitous betrothal, as he saw it. That Elizabeth did not crush Philip utterly after his letter and forever forbid him the Court, has been the wonder of ages. She could not help seeing the truth in his arguments; she must have felt, in spite of her anger, the appeal to her dignity and the dignity of her nation. Above all, she felt the satire underlying the protest. This she hated, and was deeply angry with the sheer interference in her pet scheme. The whole world waited and gaped. Languet, terribly alarmed, wrote that Philip would not find safety in Flanders, and still less in France, while Spain and Italy were closed to one of his religious opinions and Germany the only safe refuge under the circumstances. The bold young man did not fly. He braved disfavour, and returned to the country. He was more than ever weary of Courts and intrigues, scandals and schemes. He flung himself into literature—once more at Wilton.

It is not surprising that the "pastors and masters" of Penelope troubled their heads no longer about him. Had he prostituted his talents, fawned on Elizabeth, carried love-messages between France and England, and, as his reward, bounced suddenly into a title above his poor knighthood, with the appanage of rich estates, then indeed every guardian in England would have angled for him. Lord Huntingdon, as explained, had every opportunity of doing this. Yet it was he who pushed the elder of his two girl wards in the direction of a very different husband.

Before all these plans matured, Lettice Devereux had made sure of her Leicester. In secret, only a few months after the May Masque, their marriage was solemnised at Wanstead, while the unsuspecting Queen was enjoying a great pageant at Norwich. But the bride's father, Sir William Knollys, witnessed it, lest doubts of legality should arise later, when the Queen's anger burst forth.

It was about a year and a half after this that Lord Huntingdon made up his mind about the elder of his

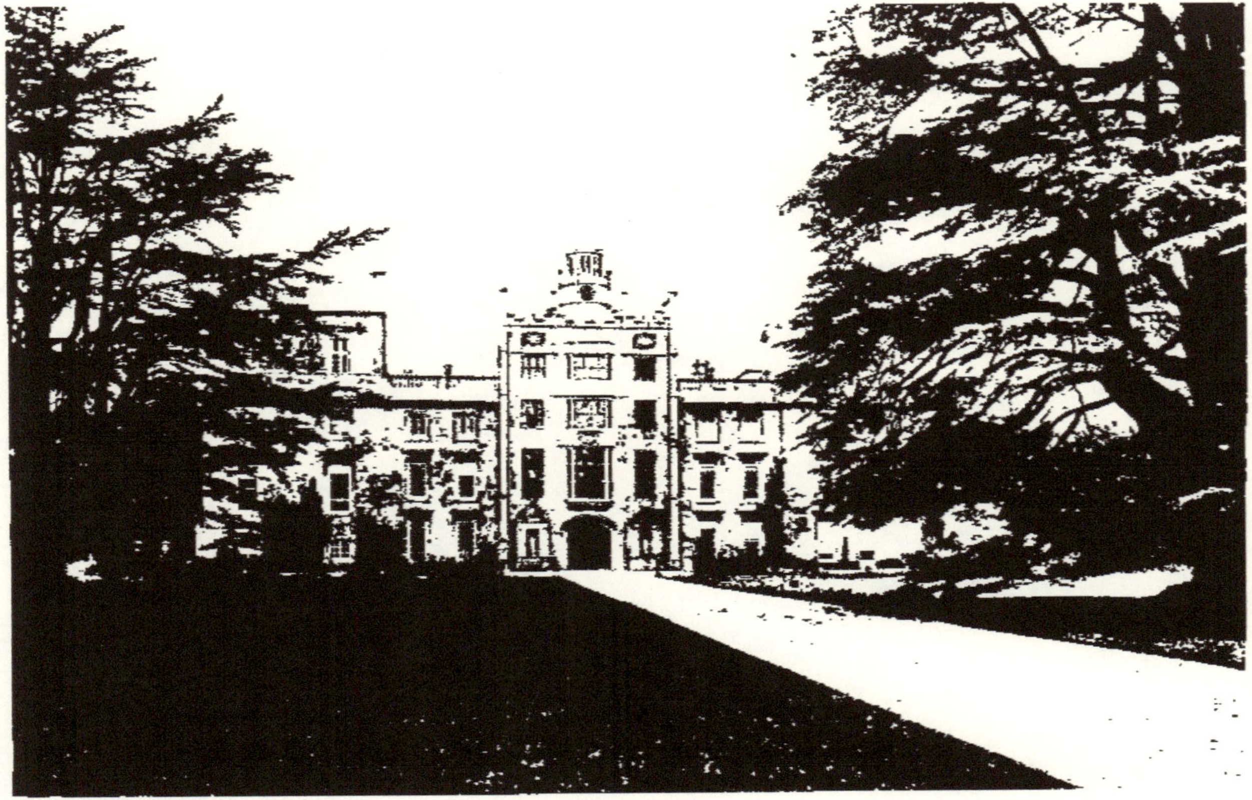

From a photograph

WILTON HOUSE

two girl wards, and wrote thus to Burghley in the March of 1580 :

" May it please your lordship, hearing that God hath taken to his mercy my Lord Rich, who hath left to his heir a very proper gentleman and one in years very fit for my lady Penelope Devereux, if with the favour and liking of Her Majesty the matter might be brought to pass. And because I know your Lordship's good affection to their father gone, and also your favour to his children, I am bold to pray your furtherance now in this matter, which may I trust, by your good means, be brought to such pass as I desire. Her Majesty was pleased the last year to give me leave at times convenient to put her highness in mind of these young ladies (Penelope and her sister), and therefore I am by this occasion of my Lord's death the bolder to move your Lordship in this matter. I have also written to Mr. Secretary Walsingham herein. And so, hoping of your Lordship's favour, I do commit you to the tuition of the Almighty."

This desirable *parti* was the son of that very Lord Rich, who preferred fleshpots to military service under the late Earl of Essex, and had been, as Devereux calls him, " the first of the deserters " in the Ulster campaign.

If you will glance back at that second letter quoted from Languet, you will see how fateful is that warning at the close. Philip's fine tribute to him in the third book of the *Arcadia*, beginning :

" The song I sang old Languet had me taught.
Languet the shepherd best swift Ister knew,
For clerkly reed, and hating what is naught,
For faithful heart, clean hands, and mouth as true,
With his swift skill my skilless youth he drew
To have a feeling taste of Him who sits
Beyond the heaven, far more beyond our wits,"

would ring more truly if he had really in this point trusted his " skilless youth " to so keen-sighted a craftsman and combined his friend's counsel with the dying wishes of Penelope's father, whom the boy really worshipped.

Languet certainly taught him how to " sing," enforced the beauty, depth, and spirituality of his nature. But Languet never wished him to endure those fires of love and passion which later rent his pupil.

CHAPTER IV

THE FATEFUL MARRIAGE

THE thing was done before any one could prevent it. Nobody need be troubled over such a matter. Here was a poor orphan who must somehow be disposed of. Here, on the other hand, was a gentleman who must simply have spelt "money" from crown to heel. He was of an excellent age for Penelope; he had his elbow well into Court matters, and though not specially favoured or famous, he was the figurehead of success.

Robert Rich—do not the alliteration and the names together tickle the ear nicely? If Lord Leicester and Lord Huntingdon had begun their chase after fortune by way of a joke, they really could not have hit upon a more grotesquely satisfactory combination. The very patronymic must have inflamed the business instincts of his progenitors. Here is his origin:

Midway in the Tudor period there rose to civic eminence in London, as sheriff, one Richard Rich, a mercer. He was a wise and thrifty tradesman, and left his business and his fortune to his son of the same name. The fortune certainly increased, while the second Rich doubtless carried out his father's precepts, and, though he did not become a sheriff, succeeded in being elected deputy of his ward. It was in the third generation that the family broke new ground. The first mercer's grandson, called after him Richard Rich, was not minded to spend his energies over bales of silk, woollen, and cotton. His aspirations were in the direction of the Bar. This meant a tolerably idle life at the outset as regards sheer fortune getting, but a busy one so far as social expansion and opportunities for self-advancement were concerned. Incidentally, he became a shrewd lawyer, and played his cards so well that in 1533 he was made Solicitor-General. He has been described as "an unprincipled roysterer among the city taverns." This knowledge of life and experience of men were exactly suited to develop his powers. He was not troubled with a tender conscience, and was invaluable to Henry VIII in many a high-handed and illegal transaction. Not the least of these was the manner in which he assisted the King to seize the goods of his first wife, Katherine of Arragon, after her death at Kimbolton Castle. Richard Rich the younger always played a double game, and played it successfully, till the moment came when the contest for political power between Protector Somerset and the Earl Warwick, from both of whom he had received marked favours, seemed likely to engulf him, when he adroitly retired—still a great man in the eyes of the world, with all the dignity of an ex-Lord Chancellor and a baron—to live the life of a country gentleman at his country house of Leighs, in Essex.

The next member of importance to us in this family is Penelope's husband-elect, grandson again of the famous, infamous ex-Lord Chancellor. Penelope's lord was known as "the rich Lord Rich." He does not seem to have been celebrated in any other capacity. He appears to have been a leech-like individual without the initiative or assertiveness of his forefathers, but with the family talent for using the right people. Captain Walter Devereux describes him as "rough and uncourtly in manners and conversation, dull and uneducated, proper in nothing but his wealth."[1]

The marriage was arranged, had the royal approval, and was celebrated many miles from Penshurst, Wilton, or the Court before Philip could realise what it meant to him. Penelope seems to have drifted helplessly up to the moment of the marriage ceremony. It is on record that she now openly expressed her unwillingness. But her environment was too strong for her.

Hereafter the first experiences of marriage and the business of a newly wedded titled lady may be said to extinguish her for some years. We have no record of her early life at Leighs. She was certainly engulfed, engrossed, overpowered by the calls upon her time, her physique, her intelligence. It is impossible that she could fully realise the tragic mistake into which her relatives had forced her, of the unholy power of what Gifford calls "the accursed Court of Wards" and its interference in marriages, which "eternally troubled the current of true love." But her eyes were gradually being opened to the shortcomings of her Robert.

This well-belaboured gentleman does not appear to have laid claim to much polish. Let this at least count for a virtue in him. We have it on his own confession that he had little culture and was no linguist. That is to say, his experience in foreign Courts, always so essential to the gentleman of any eminence of his day—was *nil.* He did not lay himself out for personal attendance on Elizabeth, nor had he the gracious qualities which would have caused the eye of Burghley to single him out for special service to State or Queen. In the fol-

[1] *Lives of the Earls of Devereux,* by Walter Devereux, Vol. I.

lowing letter written by him to Essex he paints for us the pitiless contrast between himself and Penelope's first suitor.

" I am glad any way to hear of your Lordship's good health, and sorry that I cannot entertain this gentleman it pleaseth your Lordship to commend in a place worthy his good parts.   Myself, as your Lordship well knoweth, am a poor man of no language, only in the French, having therein but a little oversight with coming over to attend my Lord of Shrewsbury's, which being now performed I look not for like occasion.   And therefore the gentleman might with me have small or no use for his gifts that way. . . . Your Lordship's poor Brother to command, Rd. Rich."

It is evident that Essex wanted employment for some needy clerk, but that Rich was too wary to trouble himself with any penniless protégé sent to him by his generous brother-in-law, who was certainly surrounded by " suitors " of every kind.   What really makes this short letter valuable is the fact that it came into Penelope's hands before it was sent off, and she added this naughty postscript :

" You may imagine my Lord Rich hath no employment for a language secretary—except he hath gotten a mistress in France."

The actual date of this letter is 1597, so that I am anticipating somewhat the course of events.   It was written after his return from France on an embassy in which Gilbert Talbot, the Earl of Shrewsbury, was his chief.   It shows that, while he wished to keep on the best of terms with his useful brother-in-law (who, by the way, had taken pains to tell Burghley just before the marriage that for many causes Rich was "most dear to him"), he was not going to put his hand in his pocket unless he apprehended some solid benefit therefrom to himself. The letter also embodies the fact that Rich, like his father, loved ease and comfort, and was never eager for foreign service. He was persuaded to go to Calais in 1596, and was one of the gentlemen whom Essex was specially deputed to enlist, while Charles Blount, Lord Mountjoy, Rich's rival (of whom more hereafter), was, on the other hand, clearly recalled from France at the time. Documents show, however, that Rich subsequently went most unwillingly on the celebrated military expedition to Cadiz.

So far, and indeed throughout her marriage, Penelope's family did their best to maintain at least an attitude of civility towards her husband. Their position in regard to her was rather difficult, seeing that her mother, brother, Lord Leicester, and Lord Huntingdon had been instrumental in thrusting her into these marriage bonds. These "heavy relations" would be very unwilling to confess so early in the day that no happiness could come out of their achievement. But there was one who realised. Not Penelope's mother, just now too disturbed over her own secret marriage to Leicester, always, possibly, too tortured by the knowledge of his light ways and easy promises, and manifestly on tenterhooks as regards the lost royal favour, to pay much heed to the happiness of her children. Neither did Lord Essex really care. Though he adored his sister, he was her junior by several years, and the matter did not personally affect him. It was Philip Sidney—fresh from his magnificent and dignified interference in the marriage proposals between his Queen and her "Frogg"—who realised—because he cared, and cared too much. His indignation, love, and sincerity did her no violence, but put forth flower and fruit, as all the world knows, in his *Arcadia* (of which Penelope is the lovely Philoclea) and in his sonnets.

As for the Rich marriage itself, it bore fruit in children. Six followed one another closely—and all the while there is no record either of Penelope's nonchalance or neglect towards her brood. She bestirred herself in worldly ways for their benefit, urged on, no doubt, by her acquisitive spouse. The following letter to Burghley, under date 1588, written evidently while she awaited the birth of a child, shows her in a highly practical light, and deals with her application of the guardianship of one of the tenants of the Crown during his minority. Such an appointment would give her the profits of the lands of the boy concerned until he came of age. That such things were permitted is amazing, but in olden days diversion of funds by State permission was apparently possible through the favour of the great. Lord Leicester brought his weight to bear on the matter also in a letter to the Treasurer which would be redundant here.

"The great favour your Lordship promised me, touching the request my Lord of Leicester made to her Majesty for Sir Robert Jermyn's son, hath now emboldened me to be an humble suitor to your Lordship for the performance of it, hoping only in your Lordship's favour, which is the means to accomplish my desire. Wherefore I beseech your Lordship to make me so much bound unto you as to set it so forward as that I may shortly hope to see an end of it ; and I will acknowledge it ever as proceeding from your Lordship's great favour, and will employ myself both to deserve it and to show all thankfulness for so great a benefit. I would have been glad to have waited on your Lordship myself, if I might have done you any service ; but my burden is such as I am fitter.to keep the house than to go any whither. Wherefore I hope your Lordship will pardon me for this time and accept these lines with the which I commend both my suit and myself to your Lordship's favour. York House, this 10th of September. By her that desires to merit your Lordship's favour, " Penelope Rich.

" 1588."

CHAPTER V

THE STARRY WAY

THUS by ring and book great wrong had been done, under colour of the best intentions, to Penelope Devereux. Little did Essex or her guardians realise what great happenings would be the issue of this easily arranged marriage, accomplished amid the high approval of her relatives, without let or hindrance on the part of Treasurer or Queen. These smiling, fatuous older persons were simply like stupid schoolboys playing with flood gates, and in such cases it is unfortunately not usually the schoolboys who suffer. It is well, perhaps, that the first really wide-awake victim of this matrimonial bungle should have had his outlet in song. His heart was certainly laid bare by his pen. How much of the actual story of the sonnets—the action, the lover's interviews, the passionate pursuit, the temptation to sin against her marriage vows on the lady's part and her fine resistance—are true no one can tell. Many minds have sat in judgment over them. Let us not afflict ourselves with controversies, but take the story as it shines through the starry poems. Let us note at the outset that even Philip, the great-hearted, could not forbear from open abuse of the successful Robert Rich. Philip was young, Rich was universally unpopular and despised. Philip had a nimble wit, and already a distinguished pen. The mental processes of Rich can only be likened to the progress of a toad over a ploughed field, and he acknowledged himself to be thoroughly unlettered. Hatred and literary vanity led Philip into this one error, and so potent was his influence that this wretched punning freak of his was made a precedent by other verse-makers. The following sonnet explains itself :—

" Rich fools there be, whose base and filthy heart
    Lies hatching still the goods wherein they flow,
And damning their own selves to Tantal's smart ;
    Wealth breeding want—more rich, more wretched grow.
Yet to those fools Heav'n such wit doth impart,
    As what their hands do hold, their heads do know ;
And, knowing, love ; and, loving, lay apart
    As sacred things, far from all danger's show.
But that rich foole, who by blind Fortune's lot
    The richest gem of love and life enjoys,
And can with foul abuse such beauties blot ;
    Let him, depriv'd of sweet but unfelt joys,
Exil'd for ay from those high treasures which
    He knowes not, grow in only folly rich ! "

That sonnet was not one of the first. It comes twenty-fourth in the long tale of them.[1]

Four years before Penelope's marriage Philip had tried his wings as a poet. In 1579 Spenser himself was at Penshurst and under that stately roof and within its pleasaunces light and sweetness were sovereign guests. The son of the house was the centre of a striking family group which, as it meets the eye, moves the heart even after the lapse of centuries. Here was old Sir Henry Sidney trying to forget his sore memories of Court life ; here too his " old Moll," who had lost her rich personal charms even as Sir Henry had lost his youth and joy and emptied his purse in the public

[1] The numbering indicated is that followed in Pollard's edition of these sonnets.

F

service. Here from time to time came the beautiful, serene, and cultured Mary, Countess of Pembroke, married but two years previously. Here, too, probably were her other brothers, Robert, later the second Earl of Leicester, and Thomas, who rose to colonel's rank. In his *Arcadia*, which Philip was incited to write, as all the world knows, by his sister Mary, there is this delicious description of a fine and durable country house, which may well have been prompted by this environment or by the peace of stately Wilton.

" The house itself was built of fair and strong stone, not affecting so much any extraordinary kind of fineness as an honourable representative of a firm stateliness. The lights, doors, and stairs rather directed to the use of the guest than the eye of the artificer, and yet, as the one chiefly heeded, so the other not neglected. Each place handsome without curiosity, and homely without loathsomeness, not so dainty as not to be trod on, nor yet slubbered up [1] with good fellowship ; all more lasting than beautiful, but that the consideration of the exceeding lastingness made the eye believe it was exceeding beautiful. The servants, not so many in number, as cleanly in apparel and serviceable in behaviour, testifying even in their countenances that their master took as well care to be served as of them that did serve."

And there are many other fragments which come from a veritable well-spring of joy, from the heart which hungers after beauty in the life of every day:

" Here a shepherd's boy piping as though he never should be old; there a young shepherdess knitting, and

---

[1] Slubbered = soiled. An entrance not sullied by the coming and going of a crowd of mere acquaintances.

withal singing—and it seemed that her voice comforted
her hands to work and her hands kept time to the voice-
music. As for the houses of the country—for many
houses came under their eye,—they were all scattered,
no two being one by the other,—yet not so far off
as that it barred mutual succour ; a show, as it were,
of an accompanible solitariness and of a civil wild-
ness."

What tenderness, what "poise," what solace in such
imaginings ! And what a picture to make all the
Little Pedlingtons of a great country blush for shame—
this ideal of intercourse without familiarity, this "mutual
succour " without scandal, this high dignity with tender
neighbourliness ! To the undying reproach of the
petty mind let this description remain for ever. This
delicate, stately mood, however, came upon Philip later.
He had first to pass through the storm and stress of
the sonnets, he had to understand that while he
was luxuriating in the muses at Penshurst the Fates
were busy cutting the slender thread which bound
him to Penelope. In the sonnets he duly flogs
himself.

He returned to Court about six weeks after the Rich
marriage. No wonder that muse gushed forth into
such verse as this "Dirge" in litany form, extraordinarily vivid in its imagery, direct and biting.

> " Ring out your bells, let mourning shows be spread,
>   For Love is dead !
> All Love is dead, infected
> With plague of deep disdain,
> Worth, as nought worth, rejected ;
> And Faith fair scorn doth gain.
> From so ungrateful fancy,
> From such a female frenzy,
> From them that use men thus,
>   Good Lord, deliver us !

" Weep, neighbours, weep ! do you not hear it said
      That Love is dead ?
His deathbed peacock's folly,
His winding-sheet is shame,
His will false-seeming holy,
His sole executor blame.
From so ungrateful fancy,
From such a female frenzy,
From them that use men thus,
      Good Lord, deliver us !

" Let dirge be sung and trentals rightly said,
      For Love is dead !
Sir Wrong his tomb ordaineth
My mistress' marble heart,
Which epitaph containeth
' Her eyes were once his dart,'
From so ungrateful fancy,
From such a female frenzy,
From them that use men thus,
      Good Lord, deliver us ! "

Then his mood seems to soften, his trust and hope
in his lady return. He knows that deep in her heart,
like a hidden tarn, lies the truer love, never yet fully
given to any man. So he ends the litany thus :

" Alas ! I lie ; rage hath this error bred !
      Love is not dead !
Love is not dead, but sleepeth
In her unmatchèd mind,
Where she his counsels keepeth
Till due deserts she find.
Therefore from so vile fancy,
To call such wit a frenzy
Who love can temper thus
      Good Lord, deliver us ! "

"Where she his counsels keepeth." Here we are on
the threshold of the door which opens into the garden
of love, the actual drama of *Astrophel and Stella*, its
songs and sonnets. The above litany, as extricated
from the poems united with a 1598 edition of *The*

Arcadia, appears, according to Pollard's arrangement, thirteenth in a separate group of sonnets as distinct from the *Astrophel* group. There seems no doubt at all that it was penned at the time of the hated wedding, because of the obvious allusion to the ringing of bells and the use of such a phrase as " false-seeming holy "—a wrong done under cover of Church rites.

With that litany we open the door and pass in to the place of stars and flowers, frosts and heats, rain of tears and dew of forgiveness, where tenderness at last lays its foot gently upon scorn, and the immensity of a great spirit triumphs over the stupendous demands of the body in all its beauty and overwhelming grace.

One last word. . . . If I take you by the hand through this "garden," I take you as one conducts a young comrade to his first sight—let us say—of *As You Like It*, or *Faust*, or one of the great masterpieces of poetry about which many books have already been written, and which in every young life mark an epoch. Accomplished students of history, chivalry, and poesy know the way alone through this Sidney romance. My journey is not specially designed for these. Nor is it for the censorious, to whom all verse is " poitry," and all the rarer expressions of love fantastic superfluities. The sonnets are very much part of our affair, because the romance they reveal is a tremendous counterpoise to the after-story of Penelope Rich, as even the pharisaical will allow.

In Sonnet I Astrophel takes his task upon him thus :

"Loving in truth, and fain in verse my love to show,
That she, dear She, might take some pleasure of my pain,—
Pleasure might cause her read, reading might make her know,
Knowledge might pity win, and pity grace obtain,—

whose work Sidney's foreign journeys had acquainted
him.

> " Queen Virtue's Court, which some call Stella's face,
> Prepar'd by Nature's choicest furniture,
> Hath his front built of alabaster pure ;
> Gold is the covering of that stately place.
> The door by which sometimes comes forth her grace,
> Red porphir is, which lock of pearl makes sure,
> Whose porches rich (which name of cheeks endure)
> Marble, mix't red and white, do interlace.
> The windows now, through which this heavenly guest
> Looks over the world, and can find nothing such,
> Which dare claim from those lights the name of best,
> Of touch[1] they are, that without touch doth touch,
> Which Cupid's self from Beautie's mine did draw ;
> Of touch they are, and poor I am their straw."

After this, as if the contemplation of the picture were
too much for him, he falls back immediately into a play
upon words, setting Love against Reason ; and again
quickly rebounds, as the ardently amorous sonnet,
beginning " Cupid, because thou shins't in Stella's eyes,"
reveals.

We pass on to Sonnet XIII where he gives us a fine
bit of heraldic painting of " Jove, Mars, and Love,"
and, as if this flight of rhetoric and fancy must have a
reaction, his fancies flow into a naïve stanza, in which
he deals with the sour comments of a friend upon his
love-sickness—" rhubarb words " he calls them :

> " Alas, have I not paid enough, my friend,
> Upon whose breast a fiercer gripe doth tire
> Than did on him who first stole down the fire,
> While Love on me doth all his quiver spend.—
> But with your rhubarb words ye must contend
> To grieve me worse, in saying that desire
> Doth plunge my well-form'd soul even in the mire
> Of sinful thoughts, which do in ruin end?

---

[1] Touch = touchwood, tinder.

> If that be sin which doth the manners frame,
> Well stayed with truth in word and faith of deed,
> Ready of wit, and fearing nought but shame;
> If that be sin, which in fixed hearts doth breed
> A loathing of all loose unchastity,
> Then Love is sin, and let me sinful be."

Now he rambles a little, discusses contemptuously the possible conjectures of the ever inquisitive world as to the source of this sombre mood :

> " The curious wits, seeing chill pensiveness
> Bewray it self in my long-sabled eyes,
> Whence those same fumes of melancholy rise,
> With idle pains and missing aim do guess—
> Some, that know how my spring I did address,
> Deem that my Muse some fruit of knowledge plies;
> Others, because the Prince my service tries,
> Think that I think state errors to redress :
> But harder judges judge ambition's rage—
> Scourge of itself, still climbing slippery place,
> Holds my young brain captiv'd in golden cage.
> O fools, or overwise : alas, the race
> Of all my thoughts hath neither stop nor start,
> But only Stella's eyes and Stella's heart."

Before that sonnet is reached he has lost heart, condemns his failure. Common sense and concentration on his plight triumphantly announce that he is a bankrupt—a wastrel " unable quite to pay even Nature's rent," deprived of his birthright of happiness, unable to show any good excuse for wasting the "goods" bestowed by Heaven, till he breaks out suddenly into the sensational warning of Sonnet XX :

> " Fly, fly, my friends ; I have my death wound ; fly ;
> See here that boy, that murdering boy, I say,
> Who, like a thief hid in dark bush, doth lie
> Till bloody bullet get him wrongful prey.
> So tyrant he no fitter place could spy,
> Nor so fair level in so secret stay,
> As that sweet black which veils the heavenly eye ;
> There himself with his shot he close doth lay.

Poor passenger, pass now thereby I did,
And stayed, pleased with the prospect of the place,
While that black hue from me the bad guest hid;
But straight I saw motions of lightning grace;
And then descried the glisterings of his dart:
But ere I could fly thence it pierced my heart."

The friend whose unpalatable criticism previously added to his smart, evidently is busy again, for immediately after the last outburst Sidney alludes to his counsel again, calling his words " right healthful caustics " which in their way are very sound, adding that the recommendations to read Plato, to dig deep with " Learning's spade" into his "golden mine of wisdom" are very well in their way. But what is the use of all these things, lovely in themselves, when Stella is so much more lovely?

Thus with Sonnet XXII he breaks away into the love-garden again. It is noon; the sun rides in the " highest way of heaven," and a cavalcade of beautiful women meet and have to face his onslaught. All of them, save one, have their shields, the help of their " well-shading fans, all—save one. Stella alone rides unarmed. Her "dainties bare" escape, for the sun which, despite all their precautions, burns the meaner beauties, merely kisses her.

A few lines later we are amongst the stars and Sidney's thoughts of them.

" Though dusty wits do scorn Astrology,
      And fools can think those purest lamps of light—
Whose numbers, ways, greatness, eternity,
      Promising wonders, wonder do invite—
To have for no cause birthright in the sky
      But for to spangle the black weeds of Night;
Or for some brawl[1] which in that chamber high

---

[1] A "brawl" in Elizabethan days was a lively dance.

They should still dance to please a gazer's sight.
For me I do Nature un-idle know,
  And know great causes great effects procure;
And know those bodies high reign on the low.
  And if these rules did fail, proof makes me sure,
Who oft foresee my after-following race
  By only those two stars in Stella's face."

There follows presently a glimpse of Love and the Lady
in a chivalric, military conceit. Her eyes serve Love
with shot, her breast is Love's tent, her nether limbs his
triumphal car to bear him on to victories, her skin his
"armour brave."

From pure fancies Sidney turns aside to greater
matters of the kingdom and of continental affairs;
but the political themes which once thrilled and
absorbed him he, a bored recluse, can now only regard
indifferently :

"Whether the Turkish new moon minded be
To fill his horns this year on Christian coast?
How Poles' right king means without leave of host
To warm with ill-made fire cold Muscovy?
If French can yet three parts in one agree?
What now the Dutch in their full diets boast?
How Holland hearts, now so good town be lost,
Trust in the shade of pleasant Orange-tree?
How Ulster likes of that same golden bit
Wherewith my father once made it half tame?
If in the Scotch court be no welt'ring yet?
These questions busy wits do frame :
I, cumbered with good manners, answer do
But know not how; for still I think of you."

One of the most delicate and naïve of the poems is
the one which appeals to the Moon, asking her if in her
world things are as they are here :

"Then, even of fellowship, O Moon, tell me
Is constant love deemed there but want of wit?
Are beauties there as proud as here they be?"

Anon he harks back, reminds himself again of his own ignorances and negligences, the root of his tragic dilemma:

> " No lovely Paris made thy Helen his,
> No force, no fraud robbed thee of thy delight,
> Nor Fortune of thy fortune author is;
> But to myself myself did give the blow,
> While too much wit, forsooth, so troubled me
> That I respects for both our sakes must show:
> And yet could not, by rising morn foresee
> How fair a day was near: O punished eyes,
> That I had been more foolish or more wise ! "

Quickly upon this ensues another sort of pun upon " Rich," in a more magnanimous vein than the one previously quoted.   He cries to his lady that she and Fame are one :

> " Honour is honour'd that thou dost possess
> Him as thy slave, and now long-needy Fame
> Doth even grow rich, naming my Stella's name."

And yet another play upon the hated, beloved word:

> " My mouth doth water, and my breast doth swell,
> My tongue doth itch, my thoughts in labour be;
> Listen, then, lordlings, with good care to me,
> For of my life I must a riddle tell.
> Toward Aurora's Court, a nymph doth dwell,
> Rich in all beauties which man's eye can see ;
> Beauties so far from reach of words, that we
> Abase her praise saying she doth excel;
> Rich in the treasure of deserv'd renown,
> Rich in the riches of a royal heart,
> Rich in those gifts which give th' eternal crown ;
> Who, though most rich in these and every part
> Which makes the patents of true worldly bliss,
> Hath no misfortune but that Rich she is."

He appeals constantly to Sleep, the elusive deity :

> " The poor man's wealth, the prisoner's release,
> Th' indifferent judge between the high and low,

Take thou of me smooth pillows, sweetest bed,
A rosy garland and a weary head;
And if these things, as being thine in right
Move not thy heavy grace, thou shalt in me,
Livelier than elsewhere Stella's image see."

Virtue and Love renew their fight in his mind, and after the course of fifteen sonnets he hurls himself against the figure of Patience, who asks too much from him.

" Fie, school of Patience, fie!   Your lesson is
Far, far too long to learn it without book:
What, a whole week without one peace of look!
When I might read those letters fair of bliss
Which in her face teach virtue, I could brook
Somewhat thy leaden counsels. . . .

.   .   .   .   .

But now that I, alas, do want her sight
What dost thou think that I can ever take
In thy cold stuff a phlegmatic delight?
No, Patience; if thou wilt my good, then make
Her come and hear with patience my desire,
And then with patience bid me bear my fire."

This brings the drama of the story much closer. The next song of importance is a piteous entreaty that he should at least be treated as fairly as his lady's lap-dog, to whom she grants favours never accorded to him:

"Dear, why make you more of a dog than me?
If he do love, I burn, I burn in love;
If he wait well, I never thence would move.
If he be fair, yet but a dog can be;
Little he is, so little worth is he;
He barks, my songs thine own voice oft doth prove;
Bidd'n, perhaps, he fetchèd thee a glove,
But I, unbid, fetch even my soul to thee.
Yet, while I languish, him that bosom clips,
That lap doth lap, nay, lets, in spite of spite,

This sour-breath'd mate taste of those sugar'd lips.
Alas, if you grant only such delight
To witless things, then Love I hope—since wit
Becomes a clog—will soon ease me of it."

She gives him a certain consolation, he tell us, in saying that he would find true love in her. But in the same breath his wine "is watered"; she cannot love a blind love, she will not have him sacrifice "birth and mind" to any ignoble course in regard to herself. So he wanders in miserable fancies till the triumphant stanza which Grosart fancifully entitles "Covenant." For Stella has confessed. Her heart is his, her courage and purity lift him up to the highest heaven.

"O joy too high for my low style to show!
O bliss fit for a nobler state than me!
Envy, put out thine eyes, lest thou do see
What oceans of delight in me do flow!
My friend, that oft saw through all masks my woe,
Come, come, and let me pour myself on thee.
Gone is the Winter of my misery,
My Spring appears; O see what here doth grow:
For Stella hath, with words where faith doth shine,
Of her high heart given me the monarchy:
I, I, O I, may say that she is mine!
And though she give but thus condition'ly
This realm of bliss, while virtuous course I take,
No kings be crowned but they some covenant make."

For a while this state of transport suffices; he will write no more of her, for "wise silence is best music unto bliss." It is enough for the seeker after truth and beauty to read in Stella—

". . . those fair lines which true goodness shew.
There shall he find all vices overthrow,
Not by rude force, but sweetest sovereignty
Of reason, from whose light those night-birds fly."

Yet still the last lines show smouldering rebellion. Very soon the covenant will become unbearable. He banishes the rougher passion because it asks too much. But it is not to be exiled. He steals a kiss while Stella sleeps, is well chidden, and retorts that the chief result in him is inspiration to verse.

We turn the pages, we explore further into the "garden," and the lady bursts upon us with her black eyes, her shining twins. Without haste she moves, at first radiant as dawn, but quickly flamboyant as the noon—a midsummer vision.

"She comes, and straight therewith her shining twins do move
Their rays to me, who in their tedious absence lay
Benighted in cold woe; but now appears my day,
The only light of joy, the only warmth of love.
She comes with light and warmth, which, like Aurora, prove
Of gentle force, so that mine eyes dare gladly play
With such a rosy morn, whose beams, most freshly gay,
Scorch not, but only do dark, chilling sprites remove.
But lo, while I do speak it groweth noon with me,
Her flamey-glist'ring lights increase with time and place,
My heart cries, ah! it burns; mine eyes now dazzled be;
No wind, no shade can cool: what help then in my case?
But with short breath, long looks, stayed feet and aching head,
Pray that my sun go down with meeker beams to bed."

From sudden pangs of jealousy, that wretched "devil," whom he declares should have horns to mark him as fiend and enemy, the poet-lover reverts to the one stolen kiss—his "breakfast of love." He spends four of his best sonnets on it. In the eighty-second Stella is a

"Sweet gard'n nymph which keeps the cherry tree"

for which his lips hunger, and immediately he turns himself into a bird, whom he whimsically addresses as "Brother Philip," a bird who has transgressed too far in billing with her lips, and is in risk of having its neck wrung.

Absence casts a veil upon love ; he must obey her and go away. Yet, in going, the revelation of her grief is his joy.

> " Alas, I found that she with me did smart.
> I saw that sighs her sweetest lips did part,
>
> .   .   .   .   .   .
>
> For me I wept to see pearls scattered so;
> I sigh'd her sighs and wailèd for her woe;
> Yet swam in joy, such love in her was seen."

Of a sudden, apparently at Court, he sees her pass, and invites malediction on the clumsy linkboy in attendance, the darkness, the driver of her equipage.

> " Curst be the page from whom the bad torch fell ;
> Curst be the night which did your strife resist;
> Curst be the coachman that did drive so fast ! "

We are nearing the end of the story and the climax. The first of the two following songs is a vivid dialogue in the garden. The hour is ripe, the moment and the place all-powerful :

> " Only Joy, now here you are,
> Fit to hear and ease my care,
> Let my whispering voice obtain
> Sweet reward for sharpest pain;
> Take me to thee, and thee to me :
> ' No, no, no, no, my Dear, let be.'
>
> Night hath clos'd all in her cloak,
> Twinkling stars love-thoughts provoke ;
> Danger hence, good care doth keep,
> Jealousy itself doth sleep :
> Take me to thee, and thee to me;
> ' No, no, no, no, my Dear, let be.'
>
> Better place no wit can find
> Cupid's yoke to loose or bind ;
> These sweet flowers on fine bed too
> Us in their best language woo;
> Take me to thee and thee to me;
> ' No, no, no, no, my Dear, let be.'

This small light the moon bestowes
Serves thy beams but to disclose;
So to raise my hap more hie,
Feare not else, none can us spie;
Take me to thee and thee to me.
' No, no, no, no, my Dear, let be.'

That you heard was but a mouse;
Dumb sleep holdeth all the house;
Yet asleep methinks they say,
Young folks, take time while you may.
Take me to thee, and thee to me;
' No, no, no, no, my Dear, let be.'

Niggard time threats, if we miss
This large offer of our bliss.
Long stay, ere, he grant'st the same;
Sweet, then, while each thing doth frame,
Take me to thee and thee to me:
' No, no, no, no, my Dear, let be.'

Your fair mother is a-bed,
Candles out, and curtains spread:
She thinks you do letters write;
Write, but let me first indite;
Take me to thee, and thee to me:
' No, no, no, no, my Dear, let be."

Sweet, alas, why strive you thus?
Concord better fitteth us;
Leave to Mars the force of hands;
Your power in your beauty stands;
Take thee to me, and me to thee;
' No, no, no, no, my Dear, let be.'

Woe to me, and do you swear
Me to hate?   But I forbear;
Cursed be my destines all
That brought me so high to fall;
Soon with my death I will please thee;
' No, no, no, no, my Dear, let be.' "

In connection with this surely comes a sonnet which
is an " exceeding bitter cry" against Desire, the " band
of all evils, cradle of causeless care, web of will," who

has taken such heavy toll of him "with prize of mangled mind."

The theme of another "song" takes us back to the garden. Once more the place and hour are fine and fit, and the picture vivid and moving :

"In a grove most rich of shade,
Where birds wanton music made,
May, then young, his pied weed showing,
New perfumed with flowers fresh growing,

Astrophel with Stella sweet
Did for mutual comfort meet.
Both within themselves oppressed,
But each in the other blessed.

Him great harms had taught much care ;
Her fair neck a foul yoke bare ;
But her sight his cares did banish ;
In his sight.her yoke did vanish.

Wept they had, alas, the while,
But now tears themselves did smile,
While their eyes, by love directed,
Interchangeably reflected.

Sigh they did : but now betwixt
Sighs of woe were glad sighs mix't ;
With arms crost, but testifying
Restless rest and living dying.

Their ears hungry of each word
Which the dear tongue would afford ;
But their tongues restrained from walking
Till their hearts had ended talking.

But when their tongues could not speak
Love itself did silence break ;
Love did set his lips asunder,
Thus to speak in love and wonder.

'Stella, sovereign of my joy,
Fair triumpher of annoy,
Stella, star of heavenly fires,
Stella, lode-star of desires ;

Stella, in whose body is
Writ each character of bliss,
Whose face all, all beauty passeth,
Save thy mind, which yet surpasseth!'"

After full praise of her he begins to be importunate :

"'Grant, O grant; but speech, alas !
Fails me, fearing on to pass :
Grant, O me : what am I saying ?
But no fault there is in praying.

Grant—O dear, on knees I pray,
(Knees on ground he then did stay),
That not I, but since I love, you,
Time and place for me may move you.

Never season was more fit,
Never room more apt for it ;
Smiling air allows my reason ;
These birds sing, " Now use the season."

This small wind which so sweet is,
See how it the leaves doth kiss ;
Each tree in his best attiring
Sense of love to love inspiring.

Love makes earth the water drink ;
Love to earth makes water sink ;
And if dumb things be so witty,
Shall a heavenly grace want pity ?'

Then her hands, in their speech, fain
Would have made tongue's language plain ;
But her hands, his hands repelling,
Gave repulse all grace excelling.

'Astrophel,' said she, 'my love
Cease in these effects to prove ;
Now be still, yet still believe me,
Thy grief more than death would grieve me.

If that any thought in me
Can taste comfort but of thee,
Let me, fed with hellish anguish,
Joyless, hopeless, endless languish.

If more may be said, I say
All my bliss in thee I lay;
If thou love, my love, content thee,
For all love, all faith is meant thee.

Trust me while I thee deny.
In myself the smart I try.
Tyrant honour doth thus use thee,
Stella's self might not refuse thee.

Therefore, dear, this no more move,
Least, though I leave not thy love
Which too deep in me is framed,
I should blush when thou art named.'

Therewithal away she went,
Leaving him to passion rent
With what she had done and spoken,
That therewith my song is broken."

The shattered lover, now masquerading as shepherd,
bids his flock go hence to find better feeding, a merrier
place, where it shall not share in his tears or in his
enforced winter when the whole world revels in the full
flood of springtide.

There are other songs on the old theme, the ardent
request, the unswerving repulse. But the fires die
down, the vision clears, the love comes out of the
manacles of the lower passion, the prisoner of desire
swings forth—a great freeman among the "citizens of
the world."

The following most fitly comes at the end of the
sonnets, as in Pollard's edition.

" Leave me, O Love, which reachest but to dust;
And thou my mind, aspire to higher things.
Grow rich in that which never taketh rust;
Whatever fades, but fading pleasure brings.
Draw in thy beams, and humble all thy might
To that sweet yoke where lasting freedoms be;
Which breaks the clouds, and opens forth the light.

O take fast hold ; let that light be thy guide
In this small course which breath draws out to death
And think how evil becometh him to slide
Who seeketh heav'n, and comes of heav'nly breath.
Then farewell, world ; thy uttermost I see :
Eternal Love, maintain Thy life in me.

The lines read like the last words of one who enters
a cloister. But Sidney's activity was in full flower. He
was pining, as ever, for a soldier's career. The life of a
statesman to him was insupportable. His nature would
never have borne for more than a few hours together
the burden of intrigue necessary to such a position, and
despite old Languet's emphatic assertions that a man
served his country more truly with brain and word than
by the sword, Philip was really never happy except when
under arms. Not the wretched violence of war, but
its difficulties and dangers attracted him, and first and
foremost he must have the cause at heart. One places
this almost swashbuckling hunger in him in a different
category to his other " parts."

But his sense of the unseen, the Godhead, was always
the dominant factor in him. Even while fresh from
college he stated in all humility in one of his letters to
Languet that in his belief a fragment at least of the divine
element existed in himself, and he knew that Languet
made appeal always to that in him. Philip always swam
in deep waters. In the *Arcadia* his questioning heart
speaks to its comrade in all ages. The thoughts are the
thoughts of to-day, the question always the old one :

"What essence destiny hath! if Fortune be or no ;
Whence our immortal souls to mortal earth do stow ;
What life it is, and how that all these lives do gather
With outward maker's force or like an inward father.
Such thoughts, methought, I thought and shamed my single
    mind,
Then void of nearer cares, the depths of things to find."

Fox-Bourne speaks somewhat disparagingly of the deleterious influence of Penelope upon his hero. This is highly unfair and unmerited. The two were playmates as we know, and their hearts were purposely inclined to one another by agencies beyond themselves. The intimate things of every day and their social life, in addition to youthful memories, would naturally draw them close. Philip was not a courtier of the Leicester type, or a man about town who deliberately chooses to play the rôle of a tame cat. He was not a wooer of young and fashionable Court matrons ; above all he was not a creature given to such dalliance. Penelope fulfilled her marriage vows without scandal or murmur throughout all the first years of her life as Lady Rich. Had she not been unhappy, Philip would assuredly not have flung his heart into such verse or passed through such red-hot ordeal as the sonnets betray. Had she been of baser stuff his self-revelation marking every stage in his development, both as man and as immortal spirit, would have revealed her also, in all sincerity, with all her glories lessened, cheapened. Fox-Bourne compares unfavourably her power over him with that of his sister, Mary, the Countess of Pembroke. Here again this chronicler is unkind. The comparison is scarcely fair. The relationship on the one hand was complex—fraught with every kind of danger to the family circle, to the social environment. It was brought about by extraordinary circumstances, in the knots of which the lovers strove vainly, as persons in a Greek tragedy. On the other hand, there was everything in the attitude of the sister and brother to conduce to peace and harmony. She was Philip's solace during his hardest soul-strife, even as "Stella" by her mere existence gave him the courage to live, conquer, and once more go forth in the world again to his fitting work. His self-conquest was not sudden. In the sonnets we get such phrases as "fumes of melancholy," while one set of the songs comes under the title "Smokes of Melancholy." And there were wilder moods, such as the one in the fifth song, which I will not quote in full, in which his repulses thrust him into a transport of tender rage. He calls upon his muse to fling defiance at Penelope, he names her "witch" and "devil" and tells her that though she is the subject of Venus and vassal of Cupid, she has played rebel :

> " Both rebel to the son and vagrant from the mother ;
> . . . wearing Venus' badge in every part of thee,
> Unto Diana's train thou, runaway, did'st fly,
> Who faileth one is false, though trusty to another.

> .   .   .   .

> You then, ungrateful thief, you murd'ring tyrant, you,
> You rebel runaway, to lord and lady untrue,
> You witch, you devil, alas, you still of me beloved,
> You see what I can say ; mend yet your forward mind
> And such skill in my Muse you, reconcil'd shall find
> That all these cruel words your praises shall be proved."

Of heaviness and depression this great spirit had his fill until he could pass, transfigured, to that last sonnet with its fine last line :

> " Eternal Love, maintain Thy life in me."

Of a truth, Philip, though he had much to make him merry, was not superficially a merry fellow. His nature was too intense to leave only the impression of comfortable laughter upon his face. Probably old Henry Sidney knew his son's tendency when he exhorted him to good cheer as the best incentive to all achievement. The youth took life hard. He made his mistakes in heat and rashness, but he never wavered after his conquest of himself in regard to Penelope. There was work enough for him. Moreover, his family must have felt, and he probably also felt, that the best curative was a decent marriage. As long ago as the winter of 1581, a few months' before Penelope's marriage, he had, in a letter to Sir Charles Walsingham, used the phrase " my exceeding like to be good friend" of that gentleman's daughter. Except for his poverty he could have had no lack of choice. One historian has left it on record that Court ladies wooed him boldly. He chose where he could trust—though his choice was not interesting —but, as Fox-Bourne points out, he may well have formed after Languet's recent death a consolatory friendship with the great " Mr. Secretary." Philip's choice, Frances Walsingham, was not in any sense brilliant, but she came of sound stock. The two fathers corresponded duly :

"I have understood of late," wrote Sir Henry Sidney to Sir Francis Walsingham, " that coldness is thought in me in proceeding in the matter of our children. In truth, sir, it is not so, nor so shall it ever be found. I most willingly agree, and protest I joy in the alliance with all my heart."

The apparent unwillingness was merely due to the consciousness that he could not give his son a decent marriage allowance, and he put it clearly in attempting, through Walsingham, to obtain assistance from the Crown :

"As I know, sir, that it is for the virtue which is, or which you suppose is, in my son, that you made choice of him for your daughter, refusing haply far greater and far richer matches than he, so was my confidence great, that by your good means, I might have obtained some small reasonable suit of Her Majesty, and therefore I nothing regarded any present gain, for if I had, I might have received a great sum of money for my goodwill of my son's marriage, greatly to the relief of my biting necessity. . . ."

The letter also contains the phrase: "The thraldom I now live in for my debts." It ends however on a happier note :

"And now, dear Sir, and brother, an end to this tedious, tragical treatise . . . ; tragical I may well term it, for that it began with the joyful love and great liking, with likelihood of matrimonial match, between our most dear and sweet children (whom God bless!) and endeth with declaration of my unfortunate and bad estate. Our Lord bless you with long life and healthful happiness! I pray you, sir, commend me most heartily to my good lady, cousin and visitor, your wife ; and bless and buss our sweet daughter. And, if you will vouchsafe, bestow a blessing upon the young knight, Sir Philip."

This knighthood, by the way, had been among the New Year honours of this date (1583), and was conferred on Sidney's " son of excellent good proof" (as his father termed him in a letter to Walsingham), in accordance with the rules of the Orders of the Garter, for which higher honour he acted as proxy for Prince John Casimir, the younger son of the Calvinistic Frederick the Third, Elector Palatine.

Of the Walsingham wedding, which took place in this year, there is no interesting record. Philip was twenty-eight, his bride only fifteen. About this time he was sorely tempted to go over seas again. The Queen actually authorised him to depart on a journey of exploration in America. Five years earlier nothing would have held him back. His imagination, ever since the Frobisher project, had been full of schemes of this sort, and this last one, which was neither a gold hunt nor an expedition of aggression, but a purely peaceful enterprise prompted by the love of adventure and travel, and the desire to improve his worldly estate, specially smiled upon him. The Queen's charter issued to him her second charter of colonisation, whereby he was empowered to hold and use across the seas no less an estate than three million acres. When he came to look into the scheme, however, he realised the financial outlay entailed in ships, men and provisions, and in the year of his marriage transferred his rights unconditionally to a friend. So while this man—a certain Sir George Peckham—set forth over the Spanish main, Sidney was quietly passing through the experiences of his first year of married life.

Three years later the claims of the Netherland War had been thrust upon him, and he and Essex and Leicester had gone forth under arms. He had not deserted his young wife in any sense. For he wrote from Bergen-op-Zoom to his father-in-law that he "delighted in it," both because "it was near the enemy, but especially, having a very fair house in it, and an excellent air, I destined it for my wife." This plan, however, he postponed owing to fears of complications at Court, "considering how apt the Queen is to interpret everything to my disadvantage." He adds that the life out there was "not fit for anyone of the feminine gender."

Nevertheless the eighteen-year-old Frances braved the sea and the hardship of war, and was "very well and merry" at her husband's side till the black hour of Zutphen in mid-autumn.

Of his disastrous death, history has left records so complete, details which are now so impressed upon the popular methods of teaching history that it is not

necessary here to reiterate the circumstances ; but we
may remind ourselves how characteristic was the unhappy cause of that fatal wound, and recall the fact
that though her gallant servant throughout his part in
the campaign risked everything for Queen and country,
Elizabeth was blind to his value till she had lost him.
I have said that service in the Low Countries had been
actually thrust upon Sidney. It is curious that he, who
had always advocated the co-operation of England with
the Netherlands against Spain, should have shown himself unwilling now to take a part in this contest. He
had in his riper years formed the opinion that there
was only one way to wound Spain in default of whole-
hearted action on the part of a European league or an
independent invasion of the country itself. The first
possibility now seemed to be a Utopian dream ; for the
second scheme he adjudged England not sufficiently
potent in this hour. He therefore planned with such
intrepid pirates as Drake, such experienced adventurers
as Ralegh, to attack Spain's West Indian stronghold
of wealth, so that, like an animal worried by a gadfly,
she should relax her European vigilance and turn to
defend herself against unexpected aggression. This
bold project was to be a secret. It was Sidney's private
venture in which he was to share the command with
Drake. And a secret it was, till apparently through
Drake's jealousy it leaked out. The Queen wanted
Sidney for the Netherlands. She sent her orders after
him to Plymouth, where he lay on the eve of departure.
But he knew they were coming, and contrived to have
them stolen on the road. This, of course, was revealed, and from Court post-haste travelled a live lord,
with commands to deliver the official paper straight to
the defaulter. A bombshell—that letter ! We are

told that it carried " in the one hand grace, in the other thunder." It gave Philip the chance of service under his uncle, Leicester, in the Netherlands, with eternal banishment from Queen and Court as alternative. So he must perforce go home sadly enough, and remained more or less idle and discontented till some definite command should be conferred upon him. This delay of several months gave him at least the chance of being under his own roof when his firstborn, Elizabeth Sidney, came into the world. Eventually he left for Holland, not a little consoled for the spoiling of his pet naval scheme by the post of Governor of Flushing —the key of the Netherlands.

He went ahead of Leicester and longed for his coming. Had he realised how much of the energy of the new Lord Lieutenant in the Netherlands would go to pompous and ambitious devices to impress his own importance on his neighbours, Philip would have done his best to keep his uncle at the other end of the earth. The first part of Leicester's time was spent in fruitless discussion, by correspondence, with the Queen, while Philip urged action and begged for reinforcements. Meanwhile private grief tugged at his heart. Sir Henry Sidney died after a week's illness, and three months later his noble wife followed him.

Their son had his chance of distinction at last, attacked and won the town of Axel, a difficult and dangerous feat, and was created a colonel. All the Queen did was to ascribe his bravery to mere ambition, because she wished the colonelcy to go to someone else not half as worthy. Meanwhile the English troops were ready to mutiny. Leicester was losing time, the Treasury was backward with the soldiers' wages. Philip wrote from Flushing to his father-in-law in despair : " To complain of my Lord

Leicester you know I may not ; but this is the case. If once the soldiers fall to a thorough mutiny this town is lost in all likelihood." Wherefore all he could do was to be in constant attendance at Arnheim and elsewhere on the superior officer he so mistrusted, and to work for the seizure of Zutphen on the Yssel. The attack was led by him with a little company of two hundred horsemen under cover of a heavy September morning mist. They faced two thousand of the enemy and the great guns of the Zutphen ramparts. His first horse was killed under Sidney. Just before he mounted a second he met Sir William Pelham, Lord Marshal of the Camp, wearing practically no " harness." Long-buried, schoolboy fool-hardiness and pride seized the other, and he cast off those portions of armour which protected his thighs. And so to horse, and a second attack, and yet a third— the fatal third ! It was as well that the terrified charger carried its fainting rider close to the spot where Leicester had taken his stand. Philip never confessed to that divine rashness. "This my hurt is the ordinance of God by the hap of war," was his humble assertion. All through his pain he thought of his Queen, " not ceasing to speak still of Her Majesty, being glad if his heart and death might any way honour her ; for hers he was whilst he lived," as Leicester wrote in a letter giving the bad news. Elizabeth's spoken appreciation in return was a far rougher matter, when later she bade one of her gentlemen keep out of needless danger and not "get knocked on the head, like that silly fellow Sidney." Nevertheless, that roughness, in which she reminds one of her father, disguised a deep sorrow shared with the whole nation.

Philip Sidney signed his will eight days after he received his wound, but lingered for nearly a month, and had the wit and pluck to write a poem, "La Cuisse Rompue," about his hurt. So do the art-instinct and the impulse towards articulation triumph over the most acute hours of physical distress.

Yet in spite of the superb dignity and courage of that lingering death, one is impatient that he should not have passed away on the field of battle under the one sharp kind fatal stroke.

Even so he died in the full tide of his life. Surely R.L.S. had him in mind in those triumphant passages in the essay, "Aes Triplex" :

"Does not life go down with a better grace foaming in full body over a precipice than insensately struggling to an end in sandy deltas? For surely, at whatever age death overtakes the man, this is to die young. . . . In the hot fit of life, a-tip-toe on the highest point of being, he passes at a bound to the other side. . . . The trumpets are hardly done blowing when . . . this happy starred spirit shoots into the spiritual land."

And so does this creature of fire and air, who walked on earth and played with the stars for a space, call us by his death once more to the heavenly ways, the while his astral fancies lie on the earth for lovers to gather and cherish. Those who do not love, and who still doubt the beauty of his fantasy, may care to know that Charles Lamb's hallmark is upon *Astrophel to Stella* in these words :

"Written in the very heyday of his blood, they are stuck full of amorous fancies, far-fetched conceits, befitting his occupation ; for true love thinks no labour to send out thought upon the vast and more than Indian voyages, to bring home rich pearls, outlandish wealth, gums, jewels, spicery, to sacrifice in self-depreciating similitudes, as shadows of true amiabilities in the beloved. We must be lovers—or at least the cooling touch of time . . . must not have so damped our faculties as to take away our recollection that we were once so—before we can duly appreciate the glorious vanities and graceful hyperboles of the passion. . . . But the general beauty of them all is, that they are so perfectly characteristical. The spirit of 'learning and of chivalry'—of which union Spenser has entitled Sidney to have been the 'president'—shines through them. . . . The verse runs swiftly and gallantly. It might have been tuned to the trumpet or tempered (as himself expresses it) to 'trampling horses' feet.' . . . They are not rich in words only, in vague and unlocalised feelings . . . they are full material and circumstantiated: Time and place appropriates every one of them. It is not a fever or passion wasting itself upon a thin diet of dainty words, but a transcendent passion pervading and illuminating actions, persuits, studies, feats of arms, the opinions of contemporaries, and his judgment of them."

From the Autolycus wares of this chapter choose what you will, think what you list. Whether the sonnets clothe a burning heart flung at your feet—a "cannon buried in flowers," as Schumann wrote of Chopin, or whether they are the fragrant evaporation of a cultured intellect fed by a story which the writer had dreamed and not lived through (because the poet proved stronger than the man), is left for each reader to determine for himself. Whatever the judgment, it remains true that Penelope was blessed for a time by the warm regard of the greatest lover of her age, the chiefest knight. That fact, at least, is without money and without price. History gives it to us with generous hands.

CHAPTER VI

GREEN PASTURES

THE splendid Philip is dead, but he lives on, not only in his work, but in his influence. Most of all, he lives on in his *Arcadia*. This has been already alluded to briefly. It is too important a work to shelve in these pages, for it, as much as the sonnets, belongs to the "Stella" period of his life. Contemplation of it comes most fitly after his death, for it was in the truest sense a memorial of him, the chief memorial. It is not to be thought that he wrote it after the sonnets. These, like all bookish enterprises undertaken during a period of intense literary activity, were tossed off while his imagination was busy with larger work. Apart from his *Apologie for Poesie* the *Arcadia* contains the best of him. It was written solely for his beloved sister, Mary, after her marriage, but it is only natural that thoughts of the imperial beauty of Penelope Rich should force themselves upon his fantasy and invention. The part she played in it shall be presently touched upon. Let us look awhile at the personality of Mary Sidney the younger, who shared with " Stella " and Languet the honour of being his inspiration.

From the point of view of the world, the marriage of this lady was an unqualified success. On her, now their only daughter, the Sidney parents concentrated their efforts. Their other girl, Ambrosia, had died in her budding

From an old painting. Photo by Emery Walker

MARY, COUNTESS OF PEMBROKE

girlhood. Mary was her mother's one hope. Like their friend, the late Lord Essex, the Sidneys felt the danger of the times, where young and beautiful women were concerned. Above all they feared, because they had intimate experience of such things, the snares of a Court. Thus they chose for her a mate highly-born, well established as to patrimony, and one who, apparently, would know how to treat a delicately nurtured lady and a wife. That he was old enough to be her father did not perturb them. So they had found for her the goodly Henry Herbert, second Earl of Pembroke, already twice a childless widower. He was old enough to be her father, and he was rich. He was the owner of great houses, Barnard's Castle, Ramsbury, and Wilton. She knew very well how to play the part of hostess in such places, following her mother's example and bearing at Penshurst and Ludlow Castle. She came but seldom to Court, and kept out of all scandals and intrigues. Her first years were lived in placid content as mother and hostess. She bore her husband two sons, the eldest of whom, William, was destined to cause her not a little grief and anxiety. She was old for her years, intensely religious, intensely literary. Later on we shall find her sorely distressed by the sordidness and meanness of her husband in his old age. For the moment all is sweet reasonableness in her life. Philip was her dearest guest in the first year of her marriage at Wilton, and it is probably during his visit to her that her eldest son was born.

From this moment we see her building up a rich and beautiful life about her at this house, which an old chronicler has most happily termed " that apiarie, to which men that were excellent in armes and arts did resort." Truly her influence and far-radiating sympathy

H

with men of letters and of science converted the place into a gay beehive. Most certainly was she one of the few who, in the modern epigram, have avoided "aiming at a salon and only achieving a restaurant." All those men who had clustered about Philip in the first days of the Areopagus Club found their way to her circle, and the Wilton school of literature came into being. This could never have been the case, nor could her sympathies with art and learning ever have been so deep had she been only a consumer of letters and not, to a certain extent, a producer. Her position was unique. Here was a woman, highly gifted, young, good-looking, very rich, with that power of consecutive industry denied to many women who have not a financial care in the world. In addition she had not to wrestle with the hostile humours of a husband who disapproved of her art interests, or deemed wasted the time which she gave to her own literary efforts. Set against this tremendous advantage over the conditions of the average literary person the fact that there is no high road to literary success. Mary Pembroke, as much as the poorest poet whom her munificence and tenderness assisted, knew that she must walk along the narrow and often rough road at the end of which shine, now gloriously, now dimly, as though obscured by a tangle of mental effort, the ideals of art. It must be remembered that we witness here at Wilton the throes of a tremendous revolution in literature. Philip and his friends had, with gay bravery, set themselves to reconstruct 'the school of English poetry. Think of those days, imagine the crowd of budding stars in letters! Here were future great authors of books, born just before or just after Sidney, as well as his actual contemporaries, such as Fulke Greville, the author-elect of

WILTON HOUSE

dramas published in the first Stuart reign in the collection under his name, entitled, *Certain Learned and Elegant Works*, and specially remarkable to the world as Philip's biographer. Already the country was the richer for the genius and work of the famous Thomas Sackville, Lord Buckhurst, who was not only part author with Thomas Norton of the first English tragedy, *Gorborduc*, but one of the most famous of the contributors to that remarkable literary serial, *The Mirror for Magistrates*, begun under the editorship of William Baldwin and continued through several editions. This, intended as a running commentary in verse upon the events and signs of history, was a fine, bold project. The material, it seems, was to consist chiefly of tragedies based upon fact, and devised to moralise " those incidents of English history which warn the powerful of the unsteadiness of fortune by showing them, as in a mirror, that 'who reckless rules, right soon may hap to rue.'"[1] George Ferrers, John Higgins, who actually achieved the publication of a first part of this ambitious work, the prolific and penniless Thomas Churchyard were among the contributors. And in this work the Elizabethan dramatists who came after them found a rich and unfailing source of plot and inspiration.

Gorborduc, so magnificently produced by the gentlemen of the Inner Temple, after a New Year masque for the Queen, was now ancient history. So was the first English comedy, *Ralph Roister Doister*. The drama had been launched when Sidney and Spenser were little boys and Shakespeare a baby of a year old .Subsequently the ranks of literature were reinforced at a hot rate. Philip knew all about Sackville, and he had imbibed the

[1] Morley's *English Literature*.

work, in sonnet and blank verse, of Surrey and Wyatt. At this moment, the years 1579–80, he was in years and literary experience well ahead of Shakespeare and Bacon. The former was still a lad of only fifteen, member of a struggling country family, the latter at eighteen, impoverished by his father's death, was applying himself to that legal study which carried him to such heights. Spenser, just twenty-seven, was publishing the *Shepherd's Calendar*, with a store of already written works at his back ; and John Lyly was bringing out, in two successive parts, that tremendous satire, his *Euphues*, or *The Anatomy of Wit*. Philip knew Ralegh intimately, and Ralegh and Spenser had served together in Ireland. Ralegh loved good verse, and just as Gabriel Harvey, Leicester's protégé, had brought Spenser to the notice of the Earl of Leicester and of Philip, so did Ralegh (whose multicoloured, many-sided experience of war and travel was to find shape later in his *History of the World*) advance Spenser's fame in regard to Elizabeth, to whom, as you remember, the *Faerie Queen* was dedicated. As to Gabriel Harvey, he cuts a lusty figure in that company, and managed his worldly affairs, thanks to Leicester, better than poor Lyly, who ineffectually sought to obtain from the Queen the official position and salary of Master of the Revels. Nothing is more piteous than his subsequent appeal to her for sustenance, in which he begs that since, "after ten years' tempest," he must "suffer shipwreck of his time, wits and hopes," she will at least vouchsafe to send him some means, "some plank or rafter" to waft him into a country where he may "in every corner of a thatched cottage, write prayers instead of plays," prayers for her long life and prosperity, and confessions of repentance for having "played the fool so long."

From a photograph

PENSHURST PLACE

Page 100

Gabriel Harvey is a more sturdy person (his father was a well-to-do ropemaker), and as such, fitted to be of that brave knot of Philip's Areopagites. From his earliest student days he had learnt the first lesson of sincerity in literature. He knew that "the style is the man," and he uttered his creed without fear. "Let every man learn to be, not a Roman, but himself," was his dictum. From Cambridge he went to meet the Queen at Saffron Walden, and managed to get a hearing for his verses to her. She noticed him, as "Leicester's man," with a friendly "I'll not deny you my hand, Harvey," and in after days he was an honoured guest of the Sidneys at Penshurst.

"Away with mere surface polish, away with over-curious phrases, rooted in unreality, away with set forms, prescribed rhythms !" was the sum of the cry of the reformers. It was easier to say than to do. The marriage of perfect grace with strong and perfect sincerity are nuptials which at all times are hard to accomplish by the most resolute of matchmakers in style. Harder still are they to celebrate when literature is in a state of transition and rapid expansion. Hence the often recondite "incredible graces" of the "Stella" sonnets, hence the tedium of portions of the *Arcadia*. But the outcome of all the bustling energy and the correspondence of these young Areopagites was the controversy between Stephen Gosson and Sidney, which elicited from the latter his *Apologie for Poesie*, most truly judged "the first piece of intellectual literary criticism" in the English language. I have not space here for more than the barest details and a short quotation. Gosson was, like Philip, a writer of pastorals, but suddenly left playwriting for an attack on the contemporary stage. This, it must be noted, was the time of storm and stress for the drama. A multitude of moralists, religious and secular, had arisen to hurl satire at the theatre. Most unluckily, universal municipal objections to the gathering of audiences were assisted enormously by the dangers brought to London by the plague. Divines pronounced delightedly upon it, and saw an intimate connection between play and plague, as the scourge of God sent upon theatre-goers. "The cause of plagues is sin. . . . The cause of sin is plays : therefore the causes of plagues are plays," was the conclusion of a preacher at Paul's Cross in 1577 ! So Gosson brought out his *School of Abuse* and dared to dedicate it to Philip Sidney. The latter was much incensed at the attack on poetry and kindred arts, modified though it was by a confession that the times were improving and that contemporary dramas were growing into a mirror of life whereby men might learn their faults. In 1581 Sidney penned his great *Apologie*. The expression is clear, the style terse, and so every word enforces his hatred of affectation, alliteration, and of far-fetched similes, "figures and flowers extremely winter-starved," as he calls them. In the opening he deplored the distaste for poetry, which he said was "fallen to be the laughing-stock of children," adding humbly, "I—who, I know not by what mischance, in these my not old years and idlest times, having slipped into the title of a poet—am provoked to say something unto the defence of that my unelected vocation." And poetry he broadly defined as all works of imagination and elegance, including romances such as his *Arcadia*, for, said he, "it is not rhyming and versing that make poetry ; one may be a poet without versing, and a versifier without poetry." To ardent students who search after the beginnings of literary criticism I must

PHILIPPVS HERIBERTVS COMES DE PENBROKE ET MONGOMERY. BARO
DE CARDIFFE ET SHIRLAND. D." DE PARRE ET ROOS IN KENDALL .
MARCHIO S." QVINTI. REGIS ANGLIÆ A CVBICVLIS'EQVES PERISCELIDIS.

Ant van Dyck pinxit   *Robertus van VoerSt fecit.*

From an etching after Van Dyck

PHILIP, FOURTH EARL OF PEMBROKE
SECOND SON OF MARY, COUNTESS OF PEMBROKE

leave perusal in full of this manly and remarkable treatise, packed with allusions to bygone poets and romancists and sparkling with illustrations of former and contemporary works. Let us return to the *Arcadia* and see how it was written. Sidney explains its delightful haphazard growth in his lovely dedication :

"To my dear Lady and Sister, the Countess of Pembroke.

"Here now have you, most dear, and most worthy to be most dear Lady, this idle work of mine, which, I fear, like the spider's web, will be thought fitter to be swept away than worn to any other purpose. For my part, in very truth, as the cruel fathers among the Greeks were wont to do to the babes they would not foster, I could well find in my heart to cast out in some degree of forgetfulness this child, which I am loth to father. But you desired me to do it; and your desire, to my heart is an absolute commandment. Now it is done only for you, only to you. If you keep it to yourself, or to such friends who will weigh errors in the balance of goodwill, I hope, for the father's sake, it will be pardoned, perchance made much of, though in itself it have deformities ; for, indeed, for severer eyes it is not, being but a trifle, and that triflingly handled. Your dear self can best witness the manner, being done in loose sheets of paper, most of it in your presence, the rest by sheets sent unto you as fast as they were done. In sum, a young head, not so well stayed as I would it were, and shall be when God will, having many fancies begotten in it, if it had not been in some way delivered, would have grown a monster, and more sorry might I be that they came in than that they gat out. But his chief safety shall be the not walking abroad, and his chief protection the bearing the livery of your name, which, if so much goodwill do not deceive me, is worthy to be a sanctuary for a greater offender. This say I because I know the virtue so ; and this say I because it may be

ever so, or, to say better, because it will be ever so.
Read it, then, at your idle times, and the follies your good
judgment will find in it blame not, but laugh at : and so
looking for no better stuff than, as in a haberdasher's
shop, glasses or feathers, you will continue to love the
writer, who doth exceedingly love you, and most, most
heartily prays you may long live to be a principal ornament to the family of the Sidneys.

"Your loving Brother,

"PHILIP SIDNEY."

He says nothing in this preface of his intentions, gives
no key to his characters, though he might well have
confided the origin of them to her, since he never intended the work for publication.   When it was two-
thirds done he seems to have wearied of it.   He could
not but feel that the intricacies of the plot and the length
were too much for him at this juncture.   Military service called him away to death, and it was left unfinished
till his sister, when the shock of his loss diminished,
sought to ease her heart by editing and completing it.

I have spoken in a previous chapter of the Cult of
the Shepherd.   This was the very moment when an
adoration of things pastoral invaded the minds of poets
and dramatists.   This wave of pastoral poetry swept
across the Continent from Italy to us.   Italy was still
the fount of literary influence ; and pastoral poetry,
which an old fable traces to the authorship of the
Sicilian Daphnis, son of Mercury, had travelled from
Italy and Spain into France.   When Sidney entitled
his long romance *The Arcadia*, he was not the first to
use the title.   The mother-work was an *Arcadia* of
Jacopo Sanazzaro, a Neapolitan (1458–1532), and was
first published in 1504.   It was in prose and verse,
divided into twelve sections of prose, each followed by

an eclogue, and the author not only introduced himself, under a shepherd's name, but also his mother. This lady died just before the beginning of the sixteenth century, when probably his book was half written. The story of the writing of Sidney's *Arcadia* is curiously like this, for some commentators assure us that it was a *roman à clef*. The circumstances of writing are slightly inverted, for it was the author who died before it was finished. Like the older work, it is a mingling of prose and verse. This he defends later in his *Apologie for Poesie*. It is very curious to find how the old classic notion is adapted to English scenery unlike that of the original mountainous Arcadia of European travellers, though, of course, it too has its happy valleys and places of pasturage. Sidney called it Greece, but it has transpired that he really took his ideas for his scenery from a part of the English coast in the neighbourhood of Hackness, a few miles north-west of Scarborough !

"This country where you now set your foot" (the hero Musidorus is told by the shepherds of Laconia, 'an unpleasant and dangerous realm') "is Arcadia. This country being thus decked with peace and the child of peace, good husbandry, these houses that you see scattered, are of men, as we two are, that live upon the commodity of their sheep, and therefore . . . are termed shepherds—a happy people, wanting little, because they desire not much."

As to the plot, it is gloriously involved. The whole thing, which sparkles with delicious descriptions and unforgettable phrases, is in the end like a medieval romance in which ideal persons of both sexes, gifted with youth and loveliness, do mighty and pathetic deeds, make play with country clowns, foil a wicked and designing ruler, wander in disguise, encounter wild beasts in forests and pirates on the seaboard, wage war against Helots and Lacedemonians, combine the pagan religion with Christian sentiments, and apparently wear armour of the Tudor period. Two cousins, devoted companions, Musidorus, Prince of Thessaly, and Pyrocles, Prince of Macedon, are separated by a wreck on the Spartan coast. Musidorus is saved, and shepherds lead him to the pastoral paradise of Arcadia, where he is sheltered and well entertained by Kalander, an Arcadian aristocrat. Unfortunately the place of green meads and fair waters knows only superficial peace. Kalander hears that his son has been taken prisoner by Spartan Helots, and it is necessary to summon the Arcadian army to defeat them and rescue the prisoner. Musidorus leads the Arcadian army triumphantly against the Helots, has a hand-to-hand combat with a mighty captain on the opposite side, who turns out to be his lost friend, Pyrocles. "Peace is concluded. Kalander's son is released, and the two friends embark upon love adventures. Basilius and Gynecia, King and Queen of Arcadia, have two daughters—majestic Pamela and sweet Philoclea. There is also a wicked queen Cecropia. Here you have the heart of the romance.

It is not necessary here to plunge into the labyrinth of the plot. The inquisitive who find the effort of extracting it from the romance itself too great, may study it in a concise form in the pages of Morley's *English Literature.* The ending is of course triumphantly happy. One feels that Philip would have it so, and his sister in her pretty patchwork so contrived it.

Some have supposed that of the two princely friends Sidney is Pyrocles, and Musidorus his friend, Fulke Greville, while Philoclea and Pamela are Stella and her sister, the other daughter of Essex, Dorothy Percy. Again, a certain wise Euarchus of the romance is presumably based upon Sir Henry Sidney, and the treacherous, cruel Queen Cecropia possibly meant for Catherine de Medici, with whose sanguinary intrigues the author had sufficient acquaintance during his foreign embassies. The contrast between Philoclea and Pamela is vividly marked, and though Fox-Bourne holds the view that the characters were not taken from life, it is practically certain that Philoclea is Penelope Rich. Every trait which Sidney instances corresponds with the dazzling details of the portrait of the Stella of his sonnets. Moreover, when Philoclea enters his pages, her beauty always transcends that of her handsome sister. From the description of the first he works up with increasing ecstasy to the entry of Philoclea. I quote the portraits of both from the first book of the *Arcadia*. We are shown Pamela fresh from the lodge in which she lives under the guardianship of the lout Dametus. As if to show obedience to her father's will and yield to her surroundings in the peasant's house, she has "taken on shepherdish apparel of russet cloth, cut in peasant fashion, with a straight body, open-breasted, the nether part full of plaits, with long and wide sleeves; but believe me," the eye-witness continues, "she did apparel her apparel, and with the preciousness of her body made it most sumptious. Her hair the full length, wound about with gold lace, only by the comparison to show how far her hair doth excel in colour. Betwixt her breasts, which sweetly rose up like two fair mountainets in the pleasant vale of Tempe, there hung a very rich diamond, set but in a black horn. . . . But when the ornament of the earth, the model of heaven, the triumph of nature, the life of beauty, the Queen of Love, young

Philoclea, appeared in her nymph-like apparel, her hair (alas ! too poor a word. Why should I not rather call them her beams ?) drawn up into a net, able to have caught Jupiter when he was in the form of an eagle, her body (O sweet body !) covered with a light taffeta garment, with the cast of her black eyes, black indeed, whether nature so made them, that we might be the more able to behold and bear their wonderful shining, or that she, goddess-like, would work this miracle with herself, in giving blackness the price above all beauty,— then, I say, indeed methought the lilies grew pale for envy, the roses, methought, blushed to see sweeter roses in her cheeks, and the clouds gave place that the heavens might more freely smile upon her ; at the least the clouds of my thoughts quite vanished, and my sight, then more clear and forcible than ever, was so fixed there that I imagine I stood like a well-wrought image, with some life in show, but none in practice."

Here, surely, poetry walks. The opening paragraph of the book shimmers with the iridescence of spring : " It was in the time that the Earth begins to put on her new apparel against the approach of her lover, and that the sun, running a most even course, becomes an indifferent arbiter between the night and day." Philoclea's fragrant grief has the true April feeling : " With that her tears rained down from her heavenly eyes and seemed to water the sweet and beautiful flowers of her face."

In a previous chapter extracts have been given describing the ideal country house—that of Kalander, the ideal country gentleman, who is chiefly memorable for his setting. He is a great lover of gardens. He has the classic feeling for a grove sacred and apart, a place of dear delight above all other places in his estate. One afternoon he leads his guest to a well arranged ground he had behind his house, as the place in which "himself more than in any other delighted." We are told that "the backside"—that is, the court or enclosure behind the house—"was neither field, garden, nor orchard," but all three in one; "for as soon as the descending of the stairs had delivered them down, they came into a place cunningly set with trees of the most taste-pleasing fruits; but scarcely they had taken that into their consideration, but that they were suddenly stepped into a delicate green; of each side of the green a thicket, and behind the thickets again new beds of flowers, which being under the trees, the trees were to them a pavilion, and they to the trees a mosaical floor, so that it seemed Art therein would needs be delightful, by counterfeiting Error, and making order in confusion."

Hard by stood a "house of pleasure," apparently a garden pavilion, adorned with delightful pictures—in effect a species of combined portrait gallery and presence chamber, such as the greater Elizabethan houses usually possessed, and which Philip must have often seen at Ludlow, in his father's Welsh home, at Penshurst and Wilton.

All through the long romance we get glimpses of the writer's heart, peeping through his inexhaustible and very tender fancy. We get (possibly) also portraits of the people he loved and idealised. In Musidorus' portrait we have, if not Fulke Greville, then a comrade such as Fulke, adorned with Sidney's most heroic thoughts. In Kalander we have the real Tory democrat, such as Henry Sidney surely was. When told of the shipwrecked stranger's arrival Kalander proves himself no snob. He refuses to trouble about the youth's parentage, but judges him by his countenance.

"I am no herald to enquire of men's pedigrees ; it sufficeth me if I know their virtues." And how the author loves comeliness! When Musidorus has recovered from his wreck "the excellency of his matured beauty was a credible ambassador." All Philip's ideal of manhood is in this portrait of a young man. Surely also this most serious of young men had not the slightest intention, in his estimate of Musidorus, of describing a prig :—"Having found in him, besides his bodily gifts beyond the degree of admiration by daily discourses, which he (Kalander) delighted to have with him, a mind of most excellent composition, a piercing wit, quite void of ostentation, high-erected thoughts seated in a heart of courtesy, an eloquence as sweet in the uttering as slow to come to the uttering, a behaviour so noble as gave a majesty to adversity, and all in a man whose age could not be above one and twenty years, the good old man was even enamoured with a fatherly love towards him."

Is there not a reflection of the Languet-Philip friendship in this attraction between Kalander and Musidorus ?

But one is tempted to quote without ceasing from the *Arcadia*, as one loses himself in its mazes, which are like the web of the tresses of Penelope, Stella, and Philoclea in one :

> "Her hair fine threads of finest gold,
>   In curléd knots man's thoughts to hold."

Here will we leave Mary Pembroke and Philip, at first together, working side by side at verse, romance, and at their joint translation of the Psalms. Never was there freer expression of his talent than in the *Arcadia*. For Mary, a woman crowned by marriage, he could write as full-blooded a romance as he desired, and to his sister the lightest fragments of his inventions were precious.   No self-consciousness marred his work on it, no fear of a censorious public nagged him.   He could here and in his *Apologie* do what his muse bade him do in the sonnets—"look in his heart and write."

Tenderly Mary Pembroke gathered his leaflets together as they reached her, or were laid in her hands after a morning's delicious study at Wilton[1]; faithfully she marshalled and stored them, and after Zutphen, when she was weaving her own exquisite wreath of mingled cypress and laurel, *The Doleful Lay of Clarinda*, in her brother's dear memory, she laboriously set herself to prepare the romance for publication, comparing her labours on it to the work of one who repairs a ruinous house.

Posterity may say what it chooses of the whole as presented in the various editions, ancient and modern. It cannot deny that Sidney's thoughts, delicate and "high erected," often drench weary minds like May dew, that he had most truly a soul "transparent as a fair casement."   And those who are not sure of their opinion may turn first to Fulke Greville's estimate, alike of its shortcomings and beauties, and again to that loving tribute to his friend, in which he likens him to a god who pours out life and radiance in his winged voyage through the world :

"All confess that *Arcadia* of his to be in form or matter as inferior to that unbounded spirit as other men's wishes are raised above the writer's capacities. But the truth is, his end was not writing, while he wrote, but both his wit and understanding leant upon his heart,

[1] On the Wilton estate was the small house or lodge of Ivychurch, where, it is opined, she withdrew for purposes of study.

to make himself and others, not in words and opinion, but in life and action, good and great."

"He was a man fit for conquest, plantation (colonisation), reformation, or whatever action is greatest and bravest among men, and withal such a lover of mankind whatsoever had any real parts in him found comfort, participation and protection to the uttermost of his power ; like Zephyrus, he giving life wherever he blew. . . . Soldiers honoured him, and were so honoured by him that no man thought that he marched under the true banner of Mars that had not obtained Sir Philip Sidney's approbation."

As Zephyrus, the fragrant, spice-laden wind, the lover of the Earth, he seems to pervade, to my thinking, both the world of literature, and the green pastures where he battled through his love story and found at last "a truce from cares." And under the roses, lilies, and violets with which Zephyrus enriches the earth his sister buries him in her pure, scented verse. "Oh! Death !" she cries,

> " What has become of him whose flower here left
> Is but the shadow of his likeness gone ?
>
> .　　　.　　　.　　　.　　　.　　　.
>
> Ah ! me, can so divine a thing be dead ?
> Ah, no ! it is not dead, nor can it die,
> But lives for aye in blissful paradise,
> Where, like a new-born babe it soft doth lie
> In bed of lilies, wrapped in tender wise,
> And compassed all about with roses sweet
> And dainty violets from head to feet."

CHAPTER VII

A SHEAF OF VERSES

THERE is no record of Penelope's feelings upon the news of Zutphen. Yet she could not but hear full details. The whole of England for twenty-five days hung upon the despatches from Arnheim. The first hope of his recovery, like all the after bulletins, "was received," says Stowe, "not as private but as public news." And when peace brought Essex and Leicester home again, both brother and uncle would tell Penelope of her lover's end. Not till four years later did she probably see her own peculiar sonnets. But she must have listened to many verses on him before Spenser penned that gracious Elegy, packed with homage to her, and including the magnificent tribute :

> " To her he vow'd the service of his days ;
> On her he spent the riches of his wit ;
> For her he made hymns of immortal praise ;
> Of only her he sung, he thought, he writ ;
> Her, and but her, of love he worthy deem'd,
> For all the rest but little he esteem'd."

Naturally, Sidney's famous pseudonym for his love gave all the elegiac writers endless opportunities. One grows quite weary of the countless devices connected with stars.

From Spenser's *Astrophel* . . . *An Elegy* :

> " And many a nymph both of the wood and brook,
> . . . brought him presents,

But he for none of them did care a whit.
For One alone he cared, for One he sighed,
His life's treasure, and his dear love's delight.

Stella the fair! the fairest star in sky:
As fair as Venus, or the fairest fair,
A fairer star saw never living eye,
Hot her sharp pointed beams through purest air;
Her he did love; her, he alone did honour;
His thoughts, his rhymes, his songs were all upon her.

Ne her with idle words alone he wooed,
And verses vain—yet verses are not vain;
But with brave deeds, to her sole service vowed
And bold achievements her did entertain.
For both in deeds and words he nurtured was,
Both wise and hardy—too hardy alas!"

The rest of the poem goes off into an absurd yet tenderly fantastic pastoral picture of his death. He is presented as a huntsman chasing big and terrible game in a far-off forest, slaying mightily, till one "cruel beast of most accursed brood" turns after him, and "with fell tooth" bites him in the thigh. He is found dying by shepherds and carried to his "lovéd lass" . . . who at the terrible sight disfigures herself to match his sorrowful condition. And when his spirit flits her soul follows, while the pitying, romantic gods transform both into a single flower, which at first is red, then turns to blue, when a constellation appears in the centre of it:

" And in the midst thereof a star appears
As fairly formed as any star in skies;
Resembling Stella in her freshest years,
Forth darting beams of beauty from her eyes:
And all the day it standeth full of dew,
Which is the tears that from her eyes did flow.
That herb of some 'Starlight' is called by name;
Of others 'Penthia,' though not so well:
But thou, wherever thou dost find the same,
From this day forth do call it *Astrophel.*
And whensoever thou it up dost take,
Do pluck it softly, for that shepherd's sake."

From another elegist, Ludovic Bryskett:

> " Lo, where engravèd by his hand yet lives
> The name of Stella in yonder bay tree.
> Happy name! happy tree!   Fair may you grow
> And spread your sacred branch which honour gives
> To famous emperors."

In the same strain wrote Matthew Roydon in his
Elegy on a Friend's Passion for his Astrophel:

> " Stella, a nymph within this wood
> Most rare, and rich of heavenly bliss;
> The highest in his fancy stood,
> And she could well demerit this.
>   'Tis likely they acquainted soon:
>   He was a sun, and she a moon.
>
> Our Astrophel did Stella love.
> O Stella! vaunt of Astrophel!
> Albeit thy graces gods may move;
> Where wilt thou find an Astrophel?
>   The rose and lily have their prime;
>   And so hath beauty but a time.
>
> Although thy beauty do exceed
> In common sight of every eye;
> Yet in his poesies when we read,
> It is apparent more thereby.
>   He that hath love and judgment too
>   Sees more than any others do.
>
> Thus Astrophel hath honoured thee,
> For when thy body is extinct,
> Thy graces shall eternal be
> And live by virtue of his ink.
>   For by his verses he doth give
>   To short-lived beauty aye to live.
>
> Above all others this is he
> Which erst approvèd in his song
> That love and honour might agree,
> And that pure love will do no wrong.
>   Sweet saints! it is no sin nor blame
>   To love a man of virtuous name.

Did never love so sweetly breathe
In any mortal breast before?
Did never Muse inspire beneath
A poet's brain with finer store?
 He wrote of love with high conceit,
 And beauty reared above her height.

Then Pallas afterward attired
An Astrophel with her device,
Whom in his armour heaven admired
As of the nation of the skies:
 He sparkled in his arms afar,
 As he were dight with fiery stars."

And so on. . . .

These fragments are quoted because they belong to the documents, of which not too many now exist, connected with Penelope. No less than two sets of funeral poems are included in her history and in the history of her two principal lovers. Meanwhile she was, in addition to "Astrophel," the heroine of other tributes. Henry Constable, one of the leading Elizabethan sonneteers, the "Sweet Constable," who "doth take the wand'ring ear and lay it up in prisonment," also expended his art on her. In his *Diana* is this sonnet, in which he had not been able to resist allusion to her surname:

"Heralds at arms do three perfections quote:
To wit—most faire, most rich, most glittering;
So when these three concur within one thing
Needs must that thing of honour be, of note.
Lately did I behold a rich, fair coat,
Which wishèd fortune to mine eyes did bring:
A lordly coat—but worthy of a king:
Wherein all these perfections one might note—
A field of lilies, roses proper bare,
Two stars in chief, the crest was waves of gold:
How glittering was the coat the stars declare;
The lilies made it fair for to behold;
And *rich* it was, as by the gold appears,
So happy he which in his arms it bears."

And again in this, which comes a series of " Sonnets to particular ladies whom he most honoured," he plays once more with her title :—

TO MY LADY RICH

" O that my song like to a ship might be,
  To bear about the world my Lady's fame :
  That chargèd with the riches of her name
  The Indians might our country's treasure see.
  No treasure, they would say, is rich but she ;
  Of all their golden parts they would have shame,
  And haply, that they might but see the same,
  To give their gold for naught they would agree.
    This wished voyage, though it I begin,
  Without your beauty's help cannot prevail :
  For as a ship doth bear the men therein,
  And yet the men do make the ship to sail,
  Your beauties so, which in my verse appear
  Do make my verse and it your beauties bear."

The same writer turned his pen to the celebration of the birth and death of a child of the Rich family.   The first he entitles :—

" A calculation upon the birth of an honourable lady's daughter borne in the yeere 1588 and on a Friday " :

" Fair by inheritance, whom born we see
  Both in the wondrous year and on the day
  Wherein the fairest planet beareth sway :
  The heavens to thee this fortune do decree—
  Thou of a world of hearts in time shall be
  A monarch great, and with one beauty's ray
  So many hosts of hearts thy face shall slay,
  As all the rest, for love, shall yield to thee.
  But even as Alexander—when he knew
  His father's conquests—wept, lest he should leave
  No kingdom unto him for to subdue ;
  So shall thy mother thee of praise bereave :
    So many hearts already she hath slain
    As few behind to conquer do remain."

But Friday proved a bad birthday, for the second poem is headed :

"Of the death of my Lady Riche's daughter : showing how the reason of her untimely death hindered her effecting those things which by the former calculation of her nativity he (the poet) foretold."

> "He that by skill of stars doth fates foretell
> If reason give the verdict of his side,
> Though by mischance things otherwise betide
> Than he foretold—yet doth he calcule well.
> A phœnix, if she live, must needs excel,
> And this by reason's laws should not have died :
> But thus it chancèd nature cannot abide
> More than one phœnix in the world to dwell.
> Now as the mother-phœnix death should slay,
> Her beauty's light did dazzle so his eye,
> As, while he blindfold let his arrow fly,
> He slew the young one which stood in his way.
>   Thus did the mother 'scape—and thus did I,
>   By good ill hap, fail of my prophecy."

So far and wide Penelope had woven a web about the hearts of men and poets that even in immortalising her mother's sorrow they must needs work in an extravagant compliment.   Yet I like this appellation of the "mother-phœnix."   It fits her future well ; for never did any woman come more triumphantly out of fiery dangers, social and moral, nor rise so wondrously from the veritable ashes of a reputation until she finally succumbed to grief and public abuse in the last chapter of her history.

One hunts in vain for any allusion in letters to the way in which Frances Sidney took the publication of all the verse in her rival's praise.   Coming so soon after her widowhood and all its tragic circumstances—for the shock of Philip's death was certainly the cause of the death in birth of their second child shortly after the battle of Zutphen—the publication of *Astrophel* must have been a somewhat bitter pill. Gossips could not refrain their comments. But Penelope Rich was of no mean nature. This first romance of her life was over, and Frances had, at the least, rich memories of a hero as her possession, added to the tender sympathy of his near relatives and her own, and the wide compassion of the Court, the nation, and those who had worked and fought with her husband in foreign parts. She had one child to rear and protect, good health, youth, and a decent dowry. The two ladies may well have met soon after the tragedy and drawn closer to one another through their memories. And their careers were, at the time, totally different. Penelope was now a fully developed woman of the world, with assured carriage and renowned charms—in herself almost a public asset. Through her, no doubt, began for Frances the acquaintance with the young Earl of Essex, which ended in a secret marriage in 1590, a year before the issue of the "Stella" sonnets. Her father, the great Secretary of State, died about this time. Otherwise, possibly, he would have prevented his only daughter's union with one whom Elizabeth jealously guarded as her own property. Walsingham would have exactly foreseen the result—Elizabeth's anger and the slow decline of Essex from favour. For though the Queen forgave the latter after a while, he had by this act asserted finally his independence as courtier and man, and given full play to his defiance of her petty tyrannies. This tacit declaration, combined with certain traits in him, could not but lead him along a road full of danger.

CHAPTER VIII

CERTAIN THEORIES

BY the light of actual facts the story of the Astrophel to Stella, sonnets has been suggested. There remains another set of sonnets which have never been fully explained—those of Shakespeare. These, to some minds, are the key to all manner of subordinate romances of which the peerless Penelope seems to have been the centre. Small wonder ! Herself a woman of great intensity, she moved amongst hot-headed, romantic, impetuous persons of her own age. Strong individualities are like hot springs ; they must gush forth, make their way to the light and to prominence, and consequently must strongly affect their environment. The closest friends of Essex were such folk—among them the Earl of Southampton and Charles Blount, Lord Mountjoy. It is entertaining to remember that with both these men he clashed at the beginning of his life. Such clashings are inevitable at Courts ; they were especially inevitable under a woman ruler such as Elizabeth. We shall come later to Mountjoy, as he is not concerned in the theories put forward in the course of nearly four hundred pages by Gerald Massey in 1866, in his work on the Shakespeare sonnets.

This good gentleman, who is convinced that a large section of the Shakespeare sonnets deals with the personality of Penelope Rich, naturally revels in his theory. He calls her " that Elizabethan Helen," and takes end-

From an engraving by S. Freeman, after a painting by Mirevelt

HENRY WRIOTHESLEY, EARL OF SOUTHAMPTON

less pains in a very discursive but pleasant volume to prove that for a while she ensnared Southampton, and that she caused jealousy between him and his lady-love, her cousin Elizabeth Vernon.

A moment, while the eye assures itself of details about these two.

He was Henry Wriothesley, third Earl of Southampton, born in 1573, orphaned in 1581, and by 1585, owing to the death of his elder brother, holder of the title. It was at this moment that he went to Cambridge, where he took his degree in 1589 and then left for London. Three years later he took his M.A. at Oxford, and entered Gray's Inn. Lord Burghley, as in many other cases where young, fatherless peers were concerned, became his guardian. (If the Buckingham of the Stuart period was truly "a man of many honeymoons," then assuredly the Elizabethan Lord Treasurer was not only "Her Majesty's Housewife," as Lord Shrewsbury called him, but a national godfather.) His "children" did not always act in the way he could have wished. For example, this Henry Wriothesley of the romantic nature was not at all an astute courtier. He started well, and sunned himself under the queenly smiles while Burghley set about his usual match-making. The Calendar of State papers records the existence of overtures between the guardian and the young Earl's mother for a betrothal between her son and Burghley's grandchild, daughter of the Earl of Oxford. We are also made aware of an expression of willingness on the part of the groom-elect. This was in the summer of 1590. But Henry Wriothesley, by the time he entered Gray's Inn, had by no means made up his mind to this match. He evaded it, partly, perhaps, by accident. For he lost ground at Court, first by giving shelter in his house at Tichford to two young bloods who had murder on their consciences, and then by conveying them to France. In addition he had met Elizabeth Vernon.

This lady was the daughter of Sir John Vernon, of Hodnet, and his wife, Elizabeth Devereux, aunt of Penelope Devereux and Essex. Elizabeth Vernon was a Court beauty, and, naturally, also a Maid of Honour. Here was pretty material for an excellent love affair under the nose of Elizabeth, who, while she herself loved to play with love, expected her men and maids to maintain the bearing of elegant icicles. At the same time, the fair Vernon's attractions at first did not prevent Southampton from standing as rival to her cousin Essex in the Queen's favour. The Secretary of Essex[1] accentuates this clearly in a piquant letter in which he says that Fulke Greville found Southampton fancying that the Queen wearied of Essex or showed "wariness" towards him. This set up all manner of complications duly recorded in the *Sidney Memoirs*, but not ending apparently in any serious breach between the cousins.

"My Lord of Essex kept his bed all yesterday : his favour continues *quam diu se bene gesseret*. Yet my Lord of Southampton is a careful waiter here and *sede vacante* doth receive favours at her Majesty's hands ; all this without breach of amity between them."

And again :

" My Lord of Southampton doth with too much familiarity court the fair Mistress Vernon, while his friends, observing the Queen's humours towards my Lord of Essex, do what they can to bring her to favour him, but it is yet in vain."

[1] Sir Henry Wootton.

Both the letters quoted from were written in 1595—the turning point, it may be said, of Southampton's and Essex's careers. This year practically made Essex and unmade Southampton, though it cemented the close friendship for which the latter so nearly paid on the gallows.

The reason that the efforts of Southampton's friends were "yet in vain" was his inability to disregard the charms of his Maid of Honour. The two at last took their courage in both hands and waited upon Elizabeth to plead their passion and ask for her sanction. She refused to see them. Thus snubbed, they had no alternative but to repress their wishes. Naturally all association with them was not helpful to Essex, and it must have been with infinite relief that the latter gallant departed next year to take part in an attack upon Cadiz, while Southampton broke away from the Court at last in 1597, under royal leave for a year's absence. The poor lady-love does not appear to have had a like outlet for her feelings. Her part, after the disturbance caused by her love-affair, was to stay at home, bearing her mistress's humours and her lover's moods, and she must have almost blessed her namesake for that. lover's absence. Yet, though Southampton finally departed—with Essex and Ralegh—to the Azores, as commander of the ship *Garland* and vice-admiral of the first squadron—though he showed unflinching purpose, high courage, and with Essex did "the only bit of warm work that was performed on the 'Island Voyage,'" the poor Vernon had little respite from sorrow, fears, and quarrels. Essex and Ralegh had fallen out on the expedition, Southampton's tactics were opposed by a fellow admiral, and he was made a scapegoat for the shortcomings of his comrades. What wonder that this made him touchy towards his lady, that his fiery nature was always goaded into outbursts, that he and Ambrose Willoughby fought like street-boys in the royal tennis-court, and that he and Earl Northumberland—who, by the way, was brother-in-law to Essex—were on the verge of a duel? The pen of Roland White in the *Sidney Memoirs* is ever at work on the subject, and we get very tragic glimpses of Elizabeth Vernon. "His fair mistress doth wash her fairest face with too many tears. I pray God his going away" (Burleigh had now intervened and was inducing his ward to fresh change of air by way of a mission to France) "bring her no such infirmity, which is, as it were, hereditary to her name." But we are comforted immediately by the entry next day hinting at the probability of speedy marriage. No use! Two days later Southampton is gone. Again the lady plays Niobe. The Earl is off over seas, "and hath left behind him a very desolate gentlewoman that hath almost wept out her fairest eyes." Nevertheless, that year saw the end of their love-tortures. Southampton hurried over from France, spent four days at Essex's house in Wanstead—where his love was with her cousin, Penelope—and there secretly married her.

Now for the sonnets. The first mention of this superb coronal of song is in a work called *Palladis Tamia*, by Meres (*Wit's Treasury*, being the second part of *Wit's Commonwealth*), published in 1598, in which this dazzling allusion occurs: "As the soul of Euphorbus was thought to live in Pythagoras, so the sweete wittie soul of Ovid lives in mellifluous and honey-tongued Shakespeare, witnes his 'Venus and Adonis,' his 'Lucrece,' his sugred sonnets among his private friends."

From a painting by Cornelius Janssens

ELIZABETH VERNON, COUNTESS OF SOUTHAMPTON

A year later two of the songs were printed in a miscellany, published by a bookseller named Jaggard, under the title "The Passionate Pilgrim." After this follows a blank of ten years. Then, in 1609, came the famous complete quarto edition published by one Thomas Thorpe, *Shakespeare's Sonnets. Never before Imprinted.* They were prefaced with the inscription : "To the onlie begetter of these insuing sonnets, Mr. W. H. all happinesse and that eternitye promised by our ever-living poet, wisheth the well-wishing adventurer in setting forth. T. T."

This is very clear, but that word "begetter" has been the source of much misunderstanding. It has been taken to signify the one person whose strong friendship and personality inspired the poet to pen the entire set of sonnets. Yet no one is ever sure who "Mr. W. H." is. The fact is that the word "beget" may well stand for "procure." "Mr. W. H.," instead of a powerful patron with a romantic career, would therefore seem to be just a private personage whose influence and social conditions enabled him to assist in collecting the "sugred sonnets" from among the private friends of Shakespeare, and obtain their sanction for publication. It is not Shakespeare who pays a tribute to "Mr. W. H.," but the adventurous Thorpe, eager to have the honour and glory of publishing them for the first time, and who, in his gratitude, wishes his good friend all the happiness and eternity with which Shakespeare seeks to endow the friends for whom, and of whom, he wrote.

This is not the place to go into all the theories which have been propounded since the beginning of last century as to the "story" of the poems. Roughly speaking, it is agreed now by Shakespearean authorities that the first hundred and twenty-six were addressed to a man friend, the rest to a woman of sinister beauty. The latter may be penned from a purely personal standpoint and embody a strong phase in the writer's own life as a truly "passionate pilgrim," or they may be inspired by a friend unconnected with the man of the earlier sonnets, whose love-story was laid bare to the poet.

Once again most authorities, after giving up as hopeless the search after the identity of "Mr. W. H." conclude that the hero of the first section was Henry Wriothesley, Earl Southampton, who, as all evidence shows, was of the intimate circle of the poet. In this section Massey's theory is preceded by a theory from Mrs. Jameson's *Romance of History*, in which it is suggested that certain of these sonnets were written at Southampton's request, as an offering to Elizabeth Vernon. Massey, who considers that the work was begun in 1593, carries his story gallantly through on these lines :

Shakespeare, adoring the young Earl, implores him again and again to marry, praises' his "parts," his intellectual and physical beauty, promises him immortality, and next, in a group which Massey characterises as "Dramatic Sonnets," plunges into the ebb and flow of the Southampton-Vernon love-story. Presently the former is going overseas, and a single sonnet divides the former "dramatic" group from a second one, which covers the parting of the lovers, his absence, and journey. A third group, similarly labelled, is supposed to suggest a sudden *rapprochement* between the Earl and Penelope Rich. Elizabeth Vernon appeals to him and to her dangerous and beautiful cousin. Later on Massey's legend gives us the cessation of jealousy and the Vernon's punishment of her earl by a flirtation of her own. After this Penelope's part in their story lapses. The rest deals with farewells, fresh journeys for the gentleman, their complete reconciliation, their marriage, and later on the imprisonment of the Earl in the Tower in connection with Lord Essex's intrigue of 1600-1, (explained here in a later chapter), crowned by Southampton's return from exile to favour and the Court after the accession of James I.

In the second part of his legend Massey boldly tackles the situation. Shakespeare's treacherous, irresistible, dark lady who has puzzled so many inquirers is, he declares, Penelope Rich. She is not the poet's own love, but the woman adored by yet another patron of his—William Herbert, later Earl of Pembroke, the younger son of Mary, Countess of Pembroke, Philip Sidney's stately, cultured sister. This, then, vows Massey, is the "Mr. W. H." of the dedication.[1] As quite a young man of eighteen he came to town in 1598 and fell in love with Penelope, who was well on in her thirties. Later on it was his puissance and knowledge of the persons with whom the entire set of sonnets dealt which enabled him to obtain, for Thomas Thorpe, the whole "copy" and the permission to publish. This does not really explain the "W. H." mystery. There are heaps of objections, counter-suggestions. But this detail does not concern our story of Penelope. The latter half of Massey's legend I deal with in Chapter XII. At this early stage of Southampton's courtship Herbert was a young child. The thing which matters is whether or not Penelope tried to steal apples from her cousin's orchard. Practically the whole question turns upon those nine sonnets which Massey

[1] The fact of his being named plain "Mr." and not accorded his title of "Lord" is ingeniously explained away by this and other commentators.

attributes to Elizabeth Vernon's jealousy. These sonnets open with the poignant No. 133 :[1]

> " Beshrew that heart that makes my heart to groan,
> For that deep wound it gives my friend and me!
> Is't not enough to torture me alone,
> But slave to slavery my sweet's friend must be ?
> Me from myself thy cruel eye hath taken,
> And my next self thou, harder, hast engrossed ;
> Of him myself and thee I am forsaken ;
> A torment thrice threefold thus to be crossed! "

Now, this portion is very plausible, but there follow these lines :

> " Prison my heart in thy steel bosom's ward,
> But then my friend's heart let my poor heart bail ;
> Whoe'er keeps me, let my heart be his guard ;
> Thou can'st not then use rigour in my jail :
> And yet thou wilt ; for I being pent in thee,
> Perforce am thine and all that is in me."

Do not these words suggest a quite different idea, namely, that the one who pleads is a man appealing to a woman, his love, who has enslaved his friend's heart as well as his own ? He loves that friend so dearly that he counts him his " next self." Let the lady immure him (the writer) as she will, in the steel prison of her heart, in which, perforce, he is pent, but while in prison he begs that at least his heart may act as guard for that of his friend.

In the next sonnet the balance, in my opinion, is once more against the Penelope theory. The very opening line—

> " So now I have confessed that he is thine "—

is a contradiction of Massey's beloved romance. What woman of beauty and position, such as Elizabeth

---

[1] The edition I have followed is that of Professor Dowden, published 1881.

Vernon, would make that confession? What poet of spirit and truthfulness would lower her to use such words? A jealous woman would make a better fight for happiness than this. Later on in this sonnet there come the lines—

> " He learned but surety-like to write for me
> Under that bond that him as fast doth bind."

And again—

> " Thou, usurer, that putt'st forth all to use
> And sue a friend came debtor for my sake."

It is evident that the third person, the friend, has gone on a mission to the beloved on behalf of the lover. The beloved ensnares him also ; hence she is a usurer, a person who turns to her own account all that comes her way. She converts the lover's ambassador, his messenger, his go-between, into a suitor on his own account ; he is made responsible for the debt of another ; he cannot escape.

Another sonnet beginning wildly :

> " Take all my loves, my Love, yea, take them all,"

which Massey quotes in support of his notion, is just as unconvincing. Midway we find :

> " I do forgive thy robbery, gentle thief,
> Altho' thou steal thee all my poverty."

Once more it is impossible that Elizabeth Vernon would commit herself to such expressions if she really cared for Southampton. If Shakespeare, even in comparative youth, put such words into her mouth, he had a great deal to learn about jealous women in love.

The fact is, the whole romance is " gendered " by Massey. There is not a trace of it in letters or in the *chroniques scandaleuses* of the day. As regards the ebb

K

and flow of love and jealousy, reproach and vindication
in the sonnets, they may have had a dozen sources in
connection with the Earl's life and romance.   For this
was, as shown, the stormiest period of his Court existence, with the exception of the Essex intrigue much
later on.   In addition, Penelope Rich always appears to
have been ready to assist this match.   It is more than
likely that she had, as a very young girl, been privy to
her mother's secret marriage with Leicester at this same
homestead where Elizabeth was staying as Essex's guest,
under Penelope's chaperonage, when Southampton hurried over from the Continent to be married.   Penelope
once again knew of the secret when Essex effected his
own marriage.   I can find no proof whatever of her
interference in any unkind manner in the affairs of
the Southamptons.   There was another influence in her
life far stronger than that which Southampton would
exercise, and according to the *Sidney Papers* her destiny
and that of this other personage, almost the only man
of her circle who survived intrigue, rebellion, family
wreckage, had been closely linked since the year 1595,
three years before the Southampton courtship ended in
marriage.

CHAPTER IX

A DOMINANT FORCE

WE have viewed briefly the supposed love complication caused by the intercourse between Penelope and her cousin, and must pass on to an affair of far greater importance. The Southampton affair—if ever it existed in the form cited by Massey—did not deeply affect the lady's history. Rowland White, that indefatigable scribe, helps us to nothing in this direction. He does, however, very clearly indicate the *rapprochement* between Lady Rich and the man who really dominated her life and fate—Charles Blount, Baron Mountjoy. In the next chapter they will be found standing as sponsors for the child of a friend, and constantly meeting in the houses of their circle.

It was through the unpromising medium of Court jealousy that Charles Blount formed a close friendship with Penelope's brilliant brother. Hostility ripened their acquaintance. Very quickly they were bosom friends.

It is well here just to glance at the origin of this impressive gentleman.

From the various other branches of the great race of Blounts this line is distinguished by genealogical writers as "The Mountjoy Branch." Its ancestor was Sir Walter Blount, from whom the Blounts of Sodington and of Mapledurham are alike descended. This Sir

Walter was the third son of Sir John Blount of Sodington, and it was upon the former that Edward IV conferred the barony of Mountjoy. His marriage is very
interesting. His wife was a Spanish lady of high
quality, Donna Sancha de Ayala, whom he met both in
Spain and at the English Court. She was the daughter
of Don Diego Gomez de Toledo (Alcalde Mayor, or
Chief Justice, of Toledo, and Notario Mayor, or Chief
Secretary of the kingdom of the same name), by his wife
Donna Ines de Ayala. According to Spanish custom,
the daughter was called by her mother's surname. The
mother's family was of royal origin, springing from
Don Vela de Arragon, Infante of Arragon, to whose son
Don Sancho Velasquez, the King of Castile (Alonzo VI)
gave the territory and lordship of Ayala in 1074.
Proud blood indeed ! For Sancha's relatives belonged
to the proudest of the proud houses of the ancient
grandees, and there is an ancient Spanish proverb which
says, " He who is connected with Ayala will never want
ancestors." Charles Blount of Elizabeth's day certainly
did not lack ancestors. All he lacked was pence.

Walter Blount and his Sancha were favourites at the
English Court, and founded a family of four sons and
two daughters. Of the sons, Sir Thomas, the second, was
the father of another Walter, created first Lord Mountjoy, in 1464, after his partisanship with the House of
York in the War of Roses. This Blount was also Lord
Treasurer of England and Knight of the Garter, and
received many grants of land, including the confiscated
estates of his compeers.

It is not necessary to give details of the barons of the
name which follow between that epoch and the one
with which this work deals. A glance at the father of
the Elizabethan Charles Blount suffices to illumine his

position. This parent was James, the sixth baron. This man did not take much part in public affairs, nor did he, like his great grandfather, Charles, court the society of bookish men, even to the exclusion of his wife when he first married. It is true that he sat in judgment with other peers at the trial of that Duke of Norfolk who was condemned to death for plotting to deliver Mary Queen of Scots from her various prisons in Derbyshire, but thereafter all one hears of James Blount is that " he addicted himself to the vain study and practice of Alchemy, in which he expended large sums, it is unnecessary to say without success." This, we are assured by the same authority,[1] he did " to repair the shattered fortunes of his family." Was there ever so sad a joke perpetrated in this world? We shall see how infectious this notion was, and how this fine excuse served the fecklessness of all his family—save the indomitable Charles.

Charles Blount was the second son of James. His family obviously had neither the thrifty instincts nor the acquisitive. An easy devotion to Court duties, a devoted habit of vague study had assisted for several generations the rapid shrinkage of their coffers. His elder brother, by the time he inherited the title, had practically ruined himself, like his father before him, with chemical experiments, and had no longer the capital to throw away on such tentative activity like a certain Northumbrian peer with whom I shall deal in the latter part of this chapter. Charles Blount was no silent witness of the fecklessness of his race. The consciousness of family decay was so ingrained in him that when his portrait was painted in boyhood he insisted upon the addition

[1] *Genealogical History of the Croke Family, originally named Le Blunt,* by Sir Alexander Croke.

of the legend " Ad reaedificandum antiquam domum."
He was not a boaster, but he laid a heavy responsibility
upon himself by such an act.   One wonders if he ever
repented it.   He could never forget it.   Every stage of
his upward progress seems to be inspired by the dogged
intention of his childhood.   These fine sayings act like
a keen spur, but they extract very heavy toll in after
life from the aspirant.

Blount's early career was very similar to that of
Southampton, his junior by ten years.   By the time that
Southampton was finishing his first year at Cambridge,
Charles Blount, not yet the eighth Baron Mountjoy, had
left Oxford, and been twice elected member of Parliament.   In 1588 he was not only ready, like the younger
peer, to have his armour scoured and set in order in pre-
paration for Spanish invasion, but had provided ships,
like other gentlemen, at his own cost, to enforce the
national fleet against the Armada.

Charles Blount was ever a single-hearted man, and no
poverty could keep him from pushing his way to the
front.   All readers of Tudor history know how he,
following the example of other gallants before him,
danced his way to Elizabeth's heart.   Like Southampton,
he went to the Bar.   But Fortune laid her hand on his
sleeve and pulled him away from law in the hour when
he danced at a masque in the Inner Temple before the
Queen.   Naunton, in his *Fragmenta Regalia*, has described
his actual introduction to her in a really delightful way :

"As Charles Blount came from Oxford he took the
Inner Temple on his way to Court ; whither he no
sooner came, but (without asking) he had a pretty
strange kind of admission, which I have heard from a
discreet man of his own, and much more of the secrets
of those times.   He was then much about twenty years

of age, of a brown hair, a sweet face, a most neat com-
posure and tall in his person. The Queen was then at
Whitehall and at dinner, whither he came to see the
fashion of the Court; the Queen had soon found him
out, and with a kind of affected frown, asked the Lady-
Carver 'What he was?' She answered, 'She knew him
not;' insomuch as enquiry was made from one to
another, who he might be; till at length it was told the
Queen, he was brother to Lord William Mountjoy.
This inquisition, with the eye of Majesty fixed upon
him (as she was wont to do, and to daunt men she
knew not), stirred the blood of this young Gentleman,
insomuch as his colour came and went, which the Queen
observing, called him unto her, and gave her hand to
kiss, encouraging him with gracious words and new
looks; and so diverting her speech to the Lords and
Ladies, she said, that 'she no sooner observed him, but
that she knew there was in him some noble blood,' with
some other expressions of pity towards his house: and
then again demanding his name, she said, 'Fail you not
to come to Court, and I will bethink myself how to do
you good.' And this was his inlet, and the beginnings
of his grace."

No Cinderella could have felt keener ecstasy at such a
moment than this youth, who had taken the rehabilitation of his race upon his shoulders.

He went to Court, he danced, he tilted, and he put
the nose of the reigning favourite, Robert Devereux,
out of joint. Naunton's picturesque and contemporary
testimony again illumines this highly diverting Court
scandal:

"My Lord of Essex (even of those that truly loved
and honoured him) was noted for too bold an engrosser
both of fame and favour; and of this (without offence
to the living, or treading on the sacred urn of the dead)
I shall present a truth, and a passage yet in memory.

My Lord Mountjoy (who was another child of her favour) . . . had the good fortune one day to run very well in a tilt; and the Queen therewith was so well pleased that she sent him, in token of her favour, a Queen at chess of gold richly enamelled, which his servants had the next day fastened on his arm with a crimson riband, which my Lord Essex, as he passed through the Privy Chamber, espying, with his cloak cast under his arm, the better to commend it to the view, enquired what it was, and for what cause there fixed. Sir Fulke Greville told him that it was the Queen's favour, which the day before, and after the tilting, she had sent him; whereat my Lord of Essex, in a kind of emulation, and as though he would have limited her favour, said, 'Now I perceive every fool must have a favour.' This bitter and public affront came to Sir Charles Blount's ear, who sent him a challenge, which was accepted by my Lord, and they met near Marybone Park, where my Lord was hurt in the thigh and disarmed; the Queen, missing the men, was very curious to learn the truth; and when at last it was whispered out, she swore, 'by God's death, it was fit that some one or other should take him down and teach him better manners, otherwise there would be no rule with him.' And here I note the inition of my Lord's friendship with Mountjoy, which the Queen herself did then conjure."

This duel episode is of considerable importance to the love-story of Charles Blount and Penelope. It would seem by this incident that until 1583—three years after Penelope's marriage—she was unacquainted with Charles Blount. But a very interesting fact has been unearthed by Sir Alexander Croke with regard to early intercourse between Penelope and Mountjoy. This author states that early in the eighties of the sixteenth century, and long before he came into the title, Mountjoy had paid his addresses to the lady. "The attachment," he adds, "was mutual, and they were privately engaged to be married to each other. But the lady's friends, considering that he was at that time a younger brother, with little fortune, disapproved of the match, and disposed of her to Robert, Lord Rich." Croke does not state his authority for this fact, and I have not been able to find any other substantiation of it. It is not at all unlikely to have taken place, and the evident desires of the guardians to secure a rich bride-groom was the obvious barrier in the way. At the same time, it sets one thinking. Curiosity is naturally aroused as to how far Penelope's repulse of Sir Philip Sidney was due to a nascent passion for Mountjoy, which gathered force day by day as the miserable reali-ties of her marriage removed her farther and farther from the nature and disposition of her husband. It is not necessary to assume that at so early a period she literally balanced the claims and the fascinations of Philip against Mountjoy. In both respects Philip cer-tainly stood first. He was the older friend, chosen for her by her father, intimately associated with her family, and she had yet to learn the full power and attraction of the grave, courtly, restrained, and equally deep-hearted Charles Blount. Yet to a woman in this dangerous case, who is bound by law, yet whose heart is groping its way out of the loveless prison of an unhappy life and the shackles of formal vows, there comes always a vision of the men who might have loved, or may love her, and of these there is often one whose personality unconsciously overpowers and restrains her. This, to my mind, was the case with Penelope. Philip made hot, heroic love. Charles Blount watched, learned, committed himself but rarely to anything definite. He never attacked her fort-

ress.   He passed to and fro outside her walls, parleyed
gracefully with her—till the gates opened.   We will
return to her later.   Meanwhile let us follow Mountjoy
as he climbs his ladder of eminence.

In 1593, at the age of thirty, he was once more elected
M.P., and the following year saw him as successor to
his brother's title and newly appointed Governor of
Portsmouth in place of the Earl of Sussex.   These
successes were not chance, but the fruit of good service
and continuity of effort.   He was determined to " get
on," but not with the assistance of the methods employed by a Lord Rich, who trusted to the favour and
prominence of others rather than to his own personal
qualities, and would stick like a limpet to the most con-
ventional social rock rather than use such brains as he
possessed.   As Naunton puts it :

" Though Sir Charles Blount wanted not wit and
courage (for he had very fine attractions, and being a
good piece of a scholar), yet were they accompanied
with the retractiveness of bashfulness, and a natural
modesty, which (as the tone of his house and the ebb of
his fortune then stood) might have hindered his progres-
sion, had they not been reinforced by the infusion of
Sovereign favour and the Queen's gracious invitation.
And that it may appear how low he was, and how much
that heretic necessity will work in the dejection of good
spirits, I can deliver it with assurance, that his exhibition
was very scant until his brother died, which was shortly
after his admission to the Court, and then it was no
more than 1000 marks per annum, wherewith he lived
plentifully in a fine way and garb, and without any great
sustenation during all her times.   And as there was in
his nature a kind of backwardness, which did not be-
friend him nor suit with the motion of the Court, so
there was in him an inclination to arms, and a humour

of travelling; which, had not some wise men about him laboured to remove, and the Queen herself laid in her commands, he would (out of his natural propension) have marred his own market: For as he was grown by reading (whereunto he was much addicted) to the theory of a Soldier, so he was strongly invited by his genius to the acquaintance of the practique of the War; which were the causes of his excursions; for he had a company in the Low Countries, from whence he came over with a noble acceptance of the Queen; but somewhat restless in honourable thoughts, he proved himself again and again, and would press the Queen with the pretences of visiting his Company so often that at length he had a flat denial; and yet he stole over with Sir John Norris into the action of Britain[1] (which was then a hot and active war) whom he could always call his father, honouring him above all men . . . so contrary he was in his esteem and valuation of this great commander to that of his friend, Lord Essex. Till at last the Queen began to take his decessions for contempts, and confined his residence to the Court and her own presence."

In fact, like Essex and Southampton, Mountjoy wearied of Court tyrannies and intrigues and escaped abroad to share in the fighting whenever possible. He went back to the Low Countries again and again. It was shortly after his duel with Essex that he had received the honour of knighthood and the command of that company in the Netherlands, from which he returned with flying colours and the royal favour. On this expedition he too was at Zutphen, and praise of Stella's Astrophel must surely have been not only in his ears but on his lips. In this way he makes a picturesque link between them. It was not till nearly ten years later that he finally gave his Queen the slip and, as

[1] Brittany.

Naunton relates, flung himself with Sir John Norris
into the causes of Henry of Navarre, in Brittany.   He
was ordered to return, but apparently made good
excuses for absences as late as the winter of this year
(1593).   Elizabeth now checkmated his flights for a
time by the Portsmouth appointment, so perforce he
gave up the voluntary sword for an official trowel and
superintended the rebuilding of the fortifications.   She
kept him in England till 1597, when he managed to
accompany Essex and Southampton to the Azores as
commander of the land forces, and, like Southampton,
had his own ship—the *Defiance.*

This Azores business lasted about six months.   It
was, as we have seen in Southampton's case, an inglorious
affair.   Certainly it was by pure luck that Mountjoy
escaped the general censure ; his post proved a sinecure,
for no landing in the Azores was possible, and he grazed
being drawn into the squabbles of his colleagues.   That
he did escape it is one of the greatest testimonies to his
extraordinary discretion, and it added a new plume to
his casque as soldier and statesman, while, without
doubt, it increased his power over the heart of Penelope
Rich.

Once more let us go back to a few dates.   Penelope
married at twenty.   In three years she was completely
disillusioned, and in the year (1583) of Philip Sidney's
marriage to Frances Walsingham, she and Mountjoy
were drawn together.   One authority states that by this
time she had " yielded to " him.   This I cannot credit.
There may have been " passages " between them.   It
was not till after Philip's death in 1586 that she must
have permitted an open declaration and, in turn, confessed love.

Is not the whole love-story which follows inevitable ?

Her fates decreed a *mariage de convenance*, and when she awoke to the misery and injustice of it, the "Elizabethan feminine" in her revolted. It is true she had a father great in every sense—a man without reproach and without fear—except that even he, like his contemporary, George Talbot, was not strong enough to brave outright the anger of the Queen, who heavily burdened and underpaid him. After all, he died as a young man —he was but thirty-five—and had he lived as long as George Talbot, he might possibly have made a final stand against Elizabeth's injustice. Had he lived to influence his children, he would have altered the course of his Penelope's life materially, the Rich marriage would surely never have come to pass, and even had her full-blooded, impulsive nature led her into difficulties, she would have had his counsel, protection, authority at every turn of the road. But she had only her mother to refer to. And her mother, with Leicester, had her share in the marriage. Moreover, the Lady Leicester, despite the fact that her own father, the highly esteemed Knollys, lived and moved in high circles, was too like her daughter to be of much use to her. Dorothy, Penelope, and Essex inherited, with the high temper, the magnanimity of Essex, the father, the passionate intensity, the fatal powers of attraction of Lettice Knollys.

Thus, at the close of 1597, she had, on Mountjoy's return from the Azores, every excuse for not repulsing him. He was her only solace among many difficulties. He was the only one of the once triumphant squadron who received honours—in the form of the Garter—on his return. Before this there was, it may be surmised, "thunder in the air" in Penelope's home life. There was surely uneasiness on the part of Lord Rich. Indeed, his part, all through this story of ill-starred marriage, is, to my thinking, that of a suppressed and muttering troll behind the clouds. In the autumn of 1595 he wrote to his brother-in-law, Essex, the following letter, wherein the mysterious allusions to the way in which great ladies are permitted to have access to Court officials without the knowledge of their husbands have been interpreted as directly touching his own domestic problems :

" My Lord.—I acknowledge with all thankfulness your Lordship's favour signified by your letters, which I received yesterday by my man ; entreating leave also to put you in mind to remember your letters into Staffordshire to your sister and to the other party. I met this messenger from thence, but durst not intercept the letters he brings, for fear these troublesome times will bring forth shortly a parliament, and so perhaps a law to make it treason to break open letters to any my lords of the Council, whereby they are freely privileged to receive writings from other men's wives without any further question, and have full authority to see every man's wife at their pleasure. A lamentable thing that this injustice should reign in this wicked age. I only entreat your Lordship, that as you hear anything farther of that matter I wrote you of, I may have your pleasure and farther directions. And so commanding your Lordship to the blessed tuition of the Almighty, I remain your Lordship's poor brother to command in all honesty.

Ro : Rich."

That ending, " Your poor brother," is piquant. And again one smiles at the phrase " in all honesty." Let us think of these later, as the story develops, and see if the phrases ring truly.

I have not the reply of Essex to this pathetic communication, but, whatever was behind it, Penelope's brother was not the man to arbitrate in her marriage quarrels, so long as they did not discountenance himself. It was a lax age. Let us leave it for the moment at that, for it helps us further to understand why this splendid, impulsive, moody Earl threw his brilliant sister not only into the company of Mountjoy, but into intercourse with renegades and " queer fish " from overseas.

Just such an one was a certain Spanish Signor Antonio Perez. The voice of the Elizabethan matron of high principle was raised in indignation against him, and one of those who spoke her mind clearly was Lady Bacon, mother of Francis and Anthony, who wrote thus in the same year to her second son, protesting against the intimacy between the Spanish adventurer and Francis, her first born :

" Though I pity your brother, yet so long as he pities not himself, but keepeth that bloody Perez, yea, as a coach companion and bed companion ; a proud, profane, costly fellow, whose being about him I verily fear the Lord God doth mislike, and doth less bless your brother in credit and otherwise in his health ; surely I am utterly discouraged, and make conscience further to undo myself to maintain such wretches as he is that never loved your brother, but for his own credit living upon him."

This other letter from a Mr. Standen is also to Anthony Bacon. It draws a very interesting picture of Penelope's caprice and her environment, and is written to apprise the addressee of her visit with Lord Essex :

" Right Worshipful. As we were at supper my Lady Rich, Signor Perez, Sir Nicholas Clyfford, and myself, there came upon a sudden into the chamber my

Lord and Sir Robert Sidney, and there it was resolved that Signor Perez must be to-morrow morning, at eight of the clock, with my Lord in Court; after which my Lord means to dine at Walsingham House, and in the way to visit Mr. Anthony Bacon; which my Lady Rich understanding, said she would also go to dine with them at Walsingham's. And my Lord asking how she would be conveyed thither, she answered, that she would go in their companies, and in coach with them, and, arrived at Mr. Bacon's house, and there disembarked, my Lord, her brother Sir Robert, should bring her to Walsingham's and return back with the coach for my Lord her brother. All which I write unto you, Sir, by way of advice, to the end you be not taken unarmed. Women's discretions being uncertain, it may be she will not dismount, and the contrary also will fall out. Now it is resolved that Mr. Perez shall not depart, for that my Lord hath provided him here with the same office those eunuchs have in Turkey, which is to have the custody of the fairest dames, so that he wishes me to write, that for the bond he hath with my Lord, he cannot refuse that office."

This leaves us with a firm impression that Anthony Bacon had been at work to get Perez out of the way, and that he is foiled by Essex, who practically posts the Spaniard as guard over the honour of the ladies of his house. What sort of a fellow Perez was may be gauged by the flowery and politely wanton specimen of his correspondence, quoted presently, which is the product of the early spring of 1595, and is addressed to Penelope and her "sisters." She had, of course, but one—Dorothy, now Countess of Northumberland. The remaining lady of the group may well be young Lady Essex, their sister-in-law. They had all left Court and were in the heart of the country, possibly at Lady Leicester's manor of Drayton Bassett. But Lady Rich

is evidently not too fond of green pastures. She is
longing for news, and does not relish being out of the
world. Above all, she finds it politic to keep in touch
with Anthony Bacon, who knows all about every one
at Court. She begins a letter to him with assurance
of "an extraordinary estimate of his virtues," as Birch[1]
expresses it. "Besides which," she wrote, "your
courtesies toward myself increase the desire I have to
requite your friendship, and to do you all honour,
praying you to believe my words, since your merits
challenge more than I can acknowledge, although I do
with much affection esteem your worth. And while I
am in this solitary place, where no sound of any news
can come, I must entreat you to let me hear something
of the world from you, especially of my brother; and
what you know of the French affair; or whether there
go any troops from hence to their aid." She ends
with a postscript about the very man Anthony dis-
trusted: "I would fain hear what becomes of your
wandering neighbour," whom Birch, with good reason,
takes to be Perez.

I cannot find Bacon's reply to the lady, but he or the
Secretary Wilson mentioned by Perez may have given
a message which put the wily one in touch with her;
whence this letter was the result:

"Signor Wilson hath given me news of the health of
your Ladyships, the three sisters and goddesses as in
particular, that all three have amongst yourselves drunk
and caroused unto Nature, in thankfulness of what you
owe unto her, in that she gave you not those delicate
shapes to keep them idle, but rather that you should
push forth unto us here many buds of those divine
beauties. To these gardeners I wish all happiness for

<hr>

[1] *Elizabeth*, Vol. I, p. 475.

L

so good tillage of their grounds. Sweet ladies mine,
many of these carouses! O what a bower I have full
of sweets of the like tillage and trimmage of gardens !
If I return again to England I shall have no need to
seek my living of anybody, for my Book will serve my
turn. But I will not be so good cheap[1] this second
time. My receipts will cost dearer. Wherefore let
everybody provide

"Of your most noble Ladyship, her
Antonio Perez "

This "book " of Perez was nothing more than the
embodiment of an audacious scheme of blackmail. The
gay scoundrel—the letter shows—intended to make the
richest use of his worldly knowledge. The volume is
full of such secrets as certain persons would not like
published. He is going abroad. When he returns he
will begin his campaign. Whatever the result, he
stands to make a comfortable living. If the libelled or
discomforted persons refuse to pay him for the suppression of his work, he will publish and rake in the
guineas which always fall to the authors of scandalous
publications.

"Three sisters and goddesses ! " It is a very pretty
picture of fair women in a gorgeous pleasaunce which
Perez suggests with such lusciousness. Either Lady
Essex or Lady Southamption was the third, and both
were beauties, so that here we have as handsome a trio
of Elizabethan ladies as ever this Spanish *roué* could
desire. Perhaps, of the three, Dorothy Percy was the
least strictly beautiful. Penelope's charms far outshone
hers. Still, she had great attraction and vitality and a
characteristic face. Her story coincides with her nature
—brimful of the keen impulse of the Devereux race,

---

[1] An Elizabethan phrase meaning 'dirt-cheap.'

and, in addition, wilful, as wilful and hotheaded as the Percy she had lately married. He was her second husband. Her romance, like Penelope's, had begun early, and, as in her sister's case, she found life in double harness a failure. Dorothy, even more than Penelope, was born to unhappiness. Her first husband died young, her second ill-treated her.

Her first marriage—a clandestine affair—took place before Dorothy Devereux was eighteen. Her high-handed wooer was young Sir Thomas Perrott, son of Sir Thomas Perrott, who for a while was Lord Deputy of Ireland, but lost his post for high treason—abuse of the Queen. He died in prison in 1592, and it was only through the entreaties of young Essex that his son, Thomas, was reinstated in his property. It was not clear what was the opposition to his marriage with Dorothy Devereux. But it was probably the disapproval of her guardian, Lord Huntingdon, and fear of the Queen's refusal to the match which persuaded the couple to a secret ceremony. The Devereux family knew of the young knight's devotion, for in State papers there is a short letter from him to Penelope, newly wedded, entreating her support in his suit. She was not present at the ceremony, of which a most extraordinary and entertaining description is given in Strype's edition of the *Life and Acts of John Aylmer*, Bishop of London, who drew upon himself the censure of the Court of High Commission for a too easy and hasty issue of marriage licences :—

" Lady Dorothy Devereux was in July 1583, residing with Sir Henry Cock, Knight of Broxbourne, in Hertfordshire, where she was married to Sir Thomas Perrott by a strange minister, two men guarding the church door with swords and daggers under their cloaks, as

had also the rest of the company, five or six in number.
One Green was then vicar of Broxbourne, to whom
that morning repaired two persons, one of whom told
him he was minister and B.D. and a preacher long time ;
asked for the keys of the church which must be open
to him, as he had a commission to examine and swear
certain men : he asked also for the Communion book ;
the vicar said it was locked up in the vestry and he
could not come at it, but offered him a Latin testament,
which the other refused.   Going afterwards to the
church, the vicar found it open, and Sir Thomas and
the lady ready to enter.   Perceiving a marriage was
intended, he endeavoured to persuade the strange
minister not to deal in the matter, and proceeded to
read an injunction against any minister performing the
marriage ceremony, save in the church of which he is
minister.   They refused to hear it, and Lewis, the
strange man, told the vicar he had sufficient authority,
and produced a licence sealed, which the vicar offered
to read.   Before he had half done, Sir Thomas snatched
it out of his hand, and offered him a rial to marry
them : he refused, when Sir Thomas ordered Lewis to
proceed ; on which the vicar resisted and shut the book.
Then Sir Thomas thrust him away, told him he had
nothing to do with it, and should answer for resisting
the Bishop's authority.   Another of Sir Thomas's party,
one Godolphin, told him he was malicious ; on which,
forbidding once more, he held his peace.   Edmund
Lucy, Esq., who also was living in Sir H. Cock's
family, came in and plucked away the book from the
minister, who told him he should answer it ; and then
went on with the ceremony without surplice, in his cloak,
riding-boots, and spurs, and despatched it hastily."

This, of course, made the Queen very angry, and she
visited her displeasure not only upon Dorothy, but
upon her brother.   So serious was the affront apparently
that when the Queen, soon after the occurrence, arrived

during one of her journeys to make a short stay at the house of one of her peeresses—Lady Warwick, at North Hall—and discovered that the sister, as well as the brother, were under this roof of their aunt and uncle, she was so ungracious and upset that Essex was forced to send Dorothy hurriedly out of the house late at night, while he himself on the following day left for Holland and the siege of Sluys. He was, however, pursued in the Queen's name and persuaded to return.

Dorothy did not have much time either to regret or enjoy her first marriage. Thomas Perrott was alive in January, 1594, but must have died soon after, for in 1596 she was a countess and a prospective mother. Her husband was the ninth Earl of Northumberland,[1] the Percy known as the "Black" or "Wizard Earl," because of his deep interest in alchemy and astrology. A few details here and there present him to the eye as a patient and rapt student poring over his "crystal globe," which was part of the laboratory outfit of such persons in olden days, and enveloped in a cloud of tobacco smoke, which he adored. Unfortunately he had an equal weakness for gambling, and thereby considerably impoverished himself. He was the son of the eighth Earl, likewise Henry (1532-1585), and grandson of the Sir Thomas Percy who was executed for his part in that northern rebellion known as the Pilgrimage of Grace. His father's end was as tragic as that of the grandfather, for the former, after starting his career as a staunch Protestant and fighting on the Queen's side against his brother, who was a northern rebel supporting Mary Queen of Scots, and resolved to free her during her English imprisonment, suddenly joined the cause of that unhappy lady.

---

[1] The title forfeited by the Dudleys under Mary had been re-conferred on the Percy family in its original form of earldom.

He was imprisoned, flung himself on the Queen's mercy, and eventually released, but only to be imprisoned a second and a third time in the Tower, where he was found dead, shot through the heart, evidently dying by his own hand.   His son, Dorothy's husband, was educated in the Protestant faith, but apparently coquetted at one time with the Scottish Queen's cause, for the Roman Catholic party was most desirous that he should wed Arabella Stuart, Mary's niece.   His marriage with Dorothy Devereux settled the matter, and weakened his rights, such as they were, as heir-presumptive to Elizabeth.[1]   He served under Lord Leicester in the Low Countries, and two years later (1588), in the fleet sent out against the Spanish Armada, received the Garter, again went to fight in Holland (1600), and was sent on a foreign mission to France.   It was with this quarrelsome lord that Earl Southampton all but fought a duel in 1602.   The domestic life of the couple was a cat-and-dog affair.   On one occasion he appears to have turned his wife out of doors.   He was also apt to indulge in pugnacious correspondence, and does not in any way present the ideal type of a serious student of physical science.   Like Essex, his brother-in-law, and even Sir Robert Cecil, he made overtures to James I before his accession, but this was chiefly with a view to ascertaining the policy of the probable future sovereign, especially in regard to the treatment of the Catholics, whose cause the Earl always had warmly at heart. His doubts about James were the cause of one of the hottest conjugal squabbles recorded, in which his lady certainly had the last word.   This incident took place evidently at the crisis of Henry Percy's hostility towards the Scottish sovereign, for he declared he would rather

---

[1] He came only eighth on this list of possible heirs.

From an engraving by Cochran, after a painting by Van Dyck

HENRY PERCY, EARL OF NORTHUMBERLAND

that James were buried than crowned, and that both he and all his friends would rather die than acknowledge this man as king. To which the Countess retorted that she was ready to eat their hearts in salt and pay for her act on the gallows, rather than that any other king should reign. The famous speech of Beatrice in *Much Ado*— "I will eat his heart in the market-place"—is said to be inspired by the above episode.

Rowland White and others give us glimpses of these "breezes." Really Dorothy must have been quite relieved when, in 1605, her husband was sent to the tower in connection with his supposed share in the Gunpowder Plot, financed so largely by his cousin, Thomas Percy, who was a constant visitor at his house. The Earl pleaded his own gentle arts as proofs of his innocence. "Examine," he told his accusers, " but my humours in buildings, gardenings and private expenses these two years past." The king was obdurate, however ; the Star Chamber found the Earl guilty, fined him to the tune of £30,000, and confined him to the Tower for life. Here his wife intervened and appealed vainly against the terrible sentence. The Earl's estates were confiscated in default of his fine, and he stayed in the Tower, cheered by his scientific studies, in which he was assisted by contemporary *savants*, and by the companionship of his daughter, Lucy, whose husband, James Hay, afterwards Earl of Carlisle, later procured his freedom. But this was not till after sixteen years of durance. It is sad to know that his wife died three years before his release, and that the two had no opportunity of smoothing over in old age the bitterness of their earlier married life.

A word, ere this chapter closes, as to Perez. Born in 1540, the son of Gonzalo Perez, Secretary of State to

Charles V, he was at the time of his English prominence a man in full prime. He had succeeded to his
father's post under Philip II. Under this monarch he
developed to the full his intriguing powers, and was
instructed, according to Machiavellian principles, to lay
a trap for Don John of Austria, who hated him, and his
secretary, Escovedo, the friend of Perez. Don John
nourished ambitions of which his brother Philip was
afraid. Perez learned Don John's secrets and betrayed
them. Meanwhile, Escovedo arrived in Spain un-
conscious of his doom. His assassination was decided
upon, and Perez was instructed to carry it out. For
this he had a special reason. Escovedo knew that he
had a *liaision* with the Princess of Eboli, to whom
Philip also paid his addresses. The murder was
achieved in 1578. The family of Escovedo demanded
justice. For a time Philip's own incriminating letters
gave his parasite the whip-hand. But the news of the
liaison swung the pendulum the other way. Perez
and the Eboli were both seized and imprisoned. He
lingered in prison under a rain of accusation of pecula-
tion and treachery till, in 1585, he was condemned to
imprisonment in a fortress and the repayment of a large
sum of money. Against this he appealed. Once
more legal proceedings went on till he delivered up the
King's letters of self-incrimination, under the hope of a
lightening of his sentence. This gave Philip the advantage, and the execution of Perez appeared a certainty. It
was, however, hard to prove him guilty, and he was put
to the torture. His confession merely, of course,
incriminated his sovereign once more, and his death
was an inevitable consequence, had he not escaped
from prison in his wife's clothes in 1590. He took
refuge in Arragon, was twice caught on the authority of

the Inquisition, twice escaped fresh torture, only, thanks to popular feeling, was set free and found repose and honour (!) in Switzerland. From thence he made his way to Henry IV of France, was pursued, and sent over on a mission to England, in order that he might give Elizabeth Spanish information. Since the Earl of Essex was in the forefront of the anti-Spanish party at Court, he naturally took an important place in the entourage of that brilliant personage. It is not unlikely that he kept a watch upon the intrigues of the society women about him. Their beauty, their position, the attitude and relationship in which they stood to the men with whom he co-operated, were all so many tools to his fiendishly cunning hand, and intercourse with them and their intimates would constantly reveal to him secrets which could be used, while he could exercise a certain check upon their words and actions. The generous nature of Essex suited his game well, and the ladies of Essex's family evidently favoured him.

As regards Mountjoy, he would need to walk warily, and especially in regard to Perez. Penelope's chief lover was extraordinarily discreet from his earliest youth ; yet, had his growing passion for the sister of Essex clashed with the desires of this serpent-like Spanish refugee, it would have been easy for the latter to wreck both lord and lady speedily.

They, too, were wary, so far as letters are concerned. One sighs over the loss of the countless messages which the two must have exchanged, over the destruction of letters which could not but have passed between them, and, however mysteriously worded, have marked the stages of their love.

CHAPTER X

ESSEX—MAN OR MASQUERADER

WHICH was he? At times I find him wholly a masquerader, regarding him as one of those people who, while called upon to play a part at a great moment in the history of a great nation, are not content to fill that part, but must needs step aside and seek after other guises and lesser rôles. That is to say, he was of a deeply theatrical nature, which implies the possession of an overpowering consciousness of self-importance. Naunton has dubbed him a great "en-grosser" of favour. All through his story Essex really wanted to play the show part. Like many another man of great energy and genius, he had the makings of a big actor. Life afforded him, in addition, magnificent chances of self-development. But he was without the staying power, the supreme control which admits of fine co-operation, and the foresight, which carry an individual through the greatest strains and tests. He had no excuse for failure. He saw his part from the very beginning. He was given first place. But he wearied of it too soon. He was ever divided between a desire to shine in that position and a longing to carry on activities of a perfectly different character. In one sense, of course, all persons placed in so dazzling a position are conscious that they are part of a great masquerade. It is their daily business to remember both this and the fact that a share of the impression they make is due to their audience, which, in the now classic phrase, "brings half" to the entertainment. Assuredly this was the case with Leicester and Philip Sidney, Ralegh, and many another of the day. But none of these ever had so goodly a share of affectionate public interest as Essex. Sidney had a fine sense of effect, but he never abused it, for the man in him ruled the masquerader. With Essex it is not so. He had all the moodiness, the petulance of the theatrical temperament, and he would have displayed a sense of effect even had he been a mere cordwainer's apprentice instead of a Queen's favourite. Yet he had a great soul, like Sidney. He was, like him whom Grosart calls "The Galahad of Elizabeth's Round Table," demonstrative, generous, passionate, highly articulate. But he was also highly mercurial, while Philip was not. Robert Devereux had spirit, backed only with erratic force. Philip Sidney had driving power and judgment far beyond his years. Philip escaped by death the bondage of difficult service to a Queen who liked to keep all her younger servants on a short leash. Essex, most unhappily, was in the position of the spoiled orphan boy who is adopted by rich folk in their old age. He was the turbulent, irresponsible item in an aged house, and acknowledged no rivals. The rivalry between himself and Mountjoy was never serious. As Brewer[1] reminds us, the way to favour was clear. Neither Hatton, nor Leicester, nor Sidney were at his elbow "to compete for the palm." Yet he was at once too big and too little to play the part which Hatton and Leicester had played so well. And he courted the anger of Elizabeth earlier than Leicester had dared to

[1] *Studies in English History*, by J. S. Brewer.

do. He was not in the least a true diplomat, for he could never forget himself entirely in the cause at hand. He had a fine proud spirit, but a "tender mouth," and Elizabeth, as one historian puts it, "rode him always on the curb."

A glance at the copious correspondence addressed to Essex suffices in show that in regard to the maintenance of his difficult position of first favourite of a woman sovereign in whom age had accentuated all her caprices and deepened her strong characteristics, her mingling of impulse with caution, her warm affection with her vindictiveness, he had at least no lack of advice and suggestions. Foremost among those who both looked on at his career and had a part in it was Francis Bacon. He could keep his finger on the royal pulse, and he must often have had cause for apprehension when, in his opinion, the Earl played his part badly and tempted Providence. There is altruism in Bacon's letters of counsel, not unmixed with a frank desire that his own position should incur no risk. For example :

"I humbly desire your Lordship, before you give access to my poor advice, to look about, even jealously a little if you will, and to consider, first, whether I have not reason to think that your fortune comprehendeth mine. . . . I said to your Lordship last time, 'Martha, Martha, *attendis ad plurima, unum sufficit*.' Win the Queen ; if this be not the beginning of any other course I can see no end. . . . In you she will come to the question of '*Quid fiet homini, quem rex vult honorare ?*' But how is it now ? A man of nature not to be ruled, that hath my affection, and knoweth it, of an estate not grounded to his greatness, of a popular reputation, of a military dependence : I demand then whether there can be a more dangerous image than this represented to any monarch living, much more to a lady, and of Her Majesty's apprehension. And is it not more evident than demonstration itself that whilst this impression continues in Her Majesty's breast, you can find no other condition than inventions to keep your estate base and low ; crossing and disgracing your actions, . . . blasting of your merit, carping with contempt at your nature and fashions ; breeding, nourishing and fortifying such instruments as are most factious against you, repulses and scorns of your friends and dependents that are true and steadfast, winning and inveighing away from you such as are flexible and wavering, thrusting you into odious employments and offices to supplant your reputation, abusing you, and feeding you with dalliances, . . . to divert you from descending into the serious consideration of your own case ; yea and . . . venturing you in perilous and desperate enterprises ? . . . I mean nothing less than that these things should be plotted and intended as in Her Majesty's royal mind towards you : I know the excellency of her nature too well. But I say, whensoever the formerly described impression is taken in any king's breast towards a subject these other recited inconveniences must of necessity of politic consequence follow. . . . For the removing of the impression of your nature to be opiniative and not reliable : first, and above all things, I wish that your Lordship would turn altogether upon insatisfaction[1] and not upon your nature or proper disposition. This string you cannot harp upon too much. Next, whereas I have noted you to fly and avoid the resemblance or imitation of my Lord of Leicester, and my Lord Chancellor Hatton ; yet I am persuaded— howsoever I wish your Lordship distant as you are from them in points of magnanimity and merit, favour and integrity—that it will do you much good between the Queen and you to allege them, as often as you find occasion, for authors and palterers."

[1] The failure to please in a particular instance.

And the following subtle bit of advice is singularly piquant :

"Thirdly, when at any time your Lordship upon occasion, happen in speeches to do Her Majesty right —for there is no such matter as flattery amongst you all—I fear you handle it '*magis in speciem adornatis verbis, quam et sentire videaris.*' So that a man may read formality in your countenance ; whereas your Lordship should do it familiarly *et ovatione fida.*"

Moreover, Essex is to masquerade at every turn. He is to show deep interest in some project which he must abandon at the first sign of the Queen's disapproval. He is to be careful to choose some quest which he knows to be distasteful to her, thus accentuating the impression of his dependence on her smiles. He may project a journey—the Queen always liked to keep a man tied to her apron strings—but it must not be a long journey ; not further than Wales, under the plea of supervising the Devereux estates there. To propose a foreign expedition at this moment (Bacon writes just after Essex has returned from Cadiz with glory) would be most unwise and dangerous. The Queen would naturally think he had no personal affection for her in wishing to get at once so far afield. After this strong recommendation for the improvement of the Earl's bearing, Bacon does not forget to give him hints about his person : "The lightest of particulars, which yet are not to be neglected, are in your habits, apparel, wearings, gestures, and the like." He is to try for a good civil office and not to seek any more military greatness, for Her Majesty "loveth peace" and "she loveth not charge," i.e. constant payment for special service. Essex is to try for the post of Lord Privy Seal, "the third person of the great officers of the Crown," with the advantage that "it hath a kind of superintendence over the Secretary." A nice hit at Robert Cecil, and an argument more likely to tempt Essex than any other! "It is a fine honour," the writer continues, "a quiet place, and worth a thousand pounds by year. . . . And it fits a favourite to carry her Majesty's image in seal who beareth it best expressed in heart." Essex must also "pretend to be as bookish and contemplative" as ever he was. More power to his elbow would be added by "the bringing in of some martial man to be of the Council, dealing directly with Her Majesty in it, as for her service and for your better assistance." Bacon even suggests who this friend shall be : "I judge the fittest to be my Lord Mountjoy." As alternative he proposes Lord Willoughby.

A part of this advice the masquerader evidently followed, but his was not the temperament which can pursue in fair weather and foul one line of action. Bacon touched a weak spot when he bid his friend, so-called, restrain his longing for foreign service. In fact, the causes for disfavour where the young men of the day were concerned were, as history shows, generally the same. Either as a young and gay gallant you grew tired of your royal mistress's moods and unfulfilled promises, and ran away upon a foreign expedition, or you married secretly. In both cases you knew there would be the devil to pay in the end. And if it was a case of marriage, your lady, of course, paid the biggest price. What wonder that Essex, moody by tempera-ment, should find this moodiness increase under such conditions and luxuriate in it? All the world knows that he has been likened to Hamlet, or rather that the character of that prince is thought by some to have been founded on his.

He wrote a great many letters, exuberant, pathetic, involved. Of these I can, unfortunately, find very few addressed to Penelope, but the following is a specimen :

"DEAR SISTER,

"Because I will not be in your debt for sending you a footman, I have directed the bearer to you, to bring me word how you do. I am melancholy, merry, sometimes happy, and often discontented. The Court is of as many humours as the rainbow hath colours. The time wherein we live is more inconstant than women's thoughts, more miserable than old age itself, and breedeth both people and occasions like itself, that is violent, desperate, and fantastical. Myself, for wondering at other men's strange adventures, have not leisure to follow the ways of mine own heart, but by still resolving not to be proud of any good that can come, because it is but the favour of chance ; nor do (I) throw down my mind a whit for any ill that shall happen, because I see that all fortunes are good or evil, as they are esteemed. The preacher is ready to begin, and therefore I shall end this discourse, though upon another text.

"Your brother that dearly loves you,

"R. ESSEX."

The next is much in the same vein and, for its cynical allusion to the "blind god," either may have been written before his marriage to Sidney's widow, or be an allusion to one of his amours. The reference to "this lady," who entreats him to indite something fantastical, is not explained ; and he is in a very unchivalrous frame of mind in spite of the fact that he. classes himself as a lover with "apes and women" :

"DEAR SISTER,

"I would have made more haste with you but that yesternight I was surprised with a fever, and this

From a painting by Isaac Oliver

ROBERT DEVEREUX, SECOND EARL OF ESSEX, K.G.

morning I have got an humour fallen down into one
side of my head, so I dare not look out of my chamber.
This lady hath entreated me to write a fantastical . . .
but I am so ill with my pains and some other secret carps,
as I will rather choose to dispraise those affections with
which none but women, apes, and lovers (are) delighted.
To hope for that which I have not is a vain expectation,
to delight in that which I have is a deceiving pleasure ;
to wish the return of that which is gone from me is
womanish inconstancy. Those things which fly me, I
will not lose labour to follow. Those that meet me
I esteem as they are worth, and leave them when they
are nought worth. I will neither brag of my good hap
nor complain of my ill ; for secrecy makes joys more
sweet, and I am then most unhappy when another knows
that I am unhappy. I do not envy, because I will do
no man that honour to think he hath that which I want;
nor yet am I not contented because I know some things
that I have not. Love I confess to be a blind God.
. . . Ambition, fit for hearts that already confess themselves to be base. Envy is the humour of him that will
be glad of the reversion of another man's fortune ; and
revenge the remedy of such fools as in injuries know
not how to keep themselves aforehand. Jealous I
am not, for I will be glad to lose that which I am
not sure to keep. If to be of this mind be to be
fantastical, then join me with the three that I first
reckoned, but if they be young and handsome, with
the first.

And so I take my leave, being not able to write more
for pain.

"Your brother that loves you dearly,
"R. Essex."

I see no good reason for deriving Hamlet in particular from Essex. The world is full of moody, ana-
lytical minds, more or less sincere in their moralisings,
and the notion pays a very poor compliment not only to

M

the imaginative powers but to the richly complex, actual individuality of the creator of the Prince of Denmark. The atmosphere in this Elizabethan Court would foster many such natures as that of Robert Devereux, beget such melancholy and dissatisfaction among the young and hot-blooded. A Shakespeare would find half a dozen such fellows in the literary and political groups about him, and withal use the type in such a way that it would be entirely merged into the strong idiosyncrasies, the far greater personality of the child of his brain. It was, at all events, a stirring epoch in Court history, and one which would feed the inspiration of living writers in the same way that the chronicles of England had inspired previous dramatists.

But to return to our masquerader : his short and eventful life shows him in a hundred guises. Of these more presently. Let us contemplate the man first. In person he had not the attractions of a Leicester or a Hatton. He was not even an adroit dancer like these or like Mountjoy. We do not hear that he was a particularly good swordsman or rider—such as Philip Sidney. He was tall and of strong physique. In sooth, he needed physical strength to carry him through his short, incessantly active life of thirty-three years. He was, we are told, able-bodied ; his movements lacked grace. He stooped a little, perhaps because of his height, perhaps because of the amount of study and letter-writing which were inseparable from his position. His face was thoughtful, and showed reserve. Like his friend, Lord Mountjoy, he was particularly silent at meals. His secretary, Sir Henry Wootton, notes this, particularly in contrast to the usual light-hearted chatter of the average persons who gather about a board. Essex said that he preferred to think out difficult matters at meal-times—not over his post-prandial tobacco, like most folk. After the first few mouthfuls he would ruminate for a while. Like all men and women on whom the business of life rests with increasing weight, he was, after early manhood, impatient of personal adornment, impatient, it would almost seem, of all tangible objects. Friends in his immediate circle thought that he pushed his carelessness in regard to dress and person almost to disrespect where the Queen was concerned. "This was his manner : his chamber being commonly crowded with friends and servitors, when he was up he gave his legs, arms, and breast to his ordinary servants to button and dress him, with little heed ; his head and face to his barber ; his eyes to his letters, and ears to his petitioners ; and many times all at once. Then the gentleman of his robes throwing a cloak over his shoulders, he would make a step into his closet, and after a short prayer he was gone. Only in his baths he was somewhat delicate." As with his dress so with his palate. Medicine and delicacies were alike to his taste. Food had no special attractions for him, except as fuel to sustain a frame exhausted by activity. "For point of diet and of luxury, he was very inordinate in his appetite ; and of so indifferent a taste, that he would stop in the midst of any physical potion, lick his lips, and then swallow the rest."

This is certainly Essex, the man, in his daily habit. Regard now the masquerader, and see him playing a part as courtier-lover of the old Queen in a little dramatic entertainment devised for her in the tilt-yard. Sir Robert Sidney's secretary, Roland White,[1] is always his careful chronicler of such things :

[1] *Sidney Papers*, Vol. II.

"Some pretty while before he (Essex) came in himself to the tilt, he sent his page with some speech to the Queen, who returned with Her Majesty's glove. And when he came himself, he was met with an old hermit, a secretary of state, a brave soldier, and an esquire. The first presented him with a book of meditations : the second with political discourses : the third with nations of brave fought battles : the fourth was but his own follower. Comes into the tilt yard unthought upon, the ordinary post boy of London, a ragged villain all be-mired, upon a poor lean jade, galloping and blowing for life, and delivered the secretary a packet of letters, which he presently offered my L. of Essex ; and with this dumb-show our eyes were fed for that time. In the after supper before the Queen they first delivered a well penned speech to move this worthy knight to leave his vain following of love, and to betake him to heavenly meditation ; the secretaries all tending to make to have him follow matters of state, the soldiers persuading him to the war : but the esquire answered them all, and concluded with an excellent, but plain English, that this knight would never forsake his mistress' love, whose virtue made all his thoughts divine, whose wisdom taught him all true policy, whose beauty and worth were at all times able to make him fit to command armies."

There is a rich touch of vanity in those concluding words, for Essex had just drawn up for the Queen's approval an elaborate scheme of home defence in anticipation of immediate invasion, bending his fantastic mind to the management and disposal of war stores, and the victualling of the home forces.

Anon Essex puts on a parson's manner and induces one of his friends to a death-bed repentance. "My Lord of Essex," records Roland White, "indeed saved his soul, for none but he could make him take a feeling

of his end ; but he died well and very repentant." It
is cheering to know that this person, who, by the way,
died " of a surfeit," had the grace to leave his goods to
his patron.

Not long after this touching episode the Earl reveals
himself as he would certainly like to appear in the eyes
of posterity through a long letter to a protégé, the
young Earl of Rutland, who was later to become his
stepson-in-law by marriage with the daughter of Philip
Sidney's widow, Essex's wife. In this letter young
Essex masquerades as Essex *père*, and almost every
word seems to ring with pathos and irony, when one
looks back on it from the close of the writer's career.
It is so hard to reconcile these greatly sententious and
often perfectly sincere and fine phrases with those of the
moody letters to Penelope. For example :

" Health consisteth in an unmovable constancy and
a freedom from passions, which are indeed the sickness
of mind." " Strength of mind is that active power
which maketh us perform good things and great things.
. . ." " When . . . active virtues are but budding
they must be ripened by clearness of judgment and
customs of well-doing. Clearness of judgment makes
men liberal. . . . . Also it leadeth us to fortitude, for
it teacheth us that we should not too much prize life
which we cannot keep, nor fear death, which we cannot
shun ; that he that dies nobly lives for ever, and he
that lives in fear dies continually. . . . If custom be
strong to confirm any one virtue more than another, it
is the virtue of fortitude, for it makes us triumph over
the fear which we have conquered . . . and hold
more dear the reputation of honour which we have
increased."

Certainly Essex was no coward, and could and did
die bravely, but his virtues were never " ripened by

clearness of judgment." His nature could not stand the spoiling of Elizabeth, and many of his friends were a stumbling-block to his fortitude. Moreover, as regards "active virtues," he was, like his Lothario of an uncle, unfortunately very much a "ladies' man." Both his Queen and his wife suffered shocks and disillusions in regard to his love affairs. While at the very height of his career, just after the taking of Cadiz and before the Azores expedition, he seems to have been fairly reckless in the way he defied popular opinion and the Queen's goodwill by his love intrigues. Unfortunately, he always picked out one of Her Majesty's ladies, and always, as a man of fastidious taste, picked the prettiest. A certain " Mrs. Brydges" seems to have been specially irresistible. Rowland White mentions the fact of the Earl's return to her allurements in a letter from which the following is an extract. The lady was a daughter of Edmund, second Lord Chandos, and later married Lord Sandys of the Vine. The scribe, by the way, often made use of cyphers, lest his letters should fall into wrong hands and draw him into trouble. Thus Sir Robert Cecil is always designated "200," Essex "1000," Ralegh figures as "24," Lady Essex is "BB," Lord Cobham "400," and so on:

"I know you will be sorry to hear what grieves me to write of. It is spied out by Envy that 1000 is again fallen in love with his fairest B. It cannot chuse but come to 1500 ears ; then is he undone, and all they that depend upon his Favour. I pray to God it may not turn to his Harm. Sure I am that BB hears of it, or rather suspects it, and is greatly disquiet. Of these Matters I would not write but to your Lordship, for they concern me not, and not fit for me to pry into them, neither do I, but they come to me by mere chance ; and I will hope that there is no such Thing, but the Malice of a wicked World wherein we live. 7000 Daughter, that lives in Court, is said to be the Instrument of these Proceedings ; you know who I mean."

It never seems to have occurred to Essex what price the lady paid in such a case.   One of his ladies, Elizabeth Southwell, bore him a son—Walter Devereux ; the "fairest B" (Brydges) and a certain "Mrs. Russell" were turned out of the Presence with words and blows from the royal lips and hands ; while young Lady Mary Howard was selected for a specially cruel snub.   She had allowed Essex, when a married man of some years' standing, with a family, to court her.   So fascinated and flattered was she that she played truant and forgot her duties.   When the Queen took the air in her garden no Lady Mary was there to "bear Her Highness' mantle and other furniture."   At meals and at prayers the Lady Mary's chair and faldstool were empty.   Further, most dreadful of all sins, she not only on one occasion was late when the time came to carry the cup of grace during dinner into the Privy Chamber, but, when scolded, made impertinent retort.   As Sir John Harrington describes it, the lady had "much favour and marks of love " from Essex, while the Queen, after her wont, never lost an opportunity of impressing upon her women her wish that they should "remain in virgin state as much as may be."   This phrase is grimly humorous.   Considering how Elizabeth adored a perpetual masquerade of love-making in connection with herself, one is not surprised that Lady Mary's head was turned, in the first place, by the attentions of a brilliant, whimsical, dashing fellow like Robert Devereux, in the second by the fact that he was her Queen's latest darling.   Such a triumph of maid over mistress has a perennial zest—for the maid.

The Lady Mary made excuses, and doubtless did penance in her own way. Elizabeth held in reserve her special punishment. This incident, extracted from *Nugent's Antiquities*, cannot be related more picturesquely than in the form in which it appears in Devereux' *Earls of Essex :*

"Lady Mary had a velvet dress with a rich border powdered with gold and pearl, which moved many to envy, and among the rest the Queen herself, who thought it surpassed her own in beauty and richness. So one day she sent privately for Lady Mary's dress, put it on, and came out among the ladies : the Queen being a great deal taller than Lady Mary, the dress was ridiculous on her ; she asked all the ladies how they liked her new suit ; at length she came to the poor girl herself, and asked her if she did not think it too short and unbecoming, to which Lady Mary was forced to agree. 'Why then,' said the Queen, 'if it become not me, as being too short, I am minded it shall never become thee, as being too fine, so it fitteth neither well.' The dress was accordingly put by and never worn till after the Queen's death, when he, to gratify whose eyes it had been perhaps originally made, was no longer there to admire its fair wearer."

It is not inapposite to include here a letter from the Earl's mother, showing how strong was the family tie between them. Indeed, between Lettice Devereux (now Lady Leicester) her erring, eldest son, and her often distraught and erring Penelope, there was an indissoluble bond, not only of blood, but of deep sympathy. These three complex, fascinating natures, so powerful for good and evil, understood one another, for the children developed on the mother's lines. The world might judge them sternly, but to help loving them, even after centuries, is impossible. Both Penelope and her mother looked up to Essex on his difficult height at Court, relied on him to help them out of their difficulties. Never since her second marriage had Lady Leicester been received at Court. Even her widowhood did not soften Elizabeth's rigidity towards her. It was necessary, therefore, to besiege the royal stronghold. Again and again Essex manœvured to bring about a chance meeting. Repeatedly was Lady Leicester introduced to the Privy Gallery; when the Queen would get wind of it and send an excuse. Once more the lady bravely ventured. This time it was to the house of Her Majesty's "Comptroller" Knollys at the "Tilt End." Says the indefatigable Rowland White, "There was my lady Lester with a fair jewel of £300. A great Dinner was prepared by my Lady Chandos; the Queen's coach ready, and all the world expecting her Majesty; when upon a sudden she resolved not to go, and so sent word."

This roused Essex from a sick-bed. "My Lord of Essex, that had kept his chamber the day before, in his Night Gown went up to the Queen the privy way; but all would not prevail; and as yet my Lady Lester hath not seen the Queen. It had been better not been moved, for my Lord of Essex, by importuning the Queen in these unpleasing matters, loses the Opportunity he might take to do Good to his ancient Friends."

Rowland White is not quite just here. Essex spent most of his influence in helping friends, old and new, throughout his life, and it is on record that his was no *mauvaise langue*.

" He never spoke ill of anyone; only against Henry, Lord Cobham[1] he forswore all patience, calling him even to the Queen, the sycophant *per excellentiam;* and one lady he called the spider of the Court."

It is highly satisfactory to turn the pages of White's next letter (to Sir Robert Sidney) a few days later, and find that the coming of Lent (Lady Chandos' " great dinner " above mentioned, by the way, was fixed for a Shrove Tuesday) or gentler counsels softened the obdurate queenly heart :

" My Lady Lester was at Court, kissed the Queen's Hand and her Breast, and did embrace her, and the Queen kissed her. My Lord of Essex is in exceeding Favour here. My Joy is so great that I forget to answer your Letters."

Lady Leicester's vivid letter which follows shows concern as to her son's public activities, and is written to him while he was in voluntary exile at Wanstead, depressed and ill, when he was again in disfavour.

" SWEET ROBIN—
          Yourself hath given me such a taste of some strange matter to be looked for, as I cannot be quiet, till I know the true cause of your absence and discontentment. If it be but for Ireland, I doubt not but you are wise and politic enough to countermine with your enemies, whose devilish practices can no way hurt you but one. Wherefore, my dear son, give me leave to be a little jealous over you for your good, and entreat you to have ever God and your own honour before your eyes ; so shall you be sure he shall dispose indeed all, as you say, for the best in spite of enemies. My friend and I cannot but be troubled with thy needs,

---

[1] Lord Cobham (who was afterwards hanged by James I), and Ralegh proved his arch-enemies at his trial.

and do wish ourselves with you, as we would soon be, if we thought our service needful, so that you would have it so ; which let us know, and we will leave all other occasions whatsoever, and will presently be with you. Well, if it be but men's matters, I know you have courage enough; if women's, you have meetly well passed the pikes already, and therein should he skilful. So praying you not to be too secret from your best friends, I end, beseeching the Almighty to bless you ever in his highest favour, while I am, your mother, dearliest loving you,   " L. Leicester."

One is not quite sure whom she means by " my friend and I." There is a possibility that this might be Lord Mountjoy's younger brother, Sir Christopher Blount, many years her junior, whom she had married as long ago as 1589, barely a year after Leicester's death. She certainly had cause enough for alarm. A most undignified and sensational episode had occurred at Court in connection with the appointment of a Governor of Ireland. Essex wanted to get rid of a certain Sir George Carew at Court, and while in council with the Queen and others nominated this man, hostile to him. Her Majesty preferred the choice of Sir William Knollys, the uncle of Essex. In every case this would have been wise, for it would have smoothed the way of Essex in Ireland later. But he would not brook it, lost his temper, and turned his back upon Elizabeth. She boxed his ears and told him to be hanged. Whereat he clapped his hand on his sword. Lord Nottingham, present, took him to task. Essex replied that he would not have countenanced such an indignity even at the hands of Henry VIII (who, as we know, was, through Anne Boleyn, his mother's uncle-in-law and his own great uncle, which made him first cousin once removed of Elizabeth), and so left the Palace and the Court in a rage.

The Court watched both parties in this duel of sulks surely with lynx eyes ! Death, however, swooped across the tittle-tattle, and diverted attention for a brief space. For Burghley died, and Robert Cecil—Roberto del Diavolo, as Perez called him—his son, stood in his shoes. The death of " Her Majesty's Housewife" could not but shake the Court and the country. For nearly half a century had he been the Queen's friend. Never had he been her lover ; as a courtier he had not essayed to dazzle either her or his contemporaries. His part was that of watch-dog and servant combined. As Rowland White phrased it, " there was no one who looked to the clock so long" as he.

Essex attended the funeral. He had made several attempts to recover his hold of Elizabeth. From Chamberlain's *Letters* we get this glimpse of the additional imbroglio connected with the marriage of his close friend, Southampton, to Elizabeth Vernon, already treated in Chapter VIII.

" The Queen says he hath played long enough upon her, and that she means to play awhile upon him. Mistress Vernon is from the Court and lies at Essex House. . . . Yesternight the Queen was informed of the new Lady of Southampton, and her adventures, whereat her patience was so much moved that she came not to the chapel. She threateneth them all to the Tower, not only the parties, but all that are partakers of the practice. . . . My L. of Essex sick at Essex House."

Evidently presence in London was considered impolitic on the part of Essex, especially while the poor bride, Lady Southampton, was harboured under his roof. So he went into exile again :

" Yesterday he took his litter towards Wanstead ; this day I was with him there ; he is in physic ; we hope that presently upon his recovery he shall be re-called to Court. The Queen hath send her physician to attend him, and this day he hath been visited by Mr. Killigrew, Mr. Greville, and Lord Harry from her."

This, of course, meant full reconciliation in a short space of time, and honours in store, among which the Chancellorship of Cambridge University in the place of Lord Burghley could not but gratify the Earl and feed the hostility between himself and the Cecil family.

CHAPTER XI

PENELOPE'S POSITION

ABOUT this time we get nevertheless a happy glimpse of the family party at Essex House, as witnesses of a domestic entertainment on a big scale. Would that Roland White, who records it, had filled in the details a little and left for posterity the names of the plays, authors, and actors !

"Sir Gillie Merrick made at Essex House Yester-night a very great supper. There were at it my Ladies Lester, Northumberland, Bedford, Essex, Rich ; and my Lords of Essex, Rutland, Mountjoy, and many others. They had two Plays, which kept them up till one o'clock after Midnight."[1]

That far too short paragraph is rich in suggestion. It presents to us the great Essex *salon*, candles burning, floor gleaming, great chairs stiff with the embroidery of the women of the family, and furnished with fringe. The walls and windows make a warm background of tapestry, damask, and velvet. It is perhaps a "first night." Gabriel Harvey, Lyly, young Shakespeare, Francis Bacon, and Anthony, his brother, are surely there, and one or other has had a hand in the production. No doubt a special group of players, probably

---

[1] Sir Gillie Merrick was one of the captains whom Essex himself knighted after the Cadiz expedition, and was one of his warm adherents.

Apparently the friends of a great man occasionally "treated" him in his own house in this way.

that same company financed in his lifetime by the great Leicester, forms the caste. One imagines that it is an exquisite moment for author, interpreters, and audience, the moment of birth of two masterpieces, or the dramatic fragments out of which future masterpieces are fashioned. Every word, every gesture is of value, infused with superb freshness !

Once again Penelope Rich is a brilliant member of her family circle—the occasion now being a christening —and once more her name and that of Mountjoy are in the list of guests. In fact, from the year 1595, when this ceremony is noted by White, one feels that the two are constantly associated in the lives and domestic concerns of their circle, in the minds and activities of their friends and acquaintance. Rowland White tells how he goes forth to invite both to the christening of a child of Sir Robert Sidney.

" I went to Holborn," he writes to his absent master, "and found my Lord Mountjoy at his house. I said my lady sent me unto him, to desire him, both in your name and hers, to christen your son that was newly born, which he very honourably promised to do ; and when I told him my Lady Rich was godmother he was much pleased at it."

But there was a slight delay in this innocent ceremonial. Lady Sidney and her baby caught the measles, and the secretary duly notified the sponsors. Penelope declared that she was not afraid of infection. "She suddenly replied that after eight days there was no danger to be feared, 'and therefore it shall be no occasion to keep me from doing Sir Robert Sidney and my lady a greater kindness.'" In fact, she would risk the infection, thereby showing her deep devotion to her friends. Rowland White thought her rash. " When

I saw her so desperate, I humbly besought her Ladyship to take a longer time to think upon the danger,
which she did till that afternoon, and then coming to
her to Essex House, she told me she was resolved."

Can you not see the underlying eagerness of the lady
and its motive ? The christening was a great opportunity
for the meeting of the lovers. Both grasped at it.
Penelope could not bear to appear intimidated by a mere
hint of possible infection after decent quarantine. She
thought it over, and was still desperately anxious that
nothing should come in the way. Presently, woman-
like, she was as anxious that it should be postponed.
And why ? She gave the plausible excuse that a certain
Lord Compton, whose presence at the ceremony was
also required, particularly asked for delay, because important business detained him in the country, and so the
baptism was not to take place till the eve of the New
Year. Wherefore the wide-awake Rowland adds slyly
his own interpretation and the easy way in which
Lady Sidney yielded to her friend, quite unaware of her
dainty vanity and the fear lest her beauty should be
even slightly marred by a spot at a time when she
wanted to look her very best. "I do rather think it be
a tetter [1] that suddenly broke out in her fair white fore-
head, which will not be well in five or six days that
keeps your son from being christened. By my Lady
Rich's desires are obeyed as commandments by my
Lady."

Things like this were a great relief, as well from the
worries and intrigues and dangers of Court, as from the
"pikes" (to quote Lady Leicester) of love matters.
Penelope Rich lived a very full life, while all her
vitality was drawn upon in her spinning of the web of

[1] An angry spot.

her fate.   Like Essex, she never grudged any effort on behalf of her friends.   As in her mother's case, her heart was always spanned to utmost tension with anxiety. Essex was a perpetual volcano of possible danger.   Her heart and head and desires were pledged to Mountjoy. The careers of both were interwoven ; envy, malice, and hatred stalked abroad.   To steer clear of danger was no laughing matter.   If life in modern days for a recluse such as Amiel resolves itself into a succession of victories, what must it have meant in Elizabethan days at the Elizabethan Court ?   In that curious and virulent work, *Leicester's Commonwealth*, already mentioned (published in 1584), in which a coterie of four private persons retire to a " large gallery," after a Christmas dinner, to discuss and deplore the infamies of that brilliant nobleman, the opinion of the lady of the party on the social situation under the ageing Elizabeth may well be instanced :

" I do well remember, (quoth she), the first dozen years of her Highness' reign, how happy, pleasant, and quiet they were, with all manner of comfort and consolation.   There was no mention then of factions in religion, neither was any man much noted or rejected for that cause : so otherwise his conversation were civil and courteous.   No suspicion of treason, no talk of bloodshed, no complaint of troubles, miseries, or vexations.   All was peace, all was love, all was joy, all was delight.   Her Majesty (I am sure) took more recreation at that time, in one day, than she doth now in a whole week : and we that served her highness, enjoyed more contentation in a week than we can now in divers years. For now, there are so many suspicions, everywhere, for this thing and for that, as we cannot tell whom to trust. So many melancholic in the Court that seem malcontented : so many complaining or suing for their friends

N

that are in trouble : others slip over the Sea, or retire themselves upon the sudden : so many tales brought us of this or that danger, of this man suspected, of that man sent for up, and such like unpleasant and unsavoury stuff : as we can never almost be merry one whole day together. Wherefore (quoth this Lady) we that are of her Majesty's train . . . we cannot but moan. . . ."

Penelope's heart was assuredly as much exercised as this good lady's over the matter. Moreover, she was not a mischiefmaker. Like Essex, she was never malicious. If she cherished violently hostile feelings against her lawful spouse, they have not survived in letters. She was always ready to help her fellows; as Rowland White attests in the following letter to his master in Ireland, apropos of Sir Robert Sidney's desire to receive an appointment connected with the Cinque Ports, for which Lord Cobham was also a candidate :

"To NN I said that I was commanded to present your service unto her, and to desire her to hold you still in her good opinion. She thanked you very heartily, and told me, she was sorry to hear the Queen say the other day you should not yet come over, and then took me aside and said, that the Queen of late, asking her what news abroad, she answered that she was glad to hear of the good choice her Majesty made of a Warden of the Cinque Ports, and named you. The Queen said she had not yet disposed of it. I took this opportunity to beseech her (Lady Rich) to do you one favour, which was to deliver this letter, (and shewed it her) to the Queen ; she kissed it, and took it, and told me that you had never a friend in court, would be more ready than herself, to do you any pleasure ; I besought her in the love I found she bore you to take some time this night to do it, and without asking anything at all of the contents of it, she put it in her bosom, and assured me, that this night or to-morrow morning it would be read, and bid me attend her."

This next communication, curiously formal in its address, shows Penelope in close touch with the Southampton couple, and is written from Chartley, where her cousin Elizabeth was evidently staying with her.

"NOBLE SIR,

"I hope my first letter will excuse some part of my fault, and I assure you nothing shall make me neglect to yield to you all the assurances I can of my affection and desires to be held dear in your favour, whose worthy kindness I will strive to merit by the faithfullest endeavours my love can perform towards you, who shall ever find me unresumably,

"Your Lordship's faithful cousin and true friend,
"PENELOPE RICH.

"Your Lordships daughter is exceeding fair and well, and I hope by your son to win my wager."

The postscript concerns a cousinly bet, made evidently as to the sex of the child whom the Southamptons expected at this time.

Once more Lady Rich addresses her cousin by marriage. She is still at Chartley, and frankly confesses a part of the trouble between herself and her husband. She is loth to go home to him and leave Lady Southampton in the lurch. Between the lines also one detects a longing for a woman's companionship, which might make the financial pother under Lord Rich's roof easier to bear.

"The exceeding kindness I receive from your Lord in hearing often from you doth give me infinite contentment, both in referring assurance of your health and that I remain in your constant favour, which I will endeavour to merit by my affection unto your Lord. My Lord Rich doth so importune me daily to return to my own house as I cannot stay here longer than Bartelmenteide,[1] which I do against his will, and the cause of his earnest desire to have me come up is his being so persecuted for his land, as he is in fear to lose the greater part he hath and his next term, who would have me a solicitor to bear part of his troubles and is much discontented with my staying so long : wherefore I beseech your Lord to speak with my brother, since I am loth to leave my Lady here alone, and if you resolve she shall go with me into Essex, which I very much desire, then you were best to write to me that you would have her go with me, which will make my Lord Rich the more willing, though I know he will be contented, to whom I have written that I will come as soon as I know what my brother and yourself determine for my Lord. I am sorry for Sir Harry Bower's hurt, though I hope it is so little as it will not mar his good face ; and so in haste I wish your Lordship all the honour and happiness you desire.

"Your Lordship's most affectionate cousin,

"PENELOPE RICH."

This makes us tolerably *au fait* with the position of this lady. Her husband at Leighs was in a specially "grabtious" mood, and apparently wishful to secure as much as possible of her property for himself, while she depended on her brother and others to protect her rights. Under the roof of Essex she was free—either at Chartley or Wanstead. At either place she could, oh ! blessed delight ! meet Lord Mountjoy without fear or censure. At the time of her brother's disgrace (after the royal box on the ear) Mountjoy was one of those whom the Earl would suffer to visit him in his retirement. By this time, indeed, Charles Blount had

---

[1] Bartholomew-tide.

long been one of the family party. But not at
"Leighs."

Probably the supreme moment in this great love
affair of the lady was the departure of Lord Rich for
Cadiz with Essex, when Mountjoy stayed behind. At
any rate, such a liaison could not have been entirely
carried on without knowledge of her family. They
certainly kept her secret loyally. From 1590 to 1599
she seems to have been very little with her husband
and constantly in the society of her notable lover. He
was undoubtedly her rock, though in the end a rock
on which the vessel of her fate was splintered to atoms.
His cool judgment alone seems to have stayed Essex
in evil moments. He was one of the few privileged to
write thus tenderly and strongly to Penelope's brother :

" By my occasion of being at the Court, I did observe
that which I was sorry and glad to see, a Court naked
without you and yet not without a longing desire to
have you there again. I heard by others how clearly
Mr. Secretary hath made report of your Lordship's
good advice in Council, how well her Majesty liked of
it, protesting that you would do better for others than
for your self. By some speeches with Mr. Secretary
I saw both his opinion that all might and would be well
and his disposition to do the best offices that lay in
him, notwithstanding your Lordship's hard conceit of
him for some things, whereof if nothing old would
satisfy your Lordship he did not doubt but time would
clear him. Her Majesty never used me with greater
grace, but yet so that I might plainly see her com-
mendations of my kindness and care to please her, to
be a secret complaint if that she could not find the like
where she most desired. I know how unfitting I am
to advise one wiser than myself in this cause, where
your honour is more dear unto you than your life, but
yet may it please your honour to consider these circum-

stances : She is your sovereign with whom you may not beat upon with equal conditions. She denieth the ground of your difference, which is a kind of satisfaction. By all likelihood she would be glad to meet you half way, if that which doth not now a little trouble her, should further distemper her upon whose life and health you know how many depend. I am assured it would be a greater grief unto you than the loss of her hand. For the other side that which you feel (as Master Cecil and other your friends at Court do wisely foresee) can be no benefit, for admit you draw her to forget her power and to yield in her affection to that which she is unwilling to do, your peace cannot be without matter of difference. In so much as she will hardly forget to what unequal conditions you brought her, whereas if you prevent her in kindness and yield to her (to whom there is no disparagement to yield to her will) all circumstances considered, you shall be nothing unworthy your self, you shall make a sure peace and come with more ease to it, which I take to be your own end ; I grant your wrong to be greater than so noble a heart can digest, but consider my good Lord, how great she is with whom you deal, how willing, with how little yielding to be conquered, what advantage you have by yielding when you are wronged, what disadvantage by forcing her, whom though you deserve never so much you must rely upon for . . . [illegible] . . . how strong you shall make your enemies, how weak your friends, and how provoked patience turneth into fury and delayed anger into hatred. What opportunity her late loss and state, present necessity may give you to benefit your self and yours, and lastly what offence the world (that honoureth your virtues) may take, when they shall find that to right your self you neglect her. But this is all in love. I refer it to your better judgment and only advise that whatsoever peace you make you use not other means but your self which will be more honourable for you and more acceptable to her."

Between the years 1597, when Sir Gillie Merrick gave that famous evening party, and 1600, Penelope travelled fast and went through much. She bore Mountjoy several children. Rowland White has left no comment on that. But he is careful to mention her recovery from a much-dreaded disease in 1597 :

" My Lady Rich is recovered of her small pox without blemish to her beautiful face."

On April 6th of this year a very odd, rather jaunty letter is extant from Lord Rich to Essex. It deals with her illness and the risk to her beauty, but also mentions a letter, enclosed, from his wife, dealing with some love affair connected with a girl—a "fair maid" in whom his wife was interested. His reason for enclosing it is that she feared the infection for the girl if sent direct, so that evidently it is not a letter written by her. This enclosure is unsealed, and Lord Rich has carefully perused it, but is quite mystified. The suggestion that, if his wife expected not to recover her looks she would not be so careful to shield a sister beauty, is tart, not to say spiteful.

" My Lord,
    " Your Sister being loth to send you any of her infection, hath made me an instrument to send you this enclosed epistle of Dutch true or false love ; wherein, if I be not in the right, I may be judged more infected than fitteth my profession, and to deserve worse than the pox of the smallest size. If it fall out so, 1 disburden myself and am free from such treason, by my disclosing it to a Councillor, who as your Lordship well knows, cannot be guilty of any such offence. Your Lordship sees, by this care of a fair maid's beauty, she doth not altogether despair of recovery of her own again ; which if she did, assured by envy of others' fair-

ness, would make her willingly to send infection among them. This banishment makes me that I cannot attend on you ; and this wicked disease will cause your sister this next week to be at more charge to buy a masquer's visor to meet you dancing in the fields than she would on (once ?) hoped ever to have done. If you dare meet her, I beseech you preach patience unto her, which is my only theme of exhortation. Thus, over-saucy to trouble your Lordship's weightier affairs, I take my leave, and ever remain your Lordship's poor brother to command,   Ro. Rich."

"Dutch true or false love" means simulated affection, "Dutch" standing for our "Greek" in the sense of mystery. Massey suggests that the enclosure was a group of the Shakespeare sonnets, those which he thinks the author intended as representing Elizabeth Vernon in a jealous mood addressing her cousin Penelope, as already explained in a previous chapter.

On the other hand, while conjugal affairs at Leighs were at their worst, the poets of the day continued to lay their offerings at her feet or indite long flatteries in prose to her. At this moment, the year 1598, knowing what we do of her family affairs, it is amusing to find her receiving from Bartholomew Young this epistle, dedicating to her his translation of a play on no less a theme than Diana—the Diana of George of Monte-mayor, from which Sidney had already translated extracts, and which, together with Sanazarro's *Arcadia*, as stated, had been the source of his own romance :

"Right Honourable,
       "Such are the apparent defects of art and judgment in this new portrayed Diana, that their discovery must needs make me blush, and abase the work, unless with undeserved favour erected upon the high and

shining pillar of your honourable protection, that they may seem to the beholder less or none at all. The glory whereof, as with reason it can no ways be thought worthy, but by boldly adventuring upon the apparent demonstration of your magnificent mind, wherein all virtues have their proper seat, and on that singular desire, knowledge, and delight, wherewith your Ladyship entertaineth, embraceth, and affecteth honest endeavours, learned languages, and this particular subject of Diana, warranted by all virtue and modesty, as Collin, in his French dedicatory to the illustrious Prince Lewis of Lorraine, at large setteth down and commandeth ; now presenting it to so sovereign a light, and relying on a gracious acceptance, what can be added more to the full content, desire and perfection of Diana, and of her unworthy interpreter, (that hath in English here exposed her to the view of strangers), than for their comfort and defence to be armed with the honourable titles and countenance of so high and excellent a Patroness. But, as certain years past, my honourable good Lady, in a public show at the Middle Temple, where your honourable presence, with many noble Lords and fair Ladies, graced and beautified those sports, it befell to my lot in that worthy assembly unworthily to perform the part of a French orator, by a dedicated speech in the same tongue, and that amongst so many good conceits, and such general skill in tongues, all the while I was rehearsing it, there was not any whose nature, judgment and censure in that language I feared and suspected more than your Ladyship's, whose attentive ear and eye daunted my imagination with the apprehension of my disabilities and your Ladyship's perfect knowledge in the same. Now, once again, in this translation out of Spanish, (which language also with the present matter being so well known to your Ladyship), whose reprehension and severe sentence of all others may I more justly fear, than that which, Honourable Madame, at election you may herein duly

give or with favour take away ?   I have no other means
than the humble insinuation of it to your most honourable name and clemency, most humbly beseeching the
same pardon to all those faults, which to your learned
and judicious views shall occur.   Since then, for pledge
of the dutiful and zealous desire I have to serve your
Ladyship, the great disproportion of your most noble
estate to the quality of my poor condition, can afford
nothing else but this small present, my prayer shall
always importune the heavens for the happy increase of
your high and worthy degree, and for the full accom-
plishment of your most honourable desires.

Your honour's

most humble devoted

BARTHOL. YOUNG."

From all such letters one gleans a sense of those
spacious times and the spacious life of these aristocratic
Elizabethans.   The masques at the Inner Temple, the
plays and devices presented at large private houses, the
circle of busy courtiers, politicians, and foreign emissaries,
the tiltings and mummings, suppers and masquerades
were the ingredients of a continuous social pageant.
The larger pageant of the nation was being played outside, while the nation, busy with its own history, had
its eye on the Court.   Every little detail of the lives
of these great ones was precious to the outside world,
for which no alert halfpenny press had arisen to waft
the more important happenings of the hour to the
humblest doorstep, while your countryman washed down
his breakfast of roughly cured bacon and rye bread
with home-brewed ale.   A halfpenny press in those
days would have found material enough for startling
headlines, for the times were large and sensational.
Life was held tolerably cheap, and each man carried some
weapon of defence ; but the nation was growing apace.

"More life, more land, more vigour, more wealth!" it seems to cry in this era. It was ever on the watch against foreign invasion, but it managed to flourish at home all the same. No Malthusian notions had infected the country. Families were large, millers grew fat. Historians at last began to complain of "corners" in grain, and the way in which they kept the most whole-some wheat beyond the reach of the labouring class. How similar is this conflict to our own in modern times! Again and again there comes to my mind that state-ment of Mme. Duclaux: "The emotions remain the same.   It is the price of bread which alters." Elizabethan bread was of many kinds, like ours, and just as elaborately defined ; and whether you ate the wholemeal loaf, the "cheaten," the "manchet," or the " ravelled," there appears to have been the same difficulty in securing a "standard" quality in each as in the present day.

With a growing birth-rate, expansion was indispensable. So, you see, not mere patriotism and inborn dread and defiance of Spain were the sole cause of piratical sea engagements, or mere personal gold-fever the incentive which made men into dazzling adventurers.   England was growing fast.   She wanted a "large room."   She ate largely, drank deeply, fought fiercely; and she could laugh roundly—as her ancient comedies show.   Read in the innumerable chronicles of the day of the tables of the rich, of the feasts served at private and public ceremonials.   Read of her festivals, her amusements, her bull-baitings, her huntings, her lively combined dances, her love of shows and ceremonies—above all, of her love of choral music.   Witness also her delight in dress—for her foreign journeys were so increased that she could now welcome apace the devices of

Southern tailors.   From Italy and Spain she drew a new ecstasy in the colour and detail of her wardrobe and a greater freedom of choice. There was no one set fashion for hair and beard. One man would show a curled head; another, long locks, like a woman's; a third might be close-cropped. Here, one had a long pointed beard, there, you would see a beard full and broad. Courtiers had taken to earrings. "We do seem," wrote Harrison in his famous contemporary *Description of England*, "to imitate all nations round about us, wherein we be like to the polypus or chameleon."   The English now learned what a good tailor meant, and how men and women must toil and stand and endure that they may be well garbed. And so they caught the trick of torturing tailor and modiste as we do to-day. "How hardly can the tailor please them in making it fit . . . !" wrote Harrison in his chapter on "Apparel and Attire."   "How many times must it be sent back again to him that made it! What chafing, what fretting, what reproachful language doth the poor workman bear away! . . . In women also it is most to be lamented that they do now far exceed the lightness of our men (who nevertheless are transformed from the cap even to the very shoe). . . . What shall I say of of their doublets, with pendant cod-pieces on the breast, jags and cuts, and sleeves of gaudy colours?   Their galligascons[1] to . . . make their attire to fit plum round (as they term it) about them, their fardingales and diversely coloured netted stocks of silk, jerdsey and such like?   Such cuts and garish colours as are worn in these days, and never brought in but by the consent of the French, who think themselves the gayest men when they have most

[1] Bustles.

diversities of jags and change of colours about them.
. . . I might here name a sort of hues devised for
the nonce, wherewith to please fantastical heads, as
goose green, pease porridge tawny, popingay blue,
lusty gallant, the devil-in-the-head, (I should say the
hedge) and such like."

Harrison could tell us a great deal more, but omits
it, more's the pity, as he says that "nothing can particularly be spoken of any constancy thereof!"

As the Elizabethans ate, so they dressed; as they
dressed, so they built and furnished. It was not always
so. Spaniards in the time of Queen Mary had been
struck by the discrepancy between the good fare
of the working classes and the miserable architecture
and condition of their wooden dwellings. But things
were slowly improving from the top downwards. Not
so long ere this the façades and general aspect of
buildings had struck foreign visitors as poor. The
English had not troubled about making a grand
domestic impression, and the level of external beauty
was low.

Till Henry VIII began to lavish his money and fancy
on royal palaces even these were nothing like as impressive as the mansions of the leading continental
aristocrats. Now domestic architecture was proceeding
by leaps and bounds. "So magnificent and stately as
the basest house of a baron doth often match in our
days with some houses of princes in old time," comments Harrison, "so that if ever curious building did
flourish in England, it is in these years, wherein our
workmen excel and are in a manner comparable in skill
with old Vitruvius, Leo Baptista, and Serlo." Glass
had become "so good cheap" that nearly everyone
could afford good windows, while well-to-do merchants,

and plain gentry, as much as lords, had their "great provision of tapestry, Turkey work, pewter, brass, fine linen, and thereto costly cupboards of plate." Even so with the lesser agriculturists, "the inferior artificers, and many farmers, who . . . have learned also to garnish their cupboards with plate, their joined beds with tapestry and silk hangings, and their tables with carpets and fine napery." For which the good Harrison, a canon, by the way, of Westminster, rejoices "to see how God hath blessed us with His good gifts."

Each great house had its group of subordinate buildings —dairy, brewhouse, stable, "all separate from the first and one of them from another. And yet, for all this, they are not so far distant in sunder but the goodman lying in his bed may lightly hear what is done in each of them with ease and call quickly unto his many if any danger should attack him."

"Call quickly unto his many!" There you have the picture of the great house which nourished the little ones, the little ones which at a signal would rally round the greater. And therein you have also the picture of the alertness in arms of the nation. Each squire, whether plain Mr., "bannaret," or peer, could furnish so many men in time of need ; each county had its fighting force, each village its tiny armoury, for which the lord of the manor was responsible. "Certes there is almost no village so poor in England (be it never so small) that hath not sufficient furniture in a readiness to set forth three or four soldiers, as one archer, one gunner, one pike, and a billman at least. No, there is not so much wanting as their very liveries and caps, which are least to be accounted of if any haste required ; so that if this good order may continue, it shall be impossible for the sudden enemy to find us unprovided."

Let us recall once more the large picturesqueness of these vital times in the fine names for the ordnance. The smallest gun was entitled a " brobonet." The rest, on the upward scale, are " falconet " and " falcon," " minion," " sacre," " culverin," " cannon," and " basilisk "—the last being the largest. Fine romantic titles wherewith to answer those courtiers brought over by Philip in the Marian days, who contemptuously and publicly opined that England would lie down before the Spanish army ! Harrison states roundly that the outcry against poverty and an increasing population on the part of a few contemptuous persons, springs from the devil's prompting, and that a " wall of men " is worth many a corn stock in days of war. When he wrote, the times, superficially, were peaceable enough, but it was just after he penned his satisfaction at the rich " contentments " of the nation that the Armada danger burst upon the country.

Spacious days ! Penelope Rich had wit enough to keep pace with them, singular opportunities for knowledge, first hand, of all the greater affairs. One supposes that she could keep State secrets—if Mountjoy and Essex ever confided them to her. She could for the greater part of her life keep her own secret, in spite of gossip. She must have possessed superhuman physique to lead so successfully those two lives—nay, three —as Lady Rich, as Court beauty and accomplished dilettante, as the beloved of Mountjoy. Long spaces there necessarily were when she sought refuge in country places. The births of her children by Mountjoy must be adroitly stage-managed lest the truth be blazed abroad. Even in these matters she maintains the large Elizabethan attitude. She was speedily the mother of two families, twelve in all. She had to cherish them somewhere, somehow. Bringing so many into the world appears to have been to her a small matter, a detail of her large life. It was inevitable—a part of her existence, her nature, the order of things. To these ends she must have been assisted by others —subordinates, discreet, orderly, deferent. Surely a woman of large method, of little fear, of a strong heart, which can never at any time of her career be termed a small one !

The life of the great householder was hers in a double sense. With her husband in the early days of marriage she had tasted the fullness of country life, was châtelaine of the great house and lady bountiful to the little dépendances of it, saw Robert Rich jog duly to the Bench, where beggars and robbers and men who used their knives too freely were haled before him, or perchance assisted his slow wits and awkward fingers to write replies to official requests for a statement of the fighting force in his village and county. With Mountjoy she studied greater things, looked more widely into the affairs of Elizabeth, the wars, the world of books. These things were the upper current of her life. Underneath flowed the deep stream of her love, bearing with it the distracting, delicious, teasing, exhausting, inexorable business of every day—the " ordering " of bread, ale, and dishes, the control of gardens, payment of men and maids, the provision of clothes for her children, the guarding of their health, the jealous care of her own beauty, correspondence with family and friends, the devising of new gowns, the constant effort to keep bedding, hangings and linen in good estate—the never-ending feminine combat with all those things which moth and rust do corrupt.

CHAPTER XII

A MELANCHOLY YOUTH

THERE crosses the web of Penelope Rich's life at this period a third young man—William Herbert, future Earl of Pembroke and son of the Lady of the Arcadia. Born in 1580, he came to Court in 1599, after extracting a most unwilling permission to do so from his father. Rowland White notes the fact duly, with the hopes of his circle that the youth would become a great courtier—for the Queen obviously favoured him. Thus he might prove, at least to White's employer, Herbert's other uncle, a means to preferment, " a ladder to go up that house," as the Secretary puts it.

White, however, soon had to record partial disappointment : " My Lord Herbert is a continual courtier, but doth not follow his business with that care as is fit ; he is too cold a courtier in a matter of such greatness." Again, Herbert is characterised as spiritless, not courageous, " a melancholy young man," and one " much blamed for his cold and weak manner of pursuing Her Majesty's favour, having so good steps to lead him unto it." He certainly did as he liked in such matters. Did Court bore him ? Here he is, glad to play truant and join in the sensation which always followed successive scares of Spanish attack.

" My Lord Herbert hath been from Court these seven days in London, swaggering it amongst the men of war, and viewing the manner of the musters."

Now, Massey works hard to prove that this impressionable, moody young man was fascinated by Lady Rich, and that he inspired his devoted friend, William Shakespeare, to tell the tale of his love and sufferings, adoration and curses, in the second section of the great sonnets. The more, however, I go into this theory, the more I am convinced, first, that if the sonnets contain Herbert's own love-story, they do not concern Penelope Rich, and, second, that the widely held theory that the first section of the sonnets, ascribed by Massey and others to Southampton's love-story and discussed in Chapter VIII, may with far more likelihood be addressed to William Herbert. He was one of Shakespeare's most ardent patrons. Massey reminds us that the former undoubtedly was a fervent patron of Shakespeare after Southampton died, that " the first play presented to King James I. in England was performed by Shakespeare's company in Herbert's house at Wilton." Moreover, in the dedication to the first folio the editors emphatically show how Herbert had stood sponsor for the plays, for the Earl " had prosecuted the Poet with so much favour that they venture to hope for the same indulgence towards the works as was shown to the parent of them."

Massey's next argument, however, is absurd. Herbert, he points out, was a friend of Penelope's family, but "he was too young or too indifferent to become a prominent partisan of Essex, or rather " he was more in love with the Earl's sister than with his cause."

Rowland White gives us no word on this subject. All he records is an occasional meeting between Lady Rich and the young man in company with friends. As will be seen by a glance at his career, he was a fellow always in love with some woman, and the

From an engraving by H. T. Ryall, after the painting by Van Dyck.

WILLIAM HERBERT, THIRD EARL OF PEMBROKE

explanation of this melancholy at Court is due to some such affair of the heart. From a certain intrigue which follows we see how he fell in love with someone whom possibly he could not marry and durst not woo openly—but not Penelope. Under the circumstances he might, however, court her counsel, as one who had been crossed in love and had experience. He was, at any rate, often in the society of Lord Mountjoy and under the roof of Penelope's brother. If he had really been infatuated about her he would certainly not have been able to resist being a partner, two years later, in the Essex conspiracy, in which Lady Rich played such a curious part as " whipper-in " of her brother's adherents at the very crisis of his raid upon the City and the Court.

As to the beauty who ensnared Herbert, and the one addressed, possibly, in the second section of the Shakespeare sonnets, it has already been suggested in these pages, on the authority of the most recent investigators, that she was a certain Mary Fitton. For a year or two later Herbert was not only banished from Court, but sent to prison for a secret intrigue with this maid of honour. At the time of his entry into Court she would be just twenty-one, and, from what one knows of her history, dangerously attractive. She was the daughter of Sir Edward Fitton and granddaughter of the knight of the same name who was formerly vice treasurer in Ireland and Lord President of Connaught. Her father was neither successful in securing office on the first Sir Edward's death, nor happy in regard to his estates and income. Therefore it was probably with a view to the resuscitation of the Queen's interest and favour that both his daughters, Anne and Mary, were introduced to the Court. Anne was maid of honour some years previously, but left the royal service on her marriage in 1595. Mary was appointed maid of honour during the close of the nineties, but by her attractions only reaped singular misfortune. Her ill-luck certainly dated from her sixteenth year, if it is true that at this early age, and before she had any experience of the world or her own temperament, she was married to a Captain Lougher. Records are so confusing on this point that it now seems possible that this gentleman was one of her early suitors, and that, though betrothed to him, the marriage never took place. A year later than the date which associates their names thus she came to Court, and no more is heard of this captain.

Very quickly Mary Fitton was plunged into love intrigues. The first was with William Herbert. Their meeting was dramatically effective. He saw her first, apparently, when she led the dances at a masque in honour of the marriage of his kinsman, Lord Herbert, son of the Earl of Worcester, with Anne Russell, also a maid of honour, and evidently the same lady with whom Essex had flirted, and whom the Queen had chastised as described.

If you take it that the latter Shakespeare sonnets reveal " Mr. W. H.'s " passion and reproaches, then there is internal evidence of Mary's first marriage—to Lougher—for the poet accuses her of breaking her legal bond with another man. Whether to escape detection by her husband or the Queen (more probably the latter) she employed amazingly audacious tactics by way of disguise. Yet it was rather like the disguise of an ostrich in more senses than one, for she only shortened her petticoats and hid her face when she went out to her trysts. The State Papers are very frank on the subject : " During the time that the Earl of Pembroke favoured her she would put off her head-tire, and tuck up her clothes, and take a large white cloak, and march as though she had been a man to meet the said earl out of Court." Both of them paid heavily for their intrigue. Pembroke confessed, "renounced all marriage" (this seems rather superfluous, under the circumstances!) and was sent to the Fleet. The lady brought a child into the world, and was punished enough by social scorn and expulsion from Court. The child died. After this she seems to have had a similar love affair with Sir Richard Leveson. This, in spite of two more children, she lived down, and married again —Captain Polwhele, early in the reign of James I. She corresponds far more strikingly than Penelope Rich with the woman of the latter Shakespeare sonnets.

Here enters Massey, armed with his darling theory, which he constructs out of a certain playful Shakespeare sonnet in Section II of his (Massey's) grouping. This sonnet puns incessantly on Herbert's Christian name, and once introduces the surname of Penelope. To my thinking, the whole matter turns on the point whether the poet meant to give prominence to that word "rich" or not. Massey gives it italics and a capital. Take away that, remove the italics, and the link vanishes :

> " Whoever hath her wish thou hast thy will
> And will to boot, and will in over-plus ;
> More than enough am I that vex thee still,
> To thy sweet will making addition thus :
> Wilt thou, whose will is large and spacious,
> Not once vouchsafe to hide my will in thine ?
> Shall will in others seem right gracious,
> And in my will no fair acceptance shine ?
> The sea, all water, yet receives rain still,
> And in abundance addeth to his store ;
> So thou, being *rich* in will, add to thy will
> One will of mine, to make thy large will more :
> Let no unkind, no fair beseechers kill,
> Think all but one, and me in that one Will."

According to Massey it is apparent that Shakespeare does not mean himself. The only other William who appears to fit the case—assuming, of course, that this sonnet really "palpitates with actuality "—is the "W. H." to whom Thorpe dedicates his edition, and who is held to be this young Earl of Pembroke-elect and nephew of Sir Philip Sidney. Gerald Massey is very positive upon this point, and not a little sarcastic in regard to the disparity of age between the lady and her newest adorer. It may or may not have been a passing fancy on her side, a romantic infatuation on his. She was coquette enough to appreciate the attentions of men far younger than herself, perhaps to overvalue them, beautiful enough and sufficiently famous socially to be a constant lodestar to young courtiers. She was, instinctively, a spinner of love-webs, but I do not feel that she consciously drew young William Herbert into her net, with the much greater personality of Mountjoy at her side. Nevertheless, Massey builds up a strong case. Once more let me say that he leaves me unconvinced. He compares the portrait of " Stella," as drawn in so richly by Sidney, with that of the dark beauty for whom William Herbert sighed, and he would have us believe, first, that she is one and the same lady ; second, that Shakespeare indulges in more than a little irony in picturing her as she appears in later years.

Look on Penelope's traits through Sidney's eyes. She had tawny, sun-kissed hair. Each thread of it was a shaft of Apollo, enmeshed. Her cheek was of a " kindly claret " in colour—that is to say, she had a ripe complexion, slightly brunette. To this she added deep black eyes—" beamy black." (*Astrophel to Stella.* Sonnet VII.) In the very next sonnet we are reminded of her " fair skin," and in another, ivory, rubies, pearl, and gold stand for her skin, teeth, lips, and head. And again we get this accentuated in her amber-coloured head, milk hands, rose cheeks, red lips, as in No. IX, in which her face is the façade of " Queen Virtue's Court," built by Nature out of "alabaster pure."

On the other hand, the dark lady of the Shakespeare group is far darker in hue.

> " Then will I swear beauty herself is black,
>   And all they foul that thy complexion lack."

It is a coincidence that both ladies had black eyes, and it is interesting that both Sidney and Shakespeare should have used the same figure of speech as " mourning eyes."

> " Thine eyes I love and they, as pitying me,
>   Knowing thy heart torments me with disdain,
>   Have put on black and loving mourners be,"

writes Shakespeare. But were there no other black eyes at Court save those of Penelope Rich? Shakespeare harps on the gloom of the lady's charm. In the following sonnet her sombre natural beauty is cited as a reproach to those who make vizards of their faces with powder and paint :

> In the old age black was not counted fair,
> Or if it were, it bore not beauty's name,
> But now is black beauty's succession here,
> And beauty slander'd with a bastard shame.
> For since each hand hath put on nature's power,
> Fairing the foul with art's false borrowed face,
> Sweet beauty hath no name, no holy bower,
> But is profaned, if not lives in disgrace.
> Therefore my mistress' eyes are raven black,
> Her eyes so suited, and they mourners seem
> At such who, not born fair, no beauty lack,
> Slandering creation with a false esteem :
> Yet so they mourn, becoming of[1] their woe
> That every tongue says beauty should look so.

[1] *Becoming of = gracing* according to Dowden.

Again the lover is made to say :

"Thy face hath not the power to make love groan."

For the lady is no triumphant beauty, resistless where all men are concerned. Yet he loves her. Let others worship fair beauties. For him her darkness is in every detail beautiful.

"Thy black is fairest in my judgment's place."

Moreover, though she is no publicly advertised beauty, no famous and peerless one, she exercises over him all the despotism of such a lady :

"Thou art as tyrannous, so as thou art,
    As those whose beauties proudly make them cruel."

How can such details be reconciled with the celebrated charms of Lady Rich ? This next sonnet only enforces the unreality of Massey's notion :

"My mistress' eyes are nothing like the sun ;
    Coral is far more red than her lips' red ;
    If snow be white, why then her breasts are dun ;
    If hairs be wires, black wires grow on her head.
    I have seen roses damask'd, red, and white,
    But no such roses see I in her cheeks ;
    And in some perfumes is there more delight
    Than in the breath that from my mistress reeks.
    I love to hear her speak, yet well I know
    That music hath a far more pleasing sound :
    I grant I never saw a goddess go,
    My mistress, when she walks, treads on the ground :
    And yet, by heaven, I think my Love as rare
    As any She belied with false compare."

Would a young man, paying his addresses to a married lady of such importance, dare to be so uncomplimentary ? And if so, why should he call her sun-kissed hair black wires, and her skin, Sidney's "alabaster pure," dun-coloured ? At the height of Sidney's anger and despair he never dared such things as abuse of his lady's charms. William Herbert or the poet was assuredly "in hell" (as expressed in the tremendous Sonnet CXXIX) and in the throes of reaping the bitter harvest of his unbridled instincts when that sonnet was written.

As to the question of the disparity in age between Penelope and Herbert, a suggestion which so detracts from the dignity of the sonnets, Massey from the first assures himself and us that the poet interprets a " playful, ironic " mood. But pray remember that she was still under forty and in no way a past beauty. Of course, you may read anything into such a sonnet as this :

> " When my love swears that she is made of truth
> I do believe her, though I know she lies
> That she might think me some untutor'd youth
> Unlearned in the world's false subtleties.
> Thus vainly thinking that she thinks me young,
> Although she knows my days are past the best,
> Simply I credit her false-speaking tongue :
> On both sides thus is simple truth supprest ;
> But wherefore says she not she is unjust ?
> And wherefore say not I that I am old ?
> O, love's best habit is in seeming trust,
> And age in love loves not to have years told :
> Therefore I lie with her and she with me,
> And in our faults by lies we flatter'd be."

You may take it that the lady laughs at her young lover, but that rather than combat her disbelief in the maturity and depth of his feelings by a discussion upon their respective ages, which might risk his cause beyond hope, he waives the question, dissimulates to please her, and swallows her misstatements.

Is it not, however, just as possible to take the second line, the sixth, and the eighth, and believe that the lover is past his prime, and that the lady is only teasing him with her disbelief in the ripe judgment and the faith of which he tries to assure her ?

This final quotation may well have been the outcome of the affair with Mary Fitton.

> " The expense of spirit in a waste of shame
> Is lust in action ; and till action, lust
> Is perjured, murderous, bloody, full of blame,
> Savage, extreme, rude, cruel not to trust,
> Enjoy'd no sooner but despised straight :
> Past reason hunted, and no sooner had
> Past reason hated, as a swallow'd bait
> On purpose laid to make the taker mad :
> Mad in pursuit and in possession so ;
> Had, having, and in quest to have, extreme ;
> A bliss in proof, and proved, a very woe ;
> Before, a joy proposed ; behind, a dream.
> All this the world well knows ; yet none knows well
> To shun the heaven that leads men to this hell."

One editor of these sonnets (the bookseller Benson), in an address to the reader, asserts that they will be found " serene, clear, and elegantly plain." So they are, if you regard them singly as expressions of varying moods. But if you seek the story behind them, Heaven help you ! Already at the end of the seventeenth century, not a hundred years after their first issue, the vaunted plainness and clearness were found to be a myth. The matter has an enormous section in literature to itself. It may, at any rate, relieve the minds of some that so great an authority as Professor Dowden dismisses as not sound the idea that they clothe Shakespeare's autobiography, and many authorities suggest that in place of the Earl of Southampton as the beloved man friend of the first section William Herbert should be substituted. This notion, as shown, is based on the enthusiasm of Herbert for Shakespeare's drama, but also on sonnets imploring him to marry

From an old engraving

HENRY, SECOND EARL OF PEMBROKE

and beget heirs.   In connection with this the sonnet
beginning :

> " Thou art thy mother's glass, and she in thee
> Gives back the lovely April of her prime "

is often cited.   There is no improbability in this notion.
Lady Pembroke adored her firstborn.   Into him she
poured all her love of literature, her fine taste, her
generous treatment of men and letters.   His future was
her constant thought, and his interests a continual distraction from the growing curmudgeonliness of her old
husband.   In some way her William repaid her nobly.
He was a good scholar, delighting in poetry and the
practice of poetry and epigram.   He was, it is recorded,
" of an heroic and public spirit, bountiful to his friends
and servants, and a great encourager of learned men."
But he was absolutely regardless of money and never
forbore to gratify any whim, whether it concerned his
own pleasures or those of others.   He was constantly
in debt, and one supposes that his mother had many
a hard tussle with her husband when William drifted
home to Wilton or Ramsbury or Barnard's Castle with
a pathetic tale of empty pockets.   He strikes me as
having adopted the pathetic rôle from the beginning, in
spite of his " heroic and public spirit."   Fortunately, the
old Earl died soon after his son appeared at Court, so
that financial matters were easier for him, but one looks
with apprehension on an historical statement to the
effect that the father, instead of entrusting the bulk
of his income to the widow for the improvident youth,
left Lady Pembroke " as bare as he could, and bestowing
all on the young lord, even to her jewels."   This, however, is not quite correct, for there is proof that she
was, by will, the owner, for her life, of plate, jewels, and
household stuff to the value of three thousand marks,

with the lease of the manor of Ivy Church and the manor and park of Devizes.

Her son's marriage was an important matter to her and to his relatives.   White reports that he showed no inclination whatever to tie himself to any particular lady, and Clarendon gives him a poor character :

"The Earl was immoderately given up to women. But therein he likewise retained such a power and juris- diction over his appetites—(Clarendon should surely have used the word 'taste' here !)—that he was not so much transported with beauty and outward allurements as with those advantages of the mind, as manifested an extraordinary wit and spirit and knowledge, and ad- ministered great pleasure in their conversation.   To these he sacrificed himself, his precious time, and much of his fortune ; and some, who were nearest his trust and friendship, were not without apprehension that his natural vivacity and vigour of mind began to lessen and decline by those excessive indulgences."

He was certainly not a vigorous young man, this creature afflicted with frequent melancholia, though the world was at his feet.   It is not surprising that he suffered at times from racking headache and sought rest at Wilton, whence his mother wrote to Germany for special tobacco—for smoking this alone gave him respite from pain.   He was another of the many young men for whom parents and guardians hoped to find a bride among the ladies of the house of Cecil.   Over- tures were once more made for the much-sought-after hand of the Earl of Oxford's daughter and Burleigh's granddaughter, Anne, but the claims of Mary Fitton or other girls were probably far stronger.   The imprison- ment of Pembroke, for by this time he had inherited the title, was short—only a month.   But his disgrace

was long. Like many another who had for a time
basked in Court sunshine and lost it, he found life now
insupportable, and begged for official permission to live
abroad. "The change of climate may purge me of
melancholy," wrote this egotistic young blood—poor
descendant indeed of Mary and Philip Sidney—"for
else I shall never be fit for any civil society." He had
the decency to wish to "wipe out the memory of his
disgraces" by long absence. However, the fleshpots of
home seem to have settled the question for him, for
soon afterwards he appears as a member of a Christmas
house-party, and before long was thrust upon the
wealthy young daughter of Gilbert Talbot, seventh
Earl of Shrewsbury, and the granddaughter of Bess of
Hardwick, as a husband. He needed her money badly,
owing to his unceasing extravagance. He died in a
good old Elizabethan fashion "of an apoplexy, after
a full and cheerful supper." Let the memory of his
mother's nobility and their joint encouragement to the
greatest poets of their day wipe away the memory of
these things. And let us retain the benefit of the
doubt about Mary Fitton as the lady with the bold
black eyes, the dun-coloured skin, the raven hair as
harsh as black wires.

Pembroke was said to be "majestic rather than
elegant" and "full of stately gravity." His marriage
was not happy. Current opinion regarded the lady as
a much gilded pill. In swallowing her money he had
to swallow her unattractive person. This is poetic
justice. There is something quite Dantesque about
this harvest of the epicurean young courtier, who was,
as Clarendon says, so inflammable where ladies were
concerned and withal so fastidious!

CHAPTER XIII

THE FAITHFUL CHARLES

WE have dismissed as untenable the claim of William Herbert to be one of Penelope's lovers. But the claim of Charles Blount, Lord Mountjoy, increases in insistence, and with every day of the closing years of the last decade of the fifteen hundreds he grows more important to her story and that of her brother. Mountjoy is ever the man-in-waiting, biding his time for greatness and for the bringing to light the facts of his love-story. For years he had been constantly associated with Essex on military and naval service. When Queen Elizabeth wrote to scold the latter in 1597 for lack of judgment, rashness, over-presumption in his conduct of certain naval affairs, and his contempt of her unwise leniency, she took pains to accentuate her trust in Mountjoy. Part of the letter is worth quoting, because it seems like a vivid allegory of that which came to pass in connection with the downfall of the favourite of her last years.

" Eyes of youth "—so it opens—" have sharp sights, but commonly not so deep as those of elder age ; this makes me marvel at rash attempts and headstrong counsels, which give not leisure to judgment's warning, nor heeds advice, but laugh at the one and despises the last. . ."

For he has been careless over naval economy and the

manning of his ships with his "full-fed men." She goes on :

"This makes me like the lunatic man that keeps a smacker of the remains of his frenzy's freak, and makes me yield to a longer proportion than a wiser in my place would ever grant unto ; with this *caveat*, that this lunatic goodness makes you not bold. . . . Also trust not to the grace of your crazed vessel. . . . You vex me too much with small regard of what 1 bid. . . . Venture not such wonders where approachful mischief might betide you. There remains that you, after your perilous first attempt, do not aggravate that danger with another in a further off climate which must cost blows of good store. . . . Be content when you are well, which hath not ever been your property. . . . Forget not to salute with very great favour good Thomas (Lord Thomas Howard) and faithful Mountjoy."

And because Mountjoy was faithful she came in the end to prefer him as a servant—though not as a courtier—to his friend. It was extraordinary that this and Mountjoy's previously expressed distrust of his friend's generalship, which he compared unfavourably with that of Sir John Norris, did not cause an irreparable breach between the men, and that the duel of their youth found no echo in their maturity. For example, when in 1598 O'Neill, Earl of Tyrone, so disastrously defeated the Royal forces in Limerick, it was Mountjoy who was suggested as commander of the expedition to crush him. According to Camden, Essex, following up his quarrel with Elizabeth over the governorship of Ireland, as already explained, followed up this after Burleigh's death, and, after a truce—one cannot call it a peace—with his Queen, by violent protestations against this nomination. His arguments were copious, and, to a superficial observer, quite enough to make

Mountjoy his enemy for ever. He was, Essex stated, not sufficiently experienced in military affairs, nor were his private means and his connections sufficiently great for so heavy a post; moreover, he was too much of a bookman for such work. (All this on the authority of Camden.) The net result of the dispute was that the Court and Society, alike afraid of the power of Essex, were glad to get him out of the country, and so backed him in his apparent desire to secure the Deputyship for himself.

Now, this highly coloured version of an incident which led to so many great things, must be balanced by the fact that Essex showed from the outset a great dislike to undertake the post. He had continually to fight his enemies at home, and previous long absences on foreign service had worked ill for his success. It is curious that if he had been filled with an egotistical thirst to fill the Deputy's seat he should have needed Francis Bacon's written persuasion to "a service of great peril." Among the gentlemen whose names were under selection he may logically have pointed out Mountjoy as unsuitable without being actuated by any personal feeling. It has been suggested that Penelope Rich dreaded the parting with him. Hence there would be cause enough for the very strong reasons adduced, in which the personal element in Essex's reasons would, by those concerned, be treated as negligible, and not as a slur on the character of the faithful one. Moreover, Mountjoy did not seem anxious to go. Chamberlain's *Letters* show the various stages of the matter and the conditions desired by Essex.

"Oct. 20, 1598 : The state of Ireland grows deeply *di mal in peggio*. Some think the lord Mountjoy shall be sent thither Deputy; others say the Earl of Essex means to take it upon him, and hopes by his countenance to quiet that country. Marry! he would have it under the broad seal of England, that after a year he might return when he will."

"Nov. 8. It is generally held that the Earl of Essex shall go to Ireland towards the spring and Lord Mountjoy as his Deputy."

"Dec. 8. The Earl of Essex's journey to Ireland is neither fast nor loose. For ten days the soldiers flocked about him and every man hoped to be colonel at least."

"Dec. 20th. The Earl of Essex journey, that was in suspense, is now, they say, quite dashed."

"Jan. 3rd. The wind is come about again for Ireland, and the disgust that made stay of the Earl's going for awhile is sweetened and removed."

"Jan. 17th. The Queen, on Twelfth-Day, to close up the holidays, and do the Danish ambassador honour, danced with the Earl of Essex very richly and freshly attired."

After this triumphant entry difficulties crop up again; Essex is "much crossed," there are difficulties of all sorts about his commission, his Irish abode, "entertainment," and his disposal of offices under his new authority. Finally he started for Ireland on March 27th, "about 2 o'clock in the afternoon," taking horse in a lane close to Great Tower Street, "with divers noblemen and many others, himself very plainly attired, and rode through Grace Street, Cornhill, Cheapside, and other high streets in all which places and in the fields the people pressed exceedingly to behold him, especially in the highways, for more than four miles space, crying out, saying 'God bless your lordship! God preserve your Honour!' etc. And some followed him till the evening. When he and his company came forth of

P

London, the sky was very calm and clear ; but before he could get past Islington there arose a great black cloud in the N.E. and suddenly came thunder and lightning with a great shower of hail and rain, which some held an ominous prodigy." [1]

The augury made itself felt promptly as regards the Essex family. Sir Christopher Blount, the latter's step-father-in-law, seems to have incurred royal displeasure before he had reached the water's edge. He was recalled, to the great irritation of Essex. Otherwise, apparently, the affair was set afoot under flying colours. Croke declares that the army which the young Earl commanded was " the greatest and most expensive of all the expeditions which Elizabeth ever fitted out . . . and was thought sufficient to overwhelm the whole country."

With what mixed feelings of fear and pride must Lettice Blount, Lady Southampton, and Penelope Rich have watched that cavalcade start from the City lane to pass through the highways of London ! As women they certainly hated the enterprise. As kinswomen of Essex, they feared it for him and for Christopher Blount. As women of the world their hearts could not but beat high with joy and pride.

It was, after all, a very short moment of ecstasy which crowned the constant, dragging uncertainties as to the decision of the Queen and her Council of War during the past six months. Family pride was speedily enough dashed by Sir Christopher Blount's return and the depression of Essex soon after his arrival. He wrote to the Lords that since he might not appoint Blount as marshal of the army—a post for which he was singularly fitted—it were really best to send him home. "I have returned Sir Christopher Blount, whom I

---

[1] Nicholl's *Progresses.*

hoped to have carried over, for I shall have no such necessary use of his hands ; as, being barred the use of his head, I would carry him to his own disadvantage, and the disgrace of the places he should serve in."

Essex and his companions arrived in Dublin on April 15, after a terribly rough passage, and he set to work, earning hardly his experience of warfare in a new and difficult country with soldiers unaccustomed to the skirmishing tactics of the Irish. He had everything to learn at once, whilst combating physical strain and environment. "What body and mind will suffice to I will, by God's grace, discharge with industry and faith," he writes to the Privy Council. "But neither can a rheumatic body promise itself that health in a moist, rotten country, nor a sad mind, vigour and quickness in a discomfortable voyage." Yet he never stinted his effort, and out of difficulties, defeats, distresses, educed a scheme of conquest which later was to form the basis of the greatest success of Penelope's lover.

I anticipate. The war in Ireland continued, and brought a new shock upon the family party. Essex, as Lord Lieutenant, empowered to appoint his own officers, after some time chose Earl Southampton to be his Master of the Horse. The Queen, who still cherished a bitter grudge against the latter for his marriage, was furious, and cancelled the appointment. Her rage begot one of the most pathetic letters Essex ever wrote, giving his full reasons for this choice : "O miserable employment," he exclaims towards the close, "and more miserable destiny of mine, that makes it impossible for me to please and serve Her Majesty at once ! Was it treason in my Lord Southampton to marry my poor kinswoman, that neither long imprisonment nor no punishment besides that hath been usual in like cases

can satisfy or appease ; or will no kind punishment be
fit for him but that which punisheth not him, but me,
this army, and poor country of Ireland ? " The Queen
had her way, and soon after, in a similar mood, pounced
upon another appointment of a Devereux kinsman—the
young Earl of Rutland, connected with the family
through Lady Essex, by marriage with Sir Philip
Sidney's daughter.

Meanwhile Mountjoy bided his time in England,
sharing with Penelope the apprehensions about her
brother. Let us glance for a moment at the testimony
of an eye-witness, Mountjoy's secretary, Fynes Moryson,
who was associated closely with him in these years, and
who left so vivid a pen-portrait of his master that it
must be quoted at full length :

"He was tall of stature, of comely proportion ; his
skin fair ; he had very little hair on his body, it was
nearly black, thin on the head, where he wore it short,
except a lock under the left ear, which he nourished,
and being woven up, hid it in his neck under his ruff.
He only used the barber for his head ; for the hair on
his chin, cheeks, and throat, growing slowly, he used
to cut with his scissors almost daily, keeping it so low,
that it could scarce be discerned, keeping also the hairs
on his upper lip somewhat short, suffering only that
under his nether lip to grow at length and fall ; yet
some two or three years before his death, he had a very
short and sharp 'pike devant' on his chin. His fore-
head was broad and high ; his eyes great, black, and
lovely ; his nose low and short, and something blunt
at the end ; his chin round ; cheeks full, round, and
ruddy ; countenance, cheerful and amiable as ever I
beheld of any man. His arms were long, his hands
long and white, his fingers great in the end, and his
legs somewhat little, which he gartered above the knee.
His apparel in Court and city was commonly of white

From an engraving by H. T. Ryall, after a painting by Juan Pantoxa

CHARLES BLOUNT, LORD MOUNTJOY, EARL OF DEVONSHIRE

or black taffetas or satin ; he wore two, yea, sometimes three pair of silk stockings, with black silk grogram cloak, guarded, and ruff of comely depth and thickness ; black beaver hat, with plain black band ; a taffety quilted waistcoat in summer ; a scarlet waistcoat and sometimes both in winter.—In the country, and in the field, he wore jerkins and round hose ; he never wore other fashion than round, with laced panes of russet cloth, and cloak of the same, lined with velvet, and white beaver hat, with plain band ; and besides his ordinary stockings of silk, he wore under boots another pair of woollen, or worsted, with a pair of high linen boot hose.—Yea, three waistcoats in cold weather, and a thick ruff, besides a russet scarf about his neck thrice folded under it ; so as I never observed any of his age and strength to keep his body so warm. He was very comely in all his apparel ; but the robes of St. George's Order became him extraordinarily well.

" For his diet he used to fare plentifully, and of the best, so as no lord in England might compare with him in that kind of bounty. Before the war[1] he used to have nourishing breakfasts, as panadoes and broths ; but in the wars he used commonly to break his fast with a dry crust of bread, and, in the springtime, with butter and sage, with a cup of stale beer, wherewith, in winter he would have sugar and nutmeg mixed. He fed plentifully, both at dinner and supper, having the choicest and most nourishing meats, with the best wines, which he drank plentifully, but never in great excess ; in his latter years, and in the wars, he used to sleep in the afternoons, and that long upon his bed.— He took tobacco abundantly, and that of the best.— He was very neat, loving cleanliness both in apparel and diet ; and was so modest, that his most familiars never heard or saw him use any liberty out of his privy chamber, except, perhaps, in his Irish journeys, when

[1] The Irish campaign in which Mountjoy is later found playing so memorable a part.

he had no withdrawing room. His behaviour was courtly, grave, and exceeding comely."

How strikingly modern is that vision of the great man, in his person, his diet, his mien, his temperate daily habits. One wonders how "in the wars" he managed to fit in that post-prandial siesta, "and that long upon his bed." One wonders whether Essex were a smoker, and, if not, whether the fragrant weed would have calmed the storms of his soul, assisted the digestion of camp fare, and warded off his rheumatism : whether he, too, wore flannel next his skin, so to speak . . . whether he, also, always under strain, never drank to excess ! And presently the mind reverts to that rather damning accusation by Essex of Mountjoy's bookishness, supposed to hamper his military judgment and statecraft. Fynes Moryson delights in his master's high scholarship :

"Touching his studies or bookishness (by the same imputed to him in distraction of his fitness to embrace an active employment) he came young and not well grounded from Oxford University ; but in his youth at London, he so spent his vacant hours with scholars best able to direct him, as besides his reading in histories, skill in tongues (so far as he could read and understand the Italian and French, though he durst not adventure to speak them) and so much knowledge (at least in cosmography and the mathematics) as might serve his own ends : he had taken such pains in the search of natural philosophy, as in divers arguments held by him of that nature with scholars, I have often heard him (not without marvelling at his memory and judgement) to remember of himself the most material points, the subtlest objections, and the soundest answers. But his chief delight was in the study of divinity, and more especially in reading of the Fathers and the Schoolmen : and I will be bold to say, that of a layman, he was (in my judgement) the best divine I ever heard argue out of the Fathers, Schoolmen, and above all, out of the Written Word (whereof some chapters were each night read to him), besides his never intermitted prayers at morning and night."

There is a simple grace about this life which is very convincing. The man described lived evidently by an iron rule of life, but to his unswerving and temperate nature it was a régime of perfect balance and ease, no harness of metal, but a doublet as stout as the jerkin he wore in the field, yet withal as easy as that satin or taffetas upon which his choice fell for Court and City use. Had he been the twin in nature of Essex, Penelope must undoubtedly have had many hours of torture during his absences from her, and I do not suppose that Lady Essex was ever quite sure that her husband had not turned his *beaux yeux* on some Celtic darling or other. But Mountjoy was not a flirt. Again Fynes Moryson comes to our aid on this point with regard to the second Irish expedition, in which, as we shall see, Mountjoy, a year later, replaced Essex.

"Touching his affecting honour and glory, I may not omit that his most familiar friends must needs observe the discourses of the Irish actions to have been extraordinarily pleasing to him : so that howsoever he was not prone to bold discourses with ladies yet I have observed him more willingly drawn to those of this nature, which the Irish ladies entertaining in him, than unto any other. And as he had it that commendable, yea, necessary ability of a good capitain, not only to fight, and to manage well abroad, but to write and set forth his actions to the full at home, so I have seldom observed any omission of like narrations in him, whereof he used to delate the more weighty seriously, and to mention the smallest at least by way of jest."

You see by this that he was not at all insensible to sex attraction, and that there was that about the Irish ladies which specially charmed him. But he never forgot his work, he never lost his head, and his sense of humour helped to keep the balance between the big things and the little. One can well imagine his writing to Penelope, in after times, descriptions of his "entertainment" by Irish women, and all the comedy and tragedy of the weary days before he reaped the success for which Essex toiled in vain.

For a moment we must leave the "faithful Charles" and see how Essex plunged into the Irish bog of his final disaster by the conclusion of the hasty truce of September, 1599, with the rebel Earl of Tyrone.

CHAPTER XIV

THE GARBOIL

THIS word "garboil"[1] is a proper old-English noun. One meets it often in Elizabethan literature. It is used in Arber's *Garner* in connection with a seething crowd penned into a church a-fire. To me it fully embraces the whole uproar, the panic, the whirlpool into which Essex, the populace, the Court, and his own family were flung by his actions and his fate.

Directly after the six weeks truce with Tyrone was signed he went to a quiet part of Ireland "to take physic" and recruit after the strain of a hard campaign, which had only resulted in indefiniteness. Little did he know what censure was in store for him. The Queen sent him a long letter of disapproval while still unaware that he had actually concluded the treaty. She criticised the whole conduct of his negociations and showed mistrust in every line. It is small wonder that her Lord Lieutenant lost his nerve. His sense of proportion was already sapped by the hourly knowledge of the schemes, at home, of those who hated him. In vain was it for Antonio Perez to conjure him to "be constant, and conquer your enemies." To be constant in this crisis meant to stay in Ireland, watch Tyrone like a cat, keep guard and wait, withdraw from active hostility only to pounce the better on the rebels, and drive the

[1] From the French *garbouille*, a commotion, confusion, mental or physical.

campaign to an end through thick and thin directly the truce ended. This he was not wise enough to do. Instead, he hurried to England, upset by the Queen's disapproval, exaggerating the power of his enemies at Court, trusting foolishly to Tyrone's word of honour. Rowland White's description of his arrival at Nonsuch Palace, where the Queen was at the time, on Michaelmas Eve, has often been quoted. Travel-stained, breathless, after posting day and night from the coast of Wales, he burst into the Queen's presence :

"On Michaelmas-Eve, about ten o'clock in the morning, my Lord of Essex lighted at the Court gate in post and made all haste up to the presence, and so to the privy chamber, and staid not till he came to the Queen's bed-chamber, where he found the Queen newly up, the hair about her face ; he kneeled unto her, kissed her hands, and had some private speech with her ; which gave him great contentment. . . . Tis much wondered at here that he went so boldly to Her Majesty's presence, she not being ready, and he so full of dirt and mire that his very face was full of it." [1]

How different a guise from that in which he danced with his Queen at the "Twelfth Day" entertainment before the Irish journey !

The Queen's favour was but a flash of light between storm and clouds. The augury of his departure was coming true. Inside a few days the Court was divided into two parties. On his side were his old associates, including Mountjoy, and Rutland, and Mr. Comptroller —his uncle Knollys. Even the sluggish Robert Rich openly sided with him still, and was not afraid to dine at his brother-in-law's table. Against Essex were many puissant peers and lords, entertained by Burghley's suc-

[1] *Sidney Memoirs.*

cessor whom Essex deemed his sworn foe. By October 1st the Queen had formally handed him over to the Lord Keeper, and he was installed at York House, closely watched, isolated from kin and friends. It seemed at first as if this were only a temporary affair. The Queen, it seemed, looked upon him as a rather unusually naughty boy who must be kept rather longer than usual in the corner. Meanwhile his wife, who about this time gave birth to a daughter, was under her mother's care at Walsingham House, while the Southamptons and Lord and Lady Rich were housed at Essex House, which was kept open "for the family," as Rowland White explains. It was even necessary for Lady Walsingham to entreat the Queen's leave that Essex might write to his agonised and anxious wife on her sick-bed. At the beginning of October White has this entry:

"The ladies Southampton and Rich were at Essex House, but are gone to the country to shun the company that daily were wont to visit them in town, because it gave offence to the Court. His very servants are afraid to meet in any place to make merry, lest it might be ill taken. . . . At the Court my Lady Scrope is only noted to stand firm to him, for she endures much at Her Majesty's hands, because she doth daily do all the kind offices of love to the Queen in his behalf. She wears all black; she mourns and is pensive and joys in nothing but in a solitary being alone. And 'tis thought she says much that few would venture to say but herself. What the Queen will determine with him is not known, but I see little hope of any sudden liberty. My Lord Southampton and Lord Rutland came not to the Court; the one doth but very seldom; they pass the time in London merely in going to plays every day."

Matters were not improved by a conjugal quarrel between Penelope's sister, Dorothy, and her lord:

"There was a muttering of unkindness between the Earl and Countess of Northumberland, on which they were parted ; she came late last night to Essex House."

And across it drifts pathetically the baptism of the newly born :

"My Lady Essex's daughter was christened by the Earl of Southampton, the Lady Cumberland, and Lady Rutland, without much ceremony."

It was at this period of the increasing "garboil" that the Queen decided to appoint Lord Mountjoy to the Lord Deputyship of Ireland. He hung back : "The Lord Mountjoy going into Ireland grows colder every day." Small wonder ! No one could have coveted that post, least of all the friend of Essex. Anon, Penelope, working on her brother's behalf, returned to London. His wife might not go to him, but leave was granted to both his sisters "to come to Court and be suitors for him."

Again the Queen insisted upon Mountjoy's acceptance of the Irish responsibility :

"The Voice continues still that my Lord Mountjoy shall go to Ireland ; but he, as men say, will find means to stay and lay it on some other."

It was well for him that he was practically forced in the end to yield and go. It saved his head and his reputation, as events will reveal. He had everything to keep him at home, apart from his love of Penelope. Essex put the utmost reliance on him, and when formally committed to confinement placed all his affairs in his hands and those of Southampton.

Mountjoy accepted the post by the end of November, 1599, and was to start within twenty days with a fresh army of thirteen thousand men. There were, however, delays—welcome enough to one evidently so loth to take the dangerous command thrust upon him. Even the emphatic encouragement of his Queen must have seemed a poor thing. Little did he know that his apparent ill fortune was the work of his good genius, by which he could escape far greater dangers than those of war. And surely he could not have dared to believe that Elizabeth's triumphant prediction of him would be fulfilled, namely, " that it would be his fortune, and his honour, to cut the thread of that fatal rebellion, and to bring her in peace to the grave." His mind could not know much peace. All about him at Court were those who agreed with some of his best friends that literary tastes, graceful manners, and a methodical and leisurely manner of life were virtues rather civilian than military. Such, too, was the impression of the Irish nation when he reached their shores. He made no fearsome or inspiring entry into Dublin, did nothing violent or effective at the outset, and set about his task with such deliberation that Tyrone contemptuously said, " The English commander would lose the season of action whilst his breakfast was preparing." Tyrone, it must be remembered, was fresh from his triumphs over Essex and his treacherous disregard of the truce. He was strongly reinforced by Spain, both as to men and supplies, and had assumed the title of Champion of the Holy Faith, and graced his headgear " with a plume made out of the feathers of a Phœnix," hallowed and presented by the Pope !

The financial arrangements consequent on the additional force for the new Lord Lieutenant delayed the

departure of Mountjoy till well into February, 1600.
This gave Essex plenty of time for plans of the most
audacious kind. The two friends were in constant
communication. How much Lady Rich knew about
their correspondence it is hard to tell. She was at least
actively engaged in securing less rigorous treatment for
her brother. She probably was aware of Essex's wild
suggestion that Mountjoy, on arrival in Ireland, should
annex the Royal army, invite the co-operation of James
of Scotland, bear down upon England, free the Earl,
and crush the Privy Council.

Mountjoy, once overseas, assumed greater prudence.
He washed his hands of all such matters. There was
work enough to do, all the loose threads of Essex's
unfinished task to gather up, and not a moment
to lose, for the faithlessness of Tyrone turned everything to the disadvantage of the English. One mar-
vels again and again at the steadiness and com-
posure even of a man so grave and controlled under
such conditions. Loving order, he found nothing
but appalling disorder ; hating unbridled emotions and
all things crude, he was plunged into the crudest,
roughest kind of warfare, obliged to employ tactics as
against savages. His personality sketched by Fynes
Moryson stands out at this juncture like a fine etching
against a lurid background. In Ireland, assuredly, was
there sufficient of a garboil without the complexity
added by Essex's affair at home or the stupendous
shock Mountjoy received shortly, when he heard of his
friend's formal arrest at York House, and the bristling
array of accusations, prepared by Francis Bacon, which
Essex must face. Had Mountjoy not been Mountjoy,
here certainly was the correct moment for panic, for a
repetition of the hasty rush of Essex from Ireland to

Court. But the faithful Charles stayed, as we know, at his post, and could, even under the greatest stress, shunt everything connected with all garboils and such things, courting sleep, as Fynes Moryson tells us, of an afternoon.

Lady Rich laboured incessantly, Essex in confinement wrote constant letters, extravagant, piteous, pathetic, humble, to his Queen. Lady Rich wrote also. Her special letter to the Queen, shall be quoted presently. As for poor Lady Essex, she hung about the Court in mourning :

" My Lady of Essex is a most sorrowful creature for her husband's captivity ; she wears all black of the meanest price, and receives no comfort in anything. . . . All she wore was not valued at £5. She came to the Countess of Huntingdon's chamber, who came not to her ; but by a second means her desire was made known, that she would have Her Majesty to give her leave to go and see the Earl of Essex, who, she heard, the night before had been in great extremity. Answer was returned, she must attend Her Majesty's pleasure by the Lords of the Council, and come no more to Court. The Earl of Essex is extreme ill of the stone, stranguillon and grinding of the kidneys, which takes from him his stomach and his rest."

Again wrote White to Sir Robert Sidney :

" Your Lordship, peradventure may hear from others of my Lord of Essex's weakness ; upon Wednesday it was said he was dead ; the Bell tolled for him. He was prayed for in London Churches, Divines watch in the night, and in their pulpits pray for him. . . . My Lady Rich was at Court upon Thursday ; her Majesty spake with her and used her very graciously. Her humble suit was to have leave to see her Ladyship's brother before he died ; that it did concern her about the matters of her jointure ; but I do not hear that she had leave to go ; for the same suit my Lady Northumberland makes.   My Lady of Essex is with him every day from morning to night, and then returns to Walsingham H^{se}. Mr. Controller (Sir William Knollys) had leave to go to him.   His friends do very much fear he cannot live out the month."

In the centre of the turmoil was the Queen, furious with everyone connected with Essex, angry even with his strongest opponent, Robert Cecil, because, forsooth, he happened at the moment to wish to take unto him a wife.   Her own godson, Sir John Harrington, lately returned from the distressful country, asked for an audience and tendered the Irish journal he had kept by command.

"She chafed much," he tells us, "walked fastly to and fro, looked with discomposure in her visage, and I remember, catched at my girdle when I kneeled to her, and swore 'By God's son, I am no queen.   That man is above me.   Who gave him command to come here so soon ?   I did send him on other business.'"

She bade him begone ; he obeyed promptly.   And when she had read his journal she " swore they were all Irish knaves and the Lord Deputy worse."

To and fro the pendulum swung in the Earl's favour. The people believed in him, popular divines offered prayers for him and preached loudly in his favour. "Pamphlets," says Devereux, " were found on the walls and scattered about the chambers of the palace, lauding him and libelling his supposed enemies.   Wild sayings in his praise were even scrawled on the panels."   This caused a special meeting of the Star Chamber, at which the accusations against the Earl were enumerated and those who interfered in the matter or showed either

From a photo by Emery Walker, after a painting in the National Portrait Gallery attributed to F. Zuccaro

QUEEN ELIZABETH

partisanship or the reverse threatened with penalty. Essex, physically, was in such sorry case, that Elizabeth not only yielded to the prayers of Lady Essex, henceforward permitted to spend from 7 a.m. till 6 p.m. at York house, but ordered a consultation of eight of her chief doctors, on their advice ordered his condition to be improved in regard to fresh air and exercise, and sent him "some broth" by the hand of a physician. Moreover, she actually visited him, in strict secrecy, accompanied by Lady Warwick, his aunt by marriage, and the Earl of Worcester. Lord Rich does not seem to have been of much use just now. "My Lord Rich deals badly with me," wrote a servant of Essex to a correspondent in the country. But Lady Leicester bestirred herself in the shape of a handsome New Year's gift, and Rowland White's news improves :

January 5, 1599.

"Her Majesty is in very good health, and comes very much abroad these holidays ; for almost every night she is in the Presence, to see the Ladies dance the old and new country dances, with the tabor and the pipe. Here was an exceeding rich New Year's gift presented, which came as it were in a Cloud, no man knows how ; which is neither received or rejected ; and is in the hands of the Controller. It comes from the poor Earl, the downfall of fortune as it is thought. His friends do hope that he shall be removed to his own house or to Mr. Controller's. He begins to recover, for he is able to sit up and to eat at a table. His Lady comes every morning unto him by 7 and stays till 6, which is said to be the full time limited for her abode there. The Ladies his sisters, my Lady Walsingham, nor his son have no liberty to go and see him as yet. Many ministers that made public prayers for him in their Churches are commanded to silence, some indeed foolishly forgetting

Q

themselves; their doubtful opinions tending to sedition."

If Penelope had now restrained herself and not written the following extravagant letter, all would have gone smoothly for a time at least :

(My Lady Rich to the Queen).

"Early did I hope this morning to have had mine eyes blessed with your majesty's beauties, but seeing the same depart into a cloud and meeting with spirits which did presage by the wheels of their chariots some thunders in the air, I must complain and express my fears to that high majesty and divine ORACLE from whence I received a doubtful answer, into whose power I must sacrifice again the tears and prayers of the afflicted that must despair in time if it be too late to importune Heaven when we feel the miseries of Hell or that word directed to your sacred wisdom should out of season be delivered, for my unfortunate brother, whom all men have liberty to defame as if his offence were capital and he so base dejected a creature that his love, his life, his service to your beauties and the State had deserved no absolution after so hard prisonment or so much as to answer in your sacred presence, who would vouchsafe more justice and favour than he can expect of partial judges, or those combined enemies that labour upon false grounds to build his ruin, urging his faults as criminal to your Divine honour, thinking it a heaven to blaspheme heaven, when their own particular malice and counsel have practised only to glut themselves in their own private revenge, not regarding your service or loss so much as their ambitious ends to rise by his overthrow, and I have reason to apprehend that if your fair hands do not check the course of their unbridled hate, that the last course will be his last breath, since the evil instruments which by their officious cunning provide for the feast, have sufficient

poison in their hearts to infect : the service they will
serve shall be easy to digest till it be tasted, and then it
will prove a preparative of great mischief, concealed
among such restive workmen as will not only pull down
all the obstacles of their greatness, but when they are
in their full strength like the giants make war
against heaven. But your Majesty's gracious conclusion in giving hope of a voider, is all the comfort
I have, which, if you hasten not before he take a full
surfeit of disgrace, they will say the spots they have
laid upon him are too foul to be washed away, and so
his blemished reputation must disable him for ever
serving against his sacred Goddess, whose excellent
beauties and perfections will never suffer those fair eyes
to return so far from compassion, but at the least that
if he may not return to the happiness of his former
service, to live at the feet of his admired mistress, yet
he may set down in private life, without the imputation
of infamy : that his posterity may not repent their
fathers were borne of so hard destinies, two of them
perishing by being employed in one Country, where
they would have done you service to the shedding of
their last blood, if they had not been wounded to death
behind by faction, that care not on whose neck they
unjustly build the walls of their own fortune, which
I fear will grow more dangerously high than is yet discovered if God does not hinder the work as the Tower
of Babel, and confound their tongues that understand
one another too well. And lastly since out of your
majesty's own princely nature and unstained virtue
there must needs appear that virtue is not far from
such a beauty, I must humbly beseech you make it
your own work and not to suffer those to take advantage that lie in ambush thinking so soon as they
discover a relenting and compassion in your worthy
mind, to take the honour upon them as means of our
salvation, not out of Charity but pride, that all must
be attributed to them and your sacred clemency abused

by forcing us to go through purgatory to heaven.   But
let your majesty's divine power be no more eclipsed
than your beauty which hath shined throughout all the
world, and imitate the highest in not destroying those
that trust only in your mercy, with which humble
request I presume to kiss your sacred hands vowing
the obedience and endless Love of

"Your majesty's most dutiful and Loyal Servant,
                                              "P. R." [1]

To which the writer afterwards added this ungram-
matical statement :—

"This letter being showed at the Council table, and
willed to make exposition thereof and what she meant
by it, I answered presently what I meant I wrote, and
what I wrote, I meant.   "P. R."

It must be remembered that during the whole of this
time Penelope had not gained permission even to visit
her own brother for a moment.   The frenzied fantasy
of this letter is therefore the more excusable.   The
Queen evidently mistrusted her influence, wherefore
her increased anger over the letter is intelligible.   It
was above all a bad moment for the delivery of such
an epistle.   Essex, in the beginning of February, 1600,
was at last to face the Star Chamber.   Robert Cecil
induced him to write a letter of submission to the
sovereign, a letter so effectual that official proceedings
consequently hung fire.   His friends were now in high
hopes of his release, when busybodies interposed.   It
came to Elizabeth's ears that the general opinion was
that the Council had been forced to abandon the inquiry
because it found no sure grounds for the accusation.
There was truth enough in this to raise anger on her
part.   She would never acknowledge such a mistake.

[1] Birch's *Elizabeth*, Vol. II.

The bare suggestion that such a notion was public talk hardened her to flint. Her rod descended on the family. Lady Essex's daily visits to York House were shortened from eleven to seven hours. Lady Leicester, the Southamptons, and other friends, who were in the habit now of frequenting a neighbouring house, from the windows of which they could see the Earl walk in the garden of York House, were snubbed and placed under a cloud, and Penelope was turned into a polite prisoner in her own mansion. From this isolation she might not venture except when summoned before the Council to give account of her letter. She at first excused herself on the ground of indisposition, only deferring the evil day of account. Is it marvellous that Chamberlain[1] records the fact that " My Lord of Essex hath been somewhat crazy this week " ?

At the beginning of March the family party were turned out of Essex House in order that the Earl might be confined under his own roof. For some time Lady Essex alone was admitted in the day time, but, later, also his mother. He played tennis, walked on the leads, tried to distract himself with books and his wife's companionship, and, morbidly sensitive, distracted by his situation, deluged the Queen with protestations of innocence and appeals for mercy :

"The prating tavern haunter," he wrote in one of his letters to her, "speaks of me what he lists; the frantic libeller writes of me what he lists; already they print me and make me speak to the world, and shortly they will play me in what forms they list upon the stage. The least of these is a thousand times worse than death. But this is not the worst of my destiny, for your Majesty, that hath mercy for all the world but me . . .

---

[1] Letter to Dudley Carleton.

and never repented of any gracious assurance you had given till now, your Majesty, I say, hath now in the eighth month of my close imprisonment, as if you thought mine infirmities, beggary, and infamy too little punishment, rejected my letters, and refused to hear of me, which to traitors you never did.   What therefore remaineth to me?   Only this, to beseech your Majesty on the knees of my heart, to conclude my punishment, my misery and my life all together, that I may go to my Saviour, who hath paid himself a ransom for me, and whom, methinks, I still hear calling me out of this un-kind world, in which I have lived too long, and ever thought myself too happy.   From your Majesty's humblest vassal,   Essex."

The rest of the story is a succession of tragedies. First there is the sour fact to swallow that the man instruc-ted to draw up the case against the prisoner was no other than Francis Bacon, recipient of his favours, bounty, friendship; that he might have evaded the sorry business by declining to serve in this matter, and did not.   Then there is that sensational signal of the public degradation of a great gentleman upon his appearance before the curious, special tribunal at York House, when not one of the eighteen peers, knights, legal barons, and judges facing him "stirred cap, or gave any sign of courtesy"; when, in their presence and that of an audience of two hundred distinguished professional men, he knelt on the floor for a long time, till one of judges, the premier Archbishop, suggested that his knees should be spared by the loan of a cushion.   Later on he was permitted to stand and eventually sit, but not till he had suffered the biting attacks of the Attorney General, faced the five main charges against him, and heard the name of his favourite sister severely denounced. After that Francis Bacon took up the tale and brought forward other details of the charge. The five points were : deliberate appointment of Earl Southampton as master of the horse in Ireland, against the Queen's wish; his creation of too many knights on the campaign ; his undignified manner of negociation with Tyrone, to whom he had extended the deference due only to an equal.of the Queen, by which he exposed himself to suspicion, and of which the result was "shameful"; that in place of pursuit of Tyrone at a critical moment he directed the course of his campaign into another part of the country ; that he returned to England without per-. mission, leaving his army to shift during his absence "like a shepherd leaving his flock to the care of a dog." As for Penelope's offending letter, it was condemned as "insolent, saucy, and malapert, . . . an aggravation of the offence."

Her ladyship is said, according to State MSS., to have "stolen into the country" at this time, after a second summons to explain her "malapert" document. It must be added that she had written again to Elizabeth, "but in other kind of language." Unfortunately, the contents of the first letter got abroad. The Earl of Essex wrote an "apology"—whether an apology for his sister's appeal or an extenuation of his own actions is not clear. At all events, this "apology," with Lady Rich's letter, was printed, "not," says a contemporary "from friendship or faction, but hope of gain." This was undoubtedly the work of a hawker of society secrets. "A few were sold, but it was soon suppressed," the State Papers record. "My Lady Rich will have the worst of it, as she has been sent for to interpret her riddles, and is come," witnesses a further entry in the Sidney papers.

At the time of this statement it was the end of May, and the inquiry at York House took place soon after, in the first week of June, 1600.   The upshot of it was that Essex was condemned to stay in his present confinement during the Queen's pleasure.   This much leniency was, however, accorded him: the knight in surveillance over him was removed, and he had within his own walls more ease and liberty.   The Queen, nevertheless, lost no opportunity of showing her disapproval by degrading his newly made Irish knights, and in every way belittling his recent activities.

Ague seized him.   He begged for leave to seek repose in the country under the roof of a relative.   In August came the joyful news of his liberty—a qualified liberty.   He must not come to Court, he must not approach his Queen, for he was still under her ban.   So he went in early autumn to Ewelme Lodge, the property of his uncle, Sir William Knollys, while Lady Rich was also permitted to walk abroad in the full enjoyment of liberty as a private lady.

Grateful enough was she, undoubtedly, for release, and well enough it befell that Lord Rich was taken dangerously ill at this crisis.   His death would have given her immunity from all her private troubles.   But she had no desire to hasten it.   She went straight to Leighs and nursed him back to life.   Nor should her action in going and his in receiving her after so many years of virtual separation supply food for satire.   He was rather a helpless person it is true.   Yet he was not anxious to die.   He had means and fine children, and though he knew full well that he had never captured his lady, he still retained a legal right over her. Various commentators have taken the point of view that he should have now repudiated her, if he was ever going to do so.   Such an idea is not " in the part," so to speak. Does a man at the point of death rouse himself to turn such a woman out of doors ?   Above all, would a Robert Rich act thus ?   The suggestion throws a horrid slur on the action of Penelope. She could not, as she doubtless longed to do, join the party at Ewelme Lodge.   This would at once give the impression of a family plot. She might have withdrawn anywhere into the country with Lady Southampton.   Here again it might be unwise. This Earl had been peremptorily ordered to join Mount-joy in Ireland. Knowing what she knew about the wild proposals of Essex in regard to these two, and the possibility of assistance from over the Border, this was certainly the moment to keep clear of the always unpopular Southampton until her assistance should be needed—if ever.   There was one alternative : she might go to her mother—but Sir Christopher Blount's recent recall again produced a not particularly happy atmosphere in the home of the poor ex-Lady Leicester, and any scandalous tongue might turn a visit there to Penelope's disadvantage.   No painfulness or public misunderstanding could attach to Leighs, especially under the circumstances.

CHAPTER XV

THE END OF "SWEET ROBIN"

ESSEX and his family are scattered in the country places. Mountjoy is in Ireland, my Lord Rich convalescent, for Penelope has saved his life. Let us go back some years and read a part of a letter written by Thomas Fowler in Edinburgh to Lord Burghley as far back as 1589, when Essex and his sister were evidently desirous to court the goodwill of James I betimes. Nicknames and cyphers, it must be understood, were the order of the day. The former were employed both in fun and earnest—in this case surely the last, for Burghley had his spies of all degrees and nationalities in every quarter and in every court.

"Your Lordship may be pleased to know that I learn that Mr. Richard Douglas, coming last from London, brought down one Ottoman (Robert Dale). The said Mr. Richard . . . himself delivered a letter from the Earl of Essex to His Majesty, with credit : both these (gentlemen) were in commission from the Earl to deal largely with His Majesty, to assure him of the Earl's service and fidelity, and Ottoman to carry back the answer, what was not meet to be committed in writing. He had a letter from this king back again to the Earl besides this. These two had to deal with the King for the like assurance of Ricardo (Lord Rich) and lady, but no writings from the lord, yet two several letters from Ryalta (Lady Rich) written to Mr. Richard Douglas,

whereby she remembers him of his charge for his friends,
and a nickname for everyone that is partaker in the
matter ; whereof the said Mr. Richard hath a long scroll
as an alphabet of cipher to understand them by.   I can
tell few of their names, but the Queen's Majesty is
Venus, and the Earl (Essex) the Weary Knight, as I
remember, but always that he is exceedingly weary,
accounting it a thrall that he lives now in, and wishes
the change.   She is very pleasant in her letters, and
writes the most part thereof in her brother's behalf, so
as they should be showed to Victor (the King), which
they were ; and the dark parts thereof expounded to
him.   He commended much the fineness of her wit,
the invention, and well writing.   For the more assurance, Mr. Douglas took back from the King both the
Earl's letters to him, and Ryalta's to himself.   The said
Ottoman had many secret conferences with the King,
which pleased him exceedingly ; and Mr. Douglas won
credit where before he had none : but I trow some of
them went too far in persuading the poor King to hope
for help shortly, and that Her Majesty could not live
above a year or two, by reason of some imperfection,
I know not what.   Ryalta writes almost every week to
Mr. Richard . . . all in their own devised terms : but
Mr. Richard hath not so much credit with the King
but he would fain have my help in these matters.
Whereupon he told me that the Earl of Essex and all
his friends would be mine in anything I had to do.
Ryalta especially would be so, and had willed him to
assure me of it, and needs he must have me write some
few words of thanks, that she might know he had done
her message, which I did ;   And he sent it, and received a letter from her to me in a short time, which
letter contains but courteous promise of her friendship
and the Earl's, when I will in particular let them know
how they may stand me in stead, and a postscript how
much Mr. Richard Douglas loves me.   This is all I
know of this matter : but this day Mr. Richard showed

the King two of her letters and expounded them. I am no further trusted in these matters, but in general terms by Mr. Richard, how much the Earl loves the King and honours him, and would fain the King were so persuaded thoroughly. I have not showed myself willing to deal in any of those matters, because I told Mr. Richard they were not secret in this country. Now have I written to your Lordship of this, that though it be no matter of great importance, yet that you shall not be ignorant of anything that is handling here : and yet if it should be discovered at least if I were the actor, it would be my great trouble and danger of life ; and sure if it be taken knowledge of there, at least a good whiles, it will be thought to come from me. To avoid these I commit it only to your Lordship, and write thereof to no living creature but yourself, nor will ; and I shall long to know that your Lordship hath received it safely."[1]

A month later Fowler once more has news of the Rich couple. A certain Roger Dalton, he says, has had secret conference several times with "Victor" (King James. He had a commission from "Ryalta" and "Ricardo," and has brought with him the lady's picture as an offering to the King. Roger Dale's companion, one Constable, who has brought the picture, has been well received by James and "would have had Victor write to Ryalta, but he could not bring it to pass, for Victor was troubled otherways."

By these extracts it is plain that when service under Elizabeth became dangerous, difficult, and insupportable, Essex and his friends looked with eagerness to the possibilities of relief which might come with a new sovereign. The Queen, despite her daily galliards, her sublime disregard of her increasing years, her love of compliments to her beauty, was marching visibly into

---

[1] Murdin's *State Papers.*

senility. To the general public she was still a great
Queen. Here and there an eye-witness breaks forth
into praise and loyalty. We have glimpses in history
of pedestrians who suddenly come upon her as she goes
to Court by torch-light, and the emotions excited by the
sudden vision of her in her jewels and splendour. But
for all that, her wrinkles and decrepitude could not be
hidden. " In her old age," testifies one who saw her,
" she had a goggle throat, a great gullet hanging out, as
her grandfather, Henry VII, is ever painted withal. . . .
And truly there was there a report that the ladies had,
gotten false looking-glasses that the Queen might not
see her own wrinkles." This sad little farce must be
played to the finish, while all about her knew that the
days of change were not very far off. All these considerations prompted the emotions which surged to
high tide in the mind of Essex when he propounded
the aforementioned plan of his rescue to Mountjoy in
combination with Scottish reinforcements.

Less risky were the alternatives suggested—that he
should escape to France and live in voluntary exile, that
he should summon the aid of friends in Wales, that he
should by a bold stroke go to Court, dominate it, and
gain the Queen's presence at last by sheer determination.
His friends were unanimous as to the wisdom of flight,
and Southampton and Sir Henry Danvers were ready to
accompany him and sacrifice their lives and fortunes as
his comrades. This prospect of exile, this fall from
greatness to poverty and unimportance Essex could not
stomach. His pride was still too great, his spirit too
untameable. As regards the Scottish matter, negotiations
on the part of himself and Mountjoy were warily in-
stituted. The latter sent an emissary North to exoner-
ate Essex from the treasonable and ambitious scheme

attributed to him—i.e. his object to claim the crown for himself as Elizabeth's successor—and to declare that the Earl's desire was to see James named as her heir in her lifetime.

When Mountjoy later was ordered to Ireland it occurred to both of them that in the event of a sudden change of sovereign at this time, the fortunes of Essex were likely to remain in abeyance for ever. Once more, therefore, the two worked to secure the support of the Scottish King. This time the suggestion was far bolder. James was to attack Elizabeth as to the succession problem, while Essex and his supporters worked on his behalf, and Mountjoy, leaving Ireland sufficiently guarded, should back up the Scottish King with a force numbering between four and five thousand. When Southampton joined Mountjoy in Ireland he carried an additional suggestion from Essex. The new Lord Deputy was now to go straight over with the above force to Wales, whence, of course, it would be far easier to menace Queen and Court. Mountjoy—as we know—refused. He was not sure of James's approval and co-operation. Without them he would risk nothing. Nor did he deem it necessary to stake so much while Essex, though in disgrace, was no longer a prisoner of state in danger of his life.

Presently Southampton returned from Ireland and went temporarily to the Netherlands while Essex turned an ear to evil counsellors. Once more he appealed to Mountjoy and was refused. Officially the latter would do nothing. His aid must he postponed till the campaign was over and he could interest himself as a private individual in the restoration and rehabilitation of the Earl. Essex did not wait for his reply or his recommendations to patience and caution. He sent an agent to King James inciting him to press his demands upon Elizabeth.

All caution was now cast to the winds, while Essex House, to which its owner now returned for the winter, became the true centre of the renewed "garboil." And now the ineradicable essence of Essex shows itself. He was too obstinate to try and co-operate with Robert Cecil, but deliberately misunderstood him, and so cut himself adrift from a group which might have saved him. Brewer, in his *English Studies*, has drawn his personality in a paragraph. He is shown " now quarrelling with his best friends for some trifle light as air, now opening his heart to his most dangerous enemies. Now the saddest soul on earth, sighing, sorrowing, languishing, wishing to die because he had offended his sovereign, and the next moment guilty of the most unpardonable rudeness. Now for all Puritan sermons, exercises, and devotions, then indulging in the profanest oaths, or intriguing with Miss Southwell or Miss Brydges—the gayest Lothario at the Court." All this was over, however. No more is he the masquerader playing several parts at once badly, but just his own part. His heritage of royal blood, his native high-handedness, his impetuosity, his imperious determination to assert himself through thick and thin, took possession of him. The last scrap of caution was thrown overboard. And on the great tidal wave of his final revolt he carried with him his too faithful friends. One sees it gather, approach, and rise to a threatening and awful crest like a *mascaret* on the Seine in autumn ; and on the crest rode Penelope Rich, now the genius of sensation and intrigue.

The doors of the Essex House were flung open, open hall was kept, access accorded to every kind of person, important or unimportant, with revolutionary principles. Once more the discontented divines had their fingers in the broth. Discourses were permitted, popular preachers held forth to large audiences. There does not seem to have been at the outset any distinct idea of preaching revolt, but the Puritan clergy who were daily welcomed under the Earl's roof were born reformers and republicans. One of them, as least, abused his opportunities and the hospitality of Essex grossly, by accentuating within those walls the fact that under the Constitution, as it was, the judges of the kingdom had the prerogative of controlling the powers of the Throne.

We pass on to the beginning of January, 1601, to find the more important adherents of Essex, composed of earls, barons, knights, gentlemen, were 120 in number, and that the Earl of Southampton, freshly returned from Holland, followed his friend's lead by holding meetings at his own residence, Drury House.[1] A committee was formed, and Essex's final choice—a plan for the seizure of the Court and the Presence—was carefully mapped out. Sir Christopher Blount was to seize the outer gate of the Palace, Sir Charles Danvers the Guard Chamber and Presence Chamber, Sir John Davis the Great Hall. Meanwhile the Earl, who was to take up his position in the Royal Mews, could make his way unmolested to the Queen, beg her to remove his enemies from her entourage, and summon a Parliament to consider his case.

During this time, it must be noted, King James, quite eager to assert his own cause, was dealing amiably with Essex's last proposal to him, that is to say, the Earl of Mar and Bruce of Kinloss were instructed to travel to England with the demand about the succession.

---

[1] On the site of which now stands the Olympic Theatre.

Essex seems to have been perfectly reckless as regards the possibility of spies, and everything apparently favoured his audacious intentions. The Scottish ambassadors might arrive at any moment, and Court and legal authorities seemed to be quiescent.

Suddenly the Privy Council sent for the Earl. The reason given was that in view of his unwise emergence from obscurity, and his entertainment of persons not altogether reputable, he needed reprimand, and must no longer abuse his private liberty. This was undoubtedly a great shock, but he was not to fall yet into the snare he had laid for himself. He pleaded illness, and disobeyed the command. Directly afterwards, on the strength of an anonymous letter, warning him of immediate danger, he held a council of war and decided to strike the first blow.

Originally, it will be remembered, on reference to facts, he had thought of seizing the Tower as the stronghold of the City, before proceeding to dominate the Court, and only abandoned this first notion because it was decided that the City was distinctly in his favour, and the stroke would therefore be unnecessary. In that frenzied last council at Essex House three possibilities were discussed : flight—thrust aside as contemptible and impossible ; the seizure of the Palace alone ; an appeal for support to the City. Fate and an evil counsellor, who can only have been a spy in disguise, cast the die for the last-named course. A messenger, ostensibly from the City, came to promise all assistance, with the support of a foremost sheriff and a thousand men of the trained bands.

Essex told everyone that Lord Cobham and Sir Walter Ralegh sought his life, and that it behoved him, therefore, to strike first in self-defence. On the Sunday

R

morning fixed for action his associates poured in steadily, till three hundred men were crowded into Essex House. Foremost among them were Lords Rutland and South-ampton. In a few moments, with two hundred of these, he was to enter the City, timing his arrival at Paul's Cross just before the end of the sermon, directly after the conclusion of which he would declare his intentions to the aldermen and Common Council, and demand their aid. If they joined him, the way to the Palace was easy ; if not, flight to some distant part of the country was the only alternative. It wanted but a minute to the time of starting, to the opening of the great gates of Essex House, till now tightly closed upon the outside world.

The Queen struck first. At ten o'clock four "great officers" of the realm knocked for admittance. The gates were not opened, but after a time a small wicket admitted the four, shutting out the servants who attended them. State papers have given the rest in detail, too long to include here. Within the gate, as we know, was tumult enough. The Lord Keeper inquired the cause of it, promising redress for all grievances. Essex, "with a very loud voice, declared that his life was sought, and that he should have been murdered in his bed ; that his hand had been counterfeited, and letters written in his name ; therefore they were assembled there to defend their lives."

The Lord Keeper answered suavely, the Earl's men clamoured to him to fly: "They abuse you, they betray you, they undo you! You lose time!" Again the Lord Keeper threw oil on troubled waters. Adroitly he conjured the company to allegiance, artfully he con-trived to followed Essex indoors under the plea of quiet discussion. Whether this would ever have led to peace one does not know, for hotheads in the crowd again shouted fear and treason in their leader's ear. " Let us shop them up ! " was the universal cry. The four officials followed the Earl to his " back chamber." Here he left them, postponing discussion, truly " shopped up," under the guard of three of his gentlemen, armed with muskets, till four o'clock in the afternoon.

And still the heated brain of the " Weary Knight " pursued his mad scheme. While his unwelcome visitors were under guard, he, at the head of his two hundred, rode to Paul's Cross, as arranged. Neither sermon nor gaping and sympathetic crowd was there to greet him. The Queen, who now sat grimly behind barricades, closed and fortified gates, in a royal building whose corridors and ways were blocked with chains, even with carriages, in the expectation of attack, had long since stopped the preaching of that particular Sunday's sermon !

Down the City streets Essex rode, shouting out his cause in the Queen's name, appealing to all possible sympathisers, stared at by the curious, shunned by the timorous, dogged by the Queen's heralds, who, in various quarters of the City, were busily proclaiming him a traitor. Even the sheriff on whose help he had relied would not face him, and fled through the back door of his own house. The Masquerader was driven back at last, late in the afternoon, upon his own house, after a skirmish with the Crown Officers, in which one of his friends was killed, Sir Christopher Blount wounded and taken prisoner, and the Earl himself shot through the hat. His intention now was to tender his submission and make a great fight for acquittal.

Once more the drama plays itself out in Essex House. It was thought in Whitehall that Essex would turn his roof into a stronghold. Orders were consequently given to surround and attack it before it could be fortified. All this while, we must remember, Lady Essex and Lady Rich were in the house. The former could not have enjoyed the terrible strain of the days which preceded this black Sunday. Penelope, on the other hand, has been likened by one of Essex's chroniclers to a bird of storm, hovering over the gathering and deepening struggle. It was afterwards shown that she was not the moving spirit in his wild plans of rebellion, yet it is impossible to say at this juncture how far she assisted him in their execution. She assuredly could wish him nothing but success; she would hearten rather than depress the always troubled Lady Essex at such a tremendous moment. Penelope certainly had the courage and energy to steal out and rally whomsoever she could to her brother's assistance. Her boldness is amazing. Later on, when many were brought to account for their supposed share in the affair, the statement of the Earl of Bedford flashes a light on her activity. This testimony is headed :

" *Earl of Bedford to the Lords of the Council from Alderman Holroyd's house with a declaration of how he did demean himself on Sunday, 8th February.* (1601.)

" That after ten o'clock prayers and sermon began the Lady Rich did come to his house and told him how the Earl of Essex did desire to speak with him, upon which he went with her in her coach, none of the family following him out of the Sermon Room, and he going unknown to his family."

About eleven o'clock the two reached Essex House, and the Earl, after finding out the state of things, extricated himself cleverly, went back to his house, got together a troop of horse, and " went towards the Court for her Majesty's service." Wherefore the poor, toiling Penelope might have spared her pains !

Inside the house we see once more the Earl and those who yet clove to him, splashed and perspiring, their clothing torn and disarranged after the foolish ride and the puerile fray in the City. The Earl had barely time for a change of shirt, for he was busy tearing up his private papers, which included "a history of his troubles," while the women looked forth from the windows to see earls, admirals, lords, and knights clustered "on the landside, on the riverside," and even in the garden, sacred to many happy and anxious hours.

Presently news of a summons rang through the house. Sir Robert Sidney (he could not have liked this mission!) came with a message requesting the besieged to yield.

In reply Essex sent Southampton, who called satirically from the roof, asking to whom the little garrison should yield. To surrender to their enemies, he pointed out, spelt perdition; to yield to the Queen amounted to a confession of treason. The only surrender possible was on condition of hostages for their safety from the Lord Admiral, who was stationed in the garden. Armed with these Essex and his company would present themselves before the Queen; otherwise it would be better to die fighting.

Robert Sidney carried the message and returned with the ultimatum to the besieged: one hour's truce to allow of the removal of the ladies in the house, and no hostages or terms for the rest.

A hurried gathering together of feminine belongings that! Coffers must be stuffed, necessaries collected in sixty minutes, a hard enough matter in those days of great farthingales and wide ruffs when your head was clear, your heart at peace, and you were only troubled by the all-too-much of your wardrobe when it came to compression into boxes. But to pack with your head and heart on edge with terror within a house which is on the eve of assault—that was an affair indeed! Up to the moment of going the women could not tell the result of the negociations. Later they would learn fast enough of Essex's irresolution, his first intention to rush out and brave the swords of the men outside, his subsequent parley asking for modified conditions in view of his surrender—a lawful hearing of his cause, a fair trial, the ministration of his private chaplain. These were conceded, and he went to the Tower, with Southampton, Rutland, Sir Charles Danvers and others. Christopher Blount was already under arrest; the remainder of their followers were clapped in various City prisons.

It was eleven days later that the great trial began, and in a roll-call of Earls, Viscounts, and Barons which preceded the indictment; Robert Rich was present to answer to his name. Out of the actual "garboil," by some wonderful luck and by his own caution, he had kept himself. But his wife, naturally, was under surveillance; State papers, in the list of persons imprisoned or detained by the law, include her name, and show that she was isolated and confined to a private house other than her own. If this seems harsh treatment it must be remembered that her constant presence at Essex House had been patent to all, and that on the night when Essex received and shirked that last summons to the Council before his revolt, the house party, chiefly of men, at the supper-table, included her. Lady Southampton, like Lord Rich, seems to have been out of the business altogether, though her brother Robert Vernon was a guest on this occasion.

The great trial went forward. The main proceedings occupied eleven hours. The examination of the associates of the Earl caused him shock after shock. Each confession incriminated him more deeply. He was condemned to death with several others, and awaited his fate in prison. Then began the worst bit of work in the whole affair. He might be reprieved, he might be put to death. No one seemed quite sure. No one knew whether the Queen, at the last moment, could bear to sign the black warrant. But his life, while it lasted, was useful. He might prove a mine of valuable information to successive interrogators. The Council, with fiendish ingenuity, set his own chaplain, Ashton, at the task. Essex believed in him, had prepared for the worst, and particularly desired his companionship and godly counsel. Ashton worked upon his feelings with reproach and appeal, called upon him to make fuller confession of his misdemeanours and to unburden his soul of all details, including the names of all friends who had worked with him at any time. Overwrought and strained, he finally yielded, and his additional statements incriminated Penelope's lover. It was a weak, crazed move, which could not improve his case in any way. It was cowardly, it was human, it was intelligible, even excusable. He might have instanced Mountjoy's share in his schemes as regards Scotland merely to accentuate the fact that, as he had repeatedly explained already, he himself had no ambitions to the Throne, but was frankly anxious, like Mountjoy, to see the succession problem ended. He might argue privately in excuse that if Mountjoy, who had shared his own emotions under disgrace and unjust disfavour, yet kept his great position at the head of the army overseas without impugnment, with unassailable integrity, the fact of his ultimate refusals to assist Essex would counterbalance all earlier participation and acquit him in the Queen's mind.

Upon Mountjoy these statements entangling his reputation fell like a thunderbolt. Of all the dire events which engulfed Essex and Penelope the Irish Lord Deputy had full details, and of all the despatches which crowded his table in camp a communication from Earl Nottingham, Lord High Admiral, appears to be the most disconcerting. Nottingham knew all the parties concerned, and as an eyewitness of the siege of Essex House and the legal proceedings, had every detail of the situation at his fingers' ends. Moreover, his position in regard to Essex was unusual, in view of previous clashings and jealousies.

This Lord Nottingham, Charles Howard, was the great Admiral of Elizabeth's day—the man who crushed the Armada. He was not the first English Lord High Admiral, for Sir Edward Howard before him (1477–1513) had held that great post under Henry VIII, and lost his life, just after acquiring that high honour in the boarding of a French man-of-war off Les Blancs Sablons, near Brest, the man who, rather than be taken alive by the enemy or roll at their feet dead with his insignia of office upon him, took this—his official whistle—and hurled it into the sea at the moment when the French pikes thrust him and his companions overboard.

Elizabeth's Nottingham (1536–1624) was the eldest son of William, Lord Howard of Effingham, and saw sea service with his father under Edward VI. His name must be joined to the roll of those high officials who exhausted their private means in the Queen's service. She never acknowledged this, though she was always ready to concede on paper their services to the country

and her own majesty and greatness. She could write :
" You have made me famous, dreadful, and renowned,
not more for your victory than for your courage ; not
more for either than for such plentiful liquor of mercy,
which may well match the better of the two." But
when it came to the dull matter of paying the out-
standing expenses, the wages of the sailors, she hardened,
and retorted that they had been well enough paid with
their share of the plunder, and that the affair had brought
her no benefit. This was particularly in connection with
the Cadiz expedition. It was over this enterprise that
the great quarrel began between Essex and this admiral.
The latter was to take precedence at sea, and Essex was
to be supreme on land, while Essex's signature to orders
was allowed to stand first. This must have been sufficiently galling to the older man. When the fleet returned, the two quarrelled as to which should have the
kudos of success—the destruction of the Spanish ship-
ping, and the dismantling of forts. In the next year
the conferring of the earldom of Nottingham, expressly
based on Howard's naval achievements at Cadiz and in
the great Armada contest, added fuel to the flame. It
is not therefore surprising that Lord Nottingham was
prepared to sit in judgment ever after on Essex. He
scarcely needed the additional triumph of securing later
the chief command on shore and at sea as "Lord Lieu-
tenant-General of all England," a post which, so far,
Elizabeth had only destined for the late Lord Leicester.
The first wife of this admiral, Catherine, daughter of
Lord Hunsdon, Elizabeth's first cousin, was the lady
round whom centres the famous and impossible romance
of the ring which Essex is said to have sent to the
Queen, and which the Countess is supposed to have
intercepted. She was the Queen's close confidante and

favourite, but her husband's views must have coloured hers, and she could not have cherished very friendly feelings for Essex.   Still, history refuses to support this legend.   Her sister, Lady Scrope, who was seen to wear mourning all through the days of Essex's imprisonment and worked so hard on his behalf, would certainly have prevented such a tragedy as the suppression of this talisman.

In returning to Nottingham and his despatches we must anticipate very slightly and assume the "end of 'Sweet Robin'" on the scaffold, for these letters were written just after.   The old lord is at once wily and witty in the way he indicates his knowledge of Mount-joy's tremendous love affair.   After a laudatory opening, in which the writer expresses his admiration of the handling of the Irish campaign and states that, at Mountjoy's wish, the military news sent to the Earl is by him conveyed to the Queen, he protests his love, respect and desire for the Lord Deputy's speedy return. "But all this power," he adds, "lieth in Her Majesty, whose pleasure in it your Lordship may understand. And now . . . I think her Majesty could be most glad to see and look upon your black eyes here, so she were sure you would not look with too much respect of other black eyes."   That sentence stabs neatly.   It showed that for Mountjoy to return now and to let himself be mastered by a love intrigue with a lady so out of favour as Penelope, would be to court dire disgrace.

Nottingham realised what that ironical sentence meant, and tried to smooth it down with a jovial thrust at himself.   "But for that," he wrote, "if the Admiral were but thirty years old I think he would not differ in opinion from the Lord Mountjoy."

The rest of the letter is far more serious; each successive sentence certainly deepened the alarm of the recipient :

"I am sure your lordship hath had the relation at large of the late Earl of Essex' proceedings, who forgot God, his loyalty to his sovereign, above all measure of a reasonable man. Yet he died like a Christian, and God hath his soul. Yet will I acquaint your lordship with some particulars. The day after his arraignment he humbly desired that her Majesty would send some of her council to him and that I might be one of them. So the next day, being Friday, Mr. Secretary and myself was sent unto him. And thus he did begin with us : 'I do humbly thank her Majesty that it hath pleased her to send you two unto me, and you are both most heartily welcome; and above all things I am most bound unto Her Majesty that it pleased her to let me have this little man, Mr. Ashton, my minister, with me for my soul. For,' said he, 'this man in a few hours hath made me know my sins unto Her Majesty, and to my God. And I must confess to you that I am the greatest, the most vilest, and most unthankfullest traitor that ever was born in this kind. And therefore, if it shall please you, I will deliver now the truth, though yesterday, at the bar, like a most sinful wretch, with countenance and words I maintained all falsehood.' Then he began to lay open the practice for the suppressing of Her Majesty and the Court; who were at the councils at Drury House, the Earl of Southampton's lodging."

Here follow the names of the various gentlemen, including Sir Christopher Blount, "whom he ever kept with him." And immediately there follows the damning sentence, "He spared none of these to let us know how continually they laboured him about it." The worst, for Mountjoy, is left for the close of the letter.

"'And now,' said he, 'I must accuse one who is most

nearest to me, my sister, who did continually urge me on with telling me how all my friends and followers thought me a coward, and that I had lost all my valour ; ' and then thus, ' that she must be looked to for she had a proud spirit ' ; and spared not to say something of her affection to you. Would your lordship have thought this weakness and this unnaturalness in that man ? This moved Her Majesty to think fit that she (Lady Rich) should be committed, and appointed me to that pleasing office. I did obey, as it became me, and sent her to Mr Henry Lakeford's house, where she remained till she was examined by myself and her secretary."

The Earl is careful to explain that Lady Rich " used herself with that modesty and wisdom, as, the report being made unto Her Majesty, she was presently set at liberty and sent unto my lord her husband's." The close is lightly deprecatory :

" I cannot forbear after all unpleasant discourse but a little to make you afraid with sending you this enclosed "—a letter from Lady Rich clearing herself from her supposed share in her brother's treason—" when you consider what a youth I am. Yet this you may be assured, that I am faithful to my friend, and my Lord Mountjoy shall so ever find me,
" Most readiest to be commanded by him.
" NOTTINGHAM."

In the postscript we learn, besides the names of the victims executed, the hope of Nottingham to save Earl Southampton. The writer prays that the letter may be burned.

Here is Penelope's interesting epistle of vindication to Nottingham :

" Worthy Lord,
I must humbly entreat you to pardon my importun-

ing you with these lines, since the obligations your favours have laid upon me are so great as they even burthen my soul with thankfulness ; . . . For my deserts towards him that is gone, it is known that I have been more like a slave than a sister ; which proceeded out of my exceeding love rather than his authority. What I have lost or suffered, besides her Majesty's displeasure " (this is a special reference to the Queen's disregard of her entreaties to be allowed access to Essex during the very early days of his disgrace) " I will not mention : yet so strangely have I been wronged as may well be an argument to make one despise the world, finding the smoke of envy where affection should be clearest."

One sees how terribly she is suffering from her brother's accusation of her in his weakest hour of physical exhaustion and mental perversion. She tries to be patient under the bitter memory :

" But God pardon such humours, and deal with me as I was free from the love or knowledge of these unruly counsels. And, lastly, I beseech your lordship to hold me in your precious favour."

The remainder of the closing paragraph is merely a bunch of compliments, but the postscript, in which she refers mysteriously to Mountjoy, is valuable, and shows her at her best, with all her love and apprehension on the alert :

" Your lordship's noble disposition forceth me to deliver my grief unto you, hearing a report that some of these malicious tongues have sought to wrong a worthy friend of yours. I know the most of them did hate him for his zealous following the service of Her Majesty, and beseech you to pardon my presuming thus much, though I hope his enemies can have no power to harm him."

Fynes Moryson had full opportunity to observe and record the effect of all this terrible news, which first reached his master by letter on February 22nd, 1601. One longs vainly for more details, but Mountjoy was caution itself. We are just told that the intelligence

" much dismayed him and his nearest friends, and wrought strange alteration in him : for, whereas before he stood upon terms 'of honour with the Secretary (Cecil), now he fell flat to the ground, and insinuated himself into inward love, and to an absolute dependency with the Secretary, so as for a time he estranged himself from two of his nearest friends for the open declaration they had made of dependency on the Earl of Essex ; yet rather covering than extinguishing his good affection towards them." [1]

Next day the deputy took his precautions, possibly with a view to flight into France, of which his secretary was fully aware. The day after the arrival of the packet he removed his private papers from the secretary's care, and the latter knew that after that day he never had his master's full friendship and confidence. Wherefore the scribe had reason for the written statement :

" In truth his Lordship had good cause to be wary in his words and actions, since, by some confessions in England, himself was tainted with privity to the Earl's practices ; so that, howsoever he continued still to importune leave to come over, yet no doubt he meant nothing less but rather, if he had been sent for, was purposed, with his said friends, to sail into France, they having privately fitted themselves with money and necessaries thereunto."

Nothing but a miracle saved Mountjoy. The Queen presently wrote, assuring him of her confidence, and

[1] Fynes Moryson's *Itinerary*.

kept him at his post. All evidence against him was deliberately suppressed. She could not afford to lose so useful a servant ere his task was accomplished.

One longs to have witnessed the tremendous revulsion of feeling through which Penelope's lover passed, when, in place of letters of arraignment, documents to remove him from his command and order his instant attendance in London before the Star Chamber, he opened a missive from his sovereign couched in the most adroit and affectionate language. The excuse for this letter is very subtle. She writes because, first, she has to inform him of the death of Essex, his friend, and secondly, because she trusts her soldier and feels that she can unbosom herself and tell him her sorrow. She declares that, in regard of his proved fidelity and love, it was an alleviation of her grief that she could pour it out to him. There is not a word of suspicion against him, or of accusation. She only implores him to be very watchful lest disloyalty should enter into his army, and bids him have a special eye to all those who owed their advancement to the Earl of Essex. With superb aplomb she adds the priceless assertion that, while she was aware of the power of the late Earl, she was ready to pardon all those, " who, by Essex's popular fashion and outward profession of sincerity, had been seduced and violently led by him."

Mountjoy's piteous appeal for recall she treated with equal diplomacy. "She wished he would conceal this his desire until those rumours which the rebels spread of a Spanish invasion should be dissipated." So did she trump up excuses in order that she might get the utmost out of her men, and sweetened this dose by a promise to recall Mountjoy before the following winter, and to provide him with a Court post.

Essex died on the block just over a fortnight after his surrender, and with him Sir Charles Danvers and Sir Christopher Blount.   Southampton was reprieved and banished.

Where Penelope hid herself during the months which intervened between these executions and the return of her lover it is impossible to say.   Lord Rich could not have been much consolation.   It must be added, from his point of view, that these latter incidents in the history of his wife's family were not likely to excite in him a desire to seek their society.   He seems to have sat down and thought out the future coolly.   He saw that no advantages could now accrue to him from that quarter.   There was no member of Penelope's circle left who could be useful to him, as Essex had been. He had nothing to gain by blinking at his wife's repeated desertions.   He was not an old man, and there were plenty of good matches in the world left for him.   He formally abandoned Penelope, according to Mountjoy's subsequent statement.   But his plans for divorce were not yet ripe.   We leave her with the thrice-widowed Lettice to their heavy sorrow, and the Queen to the belated remorse which, in the end, killed her.

CHAPTER XVI

THE NEW REGIME

AND Penelope—now the true pattern of that idealised lady of Homer—waited. No more weaving of webs for her, no more dalliance with riddles in letters, or love buried beneath sonnets. For companions she had her children by Mountjoy, her grief-stricken mother, and her sister-in-law. Mountjoy naturally did not summon his beloved to Ireland, nor could she have gone to him, even had she been free to marry him. His whole attention was engrossed by his work. It was a task big enough to daunt a much more experienced soldier. Remember, also, that it was his first big "command." He had absolute say in the matter. He needed it. To have to undertake such a business so bungled and mishandled and then to be handicapped by rivals in authority would have annulled the whole of England's final effort to produce order over there. Except within the immediate "lines," the fortified places, or the actual spots covered by camps or invested towns, there was scarcely an inch of ground that must not be reconquered. The people were half savage, wholly unsophisticated, except in regard to theft and piracy and bloodshed. Here and there travellers of the day give us glimpses of their dress and mien. When not in revolt they were a simple people, rejoicing in their olden heritage of a hand-to-mouth existence, and mostly hospitable. One explorer —a Bohemian baron—gives an astonishing picture of

s   257

his arrival some years previous at an Irish cabin, at which he applied for rest and a night's shelter. Fifteen women of various ages inhabited it with their relations. The fifteen appeared at the door amazingly unattired. Their legs were bare, their only garment a cloak and hood combined. Some of these were such " nymphs " that he was quite dazzled by their beauty, and had to be assisted into the house ! The whole company slept in a huge circle—toes to the fire. The inmates of the house, before they sought the land of dreams, dipped their cloaks in water and wrapped the folds closely about the head and shoulders.[1] The thing reads like an anticipation of the Kneipp Cure in a country where rheumatism was to be had without the asking—as Essex and Mountjoy knew to their cost.

But all the Irishwomen were not so childlike and simple. Co-existent with these naïve nymphs of the wayside cabin were such persons as Grainore O'Mailey, the amazon who so amazed and amused Philip Sidney and his father. She was the wife of Sir Richard David Bourke, surnamed "of the Iron," because he was so continually at war with his countrymen that he was always in harness. Grainore, Sir Henry Sidney wrote, was "the most notorious woman in all the coast of Ireland." He tells of her introduction to him and how she presented herself among the number of those Irish leaders and landowners who thought it wise to throw in their lot with the Queen :

" There came also to me a most famous feminine sea-captain, called Grainore O'Mailey, and offered her services unto me, wheresoever I would command her, with three galleys and two hundred fighting men, either

---

[1] At the same time one must not believe implicitly such traveller's tales !

in Ireland or Scotland. She brought with her her husband, for she was, as well by sea as by land, more than master's mate to him."

There is, however, a far sadder picture of Irish womanhood at this time than either of the above. From the beginning of the campaign, in the time of the older Earl of Essex, generals seem to have decided that the only way to suppress rebellion was not to rush after the peasants into their foxes' holes and risk death-traps in bogs or glens, but to lay waste the agricultural places deserted by the people, who would then return to their razed habitations and in the end be reduced to submission by hunger. It is extraordinary that even the poet Spenser, in actual sight of these horrors, could endorse the wisdom of such tactics and yet bear to write later of that land of corn and honey and beeves " brought to such wretchedness that the most stony heart would have rued the same." His artist's eye paints vividly the peasants as he saw them. " Out of every corner of the woods and glens they came creeping forth on their hands, for their legs would not bear them ; they looked like anatomies of death ; they spake like ghosts crying out of their graves ; and if they found a plot of water-cresses or shamrocks, here they flocked as to a feast."

As it was under Essex, so under Mountjoy. I cull this vivid, condensed passage on his enforced and horrible task from Gardiner :[1]

" When Mountjoy landed in Ireland he could scarcely command a foot of ground beyond the immediate vicinity of the Queen's garrison. In three years he had beaten down all resistance. The system by which such quick results had been accomplished was very different from that of Essex. Essex had gathered his troops

[1] *History of England* by Samuel Gardiner, LL.D., Vol. I, pp. 364-5.

together and hurled them in a mass upon the enemy. The Irish rebellion was not sufficiently organised to make the most successful blow struck in one quarter tell over the rest of the country, nor was it possible to maintain a large army in the field at a distance from its base of operation. Mountjoy saw at a glance the true nature of the war in which he was engaged. He made war on the Irish tribes more with the spade than with the sword. . . . Every commanding position . . . was occupied by a fort. The garrisons were small, but they were well provisioned, and behind their walls they were able to keep in check the irregular levies of a whole tribe. The rebels did not dare to leave their homes exposed to the attack of the garrisons. Scattered and divided, they fell an easy prey to the small but compact force of the Deputy, which marched through the whole breadth of the land, provisioning the forts and beating down all opposition in its way. . . . Famine or submission was the only alternative offered. The arrival of an English force was not a temporary evil which could be avoided by skulking for a few weeks in the bogs and forests. . . . Wherever it appeared, the crops were mercilessly destroyed and the cattle . . . driven away. Then, when the work of destruction was completed, the troops moved off, to renew their ravages elsewhere. It is impossible to calculate the number which perished . . . from Cape Clear to the Giant's Causeway, famine reigned supreme. Strange stories were told by the troopers of the scenes which they had witnessed. Sometimes their horses were stabbed by the starving Irish, who were eager to feast upon the carcases. In one place they were shocked by the unburied corpses rotting in the fields. In another they discovered a band of women who supported a wretched existence by enticing little children to come amongst them, and massacring them for food."

From such scenes, from such pitiful knowledge, a Deputy might well be thankful to turn his eyes.

Professor Gardiner in further stating that Mountjoy was drawn back to England " by the unhallowed ties which bound him to Lord Rich's wife," does not, in my opinion, make full allowance for these other factors in his longing to be relieved of office. Moreover, the Deputy had by this time done his work—let us call it the " dirty work," the hardest of the whole Irish undertaking. With the petty dissensions, the details which must ensue in the restitution and adjustment of civic rights and harbour rights, estates and so forth, he, a soldier, grew very impatient after three years of hard work in field and fort. He had beaten the rebels back almost from the walls of Dublin ; and now each inch of his slow progress had to be made sure. It was midsummer before the chief stronghold of Tyrone succumbed, and yet six months later this Earl had managed to raise a more imposing force than before, " the largest rebel army known in Ireland," while he swept to the rescue of his four thousand Spanish mercenaries in Kinsale. Mountjoy, on Christmas Eve, 1601, triumphed in battle, laid waste the disaffected districts, reinvested the citadels. The news must have brought joy to Penelope. But again the war dragged on. Reinforcements were necessary. The following Christmas, however, saw the universal suppression of the rebellion and the surrender of Tyrone. In the March of the New Year Mountjoy's cup of triumph was full. Tyrone came to Dublin to receive pardon and the restoration of his estates. Immediately after he was to travel to England and kneel to the Queen.

The full glory of that reception was dashed for the Lord Deputy by Elizabeth's death. The tedious business of securing Tyrone's fealty had now to be repeated—for the new sovereignty required it. Mountjoy, after this, asked for leave. James only reinstated him as Deputy and raised his salary. After this came ups and downs, murmurings of various towns against his administration. Five of these had to be punished ere he could set sail for England on May 26, 1603. He went straight to his house at Wanstead, and one of his earliest guests was the ex-rebel Tyrone.

Public duties engrossed him immediately. His Irish experience was invaluable to the Privy Council, of which he was at once made a member. James showered grants of land and honours upon him. And Penelope became openly the mistress of his Essex house. This last was a bold move; under modern conditions it would have meant, for the lady, complete self-extinction. Even so, it has rather the air of tempting Providence in spite of the success and the triumphs of Mountjoy. This public declaration of their liaison could not have taken place earlier. Even at this epoch it appears very risky. The curious confession of Essex and the late Queen's consciousness of the earlier " practices " of the " faithful Charles" was still too close a matter of memory. At Court these matters afforded but poor footing for one who had been so long out of the country. As for Penelope, Elizabeth, full three years before death, had done with her. The details of the protracted affair with Mountjoy stuck in the Queen's gorge. After many years and just before her end she openly showed her disapproval in regard to the lady.

Now, all was changed. Elizabeth, dead, with all her loves and hates, tenderness and cruelties, apprehension and joviality, could no longer injure the much-be-flogged family of Essex, who, in the shock of her death, must have looked back with mingled feelings of thanksgiving, hatred, and awe upon their long comradeship with the woman whose caprice maddened many an ambassador, whose vanity had been a public laughing-stock, whose diplomacy had defied the premier nations of Europe, whose sacrifice of her life and heart to England can never be forgotten. They would endorse every word of that pungent summing up of Elizabeth by the ambassador de Noailles :

"Princesse qui excella dans la politique ; habile, prudente, d'un genie souple et aisé, qui prenoit sans peine toutes sortes de formes ; caressante, fière, vindicative, cruelle même dans ses vengeances, mais sans jamais sacrifier son veritable interêt à ses ressentimens. On peut dire d'elle, que pour mieux regner elle sent se plier aux conjonctures, et mettre en oeuvre indifférem-ment, tantôt des vices et tantôt des vertus."

With a new régime life must be begun all over again. This was the immediate business of every courtier of moment and of this moment. This dis-comfortable transition process is pithily contained in the sentiments of Robert Cecil in a letter to Sir John Harrington, Elizabeth's godson, who had expressed his intentions to keep clear of the Court, owing to the curious reports of the new King's manner of dispensing justice.

"I hear," wrote Sir John roguishly, "our new King hanged one man before he was tried : 'tis strangely done . . . if the wind bloweth thus, why may not a man be tried before he hath offended?" No one, under such conditions, is really safe, he argues ; and therefore "I will keep company with none but my sheep and oxen and go to Bath and drink sack[1] and wash away remembrances of past times in the streams of Lethe."

---

[1] No wonder that ancient "cures" were impermanent!

Cecil understood and sympathised. Both he and
Harrington had suffered hard things at Elizabeth's
hands, and yet both hankered after "past times" :

" 'Tis a great task to prove one's honesty and yet
not spoil one's fortune. You have tasted a little hereof
in our blessed queen's time, who was more than a man,
and, in troth, sometimes less than a woman. I wish
I waited now in her presence-chamber, with ease at my
food and rest in my bed. I am pushed from the shore
of comfort, and know not where the winds and waves
of a Court will bear me; I know it bringeth little comfort
on earth; and he is, I reckon, no wise man that looketh
this way to heaven. We have much stir about councils
and more about honours. Many knights were made at
Theobald's during the King's stay at mine house, and
more to be made in the City. My father had much
wisdom in directing the State ; and I wish I could bear
my part so discreetly as he did. Farewell, good Knight,
but never come to London till I call you. Too much
crowding doth not well for a cripple"—a sly hit at
Harrington's gouty tendencies—"and the King doth
scant find room to sit himself, he hath so many *friends*,
as they choose to be called ; and heaven prove they lie
not in the end. In trouble, hurrying, feigning, seeming, and such like matters I now rest your true friend
                                        "R. CECIL."

Penelope Rich, of course, now had to rebuild her
social reputation entirely, as well as win back her
place at Court. Mountjoy, meanwhile, must stablish
and strengthen his.

The new King and Queen present a very ridiculous
picture on their accession. Eyewitnesses wore no
rose-coloured spectacles, and James, at the age of
thirty-seven, is pictured with remorseless details by
Weldon :

From a mezzotint engraving after an original painting

JAMES I

" He was of a middle stature, more corpulent through his clothes than in his body, yet fat enough ; his clothes ever being made large and easy, the doublets quilted for stiletto proof; his breeches in plaits and full stuffed : he was naturally of a timorous disposition, which was the reason of his quilted doublets."

The description of his eye and the way he riveted his glance upon a new-comer reminds one of Elizabeth : " His eye large, ever rolling after any stranger who came into his presence ; insomuch as many for shame have left the room, as being out of countenance."

His beard, we are told, was " very thin." His tongue " too large for his mouth ; and made him drink very uncomely, as if eating his drink, which came out into the cup each side of his mouth." When you did homage you knew that " his skin was soft as taffeta sarsanet ; which felt so because he never washed his hands, only rubbed his fingers' ends slightly with the wet end of a napkin."

His figure was badly proportioned : " His legs were very weak . . . that weakness made him ever leaning on other men's shoulders ; his walk was ever circular."

His taste in dress appears to have been of the worst. Osborn, in his *Traditional Memoirs* of King James, presents him as he looked in the first royal progress after the coronation :—

" I shall leave him dressed for posterity in the colours I saw him in . . . which was as green as the grass he trod on ; with a feather in his cap, and a horn instead of a sword by his side. How suitable to his age, calling or person I leave others to judge from his pictures."

Anne, at the time of her husband's accession, was too seriously ill to bear him company in his swift journey

South.   In truth he had some doubt as to the effect she would make upon a nation whose heart he had yet to win.   For this reason, rather than because of her health, he commanded that she must not follow him for twenty good days.   Owing to various causes of home agitation she was taken suddenly ill, her third child was prematurely born dead, and the moment she could travel she was away across the Border after her King. Her character had changed greatly since the days when James, for once valorous, braved the stormy seas to fetch her as a bride from the coasts of Norway, where she was detained by autumn storms.   She had left her father's Danish roof, and it was not considered etiquette by the admiral in command of her little fleet of escort to take her home without fulfilling his sacred commission to land her safely in the arms of James I. At this period she was so stiff and restrained that when James, after his long journey, marched in unceremoniously, ready to embrace her, she quietly repulsed him, on the plea that they were scarcely well enough acquainted for such familiarities !   For a while, though she soon appreciated and returned his demonstrative affection, she preserved at her own Court a very reserved demeanour.   Yet she soon learned to unbend, and developed a very lively spirit which, while it brought a renewal of gaiety to the English Court, was often the cause of trouble between her spouse and herself.   She was only twenty-eight when she came to receive the homage of Elizabeth's ladies.   She had far more " go " than James.   A contemporary describes her as possessing "a bold and enterprising nature, one which loved pomp and splendour, tumult and intrigue."   Her looks and person were not remarkable.   It is certain that she made the best of them and enjoyed the details

QUEEN ANNE

Queen Consort to King James the First.

From a mezzotint engraving

ANNE OF DENMARK, QUEEN OF JAMES I

of her coronation wardrobe, about which her husband held anxious correspondence with the English Lords of Council.

To return to Penelope. While Robert Rich brooded darkly on divorce matters Fate favoured the bold. The bread which Penelope had cast on the waters, in regard to the Scottish Court, came home to her after many days. With other ladies of great rank she travelled, in the full springtide of 1603, to the Border to meet James's Queen and escort her to London. Do not imagine for a moment that the lady's progress upward and forward into Court favour was uncriticised, especially by contemporaries of her own sex. Lady Anne Clifford, in later years thrice a countess, and one of the great feminine figures of English history, was also one of those who went, in company with her mother, to greet the new King and Queen, and, though quite a young girl at the time, noticed with disfavour, and afterwards recorded in her famous Diary, the fact that during the progress Queen Anne gave great dissatisfaction by slighting the stately old dames of Elizabeth's Court, while she particularly noticed all the younger, sprightly women :—

"Here we saw the Queen's favour to my Lady Hatton and my Lady Cecil ; for she showed no favour to the elderly ladies, but to my Lady Rich and such-like company."

Then began the usual fight and scramble for Court posts. Wrote the Earl of Worcester to the Earl of Shrewsbury :

"This day the King dined abroad with the Florentine Ambassador. . . . He was with the King at Play at night, and supped with my Lady Rich in her chamber.

. . . We have ladies of divers degrees of favour ; some for the private chamber, some for the bedchamber, and some for neither certain. The plotting and malice among them is such, that I think Envy hath tied an invisible snake about most of their necks, to sting one another to death."

Penelope was made a Lady of the Bedchamber, and stepped into the highest favour. Thenceforward she was invited to take a leading part in all the Court shows, and in August of the year of his accession James conferred on her "the place and the rank of the ancientest Earl of Essex, called Bourchier," whose heir her father was. The indomitable courage of this woman and her power of carrying through her purposes compels admiration. If Robert Rich married again any woman but a countess in her own right, she would only be plain Lady Rich, while his ex-wife, by right of her Devereux origin and the King's patent, took precedence at Court of all the baronesses in the kingdom and of the daughters of all Earls, with the exception of Oxford, Arundel, Northumberland, and Shrewsbury. Thus did this extraordinary lady, by sheer force of individuality and fascination, lift upon her shoulders the house of Essex from its very ashes. She had a nephew who, in due time, would take the burden on his back, and who in his turn was destined to his share of tragedy and scandal. Her successful angling for the honour just quoted is the more easily explained by the fact that her sister-in-law, within two years of Essex's execution and just at the time of the new accession, sought forgetfulness of evils in a third marriage—with Robert de Burgh, Earl Clanrickarde. That untiring letter-writer, Chamberlain, comments on the matter : "Many that wished her well," he says, "are nothing pleased." James, however, did not disapprove, for "the speech goes that the King hath taken order and sent her word that her son shall be brought up with the young Princes."

It is plain that Penelope was now in the midst of friends, and her star once more in the ascendant. Queen Anne was a vivacious person, not too rigid as regards the morals of others, and a lover of theatricals and processions. Innumerable devices, dances, plays, received their incentive from her. Penelope was always the centre of such things. Secretary Wilson wrote of it all with delicate irony : "The Court was a continued *maskerado*, where she (Lady Rich), the Queen, and her ladies, like so many sea nymphs or Nereids, appeared often in various dresses, to the ravishment of the beholders ; the King himself being not a little delighted with such fluent elegancies as made the night more glorious than the day." Dudley Carleton, however, while he estimates their apparel as rich, adds that it was " too light and courtezan-like for such great ones."

The new queen commissioned Ben Jonson in 1605 to write a masque with parts for herself and certain of her ladies, in which they should appear as Ethiopian beauties. As the author puts it, " it was her Majesty's will to have them blackmoors at first," and he explains that he founds his allegory upon the river Niger, which " taketh Spring out of a certain lake Eastward, and after a long race falleth into the Western Ocean." It was called the " Masque of Blackness," and was presented on Twelfth Night, in Court at Whitehall.[1] The scene represented a landscape consisting of " small woods, and here and there a void place filled with huntings " (presumably painted figures of the chase). This apparently fell or was moved away, revealing an artificial sea, which " was

[1] Nichol's *Progresses*.

seen to shoot forth as if it flowed to the land, raised
with waves which seemed to move, and in some places
the billows to break, as imitating that orderly disorder
which is common in nature. In front of this sea were
placed six Tritons, in moving and sprightly actions, their
upper parts human, save that their hair was blue, as
partaking of the sea-colour ; their desinent parts fish,
mounted above their heads and all varied in disposition.
From their backs were borne out light pieces of taffeta,
as if carried by the wind, and their music made out of
wreathed shells. Behind these, a pair of sea-maids, for
song, were as conspicuously seated ; between which, two
great sea-horses, as big as the life, put forth themselves ;
the one mounting aloft, and writhing his head from the
other, which seemed to sink forward ; so intended for
variation, and that the figure behind might come off
better ; upon their backs Oceanus and Niger were
advanced. . . . . These induced the maskers, which were
twelve nymphs, negroes, and the daughters of Niger and
attended by the Oceanias, which were their light bearers."
These light bearers were invariable attendants of the
maskers, and acted at once as herald and shadow of
each actor, preceding his entrance and exit, and supporting him, while placed at a slight distance, during his
action. The chief of these Nigerian nymphs was the
Queen, under the name of Euphoris, and of her five
ladies Penelope Rich personated Ocyte. The six danced
in pairs, each carrying a fan, upon which was painted the
symbols allotted to the three couples. The Queen's
fan, and that of the Countess Bedford, bore a golden
tree laden with fruit. Penelope and the Countess of
Suffolk, who appeared as Kathare, symbolised a pair of
naked feet in a river. "The maskers were placed in a
great concave shell, like mother of pearl, curiously made

to move on those waters, and rise with the billows ; the top thereof was stuck with a chevron of lights, which, indented to the proportion of the shell, struck a glorious beam upon them as they receded one upon the other ; so that they were all seen, but in an extravagant order. On sides of the shell did swim six huge sea-monsters, varied in their shapes and dispositions, bearing on their backs the twelve torch bearers who were planted there in several graces ; so as the backs of some were seen, some in purfle (profile) others in face, and all having their lights burning out of whelks, or murex-shells."

As for the "book," it is simple and naïve. Oceanus inquires of his lonely son, Niger, how it is that he has travelled so far to mix his fresh billow with the ocean's bracky stream. Niger explains that this journey is undertaken purely to satisfy his daughters, rendered miserable by the "loose and winged fictions . . . the fabulous voices of some few poor brain-sick men, styled poets here with you." These poets declare that before Phaeton "fired the worlds" with his reckless sun chariot, the Ethiopian ladies were as white-skinned as their lovely Western sisters, whose beauty so far excels theirs. These daughters of Niger had revolted against the sun and cursed their fate. One night, as they sat cooling their limbs mournfully enough in the lake whence Niger took his road into the world, the moon appeared to bid them seek a land whose title terminates with "tania," a place of temperate air, where the sun, forsooth,

> Doth never rise or set,
> But in his journey passeth by,
> And leaves that climate of the sky
> To comfort of a greater light,
> Who forms all beauty with his sight.

With his fair cortège Niger has discovered and passed through three provinces having the correct termination, but none is the longed-for country of his daughters' desires. He has travelled through " black Mauritania, swarth Lusitania and rich Aquitania." What is the new land, O Oceanus ? The blue-green god bursts out into a panegyric on " Albion the Fair." At this point vivid stage directions take up the story :

" At this the moon was figured in the upper part of the house, triumphant in a silver throne, made in figure of a pyramis. Her garments white and silver, the dressing of her head antique, and crowned with a luminary or sphere of light : which, striking on the clouds and heightened with silver, reflected as natural clouds do by the splendour of the Moon. The Heaven about her was vaulted with blue silk, and set with stars of silver, which had in them their several lights burning. The sudden sight of which made Niger to interrupt Oceanus with this present passion."

This land is the right land ; it is Britannia ! Niger is ordered to call forth his honoured daughters and invite them boldly to dance on a shore where the sun shall caress and refine their beauties. The Tritons summon, the masquers descend from their shell, severally presenting their fans. " Their own single dance ended, as they were about to make choice of their men, one from the sea was heard to call them," with a charm. This they do not heed, but engage in a mixed dance with their cavaliers, several measures and corantos, till the moon, on the wane, summons them dancing back to their shell.

In this airy entertainment Penelope and her companions were dressed alike : " the colours azure and silver ; but returned on the top with a scroll and antique dressing of feathers and jewels interlaced with ropes of pearl. And for the front, ear, neck, and wrists, the ornament was of the most choice and orient pearl; best setting off from the black." The attendant torch-bearers were in " sea-green, waved about the skirt with gold and silver; their hair loose and flowing, gyrlanded with sea-grass and that stuck with bunches of coral."

Entertainments at Court were not always so refined and graceful. Very soon the spirit of laxity encouraged by the new sovereign and his consort took effect, and moved a gentleman who knew the Court of Elizabeth intimately—that same Sir John Harrington at whom she swore and rated on his return from Ireland —to bring the dryest humour to bear upon his recital of a scene attending the reception and entertainment of the Danish King, Anne's father, in 1606 :

" The ladies abandon their sobriety, and roll about in intoxication. One day a great feast was held; the representation of Solomon his temple, and the coming of the Queen of Sheba was made, or, as I may better say, meant to have been made, before their Majesties by device of the Earl of Salisbury and others. But alas! As all earthly things do fail to poor mortals in enjoyment, so did prove our presentment thereof. The lady who did play the Queen's part did carry most precious gifts to both their Majesties; but forgetting the steps arising to the Canopy, overset her caskets into his Danish Majesty's lap, and fell at his feet, though I rather think it was in his face. Much was the hurry and confusion; cloths and napkins were at hand to make all clean. His Majesty then got up and would dance with the Queen of Sheba; but he fell down and humbled himself before her, and was carried to an inner chamber, and laid on a bed of state, which was not a little defiled with the presents of the Queen, bestowed on his gar-

ments, such as wine, cream, jelly, beverage, cakes, spices,
and other good matters. The entertainment and show
went forward, and most of the presenters went backward
or fell down, wine did so occupy their upper chambers.
Now did appear, in rich dress, Hope, Faith, and Charity.
Hope did essay to speak, but wine rendered her endeavour so feeble, that she withdrew, and hoped the
King would excuse her brevity. Faith was then all
alone, for I am certain she was not joined with good
works, and left the Court in a staggering condition.
Charity came to the King's feet, and seemed to cover
the multitude of sins her sisters had committed ; in
some sort she made obeisance, and brought gifts, but
said she would return home again, as there was no
gift which heaven had not already given his Majesty.
She then returned to Hope and Faith, who were both sick
in the lower hall. Next came Victory in bright armour,
and presented a rich sword to the King. . . . But
Victory did not triumph long ; for after much lamentable utterance she was led away like a silly captive, and
laid to sleep on the outer steps of the antechamber.
Now did Peace make entry and strive to get foremost to
the King ; but I grieve to tell how great wrath she did
discover unto those of her attendants, and much contrary
to her semblance most rudely made war with her olive
branch ; and laid on the pates of those who did oppose
her coming. We are going on hereabouts as if the
devil was contriving every man should blow himself up
by wild riot, excess, and devastation of time and
temperance. The great ladies do go well masked, and
indeed it be only the show of their modesty to conceal
their countenance. But alack ! they meet with such
continuance to uphold their strange doings, that I
marvel not at aught that happens. I do say—but not
aloud—that the Danes have again conquered the Britons,
for I see no man, or woman either, that can command
himself or herself. I wish I was at home. *O rus,
quando te 'aspiciam'?*"

One cannot but imagine that a man and woman of the calibre of Charles Blount and Penelope Rich echoed that sentiment to the full. In effect, "peace at home," to quote an excellent piece of religious doggerel, was what they most truly desired. Their situation may have been publicly brilliant. In their hearts they craved for official sanction of their bond of love and faith. At the time of the above rowdy entertainment they were actually in country solitude for a very good reason, fully explained in the ensuing chapter. For the present they were wrestling successfully with the new régime. They had begun well. Mountjoy's bookishness had taught him the art of suave letter-writing, and he indited the following epistle—the absurd fulsomeness of which appears to have been in keeping with the Court custom of the period—congratulating the King on the discovery of the Guy Fawkes plot.

" Sir,

Although it is neither my nature nor profession to fear, yet Fear is sometimes no evil Counsellor, and what shall we not fear now after a Practise that sense would have feared? But of your safety we cannot be too jealous, and if I fear too much *Tu me timidum facis*. Give me leave, therefore, I beseech you, sir, to say that in these times, wherein there is so just reason to doubt the Worst, your precious person is not so sufficiently pro-vided for as it should be, for I do know, or should know that a few well ordered, armed and accustomed to danger may do on the sudden to multitudes unarmed and in confusion. To prevent this which it is not enough that you have sentinels except you have the Body of a Watch. There be many about this City that have no other hope, but to fish in troubled streams; and they may find a Head, that will wish all our Rome had but one head, to cut off all that is good at one Blow. And the Bond between such a Head and such a body need not to be Love, but sympathy in villainy, and the satisfaction of both their ends, although perchance they be diverse. And though wisdom and virtue do best govern forces, yet Malice and Fury do soonest raise and move them on. Sir, I hope it shall never fall out that my Hand shall come to do you Service. Pardon me if I give this counsell unto whom I owe all that fame, and the fruits of my experience, if I have any; which in advice how to resist force with force I may presume something if I have had but common Reason to observe anything, for I have been chief of an acting army much longer than any other of my countrymen who do live. Yet think not, dear Master, that I presume to write this out of vanity or ambition, but to give some weight to my counsel, and way to my Desire to do you service ; as David (then but poor David) did, when he told his Master Saul that he had some times killed a Lion and a Bear, and that heretofore the uncircumcised Philistine should be as one of them. God be thanked, Sir, your country doth bring forth no Giants in power, altho' greater monsters in purpose than all the world hath ever done. God preserve you ever, and be not too careless of yourself, since God hath shewn Himself so careful for you.

"Your Majesty's most faithful Servant,

DEVONSHIRE."

To Penelope letters and dedications flowed in anew. She was extraordinarily useful to these penmen. It was at this period that John Florio included her in the five great ladies to whom he dedicated his translation of Montaigne's *Essays*, in the preface of which he describes her most finely as "one of those whose magnanimity and magnificent frank nature have so bedewed my earth when it was sunburnt, so gently thawed it when it was frost-bound, that I were even more senseless than earth,

if I returned not some fruit in good measure."
Whatever may have been the character of the remaining
four of this quintet, Penelope was in the highest sense
magnanimous. The fact just makes all the difference to
her place in history. The most holy and spotless folk
are often entirely without such a quality, and it is
possible to be at once intense of nature, resolutely
virtuous, and abominably grudging. She was intense for
good and evil, but she was also "magnificently frank"
and magnanimous. No meanness or pettiness had their
place in her.

CHAPTER XVII

THE WAY OF THE WORLD

L ORD RICH does not appear to have honoured the pageants described overleaf. He was occupied in more practical ways, both as justice of the peace and a petitioner in the Ecclesiastical Courts. It did not really matter to him that his rival in love, if one may honour Rich by using such a term, had newly received the supreme honour of the Earldom of Devonshire, in addition to a Spanish pension of £1000 a year, and the renewal of the posts of Keeper of Portsmouth Castle and Master of the Ordnance of the Realm. What Rich wanted was quiet revenge. The divorce for which he worked was granted in 1605. It was open to the others to effect their marriage, if they dared. But the matter in those days was hard to compass. Every difficulty was still in their way. The Canon Law did not countenance the re-marriage of any person divorced under certain conditions by the Ecclesiastical Courts. And it is just about this time that the usual thing happened. Mountjoy was man enough and human enough to indulge in a notion of marriage in quite a different quarter. In 1602–3 Society was given to understand that he would wed the only daughter of Thomas, tenth Earl of Ormonde. I do not like this suggestion. It upsets my notion of the "faithful Charles" completely. Yet his move is intelligible, and, humanly speaking, therefore valuable. While he could not possess Penelope as his wife, he wanted her. When she was repudiated by her husband and she was free to devote her whole life to her lover he turned his eyes for a short space in another direction. Penelope, it must be noted, was not financially dependent upon him. She received from her husband, even now, an annual allowance. While this looks like sentimental generosity on the part of Rich, it must be remembered that he had all his life made good use of such dowry as she had for his own purposes.

The Ormonde marriage, happily for romance and idealism, fell through, and Earl and Lady were left to face each other and the social situation. Both were still in their prime, both had purpose enough to lead their lives in the full blaze of Court splendour without feeling too keenly the criticisms of their neighbours. But their five children complicated the matter. With children real responsibilities returned, and in the train of responsibility came the prospect of old age. Is it strange that these two, who had set Church law and civil law at defiance, craved for that formality, that ritual which at least should publicly confirm their unity? The fact of Robert Rich's legal triumph was enough to add fuel to their wishes. So, in the peace and isolation of Wanstead—the very same house where Lettice Devereux had secretly wedded her Leicester—the great Laud, at the time only private chaplain to Mountjoy, joined their hands. He needed no little persuasion. He knew the matter was illegal, but apparently let Mountjoy blind him. Mountjoy, an ever-cautious man, apparently thought that he knew his world. Never did it occur to either of the couple that a King who could disregard the fact of their illegal union and publicly delight in their society, would turn and rend them under plea of their offence against the law and the Church. He did rend them. The world followed suit. Laud shared with them the hailstorm of abuse, the universal disgrace. If you will be at the trouble of turning back a few pages and glance at that Court orgy depicted by John Harrington, you will marvel the more at the way of the world in respect to this much-blamed marriage. Assuredly, in such a Court, Hope was drunken and feeble-handed, Faith was not sure of her footing, Peace was a mere hooligan, and Charity, who pretended to cover the shortcomings of the rest, was nothing but the poorest sycophant who had no force to stem the cruelty, the uncharity of those who had once been proud to number lord and lady among their distinguished guests.

Earl and Countess were promptly denied the Court. When Devonshire met Robert Rich, now created Earl of Warwick, in the Upper House a year after the two marriages, "foul words" were flung by each man at the other. One regrets to read that the former was worsted and "the lie given to Devon." Laud did life-long penance for his weakness, and kept the anniversary throughout his life as a solemn fast. James never forgave him, and Prynne, in the famous "Breviate," dryly inserts the statement against the date of Laud's private appointment, "Became chaplain to the Earl of Devonshire, which after proved his great happiness." The poor priest offered up Latin prayers of propitiation, and his dreams—he was a great recorder of dreams, though he pretends that he sets no store by them—include a note on one in which he was summoned to marry a friend, found no holy book placed ready for him, opened his own for the ceremony—and found the marriage office was missing !

While Laud wrote in his book of private devotions such phrases as "Scandalum ecce factus sum nomini Tuo, dum ambititioni meae et aliorum peccatis servio," his employer was writing too—not prayers, but a stout and pedantic defence of his marriage to the King. This is such a lengthy document that I have relegated it to my Appendix chapter. The Earl brought all his learning to bear on it. But, for all that, it is tedious and involved, and the subject, treated at such length, is highly unattractive. He struggles in the coils of it like a man in the embrace of a python. Far more to the point than that epistle is this shorter letter, which he addressed to James I on the same subject. It has the personal touch without the pedantry of the other tirade, and includes details about Penelope not otherwise obtainable. There is one delicious, pardonable touch of mendacity—the attempt to depict himself and his lady, scarcely in their fourth decade, as Philemon and Baucis.

"Most dear and sacred Master, unto whom God hath given Wisdom above all that went before you,

"Since it hath pleased you in favour of your servant to descend from your Higher thoughts of the Cedars in Lebanon to speak of the humble Hyssop, vouchsafe to look upon this Treatise with such an eye as God doth look upon the unworthy obligations of those that love him. It is not enough for me to satisfy mine own Conscience, except you be satisfied with the reasons that move me. And, therefore, I have been led to this with a necessity and not a desire to write, which I confess is too much for you to read, and yet too little for the matter. I have endeavoured to prove what I do myself believe, that in some cases to dissolve the bond of marriage is neither against the first institution, the Law of Nature, nor the Law of the Gospel. That the Civil

Law and the Laws of all nations did allow it, that even the Canon Law doth confess that the Contract of Marriage during life hath a not expressed condition *videlicet si illa vel ille non in legem conjugii peccaverit.*[1] I have strengthened this with the opinion of many of the Fathers, with the Practise of the Church and of all nations, with the Canon Law, with some of their censures obnoxious to that Law, with their doctrine in general that did justly forsake the errors and Tyranny of the hypocritical laws of Chastity and the Law given the Whore of Babylon ; and next if the Bond be utterly dissolved, that neither Party doth injury to any other by contracting anew, nor offence to God if it be with a mind thereby to serve Him and to avoid Sin. And finally, that if such a marriage be not prohibited by the Law of God, they are at this time lawful by the laws of this Land. And you, my Lord, who are as an angel of God, and full of Power to judge between Good and Evil, vouchsafe awhile to leave your great flock and hearken with favour unto this particular case of a poor Lost Sheep ; a Lady of great Birth and Virtue, being in the power of her friends, was by them married against her will unto one against whom she did protest at the very Solemnity and ever after ; between whom from the first day there ensued continual Discord, although the same fears that forced her to marry constrained her to live with him. Instead of a comforter he did study in all things to torment her ; and by Fear and Fraud did practise to deceive her of her Dowry, and though he forebore to offer her any open wrong, restrained with the Awe of her Brother's powerfulness, yet, as he had not in long time before in the chiefest duty of a Husband, used her as his wife, so presently after his death, he did put her to a stipend and abandoned her without pretence of any cause but his own Desire to live without her. And after he had not for the space of twelve years enjoyed her, he did by persuasion and threatenings move her to confess

[1] " If neither party has offended against the laws of marriage."

a fault with a nameless Stranger, without the which such a Divorce as he desired could not by the Laws in practise proceed.   Whereupon to give a form to that separation, which was long before in substance made, she was content to subscribe to a confession of his and her own Counsel's making, touching a fault committed before your general pardon.   Whereupon the Sentence of Divorce proceeded with as much rigour as ever was shewed to the meanest in the like case.   Now if before God the want of consent doth make a nullity of marriage, and the not performing the Duties doth break the conditions of marriage, and that dissension by Paul's doctrine doth make the woman free to marry again ; and lastly if a sentence of Divorce by a judicial Separation not prohibited by the Law of God, this Lady remaineth divers ways free from her Bond and free from her sin if she repent, namely *Impietas impii non nocebit ei in quacunque die conversus fuerit ab impietate suâ.*[1]   And you, dear Lord, that in the greatness of your Place, but more in your wonderful gifts, resemble God out of that Clemency wherein you imitate Him whose mercy doth exceed all his works, lay by the rigour of your judgment, and as you are both *fidelis et prudens Dispensator* at the least dispense and forgive them ; though it were much, seeing they have ever loved you much; and if in no other Fortune give them leave in their age to live together like poor Baucis and Philemon, who will never entertain any other guest into their hearts but God and you.   For me, if the Laws of Moral Honesty, which in all things not prohibited by God I have ever held inviolable, do only move me now to prefer my own conscience before the opinion of the world, my own better Fortunes, or the dear Respect of my Posterity, do but vouchsafe to think what a servant the same Rule of Honesty must force me to be unto you whose merit to me is so infinitely beyond any other, and my love to you so much

[1] As for the wickedness of the wicked, he shall not fall thereby in the day that he turneth from his wickedness.

above the love to a Woman as Jonathan's was to David, whom he loved as his own soul."

This letter is practically a condensation of the longer "Discourse," of which the vagueness makes it hard to get at Devonshire's application of the reasoning to himself and his case until the closing paragraph. Here he reminds himself and the world that even in Heaven forgiveness is extended to the penitent. "What offence," therefore he says, "should the like indulgence give in a fault of weakness, especially if it fall out that it be not accompanied with any other injury? For, if both parties do desire such a separation, and are content with a new contract, *volenti non fit injuria*." His contention is that since his marriage is not opposed to the word of God, it comes (as Craik puts it)[1] "within the dispensing power of His Majesty as head of the Church, even if it should be thought contrary to law, which, however, he also maintains that it is not."

The whole matter of precedent here settles the question so far as the world is concerned. For the law of those days was not what it now is. Divorce *a mensa et thoro*— separation from bed and board—did not give either party a right to re-marry. As early as the beginning of the reign of Edward VI a similar case to that of Rich was dealt with by the Courts. The Marquis of Northampton, after divorcing his wife, married again. A commission of inquiry was appointed, and he and his second lady were ordered to separate till official judgment was pronounced. This they did. The commission gave sentence in favour of Northampton, and his new wife returned to him. All the same, after a lapse of four years, it was found necessary to confirm the legality of

---

[1] Craik's *Romance of the Peerage*, Vol. I.

the union by a special Act of Parliament. Therefore
Devonshire, in view of this case, had a right to claim
the special sanction of the King. But it must be noted
that the Marquis of Northampton's case, in spite of the
controversy it excited, had not changed the law. Two
peers and two bishops protested against the Act of 1552,
which legalised the second marriage, while Cranmer,
at the head of thirty-two persons, including sixteen
divines and eight experts in Common Law, drew up the
Reformatio Legum, which suggested that the innocent
party, in the case of divorce for infidelity, should have
the right to marry again. No civil or ecclesiastical
authority, however, had been strong enough, up to the
date of our narrative, to convert this suggested reform
into law. In Elizabeth's reign the feeling of the Church
was not on the side of such an opinion. And already,
in the first year of James I re-marriage in the lifetime
of a former husband or wife was made a felony. But
there was included a proviso stating that this act should
not extend " to any persons that are or shall be at the
time of such marriage divorced by any sentence had or
hereafter to be had in the ecclesiastical court." This
looks as if the way were quite clear for the Devonshire
marriage. Yet in 1604 the following canon upsets
matters : " In all sentences only for divorce and
separation *a mensa et thoro* there shall be a caution and
restraint inserted in the act of the said sentence that the
parties so separated shall live chastely . . . neither
shall they during each other's life contract matrimony
with other persons. And, for the better observation of
this last clause, the said sentence of divorce shall not be
pronounced until the party or parties requiring the
same have given good and sufficient caution and security
into the Court that they will not any way break or

transgress the said restraint or prohibition." Again, it was decided, " that, in all proceedings to divorce, credit be not given to the sole confession of the parties themselves, howsoever taken upon oath, either within or without the Court." Moreover, if any judge, who gave sentence of divorce or separation, did not fully observe the enactment in its details, he must be suspended for one year by Archbishop or Bishop, while his sentence would be declared null.

Hence it is plain from Devonshire's letter that two at least of these details were overlooked, Lady Rich being divorced solely on her own confession, and one of a very flimsy kind. Nor was any undertaking not to re-marry given by either party. It was not a complete divorce— that is to say, it was not a complete deliverance from the marriage bond, *a vinculo matrimonio*—but merely a separation of presence. If Devonshire had pressed the matter and pleaded the benefit of the excepting clause (which exonerated from the felony of bigamy those already divorced in the ecclesiastical court) it might have gone hard with him. He, however, on his side could urge with equal safety that the canon law had not been observed on the part of the Courts pronouncing sentence. The net result was that though the law could not punish him, his marriage was null, unrecognised by law, and was in direct violation of the canon. It did not help his cause with the King that there was royal precedent enough. It was useless to quote the cases of Henry IV of France and Henry VIII of England. James, foolish, conceited, saw no extenuating circumstances in the tragic case. The Darby and Joan picture sketched by his notable petitioner left him unmoved. He could not forgive the violation of one of the first laws he had made. Even his pedantry was not flattered or enticed into counter argument. He never forgot the affair or Laud's share in it. Eleven years afterwards, when the latter sought a nomination, through the Duke of Buckingham, to the see of St. David's, the King's anger flared afresh. "You have pleaded the man a good Protestant," he conceded. "But was there not a certain Lady that forsook her husband, and married a Lord that was her paramour? Who knit that knot? Shall I make a man a prelate, one of the angels of my Church, who hath a flagrant crime upon him?"[1] As to Devonshire, the King flung insult full in his face, telling him that he had won "a fair woman with a black soul." This, and the "alteration of the King's countenance towards him and such a lessening of the value that had been set upon him," prompted the unfortunate lord's "Defence." At this point also Laud deserted his master. He even appears to have written a contradiction of his arguments.

The sudden change from renown to obscurity, from high favour to disgrace, crushed Devonshire. His lady was obviously degraded by the King's sentence of nullity. She, once the glory of the Court, was the butt of social derision and contempt—a phantom, so far as the world was concerned. The Earl dared not take part in Court ceremonies, though the King could not or would not deprive him of the offices he held. Thus, though he had some public duties left, he was but the ghost of a great man. He was like a great house of which the interior decays and only the façade remains to hide the hollowness and ruin. And ruin it was—of body and heart. Such a public rebuff following upon the strain of the Irish campaign undermined the steely strength of Charles Blount. Three months after that ugly clash of

[1] *Life of Dr. Williams, Bishop of Lincoln.*

husband and lover in the House of Lords he lay dying in his house in London—the Palace of the Savoy. He was but forty-three, but he felt dissolution in every part of him, for at the beginning of his short illness he asserted the consciousness of his danger. He lived for barely a week after this. The following two accounts give different aspects of his end :

From Chamberlain to Secretary Winwood on April 5 (two days after Devonshire's death) :

" The Earl of Devonshire left this life on Thursday last soon and early for his years, but late enough for himself, and happy had he been if he had gone two or three years since, before the world was weary of him, or that he had left that scandal behind him. He was not long sick, past eight or ten days, and died of a burning fever and putrefaction of his lungs, a defect he never complained of." ·

Fynes Moryson's record of the event, as eye-witness, is far more humane and true :

" He was surprised with a burning fever, whereof the first fit being very violent, he called to him his most familiar friends, and telling them that he had ever by experience and by presaging mind been taught to repute a burning fever his fatal enemy, desired them upon instructions then given them, to make his will ; and then he said, let death look never so ugly, he would meet him smiling, which he nobly performed ; for I never saw a brave spirit part more mildly from the old mansion than his did, departing most peacably after nine days sickness."

And again Moryson states the case fairly when he says : " Grief of unsuccessful love brought him to his last end."

His was a courageous spirit, which expressed itself in a " countenance cheerful, and as amiable " as Moryson " ever beheld in any man." " Only," he adds, " some two years before death, his face grew thin, his ruddy colour failed, growing somewhat swarthy, and his countenance was sad and dejected." This may or may not have been the beginning of physical breakdown, the inception of the pneumonia which carried him off, for the cause of mental distress did not arise till less than a year before his death.

This last summing up of his master by the secretary should be added to that portrait quoted in a previous chapter :

" He was undoubtedly valiant and wise. He much affected glory and honour, and had a great desire to raise his house, being also frugal in gathering and saving, which in his latter days declined to be a vice, rather in greedy gathering than in restraining his former bounties of expense; to that howsoever his retiredness did alienate his mind from all action ; yet his desire of honour and hope of reward and advancement by the wars, yea, of returning to this retiredness after the wars ended, made him hotly embrace the forced course of the war ; to which he was so fitted by his wisdom, valour and frugality, that in short time he became a captain, no less wise, wary and deliberate in council, than cheerful and bold in execution, and more covetous in issuing the public treasure than frugal in spending his own revenues. And his care to preserve his honour and maintain this estate made him, (though coldly) entertain the like forced course of state counsellor at home after the wars : to the managing of which affairs he was no less enabled by the same valour, wisdom, and many other virtues, had not the stream of his nature prevailed to withdraw him from attending them, further than to the only obtaining of these his private ends. But surely these

U

dispositions of nature (besides others hereafter to be mentioned) and these his private ends, made him of all men most fit for this Irish employment, wherein the Queen and State longed for an end of the war, and groaned under the burden of an unsupportable expense.

"He loved retiredness, good fare, and some few friends. He delighted in study, in gardens, a house richly furnished and delectable rooms of retreat; in riding on a pad to take the airs; in playing at shovel-board or at cards; in reading play-books for recreation; and especially in fishing and fish-ponds; seldom using any other exercises, and using these for pastimes only for a short and convenient time, with great variety of change from one to the other.

"He was a close concealer of his secrets, sparing in speech, but judicious, if not eloquent. He hated swearing, which I have seen him often control at his table with a frowning brow and an angry cast of his black eye; slow to anger, but, once provoked, spoke home; a gentle enemy, easily pardoning, and calmly pursuing revenge; as a friend, if not cold, yet not to be used much out of the highway. Lastly, in his love to women he was faithful and constant, if not transported with self-love more than the object, and therein obstinate."

And a curious assertion is included of his mixture of evasiveness and fidelity:

"He kept his word in public affairs inviolably, without which he could never have been trusted of the Irish; but otherwise in his promises he was dilatory and doubtful, so as in all events he was not without an evasion."

Nor is he represented as generous:

"To his servants he was mild, seldom reproving them, and never with ill. I cannot say that he was bountiful to them. His gifts to them were rare and sparing. Yet . . . at his death he gave £1000 by will to be divided by his executors' discretion among them."

A strange, complex being, compounded of great strength and some weakness,—no altruist, yet rather self-concentrated than selfish ; a man with immense sense of his responsibilities, whether towards himself or the authority he served ; of deeply serious nature, intensely cool and far-sighted—except in the early stage of his love-story.   And here his fidelity and that of his lady triumph over all criticism, all censure.   That which Dudley Carleton was pleased to call " the scandal " was in truth the least scandalous ingredient of the whole. The true error was the irresponsible begetting of a family all of whom were illegitimate.   The marriage itself was an act of supreme courage, a conscientious confession of the facts, with the desire to secure a social future and heritage to these children.   It was Mount-joy's hour of supreme strength, and the world jeeringly converted it into the hour of his supreme weakness.   It has been recorded by historians that for a year after the social ban was laid upon the pair "they kept a sad house together," at Wanstead.   The ban did not divide them. For it is also on record that his last caresses were on her lips and hands, that, utterly broken, she refused to leave his chamber, and long after he had passed away lay in a corner of it, prostrate, refusing alike bread, meat, and wine.[1]

[1] Johnstone's *Historia Rerum Britannicarum.*

CHAPTER XVIII

THE WIDOW'S PART

HOWSOEVER the world might disapprove of his marriage, Court and Nation made an effort at atonement in according Devonshire a gorgeous funeral and interment in St. Paul's Chapel, Westminster Abbey. Nevertheless, even in connection with this, public insult was offered to his wife in the most gratuitous fashion. The following extract from correspondence between Dudley Carleton and John Chamberlain on the 17th April, 1606, narrates the incident :

"My Lord of Devonshire's funeral will be performed in Westminster about three weeks hence. There is much dispute among the heralds, whether his lady's arms shall be impaled with his, which brings in question the lawfulness of the marriage, and that is said to depend on the manner of the divorce ; while though it run in these terms, that she was to be separated from her late husband *a thoro et mensa* . . . *propter varia et diversa adulteria confessata et commissa ea in suburbis quam intra muros civitatis* London, yet they are two in the conclusion not to marry any other. Her estate is much threatened with the King's account, but it is thought she will find good friends, for she is visited daily by the greatest, who profess much love to her for her Earl's sake ; meantime, amongst the meaner sort, you may guess in which credit she is, when Mrs. Bluenson complains that she hath made her cousin of Devonshire shame her and the whole kindred."

" 2nd May.—My Lord of Devonshire's funeral will be performed on Wednesday next, in which my Lord of Southampton is chief mourner, my Lord of Suffolk and Northampton assistants, and three other Earls. It is determined that his arms shall be set up in single, without his wife's."

It is not clear whether Penelope, bowed down with grief, was able to face the Abbey ceremony. Certain it is that the woman who had not been crushed by the death of the splendid Sidney, or even by the execution of her brilliant and well-beloved brother, had now received her death stroke of sorrow. Very little that was not bitter seems to have been spared to her in the closing of her life. Despite the scorn of the Court and Society, this creature of undying courage, of beauty yet unmarred, of perfect constitution and health, might well have looked for a ripe middle age spent in rich seclusion, had her husband summoned strength enough at the last to forget the evils of the world, the rottenness of the entourage of the new King. At Wanstead he and she, with their five children, could have gathered up the threads of life again, sending their roots deep down into the rich peace of the country, while the master of the house lived much with the books that he loved, the books which are our best friends, since they neither slander nor conspire.

A bitterer cup than any that Penelope had ever drunk was now thrust to her lips. All the influence which she had used in so many ways in previous years amongst men and women, all the tenderness she had shed upon brother and lover, all the inspiration which her mere existence and her high spirit had radiated, all the combined forces of her nature seem to have been powerless to reconstruct life for her second husband.

Of his end she had, as we know, but little warning. Condolences poured in upon her, and her friends rallied about her. Nor did the poets who had always strewn flowers on her path remain dumb. Yet small comfort was it to her that elegy writers extolled her lover's life and death and wove into their poems delicately audacious allusions to her romance. These lines remain to interest lovers of history. In addition to that striking memorial of Charles Blount in Fynes Moryson's *Itinerary*, the eulogies of the two well-known contemporary poets, Samuel Daniel and John Ford, portions of whose funeral poems are subjoined, relieve a little the stormy gloom in which Devonshire's life closed.

Samuel Daniel expatiates on his patron's love of books and the glories of the once famous library at " solitary Wanstead."

> " Which shew'd thou hadst not books as many have
> For ostentation, but for use, and that
> Thy bounteous memory was such as gave
> A large revenue of the good it gat.
>
> . . . . . .
>
> Witness so many volumes, whereto thou
> Hast set thy notes under thy learned hand
> And marked them. . . .
> That none would think if all thy life had been
> Turn'd into leisure thou could'st have attain'd
> So much of time, to have perused and seen
> So many volumes that so much contain'd."

And on his self-knowledge and control :

> In consort with thyself in perfect love ;
> And never man had heart more truly serv'd
> Under the regiment of his own care.
>
> This action of our death especially
> Shews all a man. . . .

With what amnition he did fortify
His heart, how good his furniture hath bin.

.　　　.　　　.　　　.　　　.　　　.

Thus did that worthy, who most virtuously
And mildly lived, most sweet and mildly die."

In this connection I cannot resist reminding my
readers that Daniel, a very energetic maker of verses,
adroit wooer of great patrons, who appears to have been
in receipt of a small pension from the Earl, was in some
ways a rival of Ben Jonson, especially in regard to the
production of panegyrics, masques, and entertainments.
The notable Ben succeeded in putting his nose out of
joint, and was so "surly and malignant" towards him
that he grew bitter, and retired to the neighbourhood
of London, "the more retiredly to enjoy the company
of the Muses" (according to Fuller in his *Worthies*).
Here he wrote a good deal, drawing upon his rich
experiences of life. One of his principal works,
however, *The Tragedy of Philotas*, was taken as applicable
to the unhappy Earl of Essex, while the Earl of Devonshire was mentioned in it by name.[1] The anger of
the latter elicited the following letter, not a little
pathetic, and refreshing in its sturdy self-reliance :

"Understanding your Lo. is displeased with me, it
hath more shaken my heart[2] could have done in respect
I have not deserved it, nor done or spoken anything in
this matter of Philotas unworthy of you or me. . . .
First I told the Lords I had written this 3 Acts
of this tragedy the Xmas before my L. of Essex
troubles, as divers in the city could witness. I said
the Master of the Revels had perused it. I said I had
read some part of it to your Lord : and this I said

[1] See Preface to *Works of Daniel*.
[2] Words appear to be missing here in the original.

having none else of power to grace me now in Court
and hoping that you, out of your knowledge of books
or favour of letters and me, might answer that there is
nothing in it disagreeing, nor anything, as I protest
there is not, but out of the universal notions of ambition
and envy, the perpetual arguments of all books or
tragedies. I did not say you encouraged me into the
presenting of it; if I should I had been a villain, for
when I showed it to your honour I was not resolved to
have had it acted, nor should it have been done had not
my necessities over-mastered me. And therefore I
beseech you let not now an Earl of Devonshire overthrow what a Lord Mountjoy hath done . . . the
world must or shall know mine innocency whilst I have
a pen to show it, and for it I know I shall live *inter
historiam temporis* as well as greater men, I must not be
such an abject unto myself as to neglect my reputation,
and having been known throughout all England for my
virtue I will not leave a stain of villainy upon my name,
whatsoever error else might scape me unfortunately
through my indiscretion and misunderstanding the
time."

Daniel, in 1603, was given a post as licensee of plays.
He died in 1619.

Devonshire's irritation seems rather absurd, for both
public and private characters at all times form the basis
of the works of contemporary imaginative writers.
Sidney's pronouncement in the *Apologie for Poesie* on the
subject of the source of literary inspirations, with its
delicate flattery of the romancist's power to improve
upon nature, settles the matter for all time :

" There is no art delivered unto mankind, that hath
not the works of nature for his principal object, without
which they could not consist, and on which they so
depend, as they become actors or players, as it were, of
what nature will have set forth. Only the poet, dis-

daining to be tied to any subjection, lifted up with the vigour of his own invention, doth grow in effect into another nature, and maketh things either better than Nature bringeth forth, or quite new . . . so as he goeth hand in hand with nature, not enclosed within the zodiac of his own wit."

The other principal elegiac poem on Devonshire was " Fame's Memoriall," by John Ford, a far more notable writer and dramatist than Daniel, in which these verses occur in regard to Penelope's love romance :

> " Link'd in the graceful bonds of dearest life,
>   Unjustly term'd disgraceful, he enjoy'd
> Content's abundance, happiness was rife,
>   Pleasure secure, no troubled thought annoy'd
> His comfort-sweets, toil was in toil destroy'd.
>   Maugre the throat of malice, spite of spite,
>   He liv'd united to his heart's delight.

> " His heart's delight, who was the beauteous star
>   Which beautified the value of our land,
> The lights of whose perfections brighter are
>   Than all the lamps which in the lustre stand
> Of heaven's forehead, by discretion scanned ;
>   Wit's ornament, earth's love, love's paradise,
>   A saint divine, a beauty fairly wise."

The whole panegyric is dedicated to the lady, prefaced by a letter beginning :

" To you, excellent Lady, it was intended, to you it is addressed, not doubting but whatsoever hath been of him said, and truly said, your honourable favour will allow the favourable protection of your expressest patronage, who, whiles he lived, endowed you, and justly endowed you, with all the principles of his sincerest heart and best fortunes."

The effusion contains allusion to the friendship between Essex and Mountjoy.

And then comes what one commentator calls "the worst acrostic that ever passed the press " on her full title, "Penelope, Countess of Devonshire," bombastic, stilted, involved.

Daniel was not without a companion in misfortune, for John Ford's tragedy of *The Broken Heart*, published later, was similarly said to be based on Essex, and to further combine the tragedy of Penelope and her lover, while Robert Rich is also introduced—if one insists upon pursuing the parallel literally—in the guise of a coarse, violent, elderly, jealous husband. It is indeed a wholesale tragedy, forcible but violent and unrelieved, full of coarse allusions, lacking all the graces, the vivacity and the true values of the love-story on which it was said to be based. Yet strange indeed would it be if Penelope's romance and the life of her brother were not the root of imaginative works, dramatic or other, in days when there were no clubs, coffee-houses or newspapers, and when the theatre was the resort of the great men of the day, who, as Essex surmised in his bitterest moment, came to see their fellows (and themselves!) mirrored and portrayed, now with praise, now with satire. Of such shows Madame Tussaud is surely the amiable descendant.

Penelope's sorrows now touched their high-water mark. When Devonshire's papers came to be opened, all the world knew that out of their five children, all illegitimate, he acknowledged but three. It is impossible to probe into this terribly painful point of conjugal difference. It is an ugly blot on the story, and remains a mystery. Nothing can palliate the slur which the Earl's will casts upon the lady. In the absence of all secret correspondence and family documents the matter eludes investigation. It were fairer to give the mother the benefit of the doubt. Chamberlain wrote thus to Secretary Winwood :

"He hath left his lady (for so she is generally now held to be) £1,500 a year and most of his moveables ; and of five children that she fathered upon him at the parting of her former husband, I do not hear that he hath provided for more than three ; leaving to the eldest son, as I hear, between three and four thousand pounds a year and to a daughter six thousand pounds in money. For his offices, it is thought his Lieutenancy of Ireland is or shall be bestowed upon the young Duke of York ; his Government of Portsmouth and his company of horse in Ireland on the Earl of Montgomery. The New Forest stands between the Earl of Pembroke and the Earl of Southampton ; and the Mastership of the Ordnance betwixt the Lord Chamberlain and the Lord Carew. Other things there be, which either are not bestowed, or come not within my knowledge."

By this it will be seen that Devonshire died far better off than a great many other public officials of his day.

Of his five children there were three sons, Mountjoy, Charles, and St. John ; and two daughters, Elizabeth and Anne or Lettice. Mountjoy Blount seems to have been about ten years old at the time of his father's death, and inherited the chief part of the estate, though, as a bastard, he could not keep the new and splendid earldom. So was poor Penelope shorn of her glory and her joy at one blow. Her son Mountjoy was, however, created Lord Mountjoy of Mountjoy Fort, in Ireland, in 1606, by King Charles I (in 1627), Lord Mountjoy of Thurweston, in Derbyshire ; and in 1628, Earl of Newport, in the Isle of Wight. He was appointed Constable of the Tower and Master of the Ordnance in 1641. At the marriage in 1657 of Robert Rich, grandson of Penelope's first husband, with Frances, the

youngest daughter of Oliver Cromwell, Mountjoy Blount
was present with the then Earl of Warwick, the bride's
father, Lord Strickland and others, a proof that the two
families of Penelope were on good terms.   His wife
was Anne Botteler, daughter of John, Baron Botteler,
of Bramfield in Hertfordshire.   He died at Oxford, in
St. Aldate's parish, where he had retired with the King,
on account of the plague in London, 12th February,
1665, and was buried in the south aisle adjoining the
choir in Christ Church Cathedral.   He had three sons,
George, Charles, Henry, and two daughters, Isabella
and Anne.

Penelope's second son by the Earl of Devonshire was
Charles Blount.   The third son, St. John Blount, re-
ceived the Order of the Bath at the coronation of King
Charles I, 1623.

Concerning the two daughters, historians are somewhat at variance.   Collins, in his *Peerage*, seems to
regard the second, Lettice, as the eldest, and notes her
two marriages, first to Sir George Carey, or Carew, of
Cockington in Devonshire, secondly to Sir Arthur Lake,
son of Sir Thomas Lake, Secretary of State, for whose
story readers must refer to the private history of
James I.   She was one of the victims of a sordid family
tragedy.   The whole of her husband's relatives became
notorious over a property dispute.   Arthur Lake's
eldest sister had married William Cecil, Lord de Roos,
grandson of the first Earl of Exeter, but the couple
were miserable, and could not live together.   De Roos
had mortgaged his estates to Sir Thomas Lake, who,
upon the separation, claimed the estates for his daughter.
To this Lord Exeter, who had recently married a young
wife, objected.   Arthur Lake, the husband of Lettice
Blount, assaulted his brother-in-law De Roos, while

Lady de Roos and her mother, Lady Lake, charged the latter with carrying on a guilty amour with his young stepmother. De Roos was driven out of England and died in exile, but his wife and the Lake family proceeded methodically with the fabrication of their slander, which now included an attempt, on the part of Lady Exeter, to poison her step-daughter-in-law. The letters put forward by the plaintiffs were found by the Star Chamber to be forgeries, the witnesses were discovered to have committed perjury. The Lakes were confined wholesale in the Tower, and heavy fines were imposed upon them. In the midst of the imbroglio poor Lettice, whose husband paid the smallest fine of the group, died under circumstances far from reputable. Chamberlain makes an allusion to her death in May, 1619 : " Sir Arthur Lake hath buried his lady with scandal enough, which, among the rest, is not the least *crève-cœur* to the father to see the fruits of so graceless a generation." In June the same writer gives a hint of the mystery : " Since the death of Sir Arthur Lake's lady there is a daughter of hers come to light, thought to be Dick Martin's or a greater man's ; but, by the help of good friends, lays claim to Sir George Carew's lands, because she was born in wedlock." The discovery of a former affair of the heart on the part of his wife during her first marriage would certainly have not been hushed up by a pugnacious fellow like Arthur Lake.

Of Elizabeth Blount Camden records that she became the wife of a son of Sir Thomas Smith, a Russian Ambassador, and governor of the East India Company. This was a clandestine match, and took place at the end of 1618. It does not seem to have brought much happiness, for the bridegroom left the country in July, 1619, apparently without being reconciled to his parents.

I cannot trace Elizabeth Smith further than this. She may or may not have gone with her husband, but her sister's marriage scandals must surely have involved their joint reputation, and could not have been very palatable to her relations-in-law. Craik[1] suggests that young Smith's disappearance from England was connected with the unfortunate episode. The marriage of this Elizabeth Blount is much confused with that of her natural half-sister, Isabella Rich, who also married a son of Sir Thomas Smith's about the same time, and also effected it without the consent of that worthy. This will be mentioned presently.

Mountjoy, as aforesaid, died in his prime. It was surely a triumph for Robert Rich to outlive him. The latter always seems to have scored his points in life in default of the success of others. Not after the most exhaustive search in calendars of State papers is there to be found anything of him worth recording. He never helped to make history. He just managed to scrape through his duties as a justice, a military volunteer— " adventurer" was the more romantic term in those days for gentlemen who occasionally engaged in foreign war-service without a commission—a lukewarm courtier, a quiescent and egotistical parent. He had his enemies, of course, but was mostly considered too poor a thing to be worth powder and shot. With one exception, the only kind of artillery " trained " upon him was that of contemptuous laughter—but a complete battery at that. The exception is an occasion on which a certain person called Edmund Wyndham, full of some grievance, went to his house " armed with a dag " to shoot him, and was haled before the Essex magistrates in consequence. If that shot had only come off, a great many people would

1 Vol. I.

have been the happier—including, possibly, Rich's
second wife, whom he now sought busily, flitting, so to
speak, from flower to flower, from maid to widow, till
he found a really comfortable person. He really had
some difficulty in making his choice ; or, possibly, the
ladies were not anxious to have him. Once more we
must dip into Chamberlain, under date December 21st,
1616, for the pithy, ironical details of the man's search
after what one may call a " treasure of a woman " :

" The Lord Rich, after much wooing and several
attempts in divers places, hath at last alighted on the
Lady Sain Poll, a rich widow in Lincolnshire."

The name is really St. Paul. The lady was a daughter
of Sir Christopher Wray (who was Lord Chief Justice
of the King's Bench in 1603), and the widow of Sir
George St. Paul, of Snartford, in Lincolnshire. Within
a short year of his marriage we see that Robert Rich,
though he had found the lady, was not quite sure of the
treasure, and that her legal heredity stood her in good
stead when it came to a question of marriage settlements.
Chamberlain's pen on the 11th October, 1617, is once
more deliciously busy with the matter :

" Lord Rich is said to be in great perplexity, or
rather crazed in brain, to see himself over-reached by his
wife, who hath so conveyed her estate that he is little or
nothing the better by her, and, if she outlive him, like
to carry away a great part of his."

By way of consolation, Rich clamoured for a greater
peerage than that which he had inherited. He pressed
the King to make him Earl of Clare, and was soundly
snubbed by a refusal, based on the reasons that Clare,
being identical with Clarence, was too great an honour
—as being a title too near the throne—to confer on a

nouveau riche family so recently emerged from burgher-dom and the mercer's trade. In place of it he won the vacant Earldom of Warwick, and was duly invested in August 1618. This and a crop of other earldoms, Chamberlain tells us, elicited satirical comments from " malicious poets and libellers." Among the nicknames flung at the new peers that of " Cornu Copia" fits Robert Rich like a cap.¹ With his coffers full, his mind excited by the tussles with his new wife, his head turned by his earldom, he always strikes one in the phrase used by Dudley Carleton of Lord Cobham, as *matière pour rire.* For six months only he revelled in his new glories, ere he died on March 16th, 1619, in his house at St. Bartholomew's, London, now grandly named Warwick House. His second lady, so far as one can ascertain, did outlive him. His honours devolved upon his eldest son by Penelope, another Robert Rich, who proceeded to empty his father's horn of plenty as quickly as possible.

It is good to know that Lady Rich had care for the future of her children by her first husband. She saw that her son Robert would have a good match in a great heiress, Frances, daughter of Sir William Hatton, granddaughter of Sir Francis Gaudy, Chief Justice of Common Pleas. Other parents were angling for the same prize. Old Gaudy had already entered into negotiations with Lord Treasurer Dorset, who had an eligible grandson in Richard, afterwards the third Earl. Lady Rich intervened, charmed the girl, won her for young Robert, then seventeen, and effected the marriage in secret on February 26th, 1605. The couple had children, and Robert Rich the third was thrice married.

¹ It is probable that this *sobriquet* covers a pun on the word " horn," which in Elizabethan speech signified a betrayed husband.

ROBERT RICH, EARL OF WARWICK

SON OF PENELOPE AND ROBERT RICH

He passes down the broad ways of Stuart history as the famous Warwick who held the office of Lord High Admiral under the Long Parliament, while his grandson, as aforesaid, married the youngest daughter of Oliver Cromwell. In Clarendon's rollicking picture of him one discerns very little trace of his father, and curious touches in regard to spirit and intrigue which seem like a parody of the fire and fascination of his extraordinary mother :

" He was a man of pleasant and companionable wit and conversation, of an universal jollity and such a license in his words and in his actions, that a man of less virtue could not be found out ; so that one might reasonably have believed that a man so qualified would not have been able to have contributed much to the overthrow of a nation and kingdom. But, with all these faults, he had great authority and credit with that people who, in the beginning of the troubles, did all the mischief ; and by opening his doors and making his house the rendez-vous of all the silenced ministers, in the time when there was authority to silence them, and spending a good part of his estate, of which he was very prodigal, upon them, and by being present with them at their devotions, and making himself merry with them, he became the head of that party and got the style of a godly man."

Henry Rich married the daughter and heiress of Sir Walter Cope, through whom he inherited the seat and manor of Kensington, was in 1662 made Baron Kensington, in 1624 Earl of Holland, in Lincolnshire, and received the Garter from Charles I on his accession.

His remaining brother, Charles, after having been knighted, was killed while on a military expedition with the Duke of Buckingham, at the Isle of Rhé, in 1627.

x

Of the three Rich daughters, Penelope, Essex, and Isabel, Penelope wedded Sir Gervase Clifton; Essex became the wife of Sir Thomas Cheke, of Pirgo; Isabel married twice. Her second husband, it is curious to find, was Sir John Smith of Sutton (Kent), apparently the brother of that very gentleman who, after marrying her half-sister, Elizabeth Blount, fled the country.

Sir John Smith certainly had a good deal of trouble over both his daughters-in-law. From contemporary letters I cull the following comments on this wedding:

Chamberlain to Dudley Carleton, Nov. 28th:

"The Lord Chamberlain" (the same William, Earl of Pembroke who, under Elizabeth, was so unwilling a courtier) "and others have forwarded the marriage of Sir Thomas Smythe's son of eighteen to Lady Isabella Rich, without the knowledge of the father, who at their entreaty had consented to receive her."

From a letter of the Rev. Thos. Larking, Jan. 5th, 1619:

"I forgot to acquaint you in my former letter with a matter that hath been shuffled up between Sir Thomas Smythe's son and Mrs. Isabella Rich, who finding themselves both together at Sir —— Udal's house some four days since, and liking well enough either the other, my Lord Chamberlain, who was there present, sent for his own chaplain to Barnard's Castle to make the matter sure by marrying them; who, making some difficulty for that they had no license, his Lordship encouraged him upon assurance of saving him harmless. So they were presently married; and from thence conducted to my Lord Southampton's to Dinner. . . . But the father is a heavy man to see his son bestowed without his privity and consent."

From an engraving

HENRY RICH, EARL OF HOLLAND

It is difficult to reconcile Camden and Croke with Craik and Dudley Carleton[1] on these Smith marriages. It looks as though the identity of Elizabeth and Isabella had been confused, that Camden is altogether wrong in his facts about the marriage of Elizabeth Blount, and that her fate is a mystery, while the real and only heroine of this "shuffled-up" ceremony was Isabella Rich—unless the younger generation of the Smith family, in view of a "heavy" parent who may have been a terrible martinet, had a *penchant* for clandestine matches.[2] Dudley Carleton and Thomas Larking, as contemporaries, are the most reliable authorities, and they make no allusion at all to any previous similar match.

It cannot be said that the offspring of the Rich marriage were happy in their lives and fates. As Clarendon wrote caustically of them in after years, especially in connection with the two eldest sons, Lord Warwick and Holland : "A very froward fate attended all or most of the posterity of that bed from which he and his brother had their original."

In regard to the Earl of Holland's children, two of them, both girls, had curious psychic experiences. Aubrey, in his *Miscellanies*, tells the story which he had from a reputable source, of the beautiful Lady Diana Rich, who, while walking in her father's Kensington garden in the full blaze of noon, met her own apparition, "habit and everything, as in a looking-glass." Though then in perfect health, she died a month later

---

[1] Croke distinctly gives Isabella as one of Lord Mountjoy's daughters ; while Craik (Vol. I, p. 309) says that Isabella *Rich's* second husband, Sir John Smith, was the brother of the Mr. Smith who married her half-sister, the natural daughter of Mountjoy.

[2] See *Chamberlain's Letters*. Birch Collection, James I.

of smallpox. Aubrey takes this as a presage of death, and adds that her sister, Lady Isabella (who married into the family of Thynne), "saw the like of herself also before she died." Their father came to a violent end. Overheaped with honours by Charles I he abused by wrong-headed action and by indecision in the Civil Wars both the offices conferred on him and the other favours he received. A proper "trimmer," he flung himself at last into the Stuart cause, too late for success, and met his end at the hand of the executioner five weeks after the murder of his King.

Letters from Penelope as the Countess of Devonshire are so rare that one may be excused for perhaps wearying the reader at this stage with the two below. One, dated 1605, is merely a kindly request on behalf of a needy protegée. The other is of an equally light nature, and gives us a glimpse of her warm-hearted hospitality, her unflagging interest in other people's children, in the affairs of her friends and in the business of daily life up to the moment of her great sorrow. Both are addressed to Lord Salisbury, the Robert Cecil whom Essex and his folk had so mistrusted :

"Noble Lord,

"This gentlewoman hath entreated me to commend her suit unto you, of whose good success I should be very glad because she is one I have been long acquainted with, and is of the best disposition that ever I found any of her nation. I beseech your Lord to favour her, that if it be possible she may obtain some satisfaction, if her desires be not unreasonable. And so, wishing your Lord all happiness and contentment

"I remain

"Your Lordship's most affectionate friend to

"do you service,

"Penelope Rich."

"Noble Lord,

"The rumours of your sickness I confess hath made me haste to this place, where I might receive better satisfaction by the knowledge of your health, and had the good fortune this day to meet with the messenger you sent to my Lord Clanricarde, whereby I was assured of your safe recovery, beseeching your Lord to believe that no friend you have living doth participate more of your grief or joy than myself, whose affection you have so infinitely obliged with your constant favours. While I was at Drayton[1] with my mother, the young hunters came very well pleased, until your servant came with your commission to guide my Lord of Cranbourne to my Lady of Derby, which discontentment for fear of parting three days made them all lose their suppers, and become extreme malicious, till it was concluded that their train should stay at Drayton, and they go together with two servants apiece. I fear nothing but their riding so desperately, but your son is a perfect horseman, and can neither be outridden nor matched any way. My mother, I think, will grow young with their company: so longing to hear of your safe and perfect health, I remain

"Your Lordship's most faithful to do you service,
"P. Devonshire."

[1] Drayton Bassett, the manor left to Lettice Devereux by her second husband, Leicester.

CHAPTER XIX

HARVEST

THE letters overleaf were written from Wanstead, where the Devonshires were evidently entertaining Penelope's sister-in-law, Lady Essex and her third husband, Lord Clanrickarde. It is not likely that Penelope remained in London after her Earl's funeral. In her robes of rich and deep mourning she seems to have cloistered herself in his apartments probably at Wanstead, unconsoled by children, priest, or mother, though these most certainly must have ministered to her. Most probably it was here that she died. There is no detailed record of her death, but all authorities are unanimous in stating that she lived but a few months after her second husband's decease. She was only forty-five, and in looking back upon the achievements of her life and her tremendous notoriety, one cannot but contrast it with that of her senior and equally famous contemporary, Bess of Hardwick, who died in the same year, (1607) nearly twice her age. Both women touched great causes, were involved in secret political practices, came to grief over the marriage tie. The older women was the more important householder, while both jingled the keys of several large mansions in town. Of Penelope's domestic activities as housewife and entertainer little can be gleaned. She was far more socially brilliant, elusive, fascinating than the Lady of Hardwick. Had she lived as long, her life, which

flowed at a fierce pace, would have been just as full,
judging by the amount she crowded into her last twenty-
five years. She was assuredly radio-active, assertive,
and so belongs to that great gallery of Elizabethan
women who are for all time.

It was not so hard now for her to die. Sidney,
Essex, and Mountjoy had trodden the road ahead of
her. After many errors, after her marriage infidelity,
her coquetries, and such opportunism as seemed inseparable from her circle and her conditions, she came
in those last days of anguish to the heart of all things,
to the realisation that the body was but a poor tenement
of the spirit, that life, without the highest love, was
dross, that fidelity was the one pearl of great price.
She did not, like the stupendous "Bess" aforesaid,
write over her doors "The end of all things is to fear
God." But she had learned her sharp lesson of suffering
and sacrifice.

Was she not faithful ? In the essence most certainly.
In this her character stands out strongly compared with
that of her brother, "Sweet Robin." She certainly
sinned against her vows to Robert Rich. Her excuses
for this and the great temptations which attended her
beauty and temperament have been fully set forth. Do
not her grief and death restore the balance ? If these
and her great love may not rehabilitate her, nothing
ever can.

What is the harvest of it all ? Her life, her web,
unrolls itself—a brief, complex scroll most curiously
worked in gold and rich colours, with the interruption
of a murky strand of trouble and shame, which is
accompanied by another—the black thread of family
tragedy and personal grief. It lies here for our delight,
our amazement, our pity, not for our contempt. Is it

such a little thing to have wrought so fast and travelled so far in such troubled years? Is it nothing to have brought twelve children into the world for good or evil, to have triumphed over smallpox and measles and the far greater infections of political treasons, to have faced the Privy Council and not been clapped in the Tower, to have dwelt in a house on the verge of bombardment, to have been adored by poets and bookmen, danced and acted at Court, witnessed the production of great comedies, all but overridden a divorce and lived down a social scandal, and lastly to have carried a fair body and a famous and beautiful face erect, youthful, and flawless to the verge of middle-age? These are achievements enough for one life, and though they were not all reputable, she must in these be given credit for consistency.

There is in Mr. Chesterton's[1] pages a very pretty dissertation on the subject of marriage vows and the revolt from them. In speaking of social rebels who advocate free love, he points out that love is never free, and says, "They appear to imagine that the idea of constancy was a joke mysteriously imposed on mankind by the devil, instead of being, as it is, a yoke consistently imposed on all lovers by themselves. . . . It is the nature of love to bind itself, and the institution of marriage merely paid the average man the compliment of taking him at his word." In this true sense was Penelope faithful. It was her nature to wish to bind herself where she loved, and in this light her intercourse with her lover and their forlorn wish to be taken at their word must be regarded.

[1] *The Defendant.* There is a very dry humour about the extraction of the above passage for application to St. Valentine's Day in a recently issued calendar.

When compared with certain other of her contemporaries the doings and sayings of Penelope Rich do not make a deep dent upon history. She had not the chances for public distinction of Sidney and Essex, nor the bland domestic environment and the wealth which enabled Mary, Countess of Pembroke, to shine in literature. Yet her native qualities were just as great, and she had a far prouder, more powerful spirit than Mary, a spirit which circumstances goaded into revolt. Her personal attractions were greater—beauty far excelling that of Philip's sister, and brains just as excellent, if without a fair outlet. Her power of incentive was extraordinary; her social gifts eminently surpassed those of Mary Pembroke or young Lady Essex. Penelope was a better diplomat than her brother, who was always accounted "a poor philosopher and a weak dissembler." Hers was a great nature marred by injustice, handicapped by poor training and by a one-sided education. She was plunged into life and marriage at nineteen, possibly with some accomplishments at her command, but with no weapon save her sex attraction. The marvel is that she came out of the tangle as well as she did.

Let us glance now at the great houses with which her story is concerned.

Of the buildings in which portions of the drama of her life were played Essex House stands first, as bearing the most sensational part in the list. This was the first of the great houses which originally stretched from Temple Bar along the Strand. It had changed its name several times since it was built in Edward II's reign by Walter Stapleton. This divine called it after his own bishopric—Exeter House. As the centuries rolled on rich additions were made to it, among them a great hall by Stapleton's successor in the time of Henry VI. Later it passed, by right of plunder, into the possession of the first Lord Paget, who again embellished it considerably, and promptly christened it after himself. Subsequently it was possessed by Lord Leicester and bore his title, and when it fell under his will to his nephew was again renamed. The street of the name, now sacred to publishers and lawyers, marks the site, just off the Strand of to-day.

Chartley, the country seat of the Devereux family, in Staffordshire, has already been described. A terrible fire in 1781 so completely destroyed it that only the moat remained to indicate its position.

Leighs, where the earlier portion of her married life was spent, came to Penelope's husband through his grandfather, whom Fuller neatly describes as a "lesser hammer under Cromwell to knock down abbeys; most of the grants of which lands going through his hands, no wonder if some stuck to his finger"! This place, originally a priory of Augustinian canons, founded by one Richard Gernon about 1230, stood five miles south-west of Braintree, about midway between this and Chelmsford, on its south. From Nichol's *Progresses* one learns that Lord Chancellor Rich " made it his capital mansion." He did not, however, deem it necessary to remove from the gate the monk's carven motto, " Garde ta Foi," still to be traced on the relics. It was certainly built of " capital " stuff, "all of brick," and consisted of two courts, the inner one towards the garden fenced with stone. Three parks belonged to it, long since converted into farms. It continued in the family till it passed by marriage of a daughter to the Earl of Manchester; thence by purchase to Edmund Sheffield, Duke of Buckingham, who died 1735, and by his father's will it descended to his half-brother, Sir Charles Sheffield, who sold it for £40,000 to the Governors of Guy's Hospital, who caused it all to be taken down except the gatehouse, and the lands converted into farms. Such were the beauties and conveniences of this mansion that Mr. Knightly, a Northamptonshire gentleman, said to Robert Rich's son and heir, "My Lord, you had need make sure of heaven, or else, when you die, you'll be a great loser." And Dr. Anthony Walker, in his funeral sermon for Charles, Earl of Warwick, payed it a compliment not quite so strained, when, addressing the Earl of Manchester, to whom it was bequeathed, he concluded, "Your noble uncle hath left you, after your noble aunt, a secular Elysium, a worldly Paradise, a Heaven upon Earth, if there be any such." "In 1760, at which time as much was remaining as appears in Buck's view of it, 1738, was shown a room called Queen Elizabeth's ; and in the desolated garden was a neglected fountain not unlike that which appears in the forest of the Champ de Drap d'Or." [1] Thus Penelope had at least the satisfaction of knowing that her legitimate children were brought up in a beautiful home, a fair heritage.

Next in order comes "Solitary Wanstead," which had been held by so many different members of Penelope's family. The place lies on the South Eastern edge of Epping Forest. The name is ancient, "wan" meaning "white," and "stede" a mansion. One authority vaguely describes the distance from London as "about seven miles from Whitechapel Church." In course of time it became a fortified estate. Once more the insatiable Chancellor Rich appears in connection with it. Edward VI "bestowed it," we are told, on him, and it descended

[1] Nichols' *Progresses.*

to Penelope's husband in 1577, who, long before his marriage, sold it to her uncle, Leicester. The original house, which one of the Rich family rebuilt, seems to have been most inappropriately called "Naked Hell Hawe"! The Earl of Leicester, as stated, greatly enriched the place in order that he might entertain his Queen. But he had not more than ten years' enjoyment of it. In May, 1578, Elizabeth was his guest, in the September he married Lady Essex, whom the wits dubbed his "New Testament," in 1588 he died, and left the house to his stepson, Essex, who in his turn parted with it to Mountjoy. At the time of Lord Leicester's death the library, which Mountjoy made so famous, consisted only of "an old bible, the Acts and Monuments, old and torn, seven psalters and a service book." Of these the value amounted to thirteen shillings and eight pence. For Leicester's store was not books, but good armour and plate, jewellery, camp equipage, furniture, some fine clothes, a few horses, and a ship called after himself. Yet Mountjoy was at once by far the better soldier and householder. Wanstead still held its rank as one of the royal palaces, and in the year of Penelope's death, 1607, James I stayed there after his return from a western progress. It is hard nowadays to imagine the romantic solitude of the situation of the vanished dwelling, the hunting parties in which Sidney and Leicester rode forth with their Queen, the dense wood out of which Sidney's masquers issued on an April day, or the gardens where Mountjoy sought to coax young Essex into reason during his earlier self-exile from Court.

Let us pass on to the subject of portraits. It is quite amazing that of so beautiful a woman, who must have been painted again and again in every style of dress, not a single authentic canvas remains. The picture of "Ryalta" sent to King James has not survived. There is in Lambeth Palace a portrait, on the reverse side of which is inscribed "The Countess of Devonshire." Its identity has never been established. There is a chance that it represents Penelope in her prime. For the rest the nearest likeness to her extant is that of her daughter Isabella, said to resemble her more than any of her other children. It is here reproduced. The original, by Mytens, is in the possession of the Duke of Suffolk.

So ends the story of a many-sided woman, an idealist at heart, as iridescent in her personality as the stars to to which she was likened. Yet was she no Iris, but rather one who, in the words of the Messenger of the Gods as impersonated by a masquer before Queen Elizabeth (when pleading the love-suit of Leicester under cover of the famous Kenilworth masque in 1575), found "much greater cause to follow Juno than Diana."

A like definition may be fitly applied to that creature of astounding vitality, Penelope's mother, who outlived her. Left almost alone of her generation, Lettice Devereux represents the "old guard" of the house of Essex. It may have been some consolation to her that she lived to see and caress four generations of her descendants and greet her grandchildren's grandchildren. Her life went down in a rich glow of friendship and sympathy. For another twenty-seven years she dwelt peacefully at Drayton Bassett, where, at ninety-two, she could "walk a mile of a morning." Her grandson, Gervase Clifton, son of Penelope's Penelope by the knight of that name, wrote her epitaph.[1] It is to be hoped that this young rhymester of twenty-four

[1] Craik's *Romance of the Peerage*, Vol. I, p. 331.

gratified her aged eyes by at least a rough sketch of his eulogy, which described her as :

> " She that in her younger years
> Matched with two great English peers ;
> She that did supply the wars
> With thunder, and the court with stars."

A sugared definition which, for once, was true. Her existing descendants number, through her son, the second Earl of Essex, the Dukes of Buccleuch and Buckingham, the Marquises of Aylesbury and Townshend, the Earls of Cardigan and Ferrers. Penelope's harvest of titles gives the names of the Duchies of Montrose and Manchester, the Marquisate of Anglesey, the Earldoms of Galloway, de Grey, Ripon, the Barony of Kensington. The name of Penelope's only sister, the hot-tempered Dorothy Percy, trails an even more brilliant array of titles—the Dukedoms of Somerset, St. Albans, Devonshire, Marlborough, Newcastle, Northumberland; the Earldoms of Ashburnham, Fitzwilliam, Egremont, Spencer, Beverley, Carnarvon, Bessborough, Romney, Ducie; the viscounty of Strangford; the baronies of Churchill and de L'Isle.

It must be noted that with Charles Blount's death the Earldom of Devonshire lapsed, since it could not be conferred on the illegitimate heir to his substance. It would certainly have been a master stroke, and have crowned the triumph of Robert Rich, if the title, now wrested from the Blounts, had been conferred on him in place of the much-desired Earldom of Clare. But this would certainly have raised a storm and made a very bad impression on society. The prize fell instead to William Cavendish, Bess of Hardwick's favourite son.

And so farewell to Penelope and her people, to the lady of the honey-coloured hair, the flashing black eyes,

the skin of cream and carmine.   Let this remaining
fragment of her chief lover's elegy at the pompous
hands of Samuel Daniel bring gentleness to criticism,
even as it tendered her, in the last months of her life,
dignity and consolation ; for it lifts at last the love of
this man and woman beyond contempt :

> " Summon Detraction to object the worst
>   That may be told, and utter all it can ;
>   It cannot find a blemish to be enforced
>   Against him, other than he was man,
>   And built of flesh and blood, and did live here
>   Within the region of infirmity,
>   Where all perfections never did appear
>   To meet in anyone so really
>   But that his frailty ever did bewray
>   Unto the world that he was set in clay.
>   And gratitude and charity, I know,
>   Will keep no note, nor memory will have
>   Of aught but of his worthy virtues now,
>   Which still will live ; the rest lies in his grave."

As also in hers.   But it is impossible to imagine her
beauty shut under heavy sods.   It escapes from them
and pursues the eyes of the mind continually.   For me
she walks ever in a rose-garlanded pleasaunce at noon, a
rustling, laughing, fragrant presence, eternally young—
rich in every detail, as the punsters assured her.   What
need of a painted canvas taken from the life, when we
have Sidney's whole gallery of portraits stained with
colours as rich and strong as those of the Paul Veronese
whom he met, and in whom he delighted before his
travelling days were done ?

APPENDIX

A DISCOURSE of marriage written by the Earl of Devonshire in defence of his marriage with the Lady Rich, written in Anno 1605.

As God in himself and of himself is infinite in his being, so he is in his attributes, his wisdom, his power and his goodness, out of which goodness (the nature whereof is to communicate itself with others) as it pleased him by his wisdom and power to create the world for man and both for his glory, so was it answerable to the same, to direct and make his own works to the two ends for which it was created, whereof having created man with a purpose in him and in his posterity to be served, as in his wisdom he saw that it was not good, for that end, that man should be alone, so did he create him an assistant or helper, like unto himself, which was the woman, and to them both he prescribed a rule, how in the vocation to the which he had called them they should best serve him. The law of God, though in itself it be eternal and like unto himself in purity, who is infinitely pure, yet whatsoever doth want, doth in some sort work according to the capacity of that wherein it doth want, and therefore where we are to consider what is lawful, we are not to search into the absolute will of God, which is infinite and infinitely pure, but to be directed by so much of his will as he hath pleased to reveal unto us, the which he hath sufficiently done unto us in his word, and in those impressions of nature, which, although by our fall they are

320

blotted, yet are they not utterly defaced in us, which impressions of nature, although they be not sufficient to lead us to one true end, yet in them is there nothing contrary to the word of God, nor in the word of God is there nothing contrary to them.

So as to be resolved of the nature of the bond of marriage and of the mutual duties incident thereunto, because it is both a sacred and civil contract, we must have recourse especially to the word of God, the law of nature, and so much of the law of the country, wherein we live, as is not contrary to the word of God or the law of nature; for human laws in things that are otherwise indifferent do impose a duty in conscience to observe them. But if they be contrary to the word of God or law of nature, we are bound with patience to suffer the penalty, but not in conscience to obey the law. But in case of marriage, at the least concerning the lawfulness thereof, it seemeth here in England that *Jus Poli* and *Jus Fori* are all one, for by a statute in 33 of H. 8, which remaineth still in force, all marriages (are) pronounced lawful, that are contracted between lawful persons and by the same act all persons are pronounced lawful that be not prohibited by God's law to marry notwithstanding any statute or act to the contrary. In the question therefore whether it be lawful for two between whom a marriage was lawfully contracted and consummated, after a sentence of divorce to marry with another, both parties, between whom the first marriage was, being then alive, it is only necessary to see whether by the word of God it be prohibited to marry as this case standeth, for otherwise the marriage is lawful.

In which consideration is nothing to be alleged but the word of God, although the laws of nature, nations and the judgments of the learned men may be considered towards the interpretation of so much of the word of God as shall be produced to the purpose. To determine this matter it is first fit to be handled,

Y

whether a marriage lawfully contracted and consummated may be by any means utterly dissolved and the bonds untied during the lives of both the parties, which were first married. Now, since therein we are to be resolved by the word of God Christ who is the living word and the word of life doth such (*sic*) direct us, where we must begin, and that is in the beginning and first institution of marriage, where he saith " But from the beginning it was not so." The first institution was by God in Paradise and between the first man and the first woman in the state of perfection. The final end was (because it was not good for man to be alone) that he might have a help fit for him. The efficient cause was the consent of both parties, wherein it is said, when God had made the woman, and brought her to the man he said, " This now is bone of thy bones and flesh of thy flesh." The matter and essence of marriage is the faster adhering which is expressed in these words : " Therefore shall a man leave his father and mother and shall cleave to his wife and they shall be one flesh."

The rule of marriage out of this instruction is concluded by the word and wisdom of God to be this : " Let no man therefore put asunder, whom God hath coupled together." There is no doubt but the *Contract de Jure* ought never to be broken, and that their offence is heinous and not to be excused that do break it, but the question is whether *de facto* it may be broken, because the rule is : " Let no man put asunder, whom God hath coupled together." We may as well conclude that no man may kill, because the rule is thou shalt not kill, in which case as the magistrate may both kill an offender and justly kill him, yet is it not to be said that he but Justice killeth him and the offender is guilty of his own death and not the magistrate. So, if two that are married shall, contrary to the ends and causes of marriage, instead of comfortable helps, become continual torments unto each other, instead of mutual consent do live in continual and unconsionable contention, and instead of being one flesh, by abandoning themselves to others do become one flesh with another, I see nothing left like unto a marriage, nor of the substance of a marriage, nor any danger that I can see in the first institution for the magistrate to pronounce that to be broken, which by the fault of the offender is in deed broken.

And, as God rules all suitable to his infinite pureness, yet in those rules doth he allow some exceptions agreeable to the weakness of our nature, for as the rule is " Let no man put asunder whom God-hath put together," so we must needs confess that in some cases this rule doth bear exception, for God by Malachi doth command " If thou hate thy wife put her away," and by Moses, where the children of God are commanded that if, when they go to war, they take a beautiful woman whom they desire, that then he shall take her and marry her, if after he have no favour unto her, then he might let her go whither she would, only he might not sell her, and in the 24 of *Deuteronomy*, where a man married a wife, if so she found no favour in his eyes, because he had espied some filthiness in her, he was willed to write her a bill of Divorce and give it unto her and to send her out of his house, which words in the Hebrew expressing divorce, the learned in that tongue do interpret to imply a cutting asunder and dissolution, and nothing is more plain by this place and divers others in the scriptures than that the divorce then allowed and practised, was an utter dissolution of the bonds of marriage, in such sort, that both parties did and might marry with any other, and that the Jews did know and acknowledge no other kind of divorce but this ; and this law was especially made in favour of the party wronged in the contract of marriage, that if either of them did out of the hardness of their hearts break the obligation, wherein they were bound (the which to do was never lawful) were tolerated that then it should be lawful for them to be separated, that the innocent party being defrauded of the true end wherefore they were contracted, the marriage, should again have the proper due of their own bodies, which they had conferred upon another, for these considerations and that it should be free for them to contract any other by a better choice to make reparation of their first misfortune.

And so much was also done in favour of the innocent party, that if out of the hardness of his heart his mind were so alienated, though without just cause, from his former choice, yet he (be) allowed to live without her, lest he should be tempted to seek dangerous and more wicked means to be rid of her, and it was permitted unto him to become again *sui juris* by restoring unto her the interest that she had given him in her self, and by marriage any other more agreeable to his heart to have better means to serve God in peace, which before in war and dissention he could never in that vocation do.

Now for the law of nature ; the best expositors of that law among them who had only the light of nature to direct them, do thus derive the beginning of marriage, That man being a responsible and sociable creature deriving his own mortal being, and well-being, coveteth to preserve his being in his posterity, which he could not do in himself, and his well-being in the society of others, which he could not do alone, so that as he could not give being to his posterity without a woman, so could he neither give well-being unto them without careful and good education. If every man went promiscously to every woman, no man should know his own children, and consequently no care of their education, wherein consisteth their well-being, wherefore marriage was contracted between one man and one woman; that they two as one should preserve each other's Being and well-being both in their own mutual society and in their posterity.

Now, if there happen such a marriage, where there is no hope of posterity nor mutual comfort or society, but the clean contrary, what is there in the law of nature that prohibiteth to dissolve this marriage, especially if it be done by their consents, by whose consents it was contracted; for the Civil Law (which in the generality approacheth nearest to the law of nature) saith that *Nihil est tam naturale quam eo genere quodque dissolvere quo colligatum est*, and all laws say that *consensus facit matrimonium*, and if it be said that the consent of two parties should not prejudice the interest of a third, and that God hath an interest in this bond, being a witness thereunto, it may be answered that all honest promises made by men have ever God for their witness, and yet are there many which by consent may be dissolved without offence to God, and Although this be a promise which more than most contracts doth bind us carefully to observe it; yet this is but a contract and *magis et minus non ainesificat speciem;* I do not conclude out of all this that out of natural convenience it were comely that all persons contracted by this sacred and civil bond should upon any cause or mutual consent make separation of themselves without the cognizances of the magistrate, because many things that in themselves are lawful to be done, are unlawful till they be judged fit to be done, and if it should be done only by the parties' judgment, then should they be both judges and parties in their own case, which were unjust and unnatural.

But, as I have heard some of the fathers of our law say that, if the king do grant under his great seal, which is a high contract, any office with fee and commodity absolutely in words during life without any appearing exception, yet hath the contract this silent condition included in it, that the party shall perform all those duties that are incident to his office, the breach whereof doth forfeit his grant, but it is not in the king himself to take benefit of the forfeiture and liberty to dispose of it to any other until it be judged, so that as by a solemn record, the contract was made, so by a solemn deed it shall be pronounced to be dissolved, and though a marriage be contracted during life, yet may it have in it a hidden condition to obscure those duties which are the

motives of each other's consent, and, though the marriage
may be broken upon the liking of them, yet it may not,
neither is it fit for either party to take advantage of it,
till it be adjudged so by the public judgment of it, so
the chief natural end of marriage, which was to avoid
promiscuity in generation, and uncertainty in issue, is no
more sufficiently provided than if they had continued
joined in that bond and disjoined in their hearts, for
such a bond between (bis) such so distracted in their
hearts is not only an enticement to adulteries but a cloud
to conceal them, and a warrant for a woman to intrude
an adulterous issue into the inheritance of her husband,
the danger of which and of many other inconveniences
is clearly avoided by a public and an utter separation.

And, to infer, that I do not rashly or impertinently
make some comparison betwixt this grant of an office
and the contract of marriage, which, seeming to be
absolute, yet doth not bind for ever and in all cases, even
in this case of marriage, I have the warrant of the
Common Law, which doth allow a man for fornication to
put away his wife, although when he were married,
besides the main contract he had sworn not to put her
away, and the reason is given by the same law to be
because of the same contract and such like, this
unexpressed condition must be understood *si videlicet illa
in legem conjugii non peccaverit.*

I have, as I think, produced good reason that there is
nothing in the first institution of marriage by the same
law of God, that doth make the bond of marriage so
fast, but that in some case it may be dissevered, and the
practice in this church until the coming of Christ was
doubtless in many cases to dissolve it, and likewise that
it is not contrary to the law of nature, for then it must
needs have been contrary to the word of God ; if I had
alleged no other reason, yet I think this were sufficient,
that whatsoever all nations did hold was counted the
law of nature.   But all nations did hold divorce to be
lawful, till the coming of Christ, therefore divorce was

esteemed lawful by the law of Nature till the coming of
Christ, and I could say after˜the coming of Christ till
the beginning of the Canon Law, but that will fall out
more fit to be affirmed in this part, where (having proved
divorces *a vinculo* are neither against the law of Nature
not the Nature itself) I must now make it appear that
it is not against the law of the Gospel, to which purpose
I will only allege the words of Christ, who was the law
giver of this Caution which he gaveth himself, that he
came not to take the Law but to fulfil, and as I take it
in this case not utterly to restrain the liberty given by
the former Law, but to reform the misunderstanding,
and abuse of the Liberty, and though the words themselves do seem to interpret themselves, yet I will declare how I do understand them, and what warrant I
have to understand them.

As God gave the first Law of marriage in Paradise to
man then being in the state of perfection, so Christ when
he would regenerate us into that perfection himself and
seeking to draw us with him, did first speak of marriage
in his sermon which is called, by the fathers, "in Mount,"
wherein all his rules are so right and so full of purity that
they seem ordinary to such a life as should be the right
mark we should aim to come unto, as near as we could,
and speaking of marriage these be the words : "It hath
been said also 'whosoever shall put away his wife,
let him give her a bill of divorce,' but I say, 'Whosoever putteth away his wife except it be for fornication causeth her to commit adultery ; whosoever shall
marry that is divorced committeth adultery.'" These
words I will not only interpret out of mine own
spirit, but in the words of Erasmus's paraphrase
upon this place, and not only because it is Erasmus's
interpretation, concording with mine, but because it
agrees with the doctrine and practice of the Church for
many hundred years after the coming of Christ, with
the opinions of most of the ancient fathers, and with the
opinions of most of the Church of Rome, and lastly with

all or almost all of the learned and godly writers (whom God did use as blessed instruments for the better reformation of the Church) and these are Erasmus's words:—The Law of Moses did permit that the husband, offended with any fault of his wife, should put her away at his pleasure, so that he gave her a bill of divorce, by which she might marry unto another, and by which the right in him to assure her again might be taken away, and so he did satisfy the Law, who for any cause did repudiate his wife, if at her departure he gave her such a bill, neither should she be judged as an adulteress, neither should any note her as an adulteress notwithstanding the Law did with the friendship and concord between the married continue to be perpetual, But knowing the hardness of the Jews, (lest anything more wicked should be committed, as poisoning and other murder) hath permitted divorce. But I wish that by the professors of the New Law marriage be more holy and inviolable, and therefore whosoever shall put away his wife unless she be an adulteress (for then she leaveth to be a wife, when she hath mingled herself with another) doth constrain to adultery, for if she marry another she doth not marry a husband but an adulterer; for Erasmus enlarging the words of Christ to explain his meaning, and Cardinal Caton in his commentaries upon this place concerning which this interpretation upon the words *Et, qui dimissam duxerit, adulterat,* doth add unto *dimissam* "*procul dubio absque fornicationis nota,*" which is one with Erasmus, who unto *dimissam* doth add *sic dimissam,* and doth agree that the putting away and utter dissolving of the bond as well is allowed in the Law of Moses. I do not so far overvalue the authority of these men, although I do think them to have been as learned as any that lived in their age, as I would *jurare in verba magistri,* but that they have said the same, which, if I have never read them I had so many of their reasons to say and that in these words, they do make it plain, that in this text a divorce of marriage *a vinculo* in some case is not prohibited, which is the question I now handle, and that I do infer by these words, that whosoever shall put away his wife, (except it be fornication) doth cause her to commit adultery, and whosoever doth marry a wife so put away (except) that is for some slight cause and not for adultery, doth commit adultery, but whosoever doth marry a woman lawfully put away, (and it is lawful to put her away for that great cause) doth not commit Adultery, because she is then no man's wife, and consequently no man wronged, if she marry to any other. And if Christ in this did not take away the old Law, but reform it, he leaveth the Law to be the same that it was in the cases which he doth in this reformation except, and therefore in the case of fornication, the Law of divorce remaineth still whole as it was in the time of Moses and that the Law of divorce was then an utter separation *a vinculo*. And surely, if these words of Christ touching divorce in this place have expressed no exception I see no reason but in this we might have admitted an exception in cases clean contrary to the Nature of marriage as well, as we are forced in most of the absolute precepts in this chapter read the like, as in the next verse in like manner he saith again " Thou shalt not forswear thyself, but shalt perform thy oath unto God. But I say unto you, ' Swear not at all,' " etc., and yet we find out an exception in some cases to make it lawful to swear ; and after, " If any man will sue thee at the Law and take away thy Coat, let him have this (thy) Cloak also," and yet we find out an exception to make it lawful for us both to defend our coats and our cloaks also from the advantage of the Law, and finally he concludeth "You shall be therefore perfect, as your father, which is in heaven, is perfect." The which, if we do not otherwise expound than the Letter doth import, we must needs confess to be impossible. For how can a finite and corruptible creature by infinite degrees come near to the perfection of an infinite or infinitely Creator ? Therefore, if the exception here in the matter of divorce and the same in the 14 of *Matthew* were not, yet might those places in *Mark* and *Luke* move it where there is no exception of fornication expressed, but especially now it maketh it plain, for as no one place of the doctrine of the Holy Ghost is contrary to another, so is the general rule of expounding the Scriptures to expound that which is more scant or obscure by other places of the same subject, that are more large and plain, and not to restrain that which is written more large by any other place which doth not express so much. So that unto *Luke* and *Mark* we must add the exception which is in the 19 of *Matthew*, and not take it from those places because it is not in the other. But because in the 10 of *Matthew* this matter of deep divorce doth seem more largely to be handled, it will be fit to bring these words to be considered. The Pharisees having heard, as it is likely, of the doctrine of Christ against the present opinion and practices of those times, came to him with a mind to tempt him in the matter and said to him, "Is it lawful for a man to put away his wife upon every occasion?" And he said unto them, "Have ye not read that he that made them in the beginning made them male and female and said, "For this cause shall a man leave father and mother and cleave unto his wife, and they two shall be one flesh ; Let no man therefore put asunder those whom God hath joined together." They said unto him, "Why then did Moses command us to give a bill of divorce and put her away ?" He said, "Moses for the hardness of your hearts suffered you to do so, but from the beginning it was not so. I say therefore unto you, whosoever shall put away his wife except it be for fornication, and marrieth another, committeth adultery, and whosoever marrieth her that is divorced committeth adultery." The Pharisees, as both their cause and purpose was in this business evil, so doubtless was both their opinion and practice at that time both against the first in-

stitution of marriage, and the true meaning of Moses
in this cause of divorce, and therefore as they and
their beginning so informed of the matter did put
the question to Christ, so Christ unto them, and to
this matter as it was then held and practised, doth
make the answer, and seeking to reduce them and
all men unto that estate of perfection in the which
they were first conceived, doth call them back to the
first institution of marriage, which was made when
man was in the state of perfection, and therefore doth
answer their question whether it were lawful for a man
to put away his wife upon every occasion, as they then
held, and as they verily believed to this effect, "Have
you not read in the word of God, that God made man
and woman in the state of perfection, and therefore able
to perform those duties incident to their creation and
also to his particular vocation wherein they were ordained
as to become comforters and assistants to each other, as
well by their posterity to increase his Church, as by
their mutual Love and affection to supply to each other
the defects of solitariness, and that if they should fall
to be a means by their lawful joining together to avoid
the same, with which their inordinate defects might lead
them unto, and therefore shall this bond be so straightly
observed by you, that a man shall leave father and
mother in respect of his wife, and in continual conversation and affection be joined together, so that they,
before this mutual consent were two, by this contract be
but one flesh with another, by the which the bond is
broken and they are separated, whom God did couple
together, this being contrary to that which they conceived
by Moses' Law to be lawful. They asked him again, "Why
did Moses then command to give a bill of divorce and
put her away?" to the which he answered that Moses,
"because he knew that you, being degenerate from your
first perfection through the hardness of your hearts,
which could resist all grace, did not only break of the
true ends and conditions of marriage, but out of the

same hardness of heart were apt to seek wicked and bloody means to be separated, ordained a course which by his provision was lawful by a bill of divorce to make it known how that was separated, which you by the hardness of your hearts had separated, but from the beginning it was not so, for the seed of dissention being then unsown, there was no breaking of the bond of matrimony, and therefore no cause of divorce; neither should there be any now, when you are born again to the like perfection, and shall have my grace continually to strengthen you, except the hardness of your hearts do refuse it; I say therefore unto you that whosoever shall put away his wife and marry another, except he put her away for whoredom (which ever from the beginning that it had been committed was so opposite to the nature of marriage that it did utterly break and dissolve it) he doth commit adultery, because that she that he doth put away, is still his wife, because she is not lawfully and fully put away, whosoever marrieth, that is so put away committeth adultery, because he doth marry one that being not lawfully put away remaineth still the wife of another."

And surely, but that I am fearful to add anything to the text, in the which I have not apparent warrant, I think I might expound those words " Except it be for fornication " to have a more large intent than the bare Letter doth import, and that the word fornication doth imply not only carnal but spiritual fornication and some such other great causes as are contrary to the nature of marriage, for some causes there must be allowed besides this carnal fault, for how will else the place of Paul stand with this, wherein he doth pronounce the believing woman to be free to marry another, being abandoned by her unbelieving husband: And some of the fathers, the masters of the sentences and others of the church of Rome are forced to that large interpretation to make good their titulary divorce *A thoro et mensa*, which they allowed in divorce other causes besides adultery, and many learned writers of our Church, and the Civil Laws made by most Christian Emperors must either have that Constitution for their warrant; for we must think that the Emperors living nearest to the purest times of the Church, when the Church did flourish with more extraordinary learning and piety, and those Emperors not only obedient but obnoxious to the authority of those good men would promulgate and practice laws that were contrary to the word of God; I say they were obnoxious because Theodolphus the Younger, who by his laws did allow many other causes of utter divorce, when a churchman did injuriously threaten to excommunicate him for denying him a suit, he did rather choose to satisfy him, than repeat his wrong with just power. The judgment of the fathers and stories of those times did witness much of his extraordinary piety in duty and obedience to the Church, and Socrates doth write of him that he spent much of his time in fasting and prayer, that he did strive abundantly to keep the straight rules of a christian life, that his Court was like a monastery, for he spent the mornings with his sisters in singing Psalms, he could repeat all the Scriptures so out of his own memory that of those he would dispute with the bishops as if his function had been to be one of them, he was a more careful gatherer of such books as contained the whole word of God and of such like than ever Pittolomeus Philodelphus was, and in the end of that chapter which is the 22nd of his 7th book of ecclesiastical histories he saith that the whole city for practice and consent, was as it were but one church. Shall we think then that so godly and so learned an emperor would have made or suffered a public Law, which he had thought to have been contrary to the word of God, or if the Learned men of those times had thought it to be contrary to the word of God, can it be imagined that they would not have admonished him of it? It is not likely that he who bare so much respect to them would have ruled his will to that which they told him had been the word of God, for in those times, that was the Law *quod Principi Placuit* and there was no other difficulty, but his will, to have altered it, neither did he make his Law of divorce being many other Christians, and excellent Emperors in his Law *Consensus Liber 5 titulus* 17 : he doth restrain the causes of divorce to such as he thought of greatest importance; and yet out of all this I only conclude that it is lawful for a man to put away his wife for fornication and to marry another, and that is as much as in this question I desire to prove, which is in some cases the bond of marriage may be dissolved ; neither doth St. Paul in the 7th to the *Romans* where he saith : " The woman, which is in subjection to the man, is bound by the Law to the man while he liveth " make anything against the doctrine of Christ, and therefore their exceptions (except it be for fornication) must be added; neither is it his purpose in the Law to speak anything of divorce but by the example of a general rule wherein it was necessary he should mention the exception. His purpose was to prove another matter, for else he would never have said " Know you not, brethren, for I speak to them that know the Law, for they, that know the Law, did know, that general rules have an exception," and to this effect says *Caton* upon this place *Adverte tamen, caute lector, quod hac Pauli verba inteliguntur regulariter, secus vero in casu scriebat Paulus scriebant et docti in lege Mosis, quos alloquitur quod secundum legem verbum est regulariter quod mulier aligata est quanto tempore vivit viro suo, et cum hoc sciunt quod in casu libelli repudii secundum Legem mulier soluta erat a lege viri etiam vivente viro.* "And to the married I command, yet not I but the Lord, let not the wife depart from the husband, but if she depart let her remain unmarried or let her be reconciled to her husband, and let not the husband put away his wife." These must be expounded of such slight causes, for the which Christ doth prohibit, but to put away an adulteress, which is allowed to be lawful by the opinion of all men, and therefore there is no doubt but to this place also must be added (except it be for adultery) for in the next verse he saith, "If any brother have a wife that believeth not, if she be contented to dwell with him, let him not forsake her." By which he sheweth the marriage between such to be found lawful and yet he addeth, "But if the unbelieving depart, let him depart; a brother or a sister is not in subjection to such things," which I fear the Romish Church doth expound to be free to marry another, and from thence do many learned men of our Church conclude that for the cause of discretion it was lawful for any to marry again, but his leaving of her, for in the verse going before it appeareth that it was not lawful for her to leave him except he did leave her also, though he were an Infidel.

And surely, since cohabitation joined with the other mutual duties of marriage is that adhering, which in the first institution was of the very essence of marriage, I see no reason but he, that doth wickedly and utterly abandon his wife, should by that make her as free as she was before she was married to him, especially if it be done by order and so pronounced by the magistrate, unto the which I believe the magistrate is warranted by the word of God; I could never read nor hear of any other place in the Scriptures that with any appearance is alleged against my conclusion. And therefore, since the dissolving of the bond of marriage in some cases doth appear neither to be against the first institution of marriage, nor to be against the doctrine of Christ, I may conclude that it is not prohibited by the word of God, that marriage lawfully contracted and consummated may in some cases be dissolved from the bond during the Life of both parties that were so married; and though, to enforce so much, it is enough to have alleged the word of God, yet I will as briefly as I can, and truly, touch the censure and practice of the Church touching the matter from the time of Christ until now, not minding to allege all that hath been said in so great a matter or hath been controversed by some excellent men, but rather to give some light how the state of this question hath been held and handled until the beginning of the Common Law.

The Civil Law, which was the Law of our Christian world, did allow in some causes divorces *a vinculo*, and none of the fathers until the time of *St. Jerome* and *St. Augustine* did directly impugn, but many directly allow. It is true that in some of them there may be somewhat gathered of their dislike of the abuse of divorce and of such as did rashly *Convolare ad secundas nuptias*. But was it heard that till the Canon Law any marriage made after divorce was by the judgment of any of them dissolved? St. Jerome and St. Augustine were the first that seemed dogmatically to disallow the dissolution of marriage *a vinculo*, and from them is derived the divorce, which indeed is no divorce *a thoro atque mensa*, which now the Church of Rome doth allow ; These holy fathers out of their exceeding Love of purity (but specially Jerome) did a little too hardly censure even the holy state of marriage itself ; and so careful were they in this and many other things that heathen and heretics should see nothing foul, that they sometimes rather admitted a hidden sore in the body than a mote in the face of the Church. But how strongly soever St. Jerome handled this matter, whose strongest arguments may as well be urged against all second marriages after divorce, yet doth even extol Fabriola for her piety as a miracle and excuse her fact, who during the life of her husband had married another and though after the death of her second husband she did voluntary penance, that was after done for ordinary faults, yet was the marriage never dissolved, and the penance, because that without the authority of the Church she did put away her husband, and not because she did it.

And for that St. Augustine, after that, to prove his

purpose, he hath made such interpretations of the scriptures as will hardly satisfy any man that is not more moved by his authority than by his reasons ; yet in the end he is forced that in his book *de fide et operibus*, to conclude this matter *Quisquis uxorem in adulterio deprehensam dimiserit et aliam duxerit, non videtur equandus eis, qui excepta causa adulteri ; dimittunt et ducunt et ipsis divinis sententiis ita est obscurum, ut istam quidem sine dubio adulteram licet dimittere, adulter tamen habeatur si alteram Puxerit, ut quantum existimo venialiter quisquis falitur.* And let that reverend father pardon me, if I be not satisfied with his books of this matter, since it seemeth he was scant satisfied with them himself, for this he writeth of them in his retraction *scripsi duos libros de Conjugiis Adulteriis, quantam potui secundum scripturas, cupiens solvere difficillimam questionem, quod utrum emendatissime fecerim nescio, imo vero me non pervenisse ad hujus rei perfectionem sentio,* but howsoever even by these books it appeareth, that Polutimus, a godly father, was of the contrary opinion, as I conceive it may be gathered by that treatise of Polutimas written to him to know the reasons of his opinion as being new and diverse from that which was held at that time, I will not allege all the authorities of the ancient fathers that do make for my conclusions, but repeat even out of Sextus Senensis an adversary to this cause, that Ambrose, Tertullian, Hilary, *Aucthor operis imperfecti*, Chrisostum, Enthimus, Theophilactus, Cromatius, Pope Zacharias first, and the Fathers, Ubertine, Moguntine, and the Thibertine Councils do seem to be of that besides such of the fathers as we whom he calleth heretics do allege in this case ; But it is no wonder that the Canon Law should err in this matter, which in many things, but specially in this of marriage, hath so many errors that have no apparrance to warrant them, that none but a judgment captivated, and obnoxious to the Church of Rome can allow them, and the Common Law is the fountain that hath corrupted the current of the doctors since that time, with the which even they

z

were corrupted that in their own judgment did otherwise believe, since it was so dangerous for them to
strive against the stream ; and yet I may say by the
Authority of Cardinal Caton (whom I had rather allege
in that matter than our own writers, who doth protest
both against the contrary doctrine and parties that
profess it) ; that this matter was never dogmatically
defined by the Church of Rome to be as a matter of
faith contrary to the word of God, but judicially to be
determined as fit to be observed in fact, and these are
his words upon the 9th of *Matthew, Intelligo Igitur in
Christi lege tutum esse Christianum dimittere uxorem ob
fornicationem carnalem ipsius Hactinus non apparet, nam
decretates pontifici de hac re non sunt definitu quo fidei ad
indicialis facti*, and Catharinus, Bishop of Compsa,
when in the first edition of his book of Annotations
upon Caton's *Commentaries* he had with much bitterness taxed him for many things, doth overpass this
opinion with silence ; but in his second edition in his
5th book he doth confess that he did it because, as he
saith, *Nec poteram prudenter reprehendere quod nesciebam
etiam ? idone confutare*, and he that in all things did
quarrel with Caton doth concur with him in this
opinion, and confirm it with manifest (and I do think so
strong) reasons, as can no way be answered, and doth
much like to the other conclude in these words, *Scio quod
aliter docent nunc universaliter scholae, et ego cum illis
sentio si ex fide Cogor et Captivum reddo intellectum meum
hoc tamen precor ne nimis facile censuram adhibeant satis
est quod de cretis Pontificum hanc persolvo reverentiam
ut juxta illa doceam atque Consulam*, out of which I do
infer, that the censure, how this matter in faith should
be held, was not given at that time, which was before
the Council of Trent, and that many out of reverence to
the Church of Rome did teach in this matter contrary to
their own judgments. But as soon as we began to
shake off the bondage and to judge of all things clearly
by the word of God, the stream of our godly and

learned doctors did run the contrary way, and out of the pure fountains of the living waters of the Scriptures and with one voice did conclude, that by the word of God it was not prohibited in some causes to dissolve the bond of marriage and to contract with another, the first being yet alive.

Now for the second question, whether after such a separation the parties so separated be prohibited by the word of God, to marry with another, during the life of the party to whom they were first married, I think there is need little to be said ; for it is necessarily concluded out of the proof of the first, and therefore did all the oppugners of second marriages after divorce hold the first to be indissolvable, because they saw if they granted the one, they must needs have yielded to the other, for even so doth Bellarmin argue, if after divorce in case of fornication it were lawful for the innocent party to marry again, it must be lawful for the nocent, or it must not be lawful ; if it be lawful the adulterer should reap commodity by his sin, if it be not lawful first I demand why, for when that person is from the bond of his first marriage neither doth he injury to any, neither could the innocent party marry again except the first bond were dissolved, wherefore then may not the nocent party contract marriage : if you will say the Law forbids it, but where is that law that forbids it ? Neither is any Law extant that I know that doth grant marriage to the innocent party, and why should the Law prohibit one that is free and apt to vise to marry, when there remaineth no further hope to be recalled to the first match. These be Bellarmin's words in the title of the marriage in the end of his 16th Chapter, whereby it is apparent that he confesseth out of the necessity of conscience, that if we grant a separation from the bond of marriage we must yield that it is lawful for both parties to marry again, and neither doth he or can allege any weighty reasons against this separation *a vinculo* but the inconvenience that may follow of it, which may be well answered with many more mischiefs, that doth follow from the impossibility evil joined, and worse continued marriages. Neither should the Nocent party reap always benefit by his sin, as Bellamin saith, for it is certain, that many a man that doth commit adultery with a woman had rather be judged to die than to marry again, the party with whom they committed the fault ; But as there is no law, nor *Nihil magni quod non habet aliquid iniqui,* so that there might be in the Law of divorce some inconvenience, yet might there be many ways found by the magistrate to prevent it, and weighed with the mischief that doth follow of the other it will seem nothing. But the argument of inconvenience, because they depend upon circumstances, which would require a larger treatise to examine and to balance them, with the inconveniences that ensue on the contrary, I will omit or defer to answer, and only in few words go on with my purpose, that, if such a separation from the bond be not against God's words, they that are so separated are not prohibited by God's word to marry again, but without all question by many places of the Scripture counselled or in some case commanded to marry again, for after such a separation *a vinculo* it is generally agreed that both parties are freed from any manner of obligation, the one to the other in matter of marriage, for the knot that is united is more knit, and they both parties remaining unmarried, what shall deprive them of the liberty to marry again, which God doth grant to all men, and in many cases counsel it, and in some command it ? As in the I. to the *Corinthians,* 7 Chapter, " Art thou bound to a wife, seek not to be loosed, art thou loosed from a wife seek not a wife, but if thou takest a wife thou sinnest not. If they cannot abstain let them marry ; it is better to marry than to burn. To avoid fornication let every man have his own wife, and let every woman have her own husband," of which *Zaccheus* doth well say *Preceptum illum quod non se continet nubat et generare et perpetuum est.* And since it is not good for a man to be alone, which is spoken to all that are alone to enjoy the comfort and remedy of marriage, and even for that poor adulteress, which the Pharisees did accuse to our Saviour Christ, when he had stopped their mouths, that did accuse her, with the conscience of their own guiltiness, after he had remitted her sin and bade her sin no more, if she were separated from her husband, what should prohibit her to use her lawful means to sin no more?

Shall we say because she was an adulteress, therefore, she shall not marry? Surely I think it cannot be found in the Scripture that such as have been adulterers are more prohibited to marry than other sinners. Neither is the party offending, as Augustine saith, any more after repentance to be called an adulterer, neither the fault by man to be reputed which God hath remitted, or unto them whom by his remission he hath again made Holy. And although I will not be against any punishment, how grievous severe it be, inflicted upon adulterers, yet there is not more improper and (if they be suffered to live) more unjust than to prohibit them to marry, for marriage is the lawful remedy that God hath ordained and provided for such as cannot live in chastity, and as Augustine saith of marriage *Quod sanis fuit in offensum, aegrotis datum est in remedium.* And if our Saviour Christ left His whole flock for to seek one lost sheep, shall we put a poor lost sheep out of the right way, wherein it desireth to return again to the sheepfold? What were this but to punish sin with sin, and to deny unto them whom we would reclaim to salvation the means to lead them to it? And therefore I will only say with Calvin, who in this agrees with Luther, Melancthon, Bucer, Harmingius, Beda, Unitus, and most of all the godly doctors *Quia Hactinus non tamen tenere ut decebat animadversum fuit in adulterio ut eorum vita parcatur qui violant fidem Conjugii durum esset virum quo cum divorcium fecit uxor adulterii causa aut mulierem a marito repudiatam si incontinentia laborent in totam vitam a Conjugio arcere. Itaque necesse est, ut indulgentiam una alteram trahat.*

Now since it doth not appear that it is prohibited by the word of God, and that all marriages by our laws are pronounced lawful that are not prohibited by the word of God, I may conclude that the marriage between two, of whom one of them was divorced from another during the life of that other, is lawful by the Law of God and of man ; and if not, it being contrary to the Law of God, it were contrary to the positive Law of this Land, the Prince might in some particular sort dispense with the general rule. And neither against the nature of all human Laws, in which the equity of all particular causes cannot be sufficiently provided for, now against the Justice of this realm, since (as I take it) that power is given by a Statute of the 25 of H. 8, Chapter 11, even in this case of marriage ; And, if upon great consideration, hateful, and brewing of Treason, which is never without blood and breach of faith, wherein not only the prince but every subject hath an interest, and not only given the offenders life but restored them and their posterity from infamy, what offence should the like indulgence give in a fault of weakness, especially if it fall out that it be not accompanied with any other injury, for if both parties do desire such a separation and are content with a new contract, *volenti non fit injuria.*

Habet itaque et Christum
assertatorem justi divorcii.

Tertullianus, Lib. adversus Marcionem.

INDEX

www.ingramcontent.com/pod-product-compliance
Lightning Source LLC
Chambersburg PA
CBHW030931020726
47498CB00001B/202